The Lost Truth

By Dean Fougere

Disclaimer: This is a fiction novel; all characters, even those based on real individuals or corporations, or government entities are fictitious.

Dedication:

Special Thanks to my friends and family, for letting me be myself and serving as my lifeline when I fell too deep into the rabbit hole.

Introduction:

What is truth? What is knowledge? Not long ago, we knew the world to be flat, and if we ventured too far into the unknown we would fall off the edge of the world. Ask yourself: are you the type of person who asks questions or do you take answers? Real truth is what we search for, never accepting the knowledge of the present to corrupt our reason and deprive us from searching for real truth. Real truth is the search, the idea of the infinite possibilities of the universe. This is the truth of which we most deprive ourselves. We worship and congratulate those who grant us knowledge, though knowledge in itself corrupts the mind and eliminates the possibility of the infinite unknown. The real truth is the belief that nothing is true and therefore nothing is impossible. If we can imagine it, it is true.

Many people have been trying to lead us to their truths, leaving patterns of connection right before our eyes, and steering us down a path of knowledge to serve their purposes. We are blind to the connections, too stuck in our ways to accept the obvious false revelations before us. Be it through ancient literature or modern day media, the idea of a lost past, a hidden past strikes a chord in our human interest and for good reason, as it has been well hidden from us.

So through a story of fiction and a belief in the impossible, we may see the truths of our world and may reveal a connection. This is the story I have been waiting to tell my entire life, as I try to gain knowledge but am without any truths to define what we call reality.

Some of the greatest people of all time lead us down one of two similar paths. Trying to help us understand our place on this planet, we constantly strain to see the truth yet we are so sure of ourselves in the things we "know". We need to forget what we have been led to believe, what those in power have chronicled as our history and find the real truth for ourselves. No one can instill the truth in you, you must find it for yourself or it will not hold.

"The only true wisdom is in knowing you know nothing." — Socrates, 470-399 BC

"In a time of universal deceit… telling the truth is a revolutionary act" George Orwell Author and Actor, Book and Film: 1984

"Nothing is True, Everything is Permissible" Last words of Hassan-I Sabbah, founder of the Assassin's Order, lived 1034-1124 AD

"If you would be a real seeker after truth, it is necessary that at least once in your life you doubt, as far as possible, all things." — René Descartes, Philosopher 1596-1650 AD

"As a man who has devoted his whole life to the most clear headed science, to the study

of matter, I can tell you as a result of my research about atoms this much: There is no matter as such. All matter originates and exists only by virtue of a force, which brings the particle of an atom to vibration and holds this most minute solar system of the atom together. We must assume behind this force the existence of a conscious and intelligent mind. This mind is the matrix of all matter." Max Planck, Father of Quantum Physics 1944

"The Matrix is everywhere. It is all around us. Even now in this very room. You can see it when you look out your window, or when you turn on your television. It is the world that has been pulled over your eyes to blind you from the truth. You are a slave Neo. Like everyone else you were born into bondage, born into a prison that you cannot smell or taste or touch. A prison for your mind." –Morpheus, Fictional Character in a Film, The Matrix

"And it came to pass, when men began to multiply on the face of the earth, and daughters were born unto them, That the sons of God saw the daughters of men that they were fair; and they took them wives of all which they chose. And the LORD said, My spirit shall not always strive with man, for that he also is flesh: yet his days shall be an hundred and twenty years. There were Nephilim (Giants) in the earth in those days; and also after that, when the sons of God came in unto the daughters of men, and they bare children to them, the same became mighty men, which were of old, men of renown. And GOD saw that the wickedness of man was great in the earth, and that every imagination of the thoughts of his heart was only evil continually. And it repented the LORD that he had made man on the earth, and it grieved him at his heart." Gen 6:1-6

"Reality is merely an illusion, albeit a very persistent one." Albert Einstein, Physicist

"Everything we call real is made of things that cannot be regarded as real. If quantum mechanics hasn't profoundly shocked you, you haven't understood it yet." Neils Bohr, Inventor of the model of the Atom

"And wickedness very long continued and widespread pervaded all the races of men, until very little seed of justice was in them. For unlawful unions came about on earth, as angels linked themselves with offspring of the daughters of men, who bore to them sons, who on account of their exceeding great were called Nephilim. The angels, then, brought to their wives as gifts teachings of evil, for they taught them the virtues of roots and herbs, and dyeing and cosmetics and discoveries of precious materials, love-philtes, hatreds, amours, passions, constraints of love, the bonds of witchcraft, every sorcery and idolatry, hateful to God; and when this was come into the world, the affairs of wickedness were propagated to overflowing, and those of justice dwindled to very little." Gen 6: 1-4

"A new race has been found, which had not any object of manufacture like the Egyptians: their pottery, their statuettes, their beads, their mode of burial, are all unlike any other in Egypt, and not a single usual Egyptian scarab, or hieroglyph of carving, or amulet, or bead, or vase has been found in the whole of the remains in question. That we are dealing with something entirely different from any age of

Egyptian Civilization yet known, is therefore certain. That this race was not merely a local variety is almost certain, as these strange remains are found over more than a hundred miles of country, from Abydos to Gebelen. Our own work was in the middle of this district, between Ballas and Negada.

The race was very tall and powerful, with strong features: a hooked nose, long pointed beard, and brown wavy hair, are shown by their carvings and bodily remains." Sir Flinders Petrie, World Renowned Egyptologist, 1897

"The eyes of that species of extinct giant, whose bones fill the mounds of America have gazed on Niagara as we do now." Abraham Lincoln, American President, 1848

"And now, the Nephilim, who are produced from the spirits and flesh, shall be called evil spirits upon the earth, and on the earth shall be their dwelling. Evil spirits have proceeded from their bodies; because they are born from men and from the holy Watchers is their beginning and primal origin; they shall be evil spirits on earth, and evil spirits shall they be called. [As for the spirits of heaven, in heaven shall be they're dwelling, but as for the spirits of the earth which were born upon the earth, on the earth shall be their dwelling.] And the spirits of the Nephilim afflict, oppress, destroy, attack, do battle, and work destruction on the earth, and cause trouble: they take no food, but nevertheless hunger and thirst, and cause offences. And these spirits shall rise up against the children of men and against the women, because they have proceeded from them." Enoch 15:8-12

"The greatest form of control is where you think you're free when you're being fundamentally manipulated and dictated to. One form of dictatorship is being in a prison cell and you can see the bars and touch them. The other one is sitting in a prison cell but you can't see the bars but you think you're free.

What the human race is suffering from is mass hypnosis. We are being hypnotized by people like this: newsreaders, politicians, teachers, lecturers. We are in a country and in a world that is being run by unbelievably sick people. The chasm between what we're told is going on and what is really going on is absolutely enormous." David Icke, Political Activist, Present Day

The above statements are part of a recurring theme that every person on this planet partly knows is true when they open their minds and think within themselves. Deep down we all know the truth of our world, our eyes are just closed to it. We look around our planet and the more we dig into our past the more questions are left unanswered. The more we know for sure, the less we understand.

We praise those whom have given us "truths" and grant them rewards. Those who question these truths fall under scrutiny and are dismissed, some even put to death. One must look no further than our current paradigms to see that new ideas are labeled conspiracies to ensure we do not take them seriously. Human technological progression is repressed to allow those in power to slowly control human development, to ensure no independent technology can displace their power structure.

So new ideas are mocked and seen as creations of tinfoil hat wearing lunatics yet their claims are based on evidence we are just unwilling to accept as truth because it goes against what we are preprogrammed by society to conceive. How many were interested in the secular quotes above but rolled their eyes at the religious quotes due to preprogramming? Why have we been preprogrammed by socialization to deny the existence of a spiritual dimension? Who benefits?

We can leave these questions for now. Herein you will find truths that could free all mankind but have been deliberately hidden to empower the few over the many.

Prologue

Year 1119 AD, Reims, Champagne, France

A war between good and evil has raged throughout the ages and humanity is caught in the middle of it. This war has taken many shapes and forms. Sometimes the lines are not drawn easily, and the sides can be confused. Those caught in the fray are lost, and follow those who seem to know the way. The choice of whom to follow is up to the people, thus the people are the true power. Should we follow men of religion, or men of wealth and power? Who is most fit to rule over mankind, if anyone? Who can we trust to save us from ourselves?

Leading up to the first Crusade it was a time of Kings and Holy Men. The power split between the Imperial Authority of the Kings and the Divine Right to Rule of the Holy Roman Catholic Church.

The Church, under the command of Pope Calixtus II seeing in war an opportunity to weaken independent imperial authority, set the stage for the crusades, a Holy War in which the Pope would lead the Kings and their men, thus cementing the Pope as the most powerful figure in Europe at the time; in command of the combined armies of Europe. The Pope would create the World's first League of Nations, getting the Western Nations of Europe to band together to clean the Holy Lands of Islamist Rulers not under the control or influence of the Vatican. The Holy Land before the crusades was a peaceful place, where all religions could practice in peace. The Kingdom of Israel had been gone since General Titus of the Roman Empire wiped it out in 70 AD, in response to the Jewish Revolt in Rome of 66 AD.

The Kings of the world felt justified to rule, to place themselves over the rest. Most European Kings claimed to be descendants of the first great King Solomon. Solomon's wealth and power has long held its sway over the minds of men. Even modern day King's, try to trace their lineage back to Solomon. Being a descendant of Solomon, as modern Kings would claim, they could justify their lineage was elite. Before Solomon, and in the East, Kings and Pharaohs would claim they were Gods, or had direct access to those who came to Earth from the heavens and created mankind. Kings thus would always claim they had a God-given right to rule, thus they had a divine right. Solomon traced his lineage back to Babylon and the fish King Nimrod. Of course the Nimrod bloodline did not start here. Nimrod was a descendant of Noah, then Ham, and Cush. The flood of Noah was independently recorded in the Epic of Gilgamesh, along with over 2,000 other ancient texts, from Japan and Egypt to South America; the flood of the Bible and the story of a boat was recorded. A lost civilization, a pre-flood world, through Nimrod's bloodline some secrets were passed down all the way to Solomon.

Solomon was no ordinary King because of the unique knowledge he inherited. His use of the Kabala black magic, the Ark of the Covenant and a magical ring, allowed him to control demons; who according to first hand accounts built his grand temple. Of course, this history is now seen as superstition, as demons are considered fictitious. Solomon's temple would become the richest place on Earth, filled with gold and jewels, religious artifacts and ancient texts - all of which disappeared into thin air. Some believe there was enough gold in this one cache to double the known amount of gold in the world today.

Calixtus II became Pope; Crusader Knights invaded the Holy Land, set up a main port city in Acre and pushed the Saracens back into Jerusalem. Upon news of the military campaign in the Holy Lands reaching the walls of Jerusalem, the Pope called in his largest supporter, a noble by the name of St. Bernard of Clairvoux, a man that without doubt may be one of the most influential and powerful individuals to have ever lived.

St. Bernard of Clairvoux was one of the few religious elite on the rise. A relatively young man considering his power and influence. Bernard established the Cistercian Order in 1115 AD. The Cistercian Order took the story of the Virgin Mary and used it to hide their secret worship of the Goddess Isis. The Virgin Mary was never worshipped prior to the Cistercian Order. Isis can be seen all over the modern world as the figure called Liberty, most famously depicted in the Statue of Liberty holding the flame of Alexandria's Lighthouse, which Isis built. Bernard was the type of man for whom the ends always justified the means, and he would use his Order to further corrupt the Catholic Church as his contribution to the Grand Plan.

Bernard wanted to expand his order rapidly; he had vast ambitions. Hoping to expand his order into a third Monastery, he needed financial support from the Pope, the same Pope he had used his connections to help elect. Long had the Catholic Church been run by corrupt individuals. The Emperor Constantine had seen the power the Church had over its followers and decided to use the Church to his own benefit, converting Rome to a Catholic Empire. They added crosses to the Pagan symbols, and slowly Pagan beliefs changed into a mixture of Pagan Christian ideas that resulted in a new type of Christianity, one that was already altered by man. Not the religion Jesus had intended for us, the true meanings of his teachings lost and held secret by religious clergy that would use the teaching to benefit only themselves, for control.

The religious elite tossed out an extremely important teaching called the Book of Enoch, because they knew the Great Deception of the Watchers to come in the future would be explained away by information in this book. The Book of Enoch would vanish from history for hundreds of years, until recovered in recent history with the Dead Sea scrolls.

First, Bernard would require confirmation from the Pope on his new doctrines that created the Cistercian Order. He had written some alterations to French Church Doctrine, for which he had taken some just criticism. Then to appease the religious elites of the time, he had included an apology with his doctrines. Bernard thought he was beckoned to the Pope due to this apology and his release of his new doctrines, hopefully for approval.

St. Bernard was quite young but was already known as a Pope maker. He had long family connections to the new Pope Calixtus II and had been his personal advocate when being presented to the Royal families of Europe before being elected Pope. Bernard spoke on behalf of Calixtus II until the Royal Families backed the new pope. The Pope not only owed St. Bernard a favor, he owed him his position.

Chapter 1 – A Treasure for the Ages

Year 1119 AD, Reims, Champagne, France

Pope Calixtus II was seated at his desk, his stunningly beautiful white robe adorned with gold and gems. On his desk was a golden sculpture of a Pine Comb, much like the Pine Comb that adorned his staff. The pine comb symbolizes the pineal gland in the human brain, one of the ancient mysteries that had been passed down through the ages and landed in Babylon & Egypt.

Callixtus II began, "My son you are one of the pillars of our faith, may the others see your deeds and follow in their path. I have reviewed these new doctrines sent before me and I am very pleased, though your choice of Patron Saint the Virgin Mary is quite strange, we have no female Patron Saints for any of our existing orders."

St. Bernard responded, "Your Holiness, I only wish to serve God in the best way that I can. It is all a part of the Grand Plan; I am just doing my part. Is this to mean you approve of these doctrines, despite my choice?"

"As long as they include your Apology, I shall endorse these doctrines officially. Without the Apology, the current religious elites that back my position may withdraw their support for me due to our obvious connections. Our fate is intertwined, as it seems the more powerful your order grows; the more powerful my position as Pope becomes. Though my position in the Church is not questioned we have many enemies and we need to find a way to restore the power of the Church."

"If there was anything we could do, to reacquire the Vatican from Henry V?" St. Bernard questioned.

"Though I am beholden to God to keep this information to myself, our Church is in desperate times and I know of something that could restore us to power forever and rid the Holy Roman Emperor Henry V and his fake Pope from our City. It was not to be used and hidden forever, but the times are desperate and we must take the chance whilst I command the armies of Europe. The first step in the plan was to unify Europe, under my command, which has been done. We need the army to provide cover for what you are going to extract. I should only trust you St. Bernard with this information and you are to not tell anyone of this. You understand?"

St. Bernard sat forward in his chair; a quizzical look upon his face. "With God as our witness this secret shall remain with me until death."

"Forever, not just till death. You must forget what you learn once this mission is accomplished or your very soul will be haunted for all time." the Pope remarked, the pupils of his eyes growing dark and ominous. A cool chill ran through the room, causing Bernard's hair to stand on end.

Calixtus II paused clearly giving his next statement one last thought before delivering. Calixtus II knew the importance of the information all too well since becoming Pope and learning the secrets. He also knew that the Church stood at the precipice of greatness or slow demolishment, that now and forever the Church could establish its power over all or let it slip out of its grasp. He must act, and the only way to do so was to trust his closest ally.

Reluctantly he began, "There exists a treasure that belonged to King Solomon and is unknowingly in the grasp of the Saracens, who invaded the Holy Lands. It is lying under their very feet at this moment and they have no clue of its existence. It is the reason we march on Jerusalem at this very hour, as we believe it is still there unfound by the Muslim invaders. We have had spies watching the area in which it is located since we lost the Holy city in 77 AD. For a thousand years we have waited to reclaim our prize."

Calixtus paused, looking over Bernard. He saw a wonder in Bernard's eyes, that of a small child about to open a large gift. Calixtus wondered momentarily if he had made a huge mistake. He then recalled Bernard's undisputed loyalty and the realization that

Bernard's Cistercian Order needs his financial support. With renewed confidence, Calixtus II entrusts Bernard with the information.

"This treasure to the common man would seem of simple material value, but some value is not easily perceived. There exists information with this treasure that can empower those who have evil in their hearts and greed in their minds. This power was given to mankind and it can be used for good or evil, whoever possesses it can control the world. It threatens the foundation of our church and must be returned to us for safekeeping."

"I can trust only you with this information Bernard, as I owe you everything. The existence of this treasure and archive of knowledge has been concealed since the fall." Calixtus pauses, takes a long swig of his cup of wine and motions for Bernard to come closer. "There may be unseen visitors with us, let us whisper so they may not hear." The sound of an owl coos outside. The room feels cooler now, and Bernard swears he can see his breath despite the roaring fire in the corner of the room.

Calixtus leaned closer still and whispered into Bernard's ear to ensure no one outside the room could hear.

"The treasure is well-hidden deep in the granite of Temple Mount. You will find it below the very center of Solomon's Temple. Nine Chambers below the earth; do not dig straight down for peril lies with each chamber, you must go in from an angle as depicted by this manuscript. The treasure that I seek lies within the Ark of the

Covenant; the Ark cannot be opened. The temple of Solomon itself consists of an

unbelievable amount of gold and also more importantly the mystery teachings of

Heliopolis, Egypt the ancient mystery schools. These ancient texts and knowledge must

be destroyed, they are but lies cleverly written to seem as truths, they have been used in

the past to enslave mankind, and I fear they will be used again." Calixtus paused to take

a swig of wine and listen for any eavesdroppers, then continued in a hushed voice.

"This treasure is from many lands, half-stolen from Egypt upon the departure of Moses,

the other half stolen from Rome during the Jewish revolt of 66 AD. King Solomon used

this treasure of knowledge to build his vast Kingdom, and his complex architectural

structures. Rome used the texts and knowledge before they were lost in 66 AD to build

their vast empire, much as Alexander the Great had done before. The treasure has not

been seen since, as it has been buried for almost a thousand years. I know the exact

location of this treasure and we are about to take the City. If we could retake Jerusalem,

we may recover this treasure and ensure these secrets are destroyed."

"I understood that Moses fled Egypt with nothing but women and children and the

same for the Jewish revolts of 66 AD, my Holiness?" Bernard questioned with a

puzzled look upon his face.

Calixtus very sure of himself stated, "My son, the history of these events did not happen as you have been told. We have recorded them as we feel they should be told, the average man does not need to know the whole truth."

Sensing he had Bernard's full attention, he continued, "The proof is hidden under Jerusalem in the texts. Moses was not a leader of a band of slaves, mainly women and children as you may have thought. Moses grew up in Egyptian court because the Pharaoh Hatshepsut adopted him, plucked him from the basket sent down the Nile. A story later adopted by the founders of the city of Rome, but its origins are from Moses. Moses was a great military leader, accumulated over 60 positions within the Egyptian court according to the hieroglyphs under Pharaoh Hatshepsut. Moses served for thirty years under the Pharaoh protecting the Northern lands of Egypt from invasion. Moses had an intricate knowledge of the terrain and experience moving large groups of people through that terrain in haste. Moses was in charge of a band of Hebrew warriors that were called the Habiru. These Habiru are well recorded as being the guardians on Egypt's northern border, basically protecting the Sinai Peninsula from invasion. They were considered elite warriors.

"Hatshepsut was a woman pharaoh and advanced the culture of Egyptian society more than any other Pharaoh. She worshipped at the feet of one God, and established a society to represent a One God ideology. She built the two largest obelisks in Egypt, expanded trade and ruled over Egypt during what is called a golden age. Her downfall was her worship of one God and not the many gods of her predecessors. Previous pharaohs had set themselves up as part king, part god, to ensure ultimate control: this they learned from the same texts you will destroy. The people would worship the pharaoh; and the pharaoh would use the serpent priests to create various religious teachings to keep the working class under control. The laws were of man and his invented gods, not the laws of the one true God. These Serpent priests were not a part of Hatshepsut's plans, and she was doing away with the ancient gods thanks to her interactions with Moses, whom had seen the true God.

"This change from worshipping many gods, to solely the teachings of one made the religious elite unhappy. It also was the first time a pharaoh did not claim to be part divine. Most pharaohs claimed to be genetically different, direct descendants of the gods, therefore had divine bloodlines. The Hieroglyphs do depict rather anomalous physical features for the pharaohs by comparison, including King Tutankhamen whose recovered skull was very strangely shaped. She constantly had to deal with a group of high serpent priests who felt she was not following tradition. These priests believed in upholding the idea of many gods. Even the location of her capital city Thebes was chosen as a compromise to the high priests. The priests had long held a tradition of moving the capital depending on the star signs. To compromise Hatshepsut built a beautiful city at Karnak, halfway between the two proposed sites. At Karnak she had built the Temple of Man, which angered the high priests enormously as it was an indication of the method of freedom for the people. The priests knew an enlightened human would see the truth in the configuration of this temple of Man and be set free. So they hid the meaning and covered up all her works.

"She was assassinated by Ramses III and then wiped from the history books. To the victor go the spoils. After she was dead and gone, all of her works were concealed, and her existence was wiped from the map. All of her hieroglyphs were covered over by Ramses III. The new one God idea she promoted was wiped from the map as well. Her capitol city moved and her elite band of Habiru warriors became a threat to the new Pharaoh.

"Ramses III was a proud Pharaoh and wanted to ensure the Habiru would not be able to rise up against him. So the new Pharaoh Ramses III decided to repurpose the Habiru as peasant workers, stripping them of their weapons, land, titles, and possessions. The Habiru had been mighty warriors and the demotion from warrior to peasant farmer was horrible for them. The Habiru would eventually leave Egypt, taking their families with them for freedom from their tyrannical Pharaoh under the direction of their General Moses.

"Moses, fearing for his life after his adopted mother was killed left Egypt. He went out across the lands that he had defended for Hatshepsut faithfully for years. At which point, divine intervention occurred, to ensure Moses would follow the laws of God and not the Laws of the Isis at the mountain of Sinai, telling him to go back to Egypt and save his people from Ramses III. So Moses went back to Egypt and with the help of God, seven curses fell upon Egypt allowing for Moses to free the Habiru (Hebrew) people, but Moses and his warriors didn't leave empty-handed.

"Pharaoh Ramses III took over an Egypt full of riches, and without any real enemies thanks to the successful golden years of Hatshepsut. Many letters have been seen written to the Pharaoh asking him for gold because "Gold is as dust in the land of my brother the Pharaoh" Egypt's gold and other mineral production in the ancient past was unmatched, with mines stretching up and down the Nile and into Southern Africa. This gold is mainly unaccounted for in our current time, as most is still buried in Solomon's temple, the Egyptians never recorded how much gold they held, this way they could increase the value of the Gold they already owned by making it seem rarer than it really was. Calixtus II noticed the rapt attention of Bernard, drained his cup, refilled it, and continued.

"In the end the Pharaoh Ramses III had no choice but to let Moses go. The last straw was the loss of every first-born child of Egypt. The Pharaoh didn't want to show weakness but decided he would be better off just letting his work force leave rather than having them burn down his entire Empire. So Ramses III let Moses and his Habiru warriors leave.

"Moses was leaving not just to get out of Egypt. Moses was leaving to establish a Kingdom in the Holy Lands promised to him by God. Wanting to ensure his new state would be successful, he decided to use this position to his advantage. The Pharaoh Ramses had retreated to his Capitol at Thebes in Southern Egypt with the majority of his Chariot army, leaving the Northern Half of Egypt mainly unguarded.

"Moses' Habiru warriors raided many of the cities of Northern Egypt and raided them. They took a huge amount of gold and weapons from the Pharaoh, and then raided the city of Alexandria and the plateau of Giza. More importantly they raided the Mystery Schools of Heliopolis, the schools established by the Goddess Isis. In Heliopolis they acquired the ultimate truth, pieces of information given to man by a long lost ancient civilization, those who had actually built the pyramids before the global flood. Once the Habiru had taken everything they could, they left with Moses for the desert.

"The Habiru warriors protected the civilians as they travelled. Moses used his knowledge of the terrain to position his troops for the perfect escape through the marshes of the Red Sea, the same area of desert he patrolled as a 30-year general in the Egyptian army. God assisted them as well, lighting the way with a pillar of fire in the night sky.

"Once Pharaoh Ramses III realized how much gold, artifacts and weapons were stolen, he changed his mind. He couldn't let the Habiru leave with a vast amount of his gold and the artifacts. He lost so much he decided to send his entire army of chariots after Moses and his band of warriors.

"The rest is history of which you have heard. Obviously Moses, his warriors and people escaped untouched with all the gold, and the artifact. The Egyptian Army got stuck in the mud and waters of the Red Sea. Moses knew on foot, even carrying a lot of cargo his men would be able to navigate this marshy section of the Red Sea if they left at the start of low tide. He also knew the chariots of the Pharaoh's army would get stuck in the mud and the tide would come in on them before they could get across. His planned worked to perfection.

"God had granted them a land for their own, if they could wipe the land clean of the Nephilim. Tribes of Nephilim Giants, for example Goliath was an Amalekite (vampire like demon), these tribe of Nephilim called Amalekites are the true source of stories of Vampires. The Israelites went from city to city wiping out all inhabitants on their March to Jerusalem, eliminating the remnants of the Nephilim and all the genetic strangeness that ensued from them that survived the flood. Many famous examples of this can be found.

"The city of Jericho was thought of as impenetrable due to its city walls. Until Moses arrived with the Ark, the population swelled with fear. According to the Old Testament, Moses had his men circle the city of Jericho for seven days with the Ark of the Covenant, and on the seventh day they circled while blowing their horns; and when they had done this the walls crumbled to the ground. The people of Jericho saw the great walls of their city toppled by power of the Ark of the Covenant and the blows of their horns. The Ark gave Moses power over a force that could not be seen, so it was taken as magic, rather than what it was; resonant energy in the walls being vibrated by the sound of the horns thus destroying the walls. You see they charged the walls with resonant sound energy emanating from the ark, and when they blew the horns the energy vibrated in the walls, which clashed with the frequency of the horn blasts causing them to crumble. The ark has influence on matter as all matter has a vibrational frequency. When Moses and his Army reached Jerusalem, they wiped the city clean of inhabitants. All of this is recorded in the Old Testament."

Bernard looks over to the Pope to see the gratification of a finished statement but did not receive it. "Is there more, Your Grace?" He asked sheepishly.

"Solomon's treasure from Egypt was added to when, in 66 AD the Jewish Revolt in Rome occurred. The Jewish people raided the Roman Capitol and stole important documents from the Empire, as well as, a vast amount of gold. This wealth of knowledge and financial wealth were brought to Jerusalem and added to the Temple of King Solomon. Jerusalem now had more gold than all the other kingdoms in the world combined, and most of the world's most precious sacred artifacts. Realizing the importance of what they held, they buried the treasure and the artifacts deep under Solomon's temple on Temple Mount before the city was sacked by the Saracens." Calixtus II drained his cup a second time, set it down with finality and waited on Bernard's response to this newfound knowledge.

Bernard considered what he had just heard at length. He questioned parts of the story Calixtuss II had told him, but with every query the Pope had a solid answer and evidence pointing to this story being concrete. After a few minutes of discussion, Bernard decided he did not doubt the authenticity of what the Pope had said. It was just difficult for him to process this information because it went against most of what he had been taught over the course of his life. Feigning indifference he decided to delve quickly into the logistics.

"Moving that amount of gold and sacred artifacts will hardly be secretive. We will need a large team of dedicated trustworthy men. No one but you or I can know of the true nature of this quest. How will we accomplish this my Holiness?"

"The Crusades my son, we have almost taken the city back. We told the people it was God's Will to reclaim the Holy Lands. Really, it was our will, as God acts through us, so we must get our gold and artifacts back; before they ruin us. Even if we do not hold Jerusalem we will retrieve the artifacts. We have the means already in place, my son.

"You are related to Hugh de Payan, and his eight other Knights of Christ. They are all related to you by blood or by marriage, yes? I have had them all vetted and I feel they are all trustworthy. Fortunately nine is the exact number of Knights we require, as there are nine sacred artifacts to protect according to the ancient texts. They should travel to the Holy Land under the premise they are going to help defend the roads around Jerusalem. However, have them present this letter to King Baldwin and he should allow them residence in the Temple of Solomon. Under this temple they can dig to find the treasure of Solomon. Once recovered, the nine golden chests, each containing an artifact, must to be returned to me unopened. The ninth chest you will recognize, and it must remain hidden at all times. Under no circumstances are the contents of the nine chests to be revealed, not even to those who find them, for the information contained within may destroy our faith. There is said to be over 5,000 tons of gold along with the nine artifacts. You may keep the gold as payment, but the sacred relics belong to the church. The amount of gold should suffice as payment and allow you to rapidly grow the Cistercian Order. You may increase the number of Knights in the Cistercian order for defense of the trade routes in the Holy Land, to keep this treasure trove safe upon its return" As he finished the Pope took out a seal and a candle. Sealing a pre-written letter with his seal, he handed it to St. Bernard.

"Five thousand tons of gold is worth more than all the sacred relics in the world Father. You have my word, let us begin our work". St. Bernard left the room in great haste. He now had a mission, and a plan to not only help restore the Catholic, but he would have all the assets he would need to build his new Cistercian Order.

Chapter 2 – The Greatest Lie Ever Told

Year 1128 AD, Jerusalem, Temple Mount

Andre stared across the Temple Mount and wondered how much longer it would take. He had been restlessly pursuing access to the Temple of Solomon, ever since his uncle St. Bernard of Clairvoux found the location of a great discovery. The year was 1128 AD, and his nine French Brethren had taken up residence in Jerusalem, at least for now. He knew they were about to uncover one of the most amazing treasure troves in existence. The Treasure of Solomon, the Kingdom of Israel's first King. The amount of gold was told to be legendary, and even may contain some of the most famous pieces of religious relics in the world.

Unknown to the Christian crusaders or to King Baldwin of Israel, the Temple of Solomon held far more than just gold or religious relics; it held a truth that had been forgotten, hidden. Deep beneath the Temple lay the ultimate truth. The Nine Poor Knights had used their power, wealth and influence to attain the location of this ancient treasure. Hugh de Payan had convinced King Baldwin of Jerusalem with his secret letter from the Pope, that his new order of poor warrior monks would ensure safe passage along the roads of Jerusalem in order for access and privacy in the Temple of Solomon. Seeing only a solution to a major problem, for just the price of residence, the King had granted their wishes.

God must be on their side, Andre thought, their plan had been perfectly executed thus far. Andre and his brethren had no opposition; no one else in the world knew the location of this treasure. Without knowing where to find it, the treasure would never have been found. The secret had been buried in Vatican records for a very long time as the Catholic Church was in no position to reacquire the treasure from Israel. The Holy Lands belonged to the Saracens, and they were extremely vicious under the command of Salahdin.

St. Bernard would transform the Poor Militia of Christ to the beginnings of the most powerful organization to exist on planet earth; the Knights Templar. His goal was to become personally wealthy and powerful, the end result was far more than any could have imagined.

For now, Andre knew they were very close. The Saracens had raided the Temple of Solomon, but they missed what laid below the temple, the real treasure.

The tunnel was to be dug at the entrance to a cavern roughly 100 feet straight below the floor of the Temple, precisely on the center point of the Holy of the Holies in the Temple, where the Ark had laid before the Roman Invasion of 70 AD. The nine

The Lost Truth by Dean Fougere

Templars had taken up residence in the Temple and had not interacted with anyone other than their personal guards standing watch outside. The guards had been used for logistical means more than security, as the entire Temple Mount was under heavy guard already. From outside the Temple, no one could see the major excavation that was going on. The Templars had been digging for weeks, hoping to find what had been described in the ancient manuscript.

The digging had been difficult, as the Temple Mount was built from enormous megalithic stones of bedrock. The Temple Mount itself resembled a giant flat platform, which had been built of enormous large megalithic blocks. Three major religions have built temples on the Temple Mount and all three can trace the origins of their religions to this spot; those religions being Christianity, Islam, and Judaism.

The Templars used simple metal digging tools and had a very difficult time digging through the hardened rock, which resulted in an arduous nine-year ordeal. Whoever had buried the treasure had not intended for it to be found, ever. More oddly, the path to the treasure seemed as if it had never been previously excavated, finding no natural path of least resistance, as one would expect from rediscovering an old tunnel. It seemed as if the original tunnel builders had removed the blocks of stone in their way; one huge piece at a time, then had put them back into place and practically melted the stone back together, leaving almost no seams, but strangely did not use mortar as if there had been no need, as if the blocks had been literally melted together.

The Templars had neither the technology nor the know-how to get blocks of that size out of the ground unnoticed, so they chipped up each block and removed them piecemeal. At eighty-five feet the tunnel seemed to end, however it was just a turn in the angle. This was to throw off any excavators that had gotten this far. Without knowing the angle, and the depth from the ancient manuscript St. Bernard had been given by the Pope, there would have been no way to determine where and how the tunnel should be dug. The angle was determined by the using a square and compass to determine the angle of the Great Pyramid's Queen's Chamber.

This same coded manuscript with the exact dimensions of the Great Pyramid of Giza and the tunnel to be dug into the Temple Mount was now directly in front of Hugh de Payan as he studied the pages for the millionth time. The translation he had done seemed accurate but they had no way of knowing, unless they were to find the chamber of treasure.

There was a sudden blur of excitement as Gondemar and Rosal came running across the flat surface of the Temple Mount towards Andre. Certainly, they had found the entrance to the cavern of Solomon's temple. They had finally found the largest cache of riches in the ancient world. Their excitement could not be contained.

Gondemar, blurted out to Andre, "Come Brother! We have found a hollow space, right where it was supposed to be!"

Rosal emphasized, "Our time is now upon us come Brother!"

Andre sprung to action, "We found it? It is real?"

Andre, Rosal and Gondemar walked in between the Grand remains of the two pillars Jachin and Boaz that had once flanked the Temple of Solomon and represented Sun and Moon or Day and Night. They walked up the seven steps into the Temple of Solomon and over to the entrance of the excavation. The floor of the temple was black and white checkerboard pattern, representing life and death. Standing there waiting to descend were their six other Templar Bretheren; all Frenchmen of noble blood: Hugh de Payan the Grandmaster, Geoffroi de St. Omer, Payen de Montdiddier, Achambaud de St-Amand, Geoffroi Bisol and Godfroi. These nine were to be the first to rediscover a truth buried since before the time of Christ, yet they had no idea what they had uncovered.

Hugh de Payan blessed the nine knights and they entered into the darkness of the tunnel. After descending the 100 feet down to the chamber they stepped inside one by one, led by Hugh de Payan.

At first, the scene was not as expected. The cavern was roughly 50 feet square, and the ceiling rounded. The entire space was lined with dark, basically black granite. Even with lit torches it seemed as if they were suspended in space.

In the middle of the room were nine large boxes made of what looked like gold but the gold looked green, not yellow. The boxes were floating in a triangle shape in the middle of the room, three boxes per side. In the middle of the floor over which the boxes floated was a pyramid glyph; the pyramid had thirteen steps and a glowing green capstone. One of the boxes, the box at the top of the pyramid was instantly recognizable to them and was giving off its own glow, almost as if it were an energy source. It was larger than the others slightly and had two winged angels on top. The wings of the angels came close to touching but didn't, and a stream of electricity flowed between the tips of the wings. It was the Ark of the Covenant. The other boxes had many strange symbols on them.

On the floor in front of the boxes was a strange altar symbol. The front of the altar displayed a hooked X, with an equal sign next to it and 1/0, known as a math equation today except for the strange X symbol it read X= 1/0. On the left side of the altar glowed a gold depiction of the Goddess Isis, and on the right a depiction of the God Osiris. Depicted on the side facing the nine gold boxes, away from the Knights, were three men standing together: on the left was King Solomon, in the middle standing taller than the other two and facing the West with one eye open was Horus, and on the right was the Architect of the Temple of Solomon Hiram. On top of the altar was a ring; in ancient Hebrew it had the Name of God on it. Also on the altar there was an emerald tablet, and two vials of blood. Without hesitation Hugh de Payan picked up the ring and glanced over the tablet.

To the left, the west side of the wall was a five-pointed star, the pentagram upside down, and bright red, embroidered in white on the field of black granite. In ancient Hebrew it read underneath "Energy is held within." Also in the room on the right side of the wall, the east side was a six-pointed star, a symbol they had seen, and they knew it as the Star of David. This symbol was also red with white embroidery, and stood out on the field of black granite. This symbol had in ancient Hebrew, 'As above So Below' written underneath.

On the middle wall was a map of the whole earth, though not a map the Knights recognized. It showed the world with vast lands between Asia and Europe that to their knowledge did not exist. The map had 12 evenly spread circumference lines running through it like a grid, and where the lines intersected there were markers. Thirteen of the markers had unique symbols next to them. The very middle of the map was the most profound intersection point, and it was centered on the Giza Plateau. Hugh de Payan quickly realized this map was more than just decorative and started to draw it. The other knights stared at it with awe.

Most amazing was the ceiling of the chamber; one look up and one would think they were staring at a starry night sky. The ceiling was an exact replication of the night sky above the temple mount when the chamber was constructed. A different diamond represented each star. Set into the black granite ceiling was one of the most amazing sights any of the knights had ever seen. Soon they realized that three of the constellations had been set apart being made from pink diamonds. The constellations they recognized were Orion, and Sirius. The third was a group of seven stars they did not recognize. After studying the ceiling for some time the Knights moved on to the objects on the floor.

Hugh de Payan approached the box at the top of the pyramid and dropped to his knees, and his brothers joined him. For they knew what they were looking at, and couldn't believe their eyes. It was the Ark of the Covenant. As he reached forward to touch it, with the ring on, the box started to glow more, and the gold seemed to start moving without changing form, almost as if it were a liquid. There was no lid on the Ark, it was as if the lid had been seamlessly welded into the top of the box. Andre noticed the objects on the wall had begun to glow in the light of the ark and he ordered the men to kill their torches.

As soon as the torches had been extinguished the room came alive. The diamonds on the ceiling were glowing as if they were being powered by their own light: the red stars on the east and west wall started to emit a red glow across the room, bright enough that the knights had no trouble seeing. The map on the wall revealed that at each intersection point was a bright white glowing dot. The map also changed dramatically, revealing a new landscape: the land grew, and the oceans shrank all over the world, revealing large new areas. The Mediterranean, Persian Gulf and many other areas that are now great seas or bays disappeared entirely. The mid ocean ridges closed, and the water disappeared back into the cracks. Above the map an eye appeared, with streams of light coming out of it, depicting the eye as watching over the map. The knights took in the scene with great awe and then relit their torches.

Andre de Martin moved forward toward the map, and in so doing, stepped on the top of the pyramid glyph on the floor, and with his weight just on the capstone of the Pyramid it sank into the floor slowly. The pyramid glyph sank into the ground; the base of the pyramid even with the floor of the room, each layer up the pyramid was another step down into a larger chamber beneath. The thirteen-step pyramid ended up being thirteen stairs down into a much, much larger room. Clearly there was a lot more in this temple than just nine chests.

In the room below was an enormous amount of gold, approximately 9000 tons of gold coins, gold bricks and all manner of gold objects in the room. Stacked all the way to the ceiling, there was more gold in this one room than any of the countries of Europe had combined. A large amount of ancient books had been catalogued in a library of texts lying next to the gold on the west side of the room. At first glance the Knights could not read any of the texts, as they had been written in Sumerian, Vedic and Egyptian Hieroglyphs. They then found some written in Latin that seemed to be translations of the other texts. There was only one marking on the wall: it was in ancient Sumerian text. Had they been able to read it, they would have understood it to say, "Gold belongs to the gods".

The gold was the intended prize for the knights, but curiosity on this day would change the world forever. Based on the experience they just had in the room above, the huge room of gold was far less intriguing. They decided the gold could wait, but they needed to open the chests to see what was inside, despite the Pope instructing them otherwise.

Hugh de Payan said a quick prayer, and then the nine knights spread out to each box. Despite the Pope's strict orders, the Knights had endlessly dug to reach this cavern and would rather be damned then not to learn the contents of the boxes. They would open them all at once, and determine the contents. The boxes had no locks.

As soon as Hugh gave the signal, each Knight opened their box and what was inside shocked them, made no sense to them, and would change their lives immediately and forever. Each box contained an emerald tablet, a vial of blood in a glass tube, and three of the boxes had small swords made from the stakes of Christ's cross, the three spears of destiny. Hugh de Payan began to read his tablet, "All is Number, God is All". As Hugh continued to read aloud the Gospel they all shared the other Knights each pulled out a glass vial of blood from their respective boxes, Hugh had two with him at the altar.

The ninth box, the recognizable box, was the Ark of the Covenant; its contents unreachable, as the box had no discernible lid, almost as if the lid had been melted into the rest of the box. There was no way to open it. On the side facing them was the symbol of God's Name that adorned the books from which they now read.

A long pause ensued while Hugh de Payan carefully weighed his next thought. He then read the tablet. His eyebrows rose in wonderment, and he had a very incredulous look upon his face. What seemed like hours passed, as Hugh and the nine others read carefully the text together. Upon conclusion they discussed what they had just learned.

"The secret is now known only by us" Hugh angrily declared, "The Church is a lie, the proof is obvious and we shall not be unenlightened anymore. This could not be forgery; the knowledge within is profound and powerful. No man can deny these truths, this tablet explains all."

Andre interrupted, "We must do as the Gods state, the world has been living under a false master, who allows free choice to create chaos. We can end the chaos and the pointless death, though we may not be there in the end, we can start the process and be remembered for all time for our deeds. With this new bloodline, these weapons, the ark, the ring and the spears, our children will recall our virtues and rule over mankind to establish a world of peace and truth, a world of Order under our reign and with these ancient gods helping us."

Hugh retorts, "According to this, the history of the world is in this blood, and if we consume it, we shall be the enlightened men destined to rule the world with this new-found power, over the forces of evil."

Andre and his brethren pulled out and drink nine of the ten vials, changing them physically. Hugh declared the tenth and final copy of the emerald tablets would be saved for their accomplice St. Bernard, as he was needed for their plan to work.

The nine knights used their new-found technology to seamlessly lift the countless pieces of gold and nine chests up the 100' nearly vertical tunnel. They stacked the nine chests of artifacts and the countless chests of gold in the Temple above. These nine chests were to be secretly transported from Jerusalem separately, each with a different route to a destination only known by each individual Knight and not the others, for safekeeping if they were captured. The Ark of the Covenant was to be moved first, as soon as possible, via a nearby heavily defended port city of Acre, under the watchful eye of the newly appointed Grand Worshipful Master Hugh de Payan. The tenth vial of blood was put into the Golden Chest, protected by Andre de Martin, and the vial and Gospel was to be delivered to St. Bernard before the chest was hidden.

The artifacts would be hidden away for future use. First the gold would be used to create a central banking system as described in the texts. The first step into creating a global utopia would be a global banking system run by the Templars, backed by their newly found gold.

That second evening the nine chests were loaded onto nine separate convoys all heading for the ports of Acre or over land via large convoys of newly recruited Knights into the order of the nine knights, now named the Knight's of Solomon's Temple, or the

Knight's Templar. The nine knights would establish control over the transportation of the lands around Jerusalem, and to do this they would need a large mobile force of well armed, well trained, and well funded knights. They already had the funds, but according to the new doctrine, they were not to use their newly found wealth but rather to conceal it, and by loaning it to the people it could be used as a method of ultimate control, The wealth would grow, and they could only spend the profits of their loans and businesses. Their gold had to become the backbone of a central banking system they would use to gain control of all national sovereignty.

The agreement to join was simple: a Knight's Templar was to join the order and give up all his personal free will, money, and titles. Once in the order, he would no longer need any of these, as the order would provide anything he desired and more -- the gift of enlightenment. The initiant would be rewarded with an eternal afterlife, to be known for all time as a savior of mankind and servant of the True God Enki. By devoting his life to the True God he could become a servant of him, and become his own personal Temple of God within, for man to become divine.

The nine knights did not share their knowledge of the truth with the new recruits, because they had to use the power of knowledge for their own benefit until they were powerful enough to not be destroyed by their foes. Their followers would be allowed to learn the secret truths they held by a commitment to the order and by studying the teachings of the books uncovered in the lower library.

These nine chests and teachings were destined for hidden locations in France, Scotland and England. Hugh de Payan and his brethren would return to France to leverage their newly found knowledge and wealth to gain immense support from the Catholic community, and to start carrying out their plans.

Watching over the Knights Templar had been what seemed an old man with a long white beard. He watched closely as Andre had loaded his wagon with the chest containing St. Bernard's vial, noticing one chest had been very carefully concealed on the way to the carriage. This must be something of great value to Andre thought the old man, and therefore of value to me.

The old man was dressed as a Christian Monk who had access to the grounds and the sympathy of the Knights Templars. He had gone unnoticed while; he had been observing the unusual activity at the Temple as of late. He did not care for what was taking place inside. His mission was one of vengeance: Andre de St. Bernard would pay for his crimes. He would wait until Andre left the confines of Jerusalem, then he would end his miserable existence in the most unpleasant way imaginable. Though he knew ending Andre would have to suffice, he knew nothing could bring his family back. For now Hassan-I would just be patient and wait, perhaps he would retreat to his favorite vantage point and some hashish would help calm his mind.

Chapter 3 – Rude Awakening

Modern Day – Boston, USA

I am waiting on a park bench, across from Boston Commons Loews theatre. I see my target leave the building, an Iranian foreign national here on business. He had just finished meeting with his contact in the busy theatre. I move into the crowd.

Then I see him, the man in the crowd, walking away from me faster and faster. All my focus on him directly, people passing by in a blur, no faces just shadows. Then I reach him, stick my knife in his side and twist. Feeling the blade rip through the ribs into his organs and soft tissue around the heart.

He turns to face me, and I cannot believe what I am seeing. It is my face looking back at me, then I feel the cold wet blood on my hand and I wake.

Waking up in a cold sweat, my hand in a pool of it. Must have been what I felt in the dream, I think. I head over to the sink and wash my face, trying to clear my mind. Looking outside, I'm surprised to see it is a sunny day in Boston. I had grown up in this cold, dark city and I longed for a warmer climate. For some reason I couldn't leave, never could put a finger on it, but I loved the city as well. The sports teams, the bars, the people were appealing. I had slept in after a long flight home the night before. Despite the sunny blue skies, it was a typical freezing cold day in December. So I sat down at my desk, slowly stirring my morning cup of coffee.

My name is Titus Frost, I am a warrior, a killer. Abandoned by my parents at a hospital as an infant with nothing but a diaper, a blanket, and a first name, "Titus" A British family living in Boston of the name Frost later adopted me. I never was able to locate my original parents. The Frosts raised me right and tried to change my nature, but failed and I became that which all men fear the harbinger of death. No man who had been in my cross hairs had yet lived. I strike in silence, from a distance, the target never sees me, but I see them, more closely than I have ever seen anyone else in my life.

I have had an inherit taste for death since birth. While my friends played baseball, I practiced moving through wooded areas unseen. Sometimes, I would disappear for days, staying in the woods overnight and sleeping under the moon. Other times I would find a vantage point and use my airsoft gun to shoot passersby in the woods with metal BB's. Loneliness became a joy: I always preferred to be on my own, rather than constricted by others. Something inherent in my nature made me want to walk a lonely path, a narrow path of my own.

There seemed something wrong with this world, a world in which a parent would abandon a child, even if to give me a better life; I became embittered and lacked comprehension of their possible reasoning. I never accepted my adopted parents as my own, despite their endless attempts.

I did quite well in school, like most kids without friends. I was able to drown out the torment of the others by engrossing myself in books, mainly on the history of war and bloodshed that fascinated me so.

In college I studied history focusing on warfare, especially Middle Eastern warfare. The events of 9/11 had occurred during my high school tenure and I knew the wars of the future would be against the Middle East. So I decided to study my enemy. After college I joined the armed forces, hoping to one day become a Navy Seal Sniper.

After passing through officer school in the Navy I was given the opportunity to attend Bud/S Navy Seal Training Program. Here I found the hardest challenge of my life, becoming a SEAL is the most difficult thing I had ever done by a long shot, and my accomplishment elevated me to an elite level of warrior that had never existed before on the planet. We had become more than man by the end of the training, establishing new limits on the human body that before seemed unimaginable. The training was designed to push the candidate to new limits, breaking through the physical constraints that pain causes in the mind, once the mind had been trained properly, the body could surpass the normal physical limitations. We were akin to the phoenix, reborn through fire and pain into a new form more magnificent than before, capable of reaching new heights.

I had joined the Navy Seals to take down dictators of the Middle East and the evil men of the world. Some would call me a true believer, and found that dangerous, as I truly believed in the Constitution and the United States, in freedom. However, my time in the service would be short-lived. I had come across bits of the truth during my short stint in the Navy Seals on a classified mission in Northern Iran. As the theory goes, the truth is far scarier than fiction.

We were sent into Northern Iran to recover an artifact that had been held since the time of the creation of the Fedayeen, which started as the Assassin's Order. This order had created the idea of sacrificing oneself in combat to achieve a place in paradise; the suicide bombers in modern day still used this ideology. The group Hezbollah, funded by Iran, had reinstated this practice with the Beirut Marine Barracks bombing, killing hundreds & forcing America to withdraw all troops from Lebanon. The teachings had to be destroyed or removed from Iran to ensure they did not carry on in the future, and were based upon ancient documents Hasan-I Sabbah had taken from the Templars. This was not taught in history books but was true nonetheless.

After the mission, we had been debriefed, and during this debriefing they tried to wipe our memories. My squad checked into the CIA Black Site in Pakistan after the mission. That night while we slept, the CIA gassed the bunks and knocked out my team. They then gave my team members chemical injections that caused acute amnesia, making them forget the past two months, and, replaced our mission files with a new mission to undertake in Afghanistan, and removed all the documents and data we had recovered from Iran. They were going to wipe our memories with a new serum they had developed that erased all recent memory from the mind; what a person cannot recall, a person cannot tell. The CIA wanted no one to remember we were searching for a ring in the highlands of Iran, or that we were there at all. A special artifact was not found, but we did uncover documentation proving Benghazi was a cover operation for arming ISIS terrorists in Syria with weapons, including chemical.

Just before the gas poured in, I had a dream. In my dream a voice told me to wake up, but not move, and keep my blood pure. I awoke and saw my squad mates sleeping, then heard the gas. Keeping down, I pulled my sheets over my mouth and watched as the CIA run Ghost Team (part of the JSOC special unit The Activity) entered the room and scanned for movement. The Activity moved in and started injecting the chemical into the right forearm of each of my squad mates. I used my sheet's corner and slowly and silently tied off my arm to keep any blood from flowing. I was last to be injected and the CIA team quickly left. I got up and ran to the bathroom, cut my arm and let the chemicals and blood pour into the sink. I didn't forget what I saw, and after my tour was over I would leave the Navy Seals with honor, and start my real mission. I had to maintain my ties to the intelligent services or they might try to erase me from existence out of fear of what I might know and remember.

The Lost Truth by Dean Fougere

I have a modest apartment in Boston's North End. My foster parents had passed in a car accident while I was on tour and left behind a small fortune. My taste for expensive things was gone; my mission to reveal the truth was all that was left. I thought by secretly killing off those who had taken over the world, I could bring to light the truth and free peoples' minds. I had no real hobbies, and my only passion was for putting full metal jacket rounds on target anyways.

In public I am fairly unnoticeable. I was a standard height at 6'1", with green eyes and dark brown hair in a close crop; I easily blend into most crowds, looking as comfortable in a tuxedo as I am in the jungle in camouflage. Despite having multiple tattoos none of them show with jeans and a T-Shirt on, publicly visible tattoos make it too easy to identify people. I live alone and have no significant relationship to speak of, which I. prefer as it makes life easier to conceal.

Upon retirement from the Navy I worked as a gun for hire, mainly dealing in death. My connections to the intelligence community as a Navy Seal sniper ensured after my retirement my old friends would want to hire me as a private contractor. This way I could do the things they wanted to do but could not. At first I wanted to say no, but realized I had no choice or they might find out I knew their secret. I would need someone to help me from within to carry out my ultimate plan.

They had tried to convince me to join a private contractor firm like Blackwater (Academy) after my retirement, but with my hidden ulterior motive I preferred to work independently. Blackwater had increasingly become a pawn of the corrupt officials in the white house, carrying out the dirty work, the very dirty work I wanted to expose. Joining a private firm would have cemented me in the system, and I would have been killed if I tried to expose the organization from within. The Academy, as they were now called, was operating on the ground in the Ukraine and Pakistan carrying out assassinations and starting revolution. When Blackwater the Academy called, I cited the fact I was independently wealthy; I stated I would only accept certain jobs and wanted full diplomatic protection for travel. Blackwater refused this, but JSOC didn't. Due to my unique skills, JSOC granted my protection. I would be their independent assassin. Freedom from Blackwater association was actually preferred, as Blackwater was a political mess.

I needed to use my connections to find the right targets and to be allowed to live in the US and operate freely around the world. The JSOC group shared me with CIA and NSA, along with private citizens, and they all thought they were using me, but in reality they helped me by concealing my actions. Thanks to the Navy Seals I had all the training I would need to work as a private assassin, and thanks to the CIA I had the cover to move about undetected. I had to use their own system against them, to attack from within.

Up until this point my targets had all been underworld targets, men that worshipped only their own lust, greed was their only God. Lavishing themselves on money, drugs, women, material objects while causing pain and suffering to those who stood in their way. They were no better than the men giving me the orders to kill them, so I did and was able to remain undetected in the employ of those whom I would eventually destroy.

I had just returned from my last assignment the night prior. This last target was most likely the first person I ever killed that had never shot a gun in anger. I only would take targets that I felt deserved to die, and this last target proved most satisfying. This target had been a man who profited from the enslavement of others. His main fear was that of his own death, and he had done everything he could to make his current life more sensational.

Unlike most men of the underworld, this man had decided to hide in plain sight as a banker, using his position in the bank to hide the money he made but mostly inherited. The bank he was part owner of, was one of the most influential banks in the world, a bank that was part of a web, a master system of control.

I wondered why I had the same nightmare of stalking myself again. I did not believe in foreboding or fate, so I assumed it was just most likely stress. The last kill had gone smoothly, and I had no fear of repercussions, as I had cleanly left the crime scene afterward. Or did I?

I decided to run the whole nights events over again in my head.

Chapter 4 – Look up to see the Light

Modern Day - Boston, USA

I had been hired by a contact that went by the name Prometheus. Though normally I
worked for the government, occasionally the intelligence branch would allow someone
of wealth and importance to use their "private contractors" for personal missions. The
intelligence community used all types of foul play to raise black funds for projects and
missions that could not be reported even to the Special Committees created by
Congress.

This was my first time working for this nameless gentleman. I assumed it was like any
other mission; rich man with a vengeance.

Over the phone the contact Prometheus told me a tale, though unbelievable at first, my
independent inquiry proved otherwise.

Prometheus said, "Titus, you are a good man and I appreciate the assistance you are
providing me. This man, a Rothson Family Member, has attained a fair amount of

wealth by assisting known war criminals, and laundering their assets. His family funds both sides of conflicts and earns profit from war, the same wars he and his brethren create. I need you to send a message to his brethren for me. That evil deeds will not go unpunished, no matter what bloodline you might be."

First I told him to contact the FBI He then stated, "His brethren created these institutions of Justice to serve their own purpose. There is no court for men like Rothson. He is protected by money, power, and connections. Rothson is a member of the ruling elite, an unseen hand that guides society. Even with rock solid evidence he will walk, and all that I have was obtained illegally. Though it is real evidence, the court would not allow it. That is why I come to you Titus. You will be his judge."

I replied, "Then his fate has been settled."

Prometheus stated, "He should be on his 110' sailing yacht in the harbor. In the early afternoon he will leave the bank to head to his yacht. They use his yacht to transport kidnapped children overseas, he always inspects them before they take off. The name of his boat is *La Nina* named after the ship of Columbus. He even has sails with the big red Knights Templar cross-displayed as Columbus did. Also his family is known as the Red Shield, you will see their family crest on the flag on the back of the ship. Send his brethren a message for me. This is the start of something profound. I have been waiting a long time for you Titus."

The Lost Truth by Dean Fougere

I headed down to the aquarium docks, and floating offshore on a mooring was the giant

sailing vessel. Walking down Long Wharf I blended into the crowd of younger Boston

college students, carrying a large duffel bag with my instruments of death. Thanks to

the frigid temperatures I had been able to conceal my identity from the various security

cameras and tourists iPhones, although the cold would make my next step rather

precarious.

Eyeing a large, unmanned motor vessel, a Viking sport fisher at the end of the docks, I

decide was where to set up. I panned the area to ensure no one was watching me and

that there were no security cameras on this section of the marina. Assured of the all

clear, I made my move. The fear of getting caught was subdued by the amount of

hatred I had for my target. I had researched the Rothson family, and it seemed they

represented the very core of my true enemy. This son was just one of the younger

members of the bloodline, but in the future he could have been one of the family heads,

possibly even the head of the family.

I climbed on board the Viking, and started by searching for a hidden key to the cabin.

After opening a few lockers, I found them hanging next to the fishing gaff under the

gunnel of the ship. Typical, I thought. People are way too trustworthy and predictable.

Entering the cabin, I marveled at the plush interior of the Viking. The main cabin had a

large dining table and an enormous flat screen TV. The TV was connected to the rotating satellite dish on the roof of the boat; the dish was enclosed in cylinder with a sphere top. Even at sea the rich cannot be without their television.

I opened my duffle bag on the table, ensuring not to move anything. If no one realized I was on this ship, then they wouldn't check it for evidence. I pulled out my dry suit, scuba gear, and waterproof Field Tech gun case with my trustworthy Berretta 9mm, with custom extended magazine and silencer. Three clips in the case fully equipped, two with hollow points and the third with armor piercing rounds. On my hip concealed under my garments was my custom 9" stiletto knife that I took from the first person I killed for money.

After getting into the dry suit, I peered out of the tinted windows of the cabin. Seeing no one in line of sight of the back deck, it was time to move. Grabbing the flippers, the duffel and my gun case I headed to the back of the ship. I locked the cabin door behind me and put the key back where I originally found it. I applied the flippers while Stand on the back diving platform and silently slipped into the dark murky water of Boston Harbor, hoping I didn't come across anything too disturbing on my swim to the ship a few hundred yards off shore.

Once at a depth of about 20 feet, I moved across what seemed like the bottom of the harbor, though it was too murky with debris to tell. Then I saw my target: a huge fin sticking down into the water like an upside-down shark. I swam by the keel of the enormous sailing ship to the far side of the ship from the shore.

Climbing up on the dinghy tender on the far side I quickly scanned the decks and located three patrolling guards. I slipped the respirator and tank off on the dinghy, slid back into the water, overcame the cold trying to paralyze me and I swam as fast as I could to the transom. It took every bit of strength to pull myself out of the bitter cold and onto the transom. Amazingly, the guard standing a few feet from the back of the ship did not hear anything and still had his back turned. I opened the gate to the back of the transom and slipped towards the guard. The other two guards stared out from the front of the ship over 90 feet away.

I pulled out the stiletto knife and it was time to go to work. I approached the guard, and at the last moment he felt my presence. Just as he turned, I slipped my left arm under his left arm and then up behind his head, in the same motion my right arm sliced the stiletto across his throat. He tried to scream, but only blood gurgled out the new smile on his neck. I dragged his lifeless body back through the transom and down into the water.

I swam back quickly to the dinghy I climbed on board, and glanced at the two guards on the foredeck; they were talking and pointing at something on shore. I opened my gun case and pull out a silenced berretta 92FS with hollow points, as these guards were not wearing armor. Then I got next to the hull of the ship and threw a foghorn at the back of the sailing vessel. The foghorn landed perfectly in the cockpit and right on the button sounded a quick blast of the horn. This turned the guards and they both started running to the back of the ship. As they passed by on the deck I could hear their feet pounding away. As soon as they were by I popped up into firing position, and double tapped each one with two shots to the heart. Climbing up on deck I ensured their demise with a third shot to each of their heads. No movement was heard below.

I decided not to move below decks, there is no need to fight my way through the entire ship. I moved along the deck peering down through the tinted ceiling windows on the roof of the cabin below my feet. One of the windows overlooked the galley, where two guards stood relaxing, unaware of the mayhem above. Most of the windows are above cabins.

At the mid-section of the ship, I spotted the banker.

He was in his cabin laying on his bed, naked except for a chain with a key on it, clearly interacting with someone out of sight from above. I moved to the mast of the ship and sliced the mainsail halyard from the clip it is attached to on the sail. With that end I tied a noose. Then I moved to the cockpit and grabbed the remote control for the halyard line winches. I tapped the button to ensure the winches will wind up the halyard on command. The remote had two buttons; one for up slowly, one for up quickly, none for down, not that Mr. Rothson would be coming down anytime soon. Standing above the window, I prepared for the kill.

Silently, I opened the window above my target, and could hear his British accent talking to some person, telling them to twirl. To ensure an easy struggle I shot out both of the banker's knees with two quick pops, and then I jumped down onto him, quickly throwing the noose over his head. I grabbed the key and ripped the chain off his neck. The banker tried to scream but shock had taken over his body, both his knee caps a mangled mess and pouring blood over his white Egyptian cotton sheets. The banker with the noose looked right in my eyes and said, "I am not ready to die, I still have so much to do." I looked right back into his, and I assured him, "Life is an illusion, I am setting you free."

I then pushed the red quickly up button. The electric winch cranked to a high-pitched wine as it turned pulling the mainsail halyard up. Hanging by the noose around his neck, the banker's body was pulled skyward right out of the window overlooking the cabin. Blood poured from his knees as he rose: most likely I had hit an artery in each leg.

The banker grabbed the air, flailing wildly as he ascended out of the cabin, but there was no sound other than the whine of the winch and drops of blood hitting the deck. Being pulled up the top of the mast by the halyard, he had no way to escape his fate. Even if he was to get free he was now over 40 feet in the air.

Once the banker was about 80 feet up he stopped moving, unconscious from suffocation or blood loss, his body now on display for all of Boston Harbor. My bloody public display portion of my contract complete, I turned to see who was in the room with him.

Crouched in the corner of the room, was a young girl, maybe 16 years old, scared and crying. There was nothing I could do for her, especially with the signal I just flew. I told her it would be ok and that the police would be there soon. I picked up the cell phone on the nightstand. and dialed 911, and then dropped the phone on the bed. The police would track the call if someone hadn't already called in the hanging body at the top of the mast. I looked at the large mirror over the bed, and out of the corner of my eye I thought I saw movement. Time to go.

I ascended up through the cabin window, out over the side of the ship, fired up the yacht's dinghy tender, and started motoring to shore. I looked back at the ship and saw three guards running around the decks. Ahead on my left were two coast guard boats with lights flashing, and men on the .50 Caliber machine guns on the bow, heading for the sailing yacht. I turned to the starboard and pull into the Charlestown Navy Yard, where my car was waiting nearby. I looked down at the key I took from this man. It had some very strange symbols on it that I did not recognize, and one number 33. Not knowing what I had recovered, I threw it into my duffel with the rest of my gear. Mission accomplished as always, I thought.

Chapter 5 – The Path to Enlightenment

Modern Day – Boston, USA

Today, I would visit my best friend Jonathon at Massachusetts Institute of Technology, also known as MIT. Jonathon was a geneticist and had been working on identifying the Human Genome. He was young, around 30 years of age and considered a genius by many of his contemporaries. Ever the enthusiast, Jonathon's communication style was typically excitable and frantic, so it was always a guess as to whether the subject of the conversation required the hype it had received in his missive. Jonathon's frenetic, pacifistic half full glass balanced out my reserved, violent nature; most likely the reason we got along. He hade made a discovery the night before and left a frantic, excited message typical of him on my mobile. "Titus, are you back from your hunting trip yet? I have figured it out, and it is more amazing than I ever thought. I can't wait to show you what I have uncovered; it will change the world forever! I am going to be rich, famous even, and think of all the women!"

I had dealt with a great many of Jonathon's "discoveries" over the past years. Every one of them would change the world forever, so to me this was just another of Jonathon's cooked up ideas.

Jonathon, dressed in his typical lab whites, displayed a huge grin as I entered the room.

"I figured it out! I have now deciphered more of the Human DNA than anyone else in history. The crazy thing; Titus it was so obvious. 'Junk DNA,' my ass."

At this point Jonathon got up and brought me over to his white board. I looked at my friend and quipped, "Look if this is such a big deal, why are you telling me and not all those supermodels that you dream of?"

"There will be plenty of time for that later, first I need to know if my theory works." Jonathan smiled inwardly.

I look at him confused, "What do you mean if your theory works?"

"Well Titus, as I am sure you know, all the instructions for the physical human body are contained in a very small portion of our DNA, only about 2% of our DNA contains all that information. The rest we assumed was junk DNA, or at the very least undecipherable. Our DNA can store a massive amount of information, and is basically the best information storage system on the planet. Almost, as if DNA had been engineered to store information. So it doesn't make sense that something so efficient would render 98% of itself useless." He went on.

"Though I have not deciphered the rest of our DNA in total, I believe I know what roughly a large amount of it is used for. I was lead down this path by the British researcher Dr. Ewan Birney from the United Kingdom's European Bioinformatics Institute. These scientists have developed a way to store information inside synthesized DNA. Though an expensive process, binary code can be translated into the DNA code very easily, and then decoded at 100% accuracy. Also, DNA can store more information than all the computers in the world combined. It is the perfect place to store information."

"Works like this, information like a picture on your computer is actually just a representation of ones and zeroes as interpreted by your computer software. We can take those same ones and zeroes, and translate them into a base 3 system, 0's 1's and 2's. Then we can take that base three system and make it a base four system with the four nucleic acids in DNA which are represented by the letters A, C, G and T. Then, synthesize the DNA with these four nucleic acids just like you would record a binary code. You can store that DNA for thousands of years as long as it is kept in the cold and the dark, or within living tissue. Then when you want to retrieve the information again, you just translate the data back to binary and run it through the same computer and the same picture will emerge. It is a way to store far more information than you can with a world full of computers for thousands of years, with the same accuracy and no need for electricity." I was nonplussed, yet he continued at rapid pace as if I was a

The Lost Truth by Dean Fougere

leading genomic scientist.

"Another bit of research that lead to DNA containing human memories came from transplant organ recipients. In some cases it has been found that when a person receives an organ from a donor that they actually obtain the donor's memories. This is odd, because they would have no idea whom the organ came from in most cases, as the organ donor is completely unknown to the recipient; yet the recipient in documented cases can recall specific memories from the donor."

Looking rather satisfied with my apparent comprehension Jonathon pressed on, "Now the trick is, can we take this a step further?"

"We need to go further?" I ask, rolling my eyes.

"Yes, now listen. It was while studying the great minds of our past and the animal kingdom that lead me down this next path. What if the DNA in our blood contained stored information from our ancestors? It would explain how certain animals such as birds and other creatures are born with knowledge that they did not gain from experience. The best example is the monarch butterfly, but it is not even close to the only example." Jonathon handed me a map, showing the migration patterns of the Monarch butterfly.

"The Monarch butterfly clearly passes down genetic information -- including knowledge of past experience -- to its offspring. The Monarch butterfly is born in North America in the spring. When winter comes, they travel 2,500 miles from east of the

Rocky Mountains all the way to one spot in Mexico where a certain oyamel fir tree grows. These butterflies then travel back to the North East in the spring and lay their eggs and die. When their offspring are born, they are somehow able to migrate to the same location without ever having been there before, and the location is 2,500 miles away from where they were born. So how is this possible? The DNA passed down from one Monarch butterfly to the next contains the information of past experience from one generation to the next.

"Carl Jung has come across this information as well, and determined that people have archetypes that, due to information genetically passed down, people are born with this subconscious information affecting their personality. Though it is not archetypes, it is the memories that affect us."

Taking the map from me, he handed me a document he created, all jumbled information and quotes. "Further proof came from studying the great minds of human history. Human civilization has not progressed gradually from cave men to people flying to the moon in a linear pattern. There have been times of great enlightenment during which great people lived and changed our world forever. We stand on the shoulders of these giants, who have helped us understand the mysteries of the universe with extremely new radical ideas that came seemingly from nowhere. What no one talks about is despite how strange these great minds were, they all shared one connection."

"What connection, they had nice beards?" I ask.

Jonathon laughs, and then continues; "Every one of the great minds of human history has used a device called "thought experiments," to come up with these incredible new advancements in history. In one year, just one year, Einstein used these thought experiments to come up with all of his important theories. Einstein described visually picturing himself flying through a wormhole in space and then he would come out of his meditation and write down these incredible mathematical revelations. Leonardo Da Vinci was famous for his thought experiments, and was able to create inventions that were 500 years ahead of his time, just with thought. Newton used thought experiments to come up with his theories on physics. Socrates famously fell into one thought experiment for hours during a battle, and was so consumed in thought he was totally unaware of the world around him. Thought experiments have been going on since prehistory and have been connected to every genius that has ever lived. They all granted their 'revelations' of science to these thought experiments; well a revelation comes from the word reveal. These men were not creating new thoughts, but revealing old information from within. To know thyself was always the key to their genius."

"At first, we assumed thought experiments were just the description of these great minds entering a state of deep thought. However, it was always a bone of contention; how these great minds would come up with entirely new ideas from just thinking, as if they had tapped into some unknown archive of information. Like they had access to the mythical tree of knowledge of the bible. Crazy right?" Jonathon glances at me almost laughing, reassuring me he did not believe in religious mumbo jumbo. As boys we had grown up like most kids in America today, believing in science and downplaying religion as superstition.

Jonathon continued, "After I delved deeper into the bizarre, I realized that is exactly what they had been doing. This archive of information has been described countless times over the centuries, first and most accurately by the Hindu texts of the Mahabharata. The Hindus referred to this as the Akashic Record, and was described as "holding all the knowledge of the universe." It was thought a person's mind could tap into this archive of information. What the Hindus did not know was the archive of information was not out in the cosmos but in our blood."

"You see they say, "As above so below," and it truly is. The record of the universe is within just as it is above. Not everyone can access this information, and those who can failed to comprehend exactly what they were witnessing. One recent genius, the famous Indian mathematician Srinivasa Ramanujan, claimed he was given the most modern and complex mathematic equations in modern history by the Ancient Hindu goddess Namigiri in his dreams. His statements were cast aside as nonsense: the God Namigiri, of course that is where your brilliance comes from you crazy Indian. Like most mathematicians, everyone thought he was insane."

Jonathon paused to check if I was paying enough attention to laugh at his joke.

"Half of his equations still have not been deciphered, but the ones that have, have opened new doors into the reality of the impossible. Ramanujan describes falling asleep, seeing a hand write the equations on the wall before him, then when he awoke he would write down the equations and start proofing them. Ramanujan was unaware, but his brain chemistry was altered in just the right way to access the stored information in his DNA during his dreams. He was witnessing the playback of his ancestor writing those equations on a board, like seeing the world through your ancestor's eyes like a movie. The strange thing is, all of this information being recovered must have been lost at some point in time." Jonathon looked at me inquisitively, almost asking for me to give a theory.

Not getting me to bite, Jonathon marched on. "Einstein is another example of a genius who was able to access this information but was unaware of how. Einstein's brain was the pivotal key that gave us proof of how to access this information. Einstein had a larger pineal gland, which allowed for greater abstract thought. This pineal gland is the part of the brain used to recreate or relive the memories in our DNA, by raising the EMF field levels in that part of the brain either by thought or artificially. Also, Einsten's brain had four times the normal glial connections, which are electromagnetic connections in the brain. The more connections you have, the faster information can travel from one part of the brain to another, and the higher your brain's EMF field level is. Einstein, having four times the amount of glial connections and an abnormally large pineal gland, could access parts of his DNA by thinking deeply for a long time about the idea. His natural pineal gland being larger, combined with a naturally high EMF level, activated Einstein's natural ability to access the memories in his DNA in a trance-like state. Simply, he could access the DNA memories naturally. Einstein's brain was more than unique; it was hard wired into this archive of knowledge, and something you and I cannot do. I have found a way to mimic Einstein's natural ability with machines, thus allowing a simple-minded person such as yourself, Titus, to access information in your DNA. We can pick out random thoughts or if we know the root of the thought we are looking for, like Einstein we can access the specific memory."

"Einstein would think and concentrate on a specific abstract idea such as flying across the universe. He would picture what it would feel like to travel across the universe faster than light, and his pineal gland would start to fire, more blood would flow to this part of his brain lobe, and the electromagnetics would increase. After some hours his mind would unlock the memory and Einstein could literally day dream and see his ancestor's memories. That of a person using a wormhole to travel from one part of the universe to the other, and by accessing this memory he would understand the principles behind this theory that his ancestor understood. Imagine, seeing a first person view of a human traveling across the universe? Someone who had figured out how to do it in the past?" With that Jonathon paused enough for me to interject.

"But wouldn't that mean all of these new thoughts and inventions are re-discoveries of lost information? How is that possible? What ancestor of Ramanujan or Einstein would have made those discoveries before them?" I ask.

"That is what I want you to find out Titus. I don't know how it's possible but it seems everything that has been discovered is something from our very distant past that has been forgotten somehow."

"I have figured out how to decode these pieces of information from a person's DNA. It is actually quite simple, once I figured it out. You take the correct DNA translator structures and convert them into an electro magnetic signal, then you directly feed that signal into a person's mind during a sleep state, and the person can relive those memories during their sleep. You see the memories in first person as your ancestor saw them. The trick is, as everyone's brain works differently, the electromagnetic signal will only work for the person who matches the DNA. I could feed the same signal into a hundred different people's brains and the only one who could decipher the signal is the person whose DNA the signal is coming from. Simply put, everyone's brain is a different computer program running on a different set of codes: you can enter the same binary code into two different programs and get very different results."

Jonathon walked over and put his hand on my shoulder and looked directly into my eyes. "Titus I won't lie to you, this is very dangerous. I have not yet tried this on a human subject and I fear I may never be allowed to. I can't try it on an animal because that would be pointless, as they can't exactly describe any memories that I may be able to have them experience. This could cause any number of unforeseen consequences, like the inability to turn this off during your dream state, which could drive you insane. It may be a door, that once opened cannot be closed."

Jonathon winces at the idea, and walks over to the window. Staring out at the scene below, he continues.

"Without any trials being done, I cannot guarantee the mind can interpret the signal and that there won't be any harm to the person receiving the signal. I am sure it will work, and there is only one way to find out if I am right about all this. Also, there is no way to limit the feedback of the electromagnetic signal, as only the human brain can decipher the message, there is no way to isolate and remove the sensation of pain from the memories. You will be reliving history through all the senses of the brain however; much like a movie you can't change the script. So if your ancestor loses an arm in a bloody damn battle, your brain will make it feel as if you lost your arm. Got it ace?"

I knew where this was going. I was not one to fear death, and I could have a long family history about which he did not know. I would be the ideal subject for a trial. With no known family history, I made a good control. Also, Jonathon knew that I was searching for answers about my abandonment. "So when do I get to be your guinea pig?"

Turning from the window with a huge smile, Jonathon came over and hugged me. "I was hoping you would volunteer! Imagine being the first person ever to relive history? To see how or why the pyramids were built; or to encounter someone famous from the past, Titus you will not regret this. I actually envy you, I would go myself but someone has to run the operation. I don't trust any of my colleagues with this."

"You should sleep on this information, Titus. If you decide you would like to go through with it we can give it a whirl first thing tomorrow. However, we must do this in secret, as I have not told my colleagues of my recent progress. I fear they would shut down my research, or turn me in, if they found out I ran a trial run on you."

I said my final words to him that night. "Don't worry, I can keep a secret if you can Jonathon, but then I am not the over-excited one with a big mouth! See you in the morning -- just make sure I don't end up a vegetable when you are done with me."

Chapter 6 – The Sabbah Blood Line

Modern Day – Boston, USA

The next morning, Jonathon and I exchange pleasantries. Jonathon ensures he has double-checked all of his equipment, equations and is sure that everything will work fine. He motions for me to lie down on the hospital bed, and I follow suit. He inserts an IV in my arm and then places two suction cups with wires on either side of my head. He turns on his lab cameras to film the operation; each camera stared down on me with a single red light glowing indicating it was recording. "These suction cups simply transmit the electromagnetic signal that should... well it's complicated so don't worry, just relax" says Jonathon. I just nod rolling my eyes. Jonathon places a breathing mask on me and tells me to take ten deep breaths as if I were some child.

"So when are you sending me back to" I ask.

Jonathon gives me a small disturbing smile, "That is up to you, your thoughts will determine which memory is accessed, in theory..."

For some strange reason the key I took from the banker enters my mind. I see the two barred cross as I feel my eyes starting to droop after the third breathe. Then my eyes shut and…

■■

10 Miles north of Jerusalem, July 10, 1099 AD

Hassan-I Sabbah awakes. I am seeing the world through his eyes, but instantly I knew who I am and why I am there, Sabbah's thought's playing in my head simultaneously to my own, as if they were my own thoughts, a strange voice in my head. He was an older man now, but still yearned for the future. He had a long white beard but was in exceptional physical shape for his age. Today, we travel to Jerusalem he thinks to himself, for a better life. Hassan-I had been traveling from Alumut to the Holy City of Jerusalem, in hope for work. He, I was traveling with his young wife Aisha, his son Akeem age 12 and his young daughter Alzubra age 8.

In typical fashion we had set up a small Bedouin tent for the night to rest. The journey had been long and treacherous. News was the Crusaders had taken the Port City of Acre, not far from the Holy City. He thought to himself, they would never reach Jerusalem. That city is under the Saracen rule and that would not change. He could not foresee the Crusaders ever making it to the walls of Jerusalem. He thought of how the city was peaceful before the invasion, and of how these men from Europe came to ruin such a beautiful place.

Hoping to reach the city before noon, Hassan-i awoke his wife and children. "We must depart before the sun becomes too hot."

They hastily loaded their belongings into the carriage and departed. They were only a half-day out of Jerusalem and were hoping to limit the number of bribes they would have to pay in order to reach the city safely. The roads around Jerusalem had become deadly, with bands of Saracen warriors and crusaders taking advantage of the lawlessness caused by war.

A few hours had passed and they were closing in on the City. For some odd reason the closer they got the more smoke they saw in front of them. Soon the black smoke filled the sky ahead and Hassan-I feared the worst. "Had the Crusaders reached the walls of Jerusalem?" he thought to himself.

After the carriage came over the top of the hill, the view beyond was incredible. There in the distance lay the great walls of Jerusalem, surrounding the area of the Temple Mount. Before the walls laid a sea of people, tents, fires. Clearly the Crusader army had arrived and the siege of Jerusalem was under way. How did word not get to me of this, how did they reach the city already? Thought Hassan-I. Realizing he would not be allowed to pass through the army of Christian Crusaders he decided to turn and make camp to determine his next move.

As the carriage creaked and bowed under the strain, they turned on the narrow path and headed back up over the tall hill. Then a sight came into view that could only spell serious trouble for Hassan-I. Coming up the path towards him and his family were Christian Knights, the man in front had a large Red Cross on his chest.

The Knights were on horseback coming up the path in full charge. Clearly, they were a scouting party for the Crusader Army. What Hassan-I could not have known was the Knights had just lost half their men in the scouting Party to a Saracen raid and were filled with rage and vengeance.

Leading the Knights was Andre de St. Bernard and he had fury within. After being ambushed by Saracen archers in one of the narrow mountain passes to the Northeast of Jerusalem, Andre and his remaining men were riding with haste to warn the Crusaders of reinforcements coming to trap the Crusaders between the ocean, the walls of Jerusalem and an army of soldiers from the North. Andre spotted the carriage coming towards them on the road and signaled to the Knights in formation to prepare to engage. Pulling his sword from it's sheathing Andre rode with the sword glinting in the early morning sun towards Hassan-I.

Hassan-I saw the knights moving to form up for attack, I knew he was, well we were in serious trouble. It seems his usual bribing tactic may not work in this scenario. He would have to try anyway as he was in no position to take on seven mounted knights by himself, especially whilst protecting his wife and children. He motioned to his wife and daughter to hide under blankets in the carriage. Then he stopped his carriage to appear as though he was no threat. As soon as he did so the Knight leading the charge lowered his sword. Hassan-I took a deep sigh of relief. His wife feeling the carriage had stopped asked what was happening. Hassan-I replied, "nothing to worry, just need to pay a fee and we can move on, these Christian Knights are no more pious than their Saracen counterparts, most are here to escape imprisonment, to gain riches or to inflict pain. Almost all of these men are insane, killing someone by hacking them to death over and over again has strange effects on the mind." His son nods in agreement.

Andre, the knight in the lead approaches the cart and smiles at Hassan-I with a grin that one would expect to see on the devil. I notice on Andre's chest is a bright red cross, and his cape bore another red cross. This was not a normal cross it was a double barred cross that Hassan-I had never seen before. Same as one of the crosses on the key I took from the banker's neck. Andre declares, "I am Andre de Martin, of King Richard's Army, these roads now belong to us. You shall hand over to us any goods of value."

"But Sir, these goods are all I have and my family will need them to survive." Hassan-I replies. "Maybe I could pay you for use of the road?" Hassan-I pleas.

"These roads are not for sale, your goods belong to the King's Army now. Go beg your king Salahdin for survival." Andre allowing his inner rage, a demon within to over whelm him and bring out his fury, then turns and says, "Better yet, say hello to Allah for me."

Andre then makes a signal by quickly turning left and getting out of the way. Directly behind him one of the other Knights had a crossbow already aimed right at Hassan-I's face. Then just as quickly as Andre had moved out of the line of fire, the arrow came slicing forward through the air. Hassan-I instantly reacts grabbing for his sword, as he reaches the sword the arrow slams into his right shoulder. A searing feeling of pain quickly shoots through his, my entire body. A second arrow swishes by through the air and lands in Hassan-I's son Akeem's throat, the tip of the arrow poking out the back of his neck. He instantly falls sideways, dead. A feeling of anger overwhelms the pain, and I rip the arrow from my arm and dismount. If I were going to save my family, I would have to fight and grieve later.

Hassan-I gets in stance to engage the Knights on horseback when a third and fourth arrow from the two mounted archers with crossbows slam into each of his legs in the upper thigh. I reach down, feeling more pain than I ever had experienced in my life and break the arrows off, leaving the tips in my legs, searing with pain. I look up and two knights are charging, one coming at each side. Just before they get to me an arrow hits the Knight on my right straight through the visor on his helmet, right in his left eye. Killing him instantly. As the dead Knight fell off the horse, the horse turned sharply to the right with the weight of his body. The horse crashed into the other Knight and the whole pile of the two horses and Knights came crashing down on top of me. I was pinned under the weight of a horse; face first, with arms to my side, completely unable to move.

The other five knights all turn the direction of the shot. Three of them fan out and dash towards the hill the arrow came from. Andre dismounts his horse and approaches me, Hassan-I on the ground. Andre says, "This is way too much cargo for just a man and his boy. Also seems you have a Saracen Archer watching over you! These supplies must be for Salahdin. Too bad we caught you first." Then he took his left foot and kicked Hassan-I across the face, knocking me unconscious….

After an unknown amount of time I feel heat on my face, I try to move but nothing. I open my eyes and horror. The cart with Hassan-I's wife and daughter burnt, with them in it. Their skeletons were clearly visible in the debris. The last bits of flame still burning away, black smoke rising into a clear blue sky. A guttural feeling of rage welled up inside me that I had never experienced before. I had seen it in the eyes of the jihadi's in the afghan mountains during my time as a SEAL. It is a deep, cold, un-human hatred, un-knowable to anyone who hasn't seen it, unforgettable to those who have. Now I could sense their anger. The anger filled me within, granting me energy when I should have none.

I on the other hand, Hassan-I, was in a far worse position than I could have imagined. Somehow the Knights had cut open the stomach of one of Hassan-I's dead horses and put Hassan-I inside it. Bounding his hands and feet so I couldn't move. My head was poking out the anus of the horse, and the smell was horrible. Then horrible thoughts came into my mind and I realized what they had done. Hasan-I was all too familiar with this type of torture and death.

What happens is the horse's body attracts all types of vermin to come and feast on the dead carcass. Including the vultures already circling above. These scavengers will eat the horse's body with the person alive inside of it. Until they get through the horse's outer layer and start eating me, Hassani-I alive. If it were just maggots eating the flesh it could be an awful experience taking days, you may even die of dehydration first, if one were lucky a large animal like a tiger would come along and end your suffering quickly.

No matter how hard Hasan-I tried he could not get out. Soon he heard a commotion in the bushes and then saw his worst nightmare. A quick flash of tan and grey moving left in the tree line above the path, then another ten yards to the right; then the chuckle, and another, almost as if they were laughing at me.

A group of striped hyenas had found the carcasses. Ever the scavengers of these hills, it looked like there were three of them. Then two more came from the other side of the path, and another pair came marching up the path. Seven hyenas in total, they were pack hunters, all laughing as they slowly moved in towards the group of dead bodies and me.

The Lost Truth by Dean Fougere

The first three started on the other dead horse's corpse. There had been two horses pulling Hassan-I's wagon. Then the other four started moving towards me. I could see their teeth glinting white in the sun, the foam dripping from their mouths. I knew it would be slow painful death, especially with my head exposed for them to attack. Once they realized I was alive they would kill me first, with quick not life ending attacks for maybe fifteen to twenty minutes before they ended it.

Just as I had given up hope and was praying for myself to wake up, an arrow slammed through the neck of the hyena closest to me. The two others stalking in with that hyena ran off yelping. The other two hyenas kept eating away at the other horse. Then another arrow bolt hit one of them mid section and killed it. The last hyena started running as a third arrow went through it's back leg. Screeching out in pain a fourth arrow pummeled into it's neck and ended it's fate.

Coming up the path was a female shape. As she drew closer he did not recognize her, but she seemed astonished to find him alive. She said, "I am Fatima, you are saved". The heat and the smell overcoming Hasan-I's senses he blacks out again.

As Hasan-I blacks out, I awake; in the hospital bed, Jonathon looking at me with awe. Jonathon says, "It worked didn't it? I was getting all the right readings, so it must have been. What did you see?"

I look up at him in amazement, and say you will never believe what I just saw. Then I tell him the story.

Jonathon asks, "Well what were you thinking about when you fell asleep, what brought about this memory, seems rather an odd and horrible memory to pick from random?"

I reply, "I have inherited a key from a recently passed, uh relative. This key had a symbol on it, that same symbol I saw on the Knight who called himself Andre de Martin. Must have been what triggered that memory" I pause for a moment to think.

"Maybe if we go back to these thoughts again I can figure out what the key is for?" I state.

Jonathon says, "Well couldn't hurt to identify the symbols on the key and see if they have any significance first. Do you have it on you?"

"Of course, here it is." I pull the chain with key from off my neck; it was hidden under my shirt.

Jonathon says, "You mind leaving it here with me? I will do some research tonight, after I finish recording the results from your trial run today. I need to ensure we gather all the data from today as it was a major breakthrough for science. We must ensure none of today's progress was lost. Come back in the morning and we shall discuss, till then take it easy today no alcohol or any drugs and that includes marijuana Titus, because I don't know what if any side effects you could have from today, okay?"

"Fine whatever, see you tomorrow Mom." I say perturbed with the comment he made about my personal bad habits.

Chapter 7 – The Key to Understanding

Modern Day – Boston, USA

The next morning I show up at Jonathon's office, bringing him a fresh cup of Dunkin coffee to match my own. Today I am fitting into the Boston crowd with a red sox cap, jeans, boots, blue sweater and wool university jacket. Being late twenties I could easily pass for a student at MIT or any of the other colleges in and around Boston. With multiple murders on my hands recently I had to be careful. No sticking out.

Jonathon glances at the key. "So on it is a x, with a hook on it, never seen that before. On the other side is what looks like a double crossed lower case t, not sure what this symbol is but I am sure the Internet will tell us. Under both symbols is the number 33. We'll take a photo and upload it using Google image search and see if anything similar pops up"

Jonathon uses his Iphone to take careful images of the key, and then uploaded the images to his photo shop program. After cropping the images to just include the symbols he uploaded them onto his screen.

"The lower case t, or double cross came up right away. Jonathon states, no doubt about it, it is the 'Cross of Lorraine'. Says here originated in Northeast France, and used by Knights Templar. The Cross of Lorraine symbol was given by the Pope to a disciple of someone named St. Bernard de Clairvoux, to use as a mark of authority; have you ever heard of him?"

"No, I have heard of the Knights Templar though, wasn't the knight in the Indiana Jones film a Knights Templar, the one guarding the Holy Grail?"

Jonathon chuckles, "yes of course I forgot your history is basically whatever you have seen in movies. Yes, the Knight in that film was representative of a Templar Knight, he had a big red cross on his chest; which is the symbol I always associated with them. Seems from these hits on here that this double barred cross was for use in the region of France controlled by the Templar Knights during their existence, and can be found on many flags from that region."

Oddly, it seems that the Free Masons, use the number 33 quite regularly. According to these websites, the Templars founded Free Masonry. Seems there is a talk here at MIT tomorrow on the subject.

"What about the other symbol?" I ask.

"It seems we have a few hits, but nothing conclusive. Here is something, there is a geologist, some guy named Scott Wolter who found this marking on an old rune stone found in Minnesota and wrote a book on it. He claims it ties directly to both groups the free masons and the Templars from the summary I am getting. He also has found the symbol in a few other places it seems, five in total in carvings and a few documents."

"Should we send this guy some images of our key?" I interrupt.

"No, definitely not, he has a TV show and would most likely want to put your artifact on air. Plus his conclusions don't seem to be correct, he claims the hooked x is representative of the bloodline of Christ, but I know from research the Free Masons protected the Merovingian Bloodline, not Jesus's. If you want to find out about that key without showing it to someone beholden to corporate interests or the American TV audience we'll need another expert."

"Seems we are in luck, a graduate from MIT studying geometric architecture is giving a talk tomorrow. She is talking about the connection between the Templars and the Free Masons and their connection to an ancient construction methods and astronomy. If you want we could go to the talk together, you will need a student badge or me with you to get in. Want to go?"

"Sure, I guess I could sit through a lecture, though don't test me after ok?" I smile at him, always giving him digs for growing up to be a teacher.

"So how about another go in my machine? It is all set and ready to go?" Jonathon sheeply asks.

I reply with exuberance to insure his compliance. Then I lie down in position on the bed. He goes about sticking suction cups on me and then the iv in my arm. I get the count to ten instructions and I know soon I will be asleep. I start counting 1,

As Jonathon peers down over me I see something unexpected. A small red mark on his neck and moving up, as I hit 2 in my head, I realize what it is. Before I can react I see Jonathon's head snap back, and I hear glass shattering to my left. A second later I hear the sound of a gunshot.

Why was he killed and not me, is my final thought as I hit three and the laughing gas took over and knocked me out.

Chapter 8 – For those who Remain, Vengeance is their Cause

North of Jerusalem, 1108 AD

I awake, looking down at myself, and my surroundings; I realize I am back with Hasan-I. My first thought is about Jonathon, is he dead? Will I ever wake up from this experience? Did anyone at MIT hear the shot?

Then a cold sweat starts in and Hasan-I motions to someone I cannot see. Hasan-I thinks to himself, "Today I get vengeance for my wife and children, today Andre will die."

Hasan-I knows the timing is essential for their victory and he has only one chance to kill this man. After today, Andre might never return to the Holy Lands again.

Hasan-I recalls to himself how Fatima had saved him from Andre and brought him to his hometown of Alamut, where she was also from originally. She had grown up as the only child of a fierce warrior and had been taught to fight from him, including her exceptional skill as an archer.

Together, Hasan-I and Fatima had created an order of fearless warriors. Using a drug called hasheesh before battle had allowed their warriors to lose the fear of death. "If you fear death, you are already dead" she had told him. The drug also seemed to slow the battlefield down for them, making it easier to react and make decisions mid battle. Their opponents soon started calling them the Hasheeshans, which over time became the Assassins.

Hassan-I and Fatima created this order of Assasin's in the defensive castle of Alamut, Northern Iran; to insure their own safety as they hunted the killers of Hassan-I's family. They vowed to create a free society where all men had an equal say, not just the rich. They would follow the laws of God, not laws made by man. In order to defeat their enemies they had to use their enemies' weapons against them, to fight fire with fire. Hassan-I would fight for and against both Christian Crusaders and the Muslim Saracens in order to gain wealth, power and most importantly knowledge.

Through his connections and the assassination of a few key political figures for favors and information they found Andre. Whoever Andre was, he was well protected and seemed to never leave the Temple Mount where he couldn't be touched. However, Hassan-I had been granted access to the Temple Mount. Where dressed as a Christian Monk he had been watching Andre and his nine brethren working on something. Time had passed and the Knights had started shipping out wagon loads of cargo daily to the port cites; all under extremely heavy guard. Hassan-I waited for Andre to leave the Temple Mount.

Finally the day came, Andre was the third of the Nine Knights Templar leaders to leave the temple mount. Hassan-I watched as he shook Hugh's hand and they both made a strange symbol crossing their arms in the shape of an "X" and bowing to one another. Two had left the days before him, in wagons filled to the brim with something very heavy and with a heavy guard in tote. The Knights Templar organization had grown dramatically over the past few years and now hundreds of them patrolled the Holy Lands with the emblazoned red crosses on their chests. Four knights Templar accompanied each carriage on horseback and another one driving the carriage. There was almost always a group of infantry as well, generally 8 men on foot. Though a considerable amount of men for protection of a carriage, they had almost 100 Knights and about one thousand infantry at the Temple Mount seemingly ready and waiting to move a rather large carriage under the command of the New Grand Worshipful Master Hugh de Payan."

Five Knights including himself guarded Andre's carriage, and he was driving. Andre also had a compliment of ten infantry walking behind the carriage. Though five armed knights and ten armed infantry was way too large a force for Hassan-I and Fatima alone, he did not care. Hassan-I also did not have time to get a force of his men together from Alamut. He would not risk losing Andre to Europe forever. He knew his only option was an ambush.

Hassan-I had tracked Andre to a narrow pass between Jerusalem and Acre, the obvious destination for Andre. This pass would be perfect. Hasan-I and Fatima had gone ahead of Andre by about a half day's ride to set the trap. Now they sat waiting to pounce.

Knowing action was about to take place Hasan-I filled his pipe and lit up his hasheesh. The harsh feeling of smoke entering his lungs, then as he breathed out the sweet taste apparent as a cough came out. Another drag and the feeling of mental peace came over his mind, his worries his cares all fading. The colors all around him seemingly more vibrant, then the sound of the birds and other animals intensified, to the point where he thought he could hear a leaf hitting the ground. The task at hand was all that mattered. Putting the pipe away he saw movement in the rocks below, down the path. Then emerging on the path was Andre's convoy. Hasan-I did not experience any fear, I thought to myself, feeling fear of my own as I watched through Hasan-I eyes.

As Andre 's men walked down the path, they watched the side of the narrow passage closely. On both sides the walls of the passage were about forty feet up. The passage itself just widens enough to get the carriage through at the base. As the carriage passed by Hasan-I motioned to Fatima, and started rolling a huge barrel of oil to the edge. One of the infantry caught the smell of the hashish and looked up, to see Hassan-I standing above them pushing a barrel off the edge of the small cliff. The motion was then noticed below and the men all stared up at him as he dumped the barrel over the edge while taking off its cover.

The oil spilled out of the barrel on it's way down. Covering all 10 walking infantry behind the carriage. The Fatima fired and arrow that was lit on fire into the middle of the group. Instantly they all went up in flames, ten men screaming in agony as the jelly like oil burnt their flesh off in spots. Killing them slowly and painfully.

Fatima then turned her aim on the four mounted knights. First shooting the lead horse in the neck killing it instantly and blocking the path ahead of the carriage. Now the three remaining Knights and Andre were caught between a blaze of fire and a dead horse the carriage couldn't go over or around.

Hasan-I, I jump down the side of the passage, half sliding on my feet and half sliding on my butt on the way down. As I am sliding I see an arrow go clean through the neck of one of the three remaining mounted knights. The lead Knight was running back to Andre from his fallen horse. Andre was hiding under his shield hoping to keep any arrows from finding him.

Fatima then killed another knight right through his face shield, the arrow finding it's mark in his right eye. Instantly falling off his horse. The last mounted Knight had pulled his crossbow out and shot Fatima at the same moment, not fatal but enough to keep her from the fight. Hassan-I screams out in anger as he sees her fall out of view into the brush.

Three left, the knight with the crossbow was reloading and turning to aim at me. Just as he pulled the string into place and started to aim I reach him. First I cut the two front legs of his horse in half with one sweep of my sword. The Knight fell off the horse forward, his arrow missing my neck by inches. Laying face down in full armor he had no chance to react. I stick my sword in the gap between his shoulder armor and the bottom of his helmet; accidentally cutting his head clean off. As I do this I see a flash of white to my right and duck leaving the sword sticking vertically through the neck of the downed Knight.

Andre moves behind me and his fellow Knight in front of me. With no sword I have no choice but to pull out the two small daggers I had. As soon as I was equipped the first blow came in, Andre swung with all his might down on me. I was able to deflect the swing partially, but my hand caught the tip of his blade slicing it wide open. Holding onto the knife would almost be impossible with that hand.

The other Knight then seeing me off balance thought he would make the kill. Swinging his long sword wildly at my head gave me just enough time to duck under the blade, roll forward and place my left dagger in his right thigh and pull him from the horse. Then as he dropped his sword in pain, I move behind him keeping him between Andre and myself in one motion and sliced his throat.

Andre looked over at me with anger and realized it was just the two of us. Andre blurts out "Should have killed me first" Realizing he had the upper hand with me down to one lone dagger he moved in. Though the fear of death was obvious in his eyes, slowing his reactions and fueling his anger.

I sense my predicament and as he pulled back to unleash a furious swing, one that would be too powerful for me to deflect with a dagger, I fell back. The blade swung inches in front of my neck as gravity pulled me back towards the ground, as soon as my back hit the deck my left hand grabbed a pile of dirt and rocks, and whipped them into Andre's face. As I did, I rolled to my right and Andre stabbed the ground as hard as possible hoping to spear me on the ground. His blade stuck into the ground just long enough for me to grab a sword on the ground and get back up.

Andre came back at me hard again, not caring that I had evened the odds. I easily defended the assault. Andre's fury and arrogance taking over his mind's ability to conduct proper hand to hand combat. His eyes seems as if they had gone full black, no whites or color, just solid black as if he was possessed by the anger that was fueling him. Hassan-I had remained calm and collected weighing his options without delay. The fear of death had no hold over Hassan-I and it allowed for clarity of mind that I had never experienced before. The action seemed to slow in Hasan-I's mind allowing him to move seamlessly even if for an old man, there wasn't thought it was more instinctual.

Andre swung hard again, however now his arms had tired. Upon deflection of his swing, he left himself wide open for a counterstrike. So I took it, slicing into his right shoulder almost cutting his arm off. Andre dropped his sword that had been in his right hand, clearly due to his right arm being almost severed. Then he dropped to his knees and begged for his life with his eyes alone. The eyes had returned to normal, no more anger just fear.

I kicked his sword aside and pointed mine at his throat, touching the tip of my sword to his neck. "For my wife you have slain, for my children, and for all those others you have wronged. I vanquish thee and thine brethren to hell for all eternity."

Andre looks up and scowls at me. "You have caused more problems than you could possibly comprehend. My death means nothing, when I go to Hell I will be running things. My brethren will hunt you to the corners of the world and take back what is rightfully ours. You cannot stop us because you have not seen the light."

As his last word comes out the edge of my sword cuts through his neck. Hitting his spine stopped my swing, as the blade was rather blunt. So a second hack was needed to finish it off. Andre trying to scream out in pain, but nothing but blood gargled out of his neck. His eyes died wide open in absolute terror.

Fatima and I go back and hop on his carriage. I will take the contents of this back with me to Alamut, Hasan-I thought to himself. There I can protect it. After a few hours of riding Hasan-I pulled off the trail and found a nice hidden area for the night. Knowing he would need luck to survive his trek home, he hoped no one would find him. He set up his Bedouin tent and went to sleep. As he closed his eyes, mine opened.

Chapter 9 – Better to have it and not need it, than to need it and not have it.

Modern Day – Boston, USA

I awoke on the bed in the MIT Lab. No one was in the room except for the lifeless corpse of Jonathon lying on top of me. Quickly I shove him off and notice he spent the last two hours bleeding all over me while I played in my own mind.

Realizing that this looked very, very bad and the Police would absolutely take me into custody; I had to get out and fast. I looked over at Jonathon I see the damage caused by the bullet. The bullet itself seemed to be stuck in the wall of the lab, and was a .50 caliber round at least. The exit wound was basically the entire back of Jonathon's skull, his brain matter and other material was all over the back wall. An absolute bloody fucking mess I thought to myself.

Looking out the window I see a building about a mile away, on the roof is where the shot came from for sure. Explains the delay in the noise of the gunshot being heard I thought. Also, whoever made that shot has elite military training and equipment. As an ex-SEAL sniper, I knew very well how difficult that shot was. It was placed through the window, through blinds, so the shooter must have had a thermal scope, and must have known there were two bodies in the room.

Looking around the lab I found a lab coat and some spare clothes that Jonathon must have left there. Though he was much taller than me, the clothes would do until I get out of the building and to a place to change. Then I remember the speech about the symbols and pulled out Jonathon's wallet from his back pocket. I took his faculty ID card and then headed out in haste, but took caution to not look like I was in a rush.

Reaching my apartment was no problem at all. Even in clothes way too large, as long as you didn't look foreign and looked like you knew what you were doing and acting cool, no one ever notices you. People are so tied up in the day to day, on their Iphones that almost nobody has any situational awareness in social settings anymore, making my job easier every year. Blending into a crowd barely took any effort anymore. I had checked to see if anyone had followed, but I did not notice anyone.

After a shower and a change of clothes, I go to my fridge and pop open a Beck's dark. Taking in the beer in large gulps I start to think of all the good times Jonathon and I had growing up together. Why would someone kill him, what did he ever do to anyone? Other than his obvious brilliance to me as a geneticist, he was of little value to the outside world. I highly doubt he knew of any information that would have compromised someone enough to hire a professional assassin. The only conclusion I am left with is, is the one I feared the moment I saw his head snap backwards. I was the target and I got my friend killed. Most likely someone wanted payback for one of the various people I had been hired to kill.

I take another swig of beer, and lighting up a pre rolled joint. I leaned back on my plush leather couch I turn on the big screen tv for some background noise. Allowing my mind to enter a peaceful state of mind would allow me to brush aside the anger and focus on my next move. I had never lost anyone close to me due to my line of work, and this feeling of hatred would not be easy to overcome. I will kill the man who shot my friend, but finding him will be difficult.

First, I needed to doctor Jonathon's ID to allow me free passage. By tomorrow his body would have been found and his ID will be tagged. However, the ID won't need to be swiped; just visually checked to enter the large lecture hall. So all I needed to do was alter the height, age and remove his photo for my own. Compared to altering a passport, this was child's play and I could handle it myself. Passports and real ID's I had to outsource to local authorities and are very, very expensive. My connections with CIA and NSA left me with various fake Government issued ID's but my mission was one of subterfuge, and one day I would need my unofficial fake ID's and passports to get by without Uncle Sam knowing. I wasn't sure who the killer was, so I had to assume everyone was guilty including my own government.

I had no idea if I had been compromised or not, however I knew I couldn't take the risk. I would be safe in my apartment for the evening most likely; but I would add some insurance just in case. So I triggered my home made alarm system, these were two homemade claymore mines aimed at the door, set to go off in sequence. First one set just beyond the ark of the door on the ground would set off if the door opened, the second set ten feet back from the door would delay 5 seconds then ignite filling the doorway and entire hallway beyond with shrapnel. This would give me at least thirty seconds to wake up, and get ready to fight my way out of the apartment.

I packed two duffle bags with various clothes and outfits for my different ID's. One day I could be a rich bachelor on the prowl, the next a lonely emo geek sipping coffee in a library. Appearances can be quite deceiving when you want them to be. Everyone judges based on appearance, yet appearance can be quite deceptive.

Then I walked over to my bookcase, smiled at my collection of ancient and modern texts, and pulled out my copy of "Eye of the Needle," one of my favorite fictions. I pulled the book out a familiar click sounded and the bookcase slightly popped away from the wall. Moving the case back on it's hinge, it revealed a small recess in the wall behind it. Lining the wall was the arsenal of weaponry I had accumulated since my private contracting began. On the backside of the bookcase I had a photograph of every man I had killed for money. The bookcase would soon have to grow I thought to myself, as the back was almost completely full of photos, mainly Mexican drug cartel members, my favorite targets. I likened it to ancient warriors taking the heads of their fallen foes, except a lot less gruesome.

On the wall were my allotment of arms, in a briefcase was a spare unused brand new MacBook pro, all my fake passports and drivers licenses, debit cards and credit cards to multiple bank accounts under multiple aliases, a key to a swiss bank account, 20,000 USD in various sized US bills, two Rolex watches worth over 3k each. Fortunately I was not planning on traveling overseas or bringing my "sporting rifles" would be an issue.

So I decided to pack my two Berretta 92FS 9mm pistols. These were my pistols of choice due to my training with them in the military, and their ambidextrous design, allowing me to draw two pistols in extreme circumstances. They also used 9mm rounds, which have more than enough stopping power and are easily purchased. One pistol would be concealed on me, for which I had an unrestricted class A license to carry. The other 92FS would go in the duffel with the two custom silencers that I did not have a license for. Six magazines each, half the magazines had hollow point rounds preloaded the other half were standard full metal jacket rounds preloaded.

The concealed 92FS was on my inside the belt holster and preloaded with full metal jacket rounds. I preferred FMJ because these as they had a better chance of penetrating body armor, car doors and thin walls. Hollow points are great if you are worried about inflicting mass damage on a soft target with a single shot, or reducing collateral damage by not having the bullet come out the other side of your target. In reality, FMJ rounds are better for killing armed men who wear body armor, and hollow points are better for killing civilians. This point had not been lost on some journalists who had covered the

The Lost Truth by Dean Fougere

Department of Homeland Securities recent million round purchases of hollow points adding up to over a billion rounds of ammunition, all designed for killing civilians.

With my berretta the first shot is double action, then recurring rounds are single action to allow me to double tap the target more effectively. If the bullet went in and out the other side, then I just needed to hit the target again to ensure their death.

In a metal gun case that I would conceal in the trunk of my Black Cadillac CTS, I would pack my Bushmaster ACR A-TACS rifle, with 10 fully loaded full metal jacket round clips. I had altered this gun by using some of the parts I had kept from my tour in the military to fire fully auto or semi auto. Also in this case would go my Smith & Wesson M&P 15T AR 15 Rifle, with red dot scope and silencer. This I would pack with another 10 fully loaded 5.56 NATO round clips. Neither of these weapons was even close to legal, having almost all of the deadly components that make assault rifles banned, that I added to them myself. These would need to be well concealed inside a trap I had constructed to fit this metal case in the back of the CTS.

Finally my long rifle, the Barrett .50 Cal Sniper Rifle, got packed in it's own metal case, this is the same type of rifle that was used by my enemy to kill my friend Jonathon. I was going to kill the man who killed him with this same rifle. Eye for an Eye, I thought. This rifle I had a license for, meaning it could go in a locked case in my trunk. I was deadly with this rifle up to a mile from my target. The specially modified versions I used in the Navy had a longer range, were more precise, and had special fun tools like thermal vision. The range and stopping power of this rifle are unmatched, and in the right hands one of the most deadly weapons to ever exist. No need for a silencer because of the range it allowed, giving you ample time to fire, confirm the kill and ex-filtrate from the area.

I brought my metal cases and duffels down to my CTS in my reserved parking spot in the garage across the way. Parking in Boston was a nightmare unless you were willing to pay around $300 a month to reserve a spot. Carefully loaded the metal case with the assault rifles and the duffel with my extra 92FS and silencers in the boot trap I had installed in the CTS trunk. A thorough investigation would easily find the trap, but it should be solid enough to conceal the illegal firearms in any normal traffic stop.

Deciding to get some sleep, I return to my apartment, re-armed the alarm system. Place my hip holstered 92FS on my nightstand within reach. Hit the lights and despite the traumatic events I pass right out. I had an uncanny ability to not let the events of my life disturb my sleep patterns.

Chapter 10 – An Illusion of Safety

Modern Day - Boston, USA

First a large bang, then the sound of cracking wood as my apartment doors is kicked open. I jolt up, then the deafening bang of the first claymore and I hear a man screaming in pain. Grabbing my 92FS I aim it at the bedroom door whilst I get out of bed. Already in sweatpants and a white T-shirt I just had to get my sneakers on, fire on my vest, pull my hooded sweatshirt on. By the time the second claymore fired off and the hallway recovered, I was ready to roll.

Opening the door to the living room, I see the doorway is covered in blood. I see a man in a black suit white shirt, black tie and ear bud pulling himself back out of the door, whilst calling in my position. Quickly I fire a round through the middle of his right eye. I aim up, and see another dead body next to his, must have been the first one in the door. I move over check his pocket and take out his wallet, and then I remove his radio and use his earpiece. Listening in I assess the situation.

"Bravo One, say again? Target location?"

"Sending up Charlie team, Alpha team is in position" "Fox team got anything on thermal, due you have the target location?"

Well this won't be easy I thought, they have a fire team on the stairs, another fire team coming up the elevator, and sniper support with thermal scopes most likely. This was definitely military, but why are they after me? I was expecting the police not a fucking full special operations squad. Damn, I could use that M&P right now.

Then I notice an insignia on the man's shirt Knight Templar, the Academy. Thinking back to what my colleagues told me about Blackwater it became obvious. These men were not US Government or police, they were private mercenaries working for Academy, previously called Blackwater. One of their scandals that caused the name change, was the hiring of Christian radicals, who called themselves the Knight's Templar and had joined the military or the private security corporation to kill non Christians, to purge the world of anyone not Catholic. The Academy was used to protect VIPs, but also had been used to conduct assassinations, kidnappings, and conduct drone strikes in Pakistan, Syria and Ukraine. The Academy could violate the law, under Government orders, but if caught only The Academy got burnt, it separated the politicians from the illegal actions, and therefore was used to handle the dirty work of politicians.

Keeping my gun aimed down the hall I move out, quickly getting to the elevator. Hitting the button, I see it is on the 1st floor. I move across and flip the waiting sofa opposite the elevator over. Crouching behind it aiming at the elevator I will smoke anything in the carriage when the doors open.

The elevator came to my floor and the door opened with a ding, when the door was about an inch apart a familiar cylindrical object came flying out of it. Flash bang, I duck covering my ears and closing my eyes. The grenade landed in front of the overturned couch and went off. Giving off a massive blast of sound and light. Thanks to extensive training I was ready for it and mainly un-phased.

The first guy out of the elevator was not expecting to get an accurate shot through the side of his temple from a 9mm. The second guy clearing to his left certainly was not expecting that same bullet to pass through his colleague's skull and into his own. Just as I run to the elevator double tapping the two sentries I hear another flash bang go off near the stairs.

The elevator door closes just as the fire team coming in from the stairs realizes what has happened. They fire rounds at the elevator but I hit the deck in time, as two bullets blast through the thin metal of the elevator door slamming into the back of the elevator carriage. Only in movies does the elevator door save you from gunfire I thought.

In the ear bud I hear, "Bravo team down, Charlie team is down, Alpha team is out of position, target is in elevator heading to ground level. Fox team you will have to take the target, kill on site."

The elevator opens on the first floor and I slowly emerge making sure to check the corners for another shooter. The security guard who watches the main entrance to our Lobby was not there, someone must have paid him to take the night off or his body was hidden away.

Then I heard the most disturbing thing I could imagine. "Control, the bird is in position, tracking target thermal signature now."

I knew this meant one thing; a high altitude drone had just come into the AO. This drone would not be armed but solely for surveillance. These drones were commonly used inside the US for Homeland Defense because they could provide hours of over watch without being detected and for far less cost than re-tasking a satellite. The reason I was disturbed is because this just went from being possibly an ex military hit squad dressed up as Blackwater, to being an active US Military hit squad with government support. Meaning whatever Jonathon and I had stumbled upon, had brought down the wrath of an active special operations unit on myself. I must have pissed off the wrong people. I knew an operation of this kind on American soil, would only be ordered for one reason, a cover-up by the executive office or an Intelligence branch operation that was above even the President's pay grade.

I knew the sniper team would be covering both entrances; however I also knew they were switched into thermal vision. So I decided to use the front entrance to catch them by surprise. I pulled out my bic lighter from my pocket and set a nearby stack of brochures from the apartment building on fire. Going over to the front door I fling it open and toss out the burning pages, they fan out and the increase of oxygen has them ignite even brighter. I shut the door behind it and after I heard a hail of gunfire hit the sidewalk aimed at the paper. As soon as the shots ended I hear "thermal imaging is burnt, switching" and I make my move.

Rushing out the door, I see three blacked out suburban's across the street. Behind the hood of the middle suv was another guy in a black suit. He started firing his pistol at me the moment I came out. First three shots, just miss me to the left as I jumped to the right. As I hit the deck I fire back, hitting the tire, the top of the front quarter then the guy in his shoulder. I see him fall back, I get up and start running.

I trip on the edge of the curb and almost fall flat on my face, as my head jolts forward to correct my balance, I hear a bullet whip past my head from the .50 Cal. If I had not tripped it would have killed me for sure, but my trip was unusual like a gust of wind hit me from behind causing it. After the stumble I hit full speed and started zigzagging.

I clear the four blocks to the garage and I jump in the CTS. Throw a fresh clip in the 92FS and tear off. Making full use of the sporty CTS's overpowered V8 engine. Hitting the street, and turning away from my apartment building I don't see anyone coming towards me. They probably are just going to track me with the drone until I stop and then pounce again; I doubt they would risk a high-speed pursuit through the streets of Boston or a drone strike in the city, too public. Too much paperwork, I laugh.

Fortunately Boston is an ideal city to lose a drone in. I fire the engine as I scream down the on ramp to 93 south. Entering the famous underground highway section of Boston's big dig. Just when the tunnel comes to an end, I pull a U turn around the end of middle barrier and head North on 93. The drone most likely waiting for me to emerge on 93 South a few feet from where I U- turned.

Hitting the accelerator I am bombing through the tunnel system at over 95 mph, unable to resist I crack the windows to hear the brilliant sound of the V8 Engine reverberating off the walls of the tunnel.

Emerging from the tunnel and heading North on 93, I just hope I lost the drone or I could have another surprise coming my way. I needed to get off the road for the night and find out why these people were after me.

I pull into a seedy Motel in Woburn and pay double the price for the room in cash for the night, telling the clerk to keep the extra if he we let me stay without paperwork. He accepted, money is always the key to getting people to do what you want it seems.

In the hotel room, I check the room for audio and video surveillance. Nothing, clean.

Then I fire up my macbook , and I go over google maps to determine my best route to

the lecture at MIT. Looks like I will be taking the T in as my car is probably being

watched for. I will have to switch transportation later.

After a quick run to a local liquor store. I light a joint and crack open a Beck's beer.

Soon the worries of my current situation fade away. After a few beers and some

research on basic information about Blackwater, freemasonry and the Templar Knights

connection I decide to get some rest. A long day ahead of me waits. As I fall asleep I

wonder what happened to Hassan-I and his order of Assassins?

Chapter 11 – No Turning Back

Boston, USA, Modern Day

As I fall asleep, a weird sensation occurs, a sensation I had not expected. Obviously, Jonathon had somewhat foreseen this happening, maybe it is something that once started cannot be turned off.

I awake though certainly still asleep, seeing the world through the eyes of another. I must have somehow unlocked this memory in my DNA naturally. Jonathon had said many great minds had accomplished this, yet I did not have the hardware to do this according to him. As hard as I try to understand how, the thoughts of my new host soon take over my own, as the situation is not ideal.

Alumut, Northern Iran, 1176 AD

I think to myself, who am I, and the answer instantly came, I am Hasan-I the second the son of Hasan-I Sabbah and heir to the Order he had created. I get out of my bed and start to dress in the white robes of my uniform. Today, I would be practicing my fighting techniques and meeting with my father's most trusted companion, whom has taken over Alamut until I am ready to command. I am to meet him before going on an assignment for him.

I think back to the stories my father Hasan-I had told me, just after being accepted into the order. He often spoke of his former wife and children, though he had re-married in Alamut to my mother Fatima. Hasan-I's knowledge was vast, and his teachings were new and different from other preachers of Islam. He had implemented new construction techniques, a new system of banking where all profits from loans were used to help the people of his Kingdom, and new weaponry. Hassan-I himself had no wealth, held no title but ruled with the will of the people, because he provided for them. He had told me soon I would understand where this knowledge came from, once I was ready to receive the information. We had decided to join with the Ismaili forces of the region to increase our protection, though Hasan-I would not share the secrets of our order with them or anyone for that matter until his death.

When Hasan-I had passed at a very old age. He had called me to his chamber. Just before he had named his successor, to rule whilst I was an adolescent. It was his most successful fedayin, and had carried out many public assassinations allowing our order to grow in influence by spreading fear. Hassan-I had spoken of a truth, something I had not yet understood, a secret he knew that he was using to inspire the people, but in reality it was all about control. As Hassan-I passed away, in his bed before my eyes, he pulled me in close and spoke his final words, "Nothing is true, everything is permissible."

Any leader in the modern day region of Syria and Persia that stood in opposition to our order was executed, publicly. Most of the men in power we executed were loyal to the ruler Salahdin. This had angered the King Salahdin who ruled over Egypt and the Arab Lands at this time.

Hassan-I had told me some of his secret in a story before passing. The man he killed, Andre de St. Maarten had been travelling with a sacred artifact containing a vast amount of information. This information had been written down in the archives of our order. Archives only to be viewed by Hassan-I, his predecessor and myself when the time came. Also an enormous amount of gold was recovered during Hassan-I's heist. Hassan-I though wounded in the confrontation, had taken that wagon all the way to Alamut and with the Gold he was able to buy the Castle and start the order, with the information he was able to establish a new society and place himself in complete control.

Hasan-I talked of a ring that held special power. This ring was taken from him by a messenger from God, and has not been seen since. Hasan-I claimed it was the ring of Solomon, and the Egyptian Goddess Isis before him. He did not speak more of it.

By the time the Templars had found Hassan-I; his fortress was too vast for them to capture. Hassan-I had built a ferocious and loyal Order of Assassins to protect his treasure. His Assassins were completely fearless in battle, and completely devoted to Hassan-I. Most thought he used magic to create this devotion, but the truth was far more bizarre.

He would show his warriors a beautiful garden, where they were allowed to spend a few days. This garden was filled with beautiful women and the warrior wanted for nothing but to remain in the garden. Hassan-I told his men, that upon death if they served under God and helped him vanquish the unholy from the land, they would return to this Garden forever. To not fear death, if you did not fear and served God as directed by Hassan-I, then one would return after death. So none of his men would question his orders and none feared death. This lack of fear allowed his men to fight ferociously in battle. The Templars who had the same information also had a similar practice and use it's ideas for their own order, becoming monks, not owning property and being fearless of death. The Templars were told because they were serving God, that all their violence was justified and would enter Heaven upon death. In hand-to-hand combat, fear is the greatest enemy; it slows the mind and the hands by eliminating fear the Templars and Assassin's had an advantage over every other warrior alive.

Hassan-I had indicated the artifact he took from Andre was worth far more than the gold he recovered. Our library of information was created from the knowledge he gained from the artifact and documents. He had used the gold and information he was able to gather from the texts to build his huge fortress as well. Stating that the methods

for construction he learned form the text allowed for the building of a fortress and

empire that could stand the test of time. He had picked a mountain made of hard

granite, and used the stones to build his fortress. I had never seen it, but rumors existed

of an artifact buried deep under the Castle, deep in the granite mountain below.

I thought of all this as I stared out the window, at the vast valley below, an eagle soared

overhead, surveying the town below for any vermin. Below on the rooftops, sat our

archers, doing the same, a wonderful sight, for the moment.

Then at the front wall below, the entrance to the valley, a signal fire was lit. The archers

had spotted an enemy force approaching the wall. I quickly yelled for my squire and

my armor. My squire came in haste, wide eyed and scared.

"Sir, the fires are lit, Grand Master Rashid ad-Din Sinan calls for you!"

Sensing his fear, I respond, "Quickly with the armor, these invaders shall feel the edge

of my blade soon. What does the old man of the mountain want?"

"He did not say, he is in the garden awaiting you."

With the precision of a well-practiced drill the armor is equipped to my body. Far

lighter, stronger and more agile than most armor of the time, our new sets of armor had taken years to make correctly. Only Hassan-I and myself are allowed to use this new alloy. Rashid had taken Hassan-I's armor upon his death, as it was too large for me. My armor is specially designed by my father and uses a new type of metal that he created supposedly by mixing gold, copper and iron together, it resulted in a much stronger and lighter metal. His blacksmith has told me the ingredients are not what I have been told however and the process is more secretive than the metal, so I am not sure what the metal really is. Of all the different metals and minerals Hassan-I tried to mix, it seemed he could only get this mixture correct enough to use. He had mentioned learning of others from our secret archive, but would not share what they were supposed to do. I knew he had shared the secrets of the order with Rashid, and when the day came, and it would soon, I would be told of their secrets, I was told the root of their plan was from Alchemy, self guided improvement.

Rashid now is an old man; he sits on the throne in the garden. A golden chair looking out over the garden and aimed at the view out over the cliff. Rashid's eagle is sitting on the right arm of his chair. The garden itself is the most beautiful place I have ever seen, lush green, with a fountain in the center of the clearest fresh water in all of the old world. Built on the backside of the castle, with one edge of the garden looking out over the North Side cliff of the mountain the castle is built upon. Though seemingly out in the open, one would have to fight through the Castle to gain access to the garden. The cliff is far too steep for anyone to climb but an eagle.

Hassan-I had created it to resemble the Garden of Eden, the place where mankind was created. He had filled his garden with the most beautiful women he could find. Only the top members of our order have ever been in the garden. Upon entering one felt as if they have died and gone to the paradise often described as the afterlife.

As I approach Rashid, I listen in to what he is saying. He has gathered the women of the garden together.

"You must leave this place, if Alamut falls you shall be tormented by the men of Salahdin. Or you will starve to death in the siege that is to come. You shall take my wife and daughters with you (Rashid had no sons, no heir to take my place in the line of succession). Only when my Eagle or Hassan-I the second, who just arrived, comes for you are you to return. Take the tunnel out to the North, and do not turn back for any reason, you must leave immediately!"

The women all nod, and start to head for the exit. If there is a tunnel through the granite that leads out of the north face of the cliff I was unaware of its existence. Rashid calls me over to me.

I approach his throne; his eagle turns to look at me from the side and then takes off. "Mualim, how may I serve?"

Rashid stands up and out of his thrown. His long white beard matched his flowing white robes. He has a presence of wisdom and power about him. Rashid has welcomed his nickname Old Man of the Mountain, as it projected fear and a sense of his power over all those under him. He puts his arm around me and says, "let us talk quietly, for I fear who may be listening, his great eye see's all and now he comes for us, using his agent Salahdin. I have long feared this day".

Standing tall and defiantly, Mualim turns towards me, his eyes grey with age but fiery with rage.

"Someone in the order has betrayed us, and led the forces of Salahdin here. The ascended master has spoken to me, and I know whom and what they have told the Sultan. Salahdin knows of our archive and has come to return what we have to Egypt, where he believes it originally came from. You shall send a message to Salahdin for me. His forces will never breach the walls of Alamut, however we will starve if he blocks us from the valley below. This is our only chance to stay free from his clutches."

"I have devised a way to hold off his forces, and to ensure our continued existence without giving him what he came for. Though his army is far larger than ours, they lack dedication and determination. A slave warrior will never have the discipline or the will of a free mind. Though our men are subservient to me, it is important they feel that it is their choice to do so. Salahdin's weakness is fear, fear of his own demise, he will not risk his own life for what we possess."

"First I need your trust, to prove to the men of Salahdin that we are fearless."

Worryingly, I reply, "Yes Mualim, whatever you command".

Maulim (The Teacher) describes to me what he has in mind, hands me my father's dagger and a green metal vest and wishes me fair well. The vest felt as smooth as glass and the form was solid, even though the metal itself seems to be shifting as if liquid. He helps me put the vest on. He says, "Our bodies are but dust, but we are eternal. Only through victory shall our actions be remembered. In your blood is the secret, only the vigilant should remain, you cannot die until you bare a child or everything will be lost. If Salahdin does not flee, you will join the women and wait for vengeances until after you are a father."

After which, I retreat from the garden, and I head down to the main wall of the fortress. Looking out over the valley passage up to the wall of our main gate, I see an army of thousands. Salahdin sent a massive force to Alamut in anticipation of our fierce defense of this impenetrable mountain castle. I can hear the cries of women and children in the valley below being slaughtered and raped, the devil, the daijjal, was certainly within the hearts of these men, greed overcoming their sense of honor. Anyone who didn't make it inside the castles walls would be at the mercy of the invaders.

The Lost Truth by Dean Fougere

As instructed; I head to the East Tower and climb to the top. I step out on the small balcony and look down. The east side of the main wall ended on the edge of a cliff, the tower looming magnificently high next to it. Flying around the tower below me was Rashid's eagle, meaning Rashid was about to appear on the wall to address the invaders as he has mentioned.

Then stepping out in the middle of the wall I see Rashid, someone from the invading Army below steps out to converse with Rashid from the bottom of the wall. Mualim must be giving them his speech about our fearlessness I think, hundreds of feet below it is well out of earshot. I look down at the vest, I have no idea how it is supposed to work, but I trust Mualim with my life. He also needs for me to live to carry out his plan.

I step up onto the edge of the balcony, barely able to keep my balance. I look down for a split second and see the few thousand feet drop, knowing soon I would descend. I look back down towards Rashid and the thousands of men below, on either side of the Wall. Then I see Rashid point up at me, no turning back now. My gut has a terrible feeling, as I knew what was about to happen. For an obvious reason I Titus seeing this through the eyes of Hasan-I 2nd, am quite scared. He intends to leap off this tower and thinks he will live, I know a drop like this with no parachute and nothing but a green gold vest will end badly, very badly. Hopefully I will wake up before I hit the deck.

Rashid's arm that is pointing at me drops, no turning back now. Rashid had explained, "Hesitation cannot happen as we must show we do not fear death, when my arm drops so do you." So I jump, diving head first off the balcony.

My body accelerates rapidly and before I can even think I pass right by Rashid's eagle, hearing it screech as I fly past downward. Watching the ground coming towards me at an increasing rate. Wake up, wake up, I keep thinking, even Hassan-I's thoughts betray him as fear overcomes his trust in Rashid, why am I not stopping, thinks Hassan-I Jr? I miss the edge of the cliff at the base of the tower by what seems like inches. The sheer vertical drop of the cliff has nothing for me to grab on to as it flies by at over 180 mph. I have attained maximum drop velocity, a feeling I am familiar with from my HALO drop training as a SEAL, though normally I have two parachutes on my back. Half way down the cliff I see a green square on the ground, as I draw closer by the millisecond it seems to have form, and it seems I would land right on it, dead center. The square grows larger and larger as I fly down at maximum vertical velocity. Just before I hit the square I close my eyes expecting the worse.

Just as my eyes shut, I feel the strangest sensation of my life. The vest starts to pull against my body, first slowly, but with every inch downward it pulls upwards harder. Almost as if the vest is attached to a parachute I can not see. Then just a few feet before I slam into the ground, I come to a full stop. Hovering a few feet over the ground, being lifted into the air by the vest entirely. The Green metal of the vest has started to glow, very brightly whilst holding me in place about two feet from the ground. Bending my legs down I push off the ground to float to the side of the green square. As I come off the edge of the square the invisible force that held me off the ground subsides and I drop onto my feet.

Hassan-I Jr searches his thoughts for what this magic is but had no clue. I deduce that the vest and the square are metal, maybe something highly conductive as I can almost feel pings of electricity coming off the vest. Most likely I think to myself it has something to do with magnetism, maybe the square on the ground gives off a magnetic charge that repels the magnetic charge in the vest. Hassan-I Jr in his thoughts has decided it is the work of magic.

My journey has just begun. I follow the mountain stream down into the valley below. The army of Salahdin must have assumed I had jumped to my death, why wouldn't they?

In the town below I spot the Sultan Salahdin's private guard. There in the middle of the town is his tent, elaborate and enormous. Though the Arab's loved their Bedouin heritage, their tents have come quite a long way from that of their ancestors. Salahdin's tent is quite large, larger than most modern homes in what will one day be America.

I watch from the nearby tree line as Salahdin and his men return from the front line to their tents. Soon night fell on the valley and I move into the village. Slipping quietly past the first guards; I get to a choke point in the protection. The only way through is to either kill the archers on the roof or kill the four guards in between the tent and myself. Well I could handle the four easily, however it would alert the rest of his camp. Just then by some miracle, two of the four guards wander off. Patience it seems has paid again.

I pull out my bow, place two arrows in front of me. I then place my first arrow in my hand and fire. Before the arrow hit's its mark, I already have loosed a second bolt. The first arrow slams into the neck of my target, cutting off his breathe and soon his life as he wriggles on the ground in pain and terror. The guard with him quickly turns into my direction to see where the shot came from. As soon as his head turns my second arrow plunges into his left eye, killing him instantly. I quickly move up and drag their bodies behind a low cut wall. Hoping their two comrades will not return quickly to find them missing from their post.

Slipping into the tent I can hear the Sultan snoring away. I head directly for the sound, and there lying on his bed is Salahdin. I could easily take the dagger and slice his throat, covering his bed in that royal blood he claims. Hassan-I's anger and hatred of Salahdin taking hold, then a sense of honor and duty overcame him. I, Hassan-I, pull out the dagger and cover it in poison. Then I take the note from Rashid and stab the pillow next to Salahdin with the note in the middle. The note simply states, "You cannot rule those who do not fear death". As I turn to leave a beautiful Persian woman is standing in the doorway, completely naked but the chains bounding her hands and feet. She's one of Salahdin's concubines, most likely from the area. I put my finger to motion for silence. She nods in agreement; hopefully realizing her life was at risk.

I turn and dart out of the tent, making my way back to the guard post. When I return the other two guards were still missing, the two dead bodies where I left them. I steal a horse and ride for the Northern tunnel entrance. By the time I find the entrance and climb the massive staircase built in the granite mountain it is dawn.

That morning, Rashid beckons for me to come with him to the wall. As we reach the top I expect to see Salahdin's army below, sieging us in the city. Instead, I see an empty valley.

Mualim's plan has worked, I have scared Salahdin away and more. Rashid informs me that Salahdin had met with him before my return and they have come to an agreement. We will spare the Sultan's life, and assist his campaign against the Crusaders, if he would leave our Ismaili state alone forever and assist us if needed.

Chapter 12 – X Marks the Spot

Boston, USA – Modern Day

I awake from my long slumber. Seems like I slept forever, as my dream was quite long. I look up my experience on the Internet to make sure it wasn't just a dream and might have actually happened. It seems some of the things I experienced were recorded in myth, no one knows for sure if they happened, but I now know them to be true, as I have just relived them first hand. A thought crossed my mind, if DNA holds memories, maybe the Government does not want people find out the true history of the World, as history is written by the victors, they may want to keep it that way if they feel they are winning.

Then it hits me, the talk. What time is it? I look over at the clock on the bed stand. Somehow I have slept for 12 straight hours? Damn, the talk starts in an hour. No time to take the T into the city. I will have to risk driving in.

Minutes later I fire up the CTS and blast down the side roads. Turn off the traction control, and switch the gearbox into S drive. Using the entire overpowered CTS engine, gripping the corners I make it onto 93 S in minutes. Fortunately without popping a tire, as the roads in Boston are awful. If I have good luck with the traffic I could actually make the talk and have enough time to scope out an exit.

Pulling up outside the lecture hall in Cambridge, MA about five minutes before the lecture there is not a parking spot in sight. Then by some miracle, about a hundred meters ahead I see a car turn on the left indicator and pull out of a spot. I slam the gas and instantly am behind them waiting to parallel park. I hop out and throw some quarters in the meter, two hours max. I had dressed as a MIT graduate student or young professor today, wearing a blazer, jeans, brown boat shoes and a button down shirt tucked into my jeans. All I need is Starbucks in my hand, a President O'Brien sticker on my Prius and an iphone in my ear playing some trendy mainstream trash and I would have been lost in the crowd of Cambridge.

Running into the lecture hall, I almost forgot to present my badge to the person taking attendance. The student saw my badge and for a second gave me an odd look. God I hope they didn't have Jonathon as a teacher, I thought. Then she smiled up at me and said enjoy. So I enter the hall and take a chair at the back, so I can see everyone in the room.

Right on time, the young MIT Graduate in Archaeology came onto the stage. She has a petite skinny frame, shoulder length reddish brunette hair, and is absolutely beautiful.

My first thought is I could listen to her for hours about nothing. However, her knowledge may hold the answers I need to find whom killed Jonathon and why.

She begins the lecture, "I am very excited to speak with all of you today. However, as some of my findings are not widely accepted by my colleagues I shall ask you to hold your questions until after I have finished." I notice she glances at one individual in the front row, an older gentleman with white hair, most likely a MIT professor from the look of him.

She then turns on a projector and a big red cross on a field of white is displayed behind her. She begins, "The symbol of the Knights Templar" then clicks the display and reveals the square and compass surrounding the letter G all in gold. "Two organizations, that according to our history books, never existed at the same time, separated by a few centuries only by disinformation. The Knights Templar 'officially' was imprisoned, exterminated on Friday the 13th, 1307, so we are told. According to Freemasonry, their order did not exist until sometime between 1500, and 1600 AD. However, my research has indicated that the groups are one and the same. From my research, it would seem that once the Knights Templar was disbanded they hid in secret until creating the Free Mason order and stepping back into the light of public view."

"The evidence is clear yet highly disputed. Luckily they have hidden their secrets in plain sight, and it is obvious that the mystery schools they reference with symbolism harken back before even the time of Egypt. They seem to be protecting knowledge in plain view by encoding it in their buildings; the knowledge seems to come from the oldest structures on the planet and the heavens above. This love of sacred number, and belief in the Pythagorean ideology that "All is Number" and that "As Above so Below" is a main connection between the two groups. From this stems their use of the same coded language, a system of banking, similar symbols and architecture, and most importantly their shared reverence of King Solomon's Temple, which according to both the Freemasons and the Templars is the perfect Temple."

"The Knight's Templar got their name from the place of their creation, King's Solomon's Temple. Though the origins of their name is associated with the Temple Mount, rather than the specific King Solomon's Temple itself. However, they depict King Solomon's temple and his architect Hiram in many of their statues and architectures. Many of their garments, symbols, and buildings incorporate architectural design from either the Great Pyramid, or the Temple of Solomon. The Temple of Solomon was famous for it's two Pillars Jachin and Boaz, which represented Sun and Moon or Day and Night. Also, the checkerboard floor pattern is quite commonly found, the checkerboard floor represents day and night, and the spiritual and physical world intermingling. Sun symbolism, serpent symbolism, and Gnosticism are seen in both societies. Other common symbols include the pentagram and octogram star, buildings that are built to fit an ad-quadratum design also called "of the square".

"The Free Masons, Templar Knights, and two other important secret society's also revere Solomon's Temple, as the ideal temple. In the Grand Lodge of England, there is a depiction of King's Solomon's Temple. They describe the temple as being the most perfect temple ever constructed, and to become a Master Mason, you must become like the temple of Solomon. The relief also shows the Ark of the Covenant entering the Temple."

"The Knight's Templar has long been heralded as the keepers of the Ark and the Holy Grail. They were all religious men, warrior monks, and required that they devote their lives to God. However, the Church labeled them as heretics in 1307, because many thought it was not the same God as the Catholic Religion they were worshipping. They accused them of worshipping the devil, which was common for the time."

"In similar manner the Free Masons require a belief in a God, and they have a different view of The One True God, referencing him as the Grand Architect. Both orders seem to have been worshipping a different god than any other religion. The Knight's Templar claimed in private documents to be in communication with a deity called Amadeus, and his face can be found in many Knight's Templar Churches from Rosslyn Chapel to Round Temple, and so on. According to Albert Pike, one of the most influential Free Masons to ever exist, their grand Architect is Lucifer, and that would coincide with the charges of devil worship levied at the Templars."

"Banking, maybe the most important connection due to the amount of wealth that is still unaccounted for. The Knight's Templar created the world's first banking system shortly after returning from Temple Mount. They quickly amassed huge amounts of wealth and spread their gold reserves across Europe in Templar Commandaries. These commandaries or banks as we would know them today, established the first system of credit in known history. Making travel to the Holy Lands possible without fear of being robbed of all your wealth."

As she was talking, I noticed a man entered the room and took a one of the only seats left, across the aisle and three rows ahead of me. He sort of stood out from the crowd due to his obvious physical attributes. He was roughly 6'4" and rock solid, short close crop hair and was dressed in an all black suit, with black Oakley sunglasses propped up in his hair. Looked much like secret service to me, just no earpiece. I couldn't tell if he was armed or not, but his sheer size alone made him a threat. He scanned the room and I pretended to look down at my iPhone as he did. To me he looked like someone out of the Special Forces secret surveillance group directly under JSOC Command, a group that has no name, but is called the Activity.

Jocelyn continues on, completely oblivious to the newcomer, "A person would go to the Templars and deposit their money. The Templars used an unbreakable coding method and would hand you what amounts to a credit chit. This chit using a symbol Templar coding system, allowed the traveler to go along and take money from other Commandaries when needed and they would mark the chit with coded symbols as you withdrew money from the Templar commandaries as you traveled. Then when you returned home or wanted to get the rest of your money out, they would check the balance on your chit and know how much you spent. This meant you could travel across Europe and never have all your wealth on you, but still access it at any Templar Commandery along the way."

"The Templar's banking system did not end with small personal credit cards. They started handing out loans, mainly to VIP clients such as the heads of state. At the time it was estimated (though never audited) that the Templars had more gold than all of the Kingdoms of Europe combined. To help pay for the Crusades King Phillip of France borrowed more than he could pay off, which eventually led to the Templar's demise. However, before they vanished they controlled the economy of Europe because they controlled the flow of money by banking. In essence they created the world's first International Credit system, basically out of nowhere."

"The Templars used the wealth to create the world's first truly modern professional army. The soldiers did not want for anything, devoted to serve their God, could not marry, and could not own property. Yet lived in some of the plushest palaces and castles, all owned by the Templar Order and not an individual. This kept the wealth growing and free from the threat of the wealth being destroyed by the actions of a private individual, as each Knight had no wealth, just access to wealth. From the Assassins, their rivals, they learned how to fight without fear, to kill swiftly and silently. They were the literal warriors from the ideal of Plato's Republic, being separate from society, held with high esteem, not owning property, but did not want for anything. They used this system to recruit a large amount of Knights and build a small army of well trained, well equipped warrior monk Knights."

"The Templars and their Cistercian counterparts were not just making money through banking. They also became great agriculturists, and made a fortune especially in England and Denmark through sheep farming. The wool was referred to as white gold because it was so profitable. They had a vast fleet of merchant ships as well, these ships carried many goods and people to and from the Holy Lands for vast profit. The Templars used their organization to create a class of businessmen that all worked together for the order. Secret pacts helped them to eliminate competition as a collective, we still see the Free Masons use this in business today Through groups such as Bilderberg and other such as Skulll & Bones they make pacts to work with one another and through secret pacts they have eliminated any competition, which they hate."

"Eventually the Templars had control of the region of France known to us today as Champagne, and the area became almost a state within a state. The King of France became worried with the Templars and had borrowed more money than he could pay back to fight the crusades. The Templars learned from the beginning that the only way to truly win a war is to fund both sides of the conflict, double the profit and ensures you always back the winner. The same Crusades that made France broke, made the Templars enormously wealthy. The Templars had learned that debt meant money, money meant power. The individual person would only borrow so much, but a Government would borrow vast amounts, especially in times of war. So to create wars and to loan money to both parties was the best way to make money and gain power."

So King Phillip appeased to the Vatican for their help eliminating the Templar threat, and they obliged. Documents and confessions of Luciferianism and the practice of reflection rooms, worshipping a human skull spread rumors that the Templars were devil worshippers and other strange things, though far fetched it was true. Then on Friday the 13th 1307, the King of France and the Inquisition in Spain, King of England and the Vatican all rounded up as many Templars as they could, raided all their commandaries. King Phillip would be clear of his debt and they all would inherit the massive Templar wealth and secret archives of knowledge, or so they thought."

"Turns out all the Templar commandaries were empty, no gold to be found. The archives of knowledge, empty, all the old documents and knowledge gone. Their supposed treasure; the Ark of the Covenant and the Holy Grail not found. Estimated that roughly 80% of the Templar Knights escaped as well, though not the Grand Master Jaques De Mo Lay. He and his brethren were tortured into confession of Satanism before being burnt at the stake for heresy."

"Oddly the entire vast fleet of Templar ships had been amassed at New Rochelle France the day prior, and all sailed off on the 12th. This fleet of ships was never seen again. Many believe Prince Henry St. Claire guided these ships and their stores to North America. The proof being sites along the Maine Coast that show signs of European influence, especially sheep herding in the 1300's. Far before Columbus and long after the Vikings."

At this point the man in the front row turned and saw the large gentleman in the black suit. I noticed a sign of fear in his eyes when he saw this man. He turned back to face the speaker. The man in the black suit, quickly texted something on his cellular phone.

"The Templars themselves did show up again. In Portugal the Templars were not arrested but allowed to change their name and remain hidden. They became the 'Ordem Militar de Cristo, or Military Order of Christ'. A name that should seem odd as Jesus Christ did not believe in war or killing, especially in his name."

"Also, two other places they show up as well. First hand accounts tell of white Knights bearing red crosses fighting alongside Robert the Bruce of Scotland and helping turn the tide for Scotland in their fight for independence from England. The Templars here create the Scottish Rite of Free Masonry. Also, in the Mountains of Switzerland two strange things happened. A land that had nothing but peasant farmers overnight developed a banking system, using coded symbols and numbers out of nowhere. Also their military went from being a colossal joke, to being the most fierce and feared military in Europe. Winning battles against much larger feudal forces from Italia, Germany and France, it was said White Knights bearing red crosses started fighting with the Swiss. All of this points to the Templars just moving and hiding in plain sight out of the reach of the Church or the King's of Europe."

"The evidence was left in plain sight for us to see. You have to understand they worshipped number, sacred geometry and the universal idea of math as an explanation for the entire Universe. The use of sun symbolism, the worship of the Goddess Isis as the Virgin Mary, the passing down of knowledge from ancient mystery schools continued with the Priory of Scion, the Theosophical society, and the Free Masons. They believed in rational, logical thought and they saw the evidence of their idea's in the heavens above and in the structures they found from past civilizations, and in the human body itself. To the Freemason's "All was really number".

"If you look at the Chartres Cathedral France, the Washington Monument, Stonehenge, the Great Pyramid, the layout of DC, the layout of Paris, the layout of San Francisco. You will find the same geometrical patterns. Everyone one of these patterns can be deciphered and the knowledge gained from them by using two simple tools, the square and compass. The square and compass is the key to unlocking any of their sacred geometric designs."

"Using these structures and planned cities the secret Free Masonic and Templar heads of state and visionaries have been encoding the sacred numbers of the ancient past into our buildings and street grids. Along with ancient symbols that have new meanings for the profane, the elite Free Masons saw the same symbols and see something entirely different than what an average person sees."

"In the past this worship of number would have be viewed as heresy and the people killed. As we advance into a more scientific age, brought on by the same thinkers of the enlightenment that created Free Masonry. We grasp a better and fuller understanding of the geometric principles of the Universe. The Freemasons learned this and used the information left behind by the creators of the Great Pyramid and places like Stonehenge to decipher the universe geometrically and then build their cities and monuments in coordination with the larger Universal Geometric pattern. Almost as if the entire Universe was built upon a decipherable grid, and all the temples of the past were already built on this grid, so we started building our own new temples with the same geometric proportions, and on the same geometric grid that resonates across the entire universe. To the profane the sacred sites are scattered and all uniquely designed, to the top level masons, these sights are all connected and part of a larger singular design."

"The Octogram star, is a part of their sun worship and symbolism. They use it to represent Earth's path around the sun, it was the basis for many calendars, including the famous Mayan Long count calendar. The basic symbol can be found as the controlling geometry for many religious symbols, such as the wheel of Buddha. However, it is really a depiction of our solar system as viewed from Earth. See these five images, one showing the basic diagram, then the wheel of Buddha, the current depiction of the Calendar, the Celtic Calendar and the Mayan Calendar."

Octogram Star, Catholicism & Islam, 10/14/14,
http://saraarienti-
characteristics.weebly.com/characteristics---
islam.html

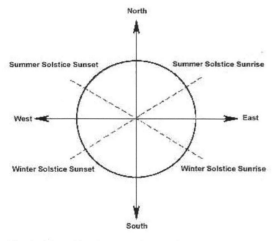

Four Fold Astrology, Sacred

Geometry, 10/3/14,

http://bothsidesofthesky.com/Sacred_Geometry.html

Buddhist Wheel of Life, Ibucket, 10/3/14,

http://i1084.photobucket.com/albums/j411/jhananda/Buddhist%20Iconography/Dharma

-Wheel-pic_zpsb85cdc88.jpg

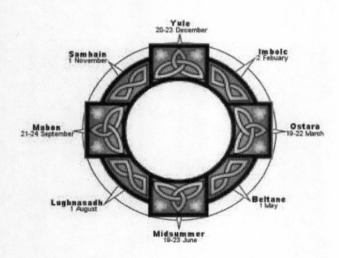

Celtic Calendar, Irish Celtic Traditions, 10/14/14,

http://thecelt.hubpages.com/hub/Irish-Celtic-TraditionsImbolc-Celebration

Mayan Long Count Calendar, 2012 – The end of the World?, October 15, 2014,
http://www.ltradio.org/articles/?admin=linkto&link=257&quick=y

These Calendar's shown on the screen use the ancient astrology and are extremely accurate, as they were based upon the sacred geometry of the Universe. They rival our modern day calendars in terms of accuracy. The Mayan Long count calendar is the same and depicts at it's center the Black Sun Symbol, which for the Mayan people was a Sun God, but for the elite it represented the center of the Milky Way Galaxy that their long count calendar was based upon, one full calendar cycle was one full cycle of earth around the center of the milky way Galaxy. How the ancients gained this knowledge we shall never know, but we do know the religious elite kept this information secret from the people of these ancients cultures normally for power and control."

"If you knew the movements and patterns of the stars, moon and Sun this knowledge could make you very powerful. In the Mayan Culture the priests knew the patterns of the heavens, and could accurately predict eclipses. They would warn the people that the

Moon God was going to devour the sun God unless they did as they were told. The people would do anything to appease the Priests and rulers especially once the eclipse began and the Sun starting disappearing as warned, the same Sun they depended on for growing food. The people would even offer themselves over to human sacrifice to save the Sun from the Eclipse. The priests would pretend their offerings had satisfied and then the Sun would reappear from behind the Moon and the people would completely believe the Priests had saved them thanks to their offerings. Thus making the Priests god like figures who had the power to take away the Sun in conjunction with the Gods. Of course this was all done for control, because the Priests knew the Sun disappearing was predictable and nothing to fear."

"The Free Masons have done the same thing today, considering the public the profane and not informing them of the true meaning of their symbols, such us the Templar equidistant cross. Or how they know this Universe is a mathematical, quantum construct that can be broken down into geometric design. The Universe to them was created by a grand architect and it is obviously not the end result of pure chaos. Their symbols, architecture, teachings all point to the fact that the Free Masons know the Universe due to it's fine tuning, with the cosmological constant, the Fibonacci sequence in so much of nature, the geometric universe is what they are keeping secret from us."

"The equidistant cross, for most is a religious symbol. However, it has nothing to do with religion to the enlightened, it is the symbol of Earth. It shows how Earth crosses the path of the sun or the solstice paths. So the North, South, East, West directions of the eight-sided octogram star, represented Earth. The Templars, took the symbol of Earth as their own, as seen here, over time it was slightly varied to incorporated Pythagorean triangles of course. The Templar's believed they were to be the Army of Earth, and eventually rule over the entire planet, which is why they adopted this symbol. This second symbol of the Templar's can be seen in the graph of DC, with the Cross Centered on the White House"

"Most people see the pentagram star in the street design of DC, but that is just the start, the DC streets encode all of the symbols of sacred geometry. One easy connection to make is the obvious overlay of the compass on DC street grid, the two points of the compass sitting on the White house and Jefferson Memorial, however the interesting thing is the tips are spread exactly one royal mile apart. The royal mile is the same as the Royal Mile encoded in the street of Edinburgh. However the royal mile's actual beginning was, the dimensions of the Great Pyramid, which encode the use of the Royal foot. It was so obvious the foot was used in the design of the pyramid, that the first person to survey the pyramid accurately added the English foot to the wall of the King's Chamber and left a sign, "To be observed by all Nations" underneath. Clearly the foot derived from Geometry, the measure of the Earth, which is encoded in the Great Pyramid, and not from some Old English Kings foot as the myth goes. The knowledge of the foot, and it's universal geometric significance was carried by the Templars into Scotland, where the one royal mile of Edinburgh came from. Scotland also benefited greatly from the knowledge of medicine the Templars brought with them, and for many years was the leading medical city in the world."

"DC from above encodes many different important symbols to the free masons, some obvious like the Pentagon, but others also fit the scheme as seen from above. The geometric perfection of the design is almost unbelievable, only master Free Masons starting from scratch could have designed a city so full of esoteric symbolism just in the street layout, never mind build it so it could be added to later with buildings such as the Pentagon fitting into the geometric shape perfectly. Most would believe this amount of careful planning and brilliant execution would be celebrated, but due to the nature of the symbols, it is not talked about. Almost as if they were trying to show that they had figured out the Universe and have encoded it with mathematical precision in their buildings and street designs, but didn't want anyone to know about it. They seem to worship sacred ratios such as 6:5 Microcosm to Macrocosm, or the definition of Phi which is 7:11"

"They have encoded the Cube, the pentagram star, the tree of life diagram, the flower of life diagram in the street plans of Paris and Washington. The Pythagorean triangles fit the scheme as well, with the easiest to detect being the Federal Triangle. In Paris the Arc de Triomphe sits amid an obvious depiction of the sun from above."

"Interestingly, one of the most famous diagrams is called "squaring the circle" and it is the overlay of the circle over a square, where both the circle and square have the same area. Of course as Pi is an unfeasible number, this is actually an impossible diagram to draw, but you can get very close to 100% percent accurate. The crazy thing is how it encodes not only the Great Pyramid, but the sizes of Earth and Moon."

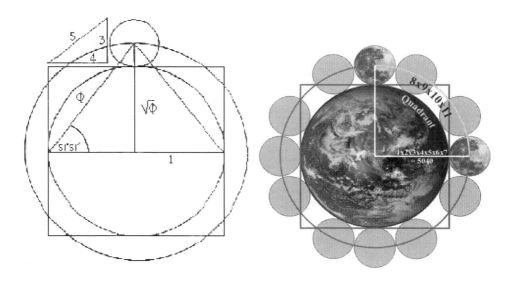

Left image: <u>Mathematical Calculations: The Giza Pyramids, Egypt</u>, Exclusive Moriko Mori Bends Space and Time, 10/14/14, https://hubculture.com/groups/47/news/102/

Right Image: <u>Earth Moon Quadrants</u>, Earth Moon Squared Circle T-Shirts, 10/14/14, http://www.constructingtheuniverse.com/Earth%20Moon%20T-Shirts.html

"You see the Earth is the middle circle that the left and right corners of the Great Pyramid touch. The top of the pyramid extends, outside the square, and therefore outside of earth and directly to the center of the moon, which is the small circle. These sizes are proportionally accurate to 99.9994% accuracy. Thus the Great Pyramid was an accurate representation of the proportion of Earth to Moon. It also encoded the math for the Pythagorean triplets, and the math needed to create Phi and Pi two of the most important numbers in math."

All of these can be created by the double vesica Pisces, by conjoining the circle with the square; you can create all geometric shapes. You can go from the basic vesica Pisces to the elaborate diagram next to it. The relationship of 6:5 is supposed to mimic the Micro-Cosm and the Macro-Cosm.

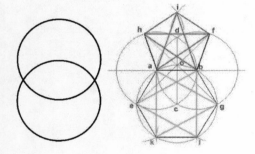

Both Images: From Wikipedia Commons Free Images

It would seem obvious upon review that many important symbols, such as the Great Seal of the United States, Chartres Cathedral and Stonehenge were created using the Geometry of the Vesica Pisces as the basis, then using straight lines connecting the intersection points. As seen here:

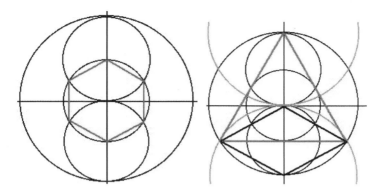

Left Image: <u>Hexagon & Vesica Pisces</u>, Doubling the Circle, October 15, 2014,

http://dcsymbols.com/double_circle/double.htm

Right Image: <u>Vesica Pisces Triangles</u>, Doubling the Circle, October 15, 2014,

http://dcsymbols.com/double_circle/double.htm

This shows how the Vesica Pisces can be used to create straight lines and expand into much larger geometric uniform shapes. The Vesica Pisces is the creator. From connecting straight lines and expanding you can great symbols, building designs and much more. As seen in these photos:

Left Image: <u>The Observer</u>, DC Symbols, October 15, 2014,

http://dcsymbols.com/myideas/ideas4.htm

Right Image: <u>Great Seal Eagle</u>, DC Symbols, October 15, 2014,

http://dcsymbols.com/myideas/ideas4.htm

It seems obvious the Great Seal was designed using the Vesica Pisces and connecting

the straight lines to form the Six Pointed Star. Same can be seen at the above view of

Stonehenge, or the design view of Chartres Cathedral, were these all designed by the

same architect? Makes one wonder?

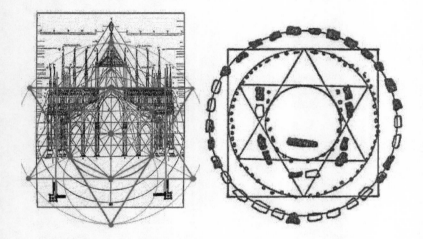

Left Image: <u>Chartres Cathedral</u>, Doubling the Circle, October 15, 2014,

http://dcsymbols.com/double_circle/double.htm

Right Image: <u>Stonehenge</u>, Doubling the Circle, October 15, 2014,

http://dcsymbols.com/double_circle/double.htm

The Washington Monument from above the walkways shows a vesica pisces, which is

the female symbol of creation; the monument itself is representative of the phallus. The

Monument is a depiction of the conjoining of the male phallus and the female, thus symbolizing creation. The conjoining of Osiris and Isis created the Egyptian God

Horus, and that is what this monument represents. The eye of Horus is on the back of

every dollar bill printed since 1933, and is called the All Seeing Eye. Horus is also

represented by the Sun, or winged disk that can be seen on the elevator inside of the

Washington Monument."

The height of the Washington Monument is 6660 inches, also known as 555'. This

ratio of six to five is represented in many Templar and Masonic creations. These two

stars, the six-sided star and the five-sided star when conjoined are supposedly magical

talismans granting those who create them power. This is up for interpretation

obviously. Some people point to the height of the Monument as a clue. The height

including the 111' feet underground, measure out to 666 feet tall, a very specific

number in Christian religion."

"The point is that Free Masons, wherever their influence was felt, created a copy of the

stars above on the Earth below. As above so below, to make Heaven on Earth, or the

conjoining of Heaven with Earth, I am not sure. This above so below theme is also seen

in the hand of the mysteries, with three fingers pointing up, two down."

"Upon research of as above so below it leads to one ideology, or one ancient promise it

seems. The mystery schools, Templars, Priory of Scion, Babylonian Mystery schools,

Free Masons, etc. All seemed to care a great deal about this as above so below

symbolism. Da Vinci put the hand of mysteries in his last supper painting, and in his painting of John the Baptist, which was originally titled Angel in the Flesh. I believe they were symbolizing the convergence of the heavens, or some spiritual dimension with our own. But of this I cannot be sure."

"What I am sure of is, they saw Geometric shapes in the heavens that seemed to match important sacred numbers. Buildings such as the Transamerica Pyramid in San Francisco, the new Freedom Tower in NYC, and their various Temples all show this sacred geometry and point to as above so below."

"George Washington and L'Enfant, created the street plan for DC, and Paris based upon ancient worship of number. These are encoded everywhere. You can see the street plan of DC is actually a depiction of this extremely complex diagram and is confirmed by buildings like the Pentagon that fit perfectly to the edge of this diagram."

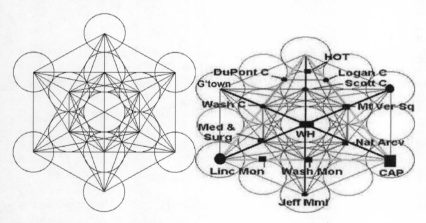

Left Image: Metatron's Cube, Metatron's Cube, October 15, 2014,

http://dcsymbols.com/cube/page5.htm

The Lost Truth by Dean Fougere

Right Image: <u>Washington Cube</u>, Metatron's Cube, October 15, 2014,

http://dcsymbols.com/cube/page5.htm

"Within this diagram, you can make many smaller symbols. Such as the pentagram star, the cube, the six-sided star commonly referred to as the Star of David. It encodes the math of 6 circles fits around 1 circle and 12 spheres fit around 1 sphere."

"The deeper you delve into this geometry, the more shapes you can create. Eventually you realize that this sacred geometry and the shapes that seem to represent the whole universe are a depiction of our entire reality. That really all can be explained by number, but the numbers are all just slightly off from what we would expect because of some interaction between the Microcosm and Macrocosm, or some sort of dimensional barrier."

"The great Pyramid seems to be the key to the whole mystery. Somehow the math used to create it was as advanced as what we have now. The pyramid also seems to encode the Speed of Light, not only in it's design, which is an extremely complex set of numbers I won't bore you with but also it's location. The speed of light is 299,792,458 m/s, and the Pyramid's Main Chamber is located at precisely a latitude of 29° 58′ 45.28″ N = 29.9792458° N. Seems the Pyramid has too many perfect coincidences, and was built to a mathematical perfection for a purpose. A way to permanently record knowledge to ensure future societies are able to decipher and use the information because it was all left in the language of math and the cosmos."

"The big secret they seem to be encoding is quite dramatic. It is called a Hyper-Cube, and it is the geometric representation of a fourth spatial dimension that exists. Maybe what they were trying to do by copying the heavens was somehow access this fourth spatial or dimension of energy, possibly a spiritual dimension. Some say the Cube is connected to the Planet Saturn through symbolism. This picture is of a Cube within a Cube, and to see the fourth dimension it has to be in motion."

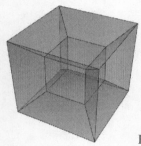

Image: From Wikipedia Commons Images

Also my research has lead me to believe the Free Masons are keeping this fourth spiritual dimension a secret for their own benefit. The lower level Masons, anyone below the 33rd degree seem unaware of this knowledge, and a letter written by George Washington seems to explain why. I believe the Free Masons have been infiltrated and are now being run by an inner circle of 33rd degree masons and above called the Illuminati."

She displayed the letter written by George Washington and stored in the Library of Congress.

Mount Vernon, October 24, 1798.

Revd Sir: I have your favor of the 17th. instant before me; and my only motive to trouble you with the receipt of this letter, is to explain, and correct a mistake which I perceive the hurry in which I am obliged, often, to write letters, have led you into.

It was not my intention to doubt that, the Doctrines of the Illuminati, and principles of Jacobinism had not spread in the United States. On the contrary, no one is more truly satisfied of this fact than I am.

The idea that I meant to convey, was, that I did not believe that the Lodges of Free Masons in this Country had, as Societies, endeavoured to propagate the diabolical tenets of the first, or pernicious principles of the latter (if they are susceptible of seperation). That Individuals of them may have done it, or that the founder, or instrument employed to found, the Democratic Societies in the United States, may have had these objects; and actually had a separation of the People from their Government in view, is too evident to be questioned.

-George Washington

"What our first President George is telling us is extremely important. This letter was dated 1798, and is still in the Library of Congress, is a full fourteen years after the Illuminati was supposedly abandoned according to Bavarian Law in 1784. This proves the Illuminati doctrine had been carried over to the United States and continued long after 1784."

The man in the front stood. "Excuse me however I have to interrupt this nonsense. None of what you are telling these people is backed with solid evidence and I shan't allow you to continue rambling. As an archaeologist you show no evidence for how these Ancient Egyptians were able to come up with this incredible math. You make assumptions that certain shapes and symbols are the basis for these structures without any credible proof! Of course the icing on the cake is the mythical Illuminati, I think you have been watching too many movies my dear. This is a total farce and full of misinformation, next thing you will suggest Martians built the pyramids with the Illuminati!" The professor standing defiant, telling the audience to leave with his hand gestures.

"Sir, I have been presenting evidence based upon the knowledge that is already established!" Jocelyn fires back at the professor.

I turn to see the man in the black suit, but somehow he vanished out of the auditorium without me noticing. Most likely concealed with the movement of people towards the exit.

The speaker tried to argue with the professor but it was no use, half the audience was already out of the room by now. I couldn't hear the words but she was screaming at him and he was flanked by two obvious colleagues who seemed to all be speaking down to her.

As I drew closer I heard the man in the middle say, "Had you stuck to the preapproved speech you handed to me this morning, I would have let you continue. A fourth dimension, really what have you been smoking? You want to have the floor then you will only convey verifiable facts. You will not embarrass this Institution, good day."

As he finished a mini-speech of his own, the professor and his colleagues turned and marched out. The young grad student turned and snatched her written speech from the podium and turned off the projector with the remote. Then she turned, her hair swingy gently as if she was modeling and made eye contact directly with me. Instantly tensed up and didn't know what to do so I smiled and approached her.

"Jack Davis pleased to meet you" I say as I extend my hand.

"Jocelyn Kirkbridge and thank you for staying" She replies in her thick British accent as she shakes my hand. Clearly not wanting to come off as too feminine as she attempted to actually squeeze my hand. "Did you have something you wanted to ask me or did you want to reprimand me for my speech like the others?"

"I was really enjoying your speech, though I am not an expert on that subject. I had some questions regarding an artifact I found that may belong to the Templars or Freemasons or both. I was hoping with your expertise you may be able to assist. Maybe we could discuss this over coffee across the street?"

The Lost Truth by Dean Fougere

"I don't really have the time, I have a class scheduled for right after this speech, and my speech was only going to be thirty minutes. You see I am still in graduate school, that is why I was cut off by my professor and his colleagues."

"Well, have a quick look at this key and if you want to discuss it we can, I'll be in the coffee shop across the way getting some work done on my computer before my evening class that I teach. If you want to join me after your class, feel free to do so." I pull the key from the banker from my pocket and hand it to her.

She looks at the key and gasps, "This is remarkable, is this authentic, where did you get this?"

"A colleague inherited it and had no idea what it was for, maybe you could assist, have you seen these symbols or the strange writing?"

"Yes, these are Masonic and Templar symbols, this key looks very old. The writing seems familiar I will look through my notes to see what it is. Forget my class I will grab my notes and meet you in five."

"See you there, can I grab you a coffee?" I say with a smile.

"Sure, I will have a skinny vanilla latte." She says as she turns and whisked away.

"No problem" I reply, basically to no one as she was halfway out the door already.

In the coffee shop I ordered two drinks, one coffee and whatever that concoction she asked me to order for her was. She arrived completely out of breathe, somehow in a completely different outfit and hairstyle no more than ten minutes later with two notebooks and a magnifying glass.

She apologized for the being late and thanked me for the latte. Then started studying the key ever so carefully.

I said, " I don't think it needs to be handled with extreme care, it has been through quite a bit since I have had it and it's fine." She just smiled at me and kept doing her thing.

She asked if I had noticed a strange guy in a black suit around, I replied I had, and she stated he seemed to follow her from the lecture then back to the shop, but she had no idea why. She pushed it aside as nothing.

Eventually she had gone over the key enough and had formulated something to tell me. She started rather excitedly. "This key is either a forgery to get my attention or a piece of evidence that directly connects the Templars and the Free Masons. I assume you have not gone to the location on the key to find what this unlocks?"

"No, I did not realize there was a location listed." She now had my full attention.

First off the key has the number 33, that number you see is very important to the Free Masons. They identify the highest degree a person can reach in their order is the 33rd degree. This means this key most likely belonged to a 33rd degree Free Mason.

"The hooked x symbol is also important to both groups. The Templars put this symbol on monuments and in Cistercian Monasteries. Like I said before it is a symbol of the connection between male and female. The hooked X is rare, though it has been found in the Rosslyn Chapel and it is said free masons, make an X with their arms while praying and often will put one thumb up to make the hook of the X. Very important symbol to both groups. Some sights on the East Coast have this marked engraving on them."

"The other symbol, the double barred cross, this is the Cross of Lorraine. This is a Templar Cross, they used this in the Champagne Region of France when they controlled the area after 1129 AD until they vanished in 1307 AD. However, the date on the key doesn't make sense."

"What date?" I ask

"I wonder did you notice the writing along the spine of the key?"

"No, I did not, what writing?"

"Here" she hands me the magnifying glass and key; look right here at an angle. As I did tiny letters appeared on the key. She said, these letters are from the Easter Table that was used by the Templars as a coded language. Substituting symbols for letters."

"Using the Easter Table that I can pull up on my ipad, I can decode the letters. It reads as follows, 'Newport Keystone and there is a date, written twice, 1392. If the date is correct, then the key was made by the Templars or someone using their symbols 85 years after they vanished as an organization.'"

She continues, "There is a Newport Tower, that is under some controversy and it just so happens that the Templars are said to have been the builders. Maybe this keystone is in the tower, want to go find out? It is about two hours from Boston to Newport by car? "

I look at her and smile, "Newport two hours? I could drive in reverse and make Newport in two hours. Can you go now?"

"Yes, I can always get class notes and my work done later. This is true-life research anyways and I may be able to add this to my thesis. Where did you park?" She is grinning ear to ear.

As I opened the door to my Cadillac CTS for Joeclyn, she utters, "nice car". As I shut the door I notice about 100 yards down the road a Chevy Suburban fired up it's engine. I climb in my car and watch through the rear view, the Suburban stayed put. Fearing there was a car bomb, I turn the key to fire the engine with great reluctance, looking into Jocelyn's bright blue eyes as I heard the V8 engine roar to life. I pull out of the parking spot and after I had driven about 60 yards, the suburban pulled out to follow.

I say to Jocelyn, "I like to drive kinda fast, hope you don't mind?"

She replies, "Go for it."

Seeing a light ahead stuck on green I determine I may be able to lose the tail if I punch the gas. Drop the engine down into third and slammed the pedal hard, the traction controlled did all it could to put the power to the back wheels without letting them spin. The CTS launched forward easily hitting 60 mph on the busy Cambridge back road. The light turned yellow, I crush the pedal even further, Jocelyn grabs for the "oh shit bar" above the passenger window. Just as I am about at the stop line the light turns red, and I don't even hesitate, blowing through the red light at about 65 mph. Thankfully the Boston Police were nowhere in sight. I look in the rear view and see the suburban parked at the red light with crossing traffic blocking his path. I take a turn so he can't spot me any longer and head the new direction for the highway.

Chapter 13 – Hidden in Plain Sight

Newport, RI – Modern Day

An hour and fifteen minutes later we arrive at the Newport Tower. Jocelyn looks at the time and says, "If you drove any faster you would have blown my clothes off on the way down here."

I smile awkwardly taken aback by the flirtatious comment and reply, "The thought had crossed my mind." I pause and look around the village green area. First thing was the spot; the tower was built on the highest hill in the area, right on the top of the hill. Small trees in a village green type area surrounded it. I did not see any government looking vehicles or any people passing by. "Well, there it is, the grand Newport Tower, let's have a look."

Jocelyn delighted to be at the site in person goes into tour guide mode, "The Tower itself, seems out of place compared to the other structures in the New England Area. Officially attributed to being built by Benedict Arnold in the 18th Century as a copy of a windmill in Denmark, the stones tell a different story. The three story windmill is now just a stone skeleton of it's former self, the stones are very old and carbon dating has been unable to determine an accurate date for the site."

Jocelyn explains, "The tower is built in the style of the Templar's, basically an exact copy of the Round Church in England. The concept of this being a windmill designed after one in Denmark holds little water for me. The Windmill in Denmark is built with six pillars supporting six arches, not the eight pillars supporting eight arches seen here."

"The eight pillars aren't the only dead giveaway that this was a Templar or Freemasonic Construction. The Building is aligned with both Venus and the Summer Solstice. The Eight Pillars mark as eight points of the octogram star. This means if something is hidden hear it should be right in the middle of the space. This like Stonehenge is a large version of a Sun dial or calendar. Not just some windmill built by a traitor Benedict Arnold."

"This seems to be a part of a round ambulatory church that was designed in Norman Gothic Style, much like the churches it seems to have been built after. Time it would seem destroyed everything but the stones themselves. The design is too familiar with the Round Church of England; this Round Church was a copy of the Temple Church of England but on a smaller scale. The Temple Church was built by the Knights Templar in their traditional Norman Gothic Style and supposedly designed after the Holy Sepulchre Church of Jerusalem. In reality all their buildings were built with the Sacred

Numerology they inherited from Egyptian mystery schools and teachers like Pythagorus."

"The tower has obviously been renovated in the 16th or 17th century, which has lead to confusion in the carbon dating. Seems like someone came across the old tower and tried to change the look of it by coating the entire outside in plaster, most of which has withered away now. I believe the build date of the tower is roughly 1300-1400 AD. This means this tower is absolute proof Templar Knights ventured to New England after they were destroyed in 1307 and long before Columbus sailed across the ocean in 1492. Furthermore, Columbus was also a member of an offshoot of the knight's Templar that had survived in Portugal under a new name. So Columbus would have known of any Templar expeditions previous to his own, possibly this is why he was so sure he could cross the ocean."

"That would make sense." I say. She ignores my agreement and drones on.

"Also, the pillars as you can see are sticking out further than the walls of the upper floors. Meaning a windmill is not the likely purpose as the lower columns may get in the way of the fans of the mill."

I look up at the inside of the mill and notice, there are two windows in the side of the tower, and a third window that is walled in. I point at the walled in window and before I can speak.

"Yes, you noticed it the second floor fireplace, notice the color change in the walls from the smoke?"

"Absolutely" I reply.

"There aren't windmills with fireplaces inside because the grain being milled would have made the inside of the mill a dangerous place for even a candle, never mind a fireplace."

"Of course, other than the obvious design changes there are two keystones centered in the archways. And some unusual alignments that signify the solstice, and Venus rising. When you cross the alignments for Venus and the solstice line you get an X, a symbol very popular with both the Free Masons and the Templars. Also, there is another alignment through the keystones that point to a controversial medieval runestone dug up in Minnesota. The astrological alignments are very accurate if the date of the build was around 1390 or even yesterday."

"The astrological alignments in this tower are not the only ones in the Northeast that have been discovered. A much, much older site in New Hampshire called the American Stonehenge is connected to this Newport Tower by the solstice line. The summer solstice alignment in the tower lines up with a Stonehenge in New Hampshire. This Stonehenge solstice line if carried over the Atlantic Ocean goes directly through the

Solstice marking stones of the famous Stonehenge in England. If you continue the line further in ends up in Lebanon at Baalbek, which would have been the Phoenicians. It seems the Newport Tower, Stonehenge, The New Hampshire Stonehenge, Viking Forts in Denmark, and the Phoenician culture are all connected by this one alignment they all must have been aware of to get so perfectly precise with the placement of their sacred sites. It is too perfect to be coincidence."

"Let's see the Keystones" I say pulling the key from my pocket. As I do I check the perimeter, and see nothing but the trees and the leaves shaking in the breeze. No one will notice.

Hopping the small fence that protects the Tower from the public, I just hope no one is watching. Jocelyn points out some small rocks embedded in the tower, she mentions they are cumberlandite and have special magnetic properties. I asked her if they were placed with any significance throughout the tower and she says none that anyone has picked up on yet.

One of the keystones, was egg shaped and on the summer solstice the sun shown through one of the windows and illuminated the egg shaped keystone. The other keystone was on the outside of the tower, and resembles the shape of the book held by the Statue of Liberty, a masonic structure.

The Lost Truth by Dean Fougere

First examining the outer keystone I tried to insert the key into cracks around the outside and nothing happened. Seems the Statue of Liberty Book Keystone did not hold the secret of the key. The egg shaped Keystone was our next attempt.

I tried to insert the key in a few cracks next to the stone but nothing. Then I ran it underneath the stone and it fit into some small cracks under the stone perfectly. As it fit into the stone, it got pulled up almost by a magnetic force. Trying to pull the key out from the stone wouldn't work, it didn't budge, completely held in place by what had to be something magnetic in the Keystone.

At this point something incredible took place, totally unexpected yet spectacular. The key grew very hot so I released it. Then a spark of electricity shot from the key to the far wall of the tower right at a piece of cumberlandite, the spark large enough to be easily seen almost like a small bolt of lightning. When the spark hit the rock on the far wall it did so hard enough to split the rock into two pieces. The rock then fell in pieces to the ground and revealed two small coins and a letter. The coins made of a strange green metal that looked almost gold like; the electricity from the spark seemed to be flowing in the metal coins, as they almost appeared liquid despite being solid.

I reach forward to grab the coins, but stop short when I feel a hand on my shoulder. Jocelyn says, "Don't touch anything, we could contaminate the"

As I stopped, I felt the whoosh of a bullet go ripping by where my face should have been had she not stopped me. Then a second shot hits me dead square on my body armor right where my heart should be. Instantly knocking me back off my feet, stunned. Fortunately the armor had taken the round and I was fine.

Jocelyn screams in horror, and I see the shooter moving out from behind one of the larger trees on Truoro Park. I pull my Berretta out, but before I can return fire three more bullets hit the metal fence between us, one of the bullets shatters and the shrapnel hits me in the arm and leg then another piece clips Jocelyn's arm. I quickly aim and fire, I unloaded 7 shots, I see at least 3 hit their target. The man in the black suit falls over, still firing away with his silenced pistol, but missing wildly. I stand aim and deliver three rounds at his cranial vault, two miss him completely but the middle shot plows right through his left eye and out the back of his skull. I pop the empty clip out of the berretta and quickly replenish the ammo with a fresh clip and scan the horizon for more targets. Seeing none I turn to Jocelyn.

"Are you ok?" I ask Jocelyn and she just starts crying in shock. I did not have the silencer on my pistol and I had to have woken up the entire Police Force of Newport by now. "Let's get out of here, go to my car I'll meet you there"

Grabbing the two coins and the letter, I stuff them in my jacket pocket. Then I run over to the dead body of the secret service agent. Looks like I hit him twice in the armor on his chest and once in the neck, before the death shot that went through his eye. "No open casket for you my friend" I say to his lifeless corpse. I pull out his wallet to ID

him. He has a badge in his pocket. National Security Agency, "The NSA, that isn't

good what have I gotten myself into?" I pull out his wallet and notice a chain hanging

around his neck. I grab the gold chain and pull it out, on the chain is a gold cross, the

double barred cross of Lorraine. Then I hear a siren coming up the hill to the South.

I run as fast as possible for the CTS, and reach it just as I see blue lights on the far side

of the park. I hand Jocelyn the items and she says, "Good the police, we need their help,

who was shooting at us?"

I just reply, "The cops were shooting at us" and slam the car into first gear and peel off

down the road. "We need to get off the roads and change vehicles. Take a look at the

coins and the letter and see if you can find a direction for us to head in, we have clearly

found something the Government is willing to kill to keep hidden so let's try to figure

out what it is before we end up dead ourselves. Are you injured?"

"I am fine" she replies, "just a small cut, the shrapnel just nicked me."

Looking at my arm and my leg, I notice neither wound is still bleeding, just small

pieces of shrapnel barely under the surface of the skin. Easy enough to pull out once we

have stopped.

"If you have a cell phone, or any electronics on you, get rid of it out the window, I'll replace it for you later." As I said this I tossed my iphone and blackberry out the car and asked her to throw out my ipad. "The NSA tracks this stuff regularly, they could just sit back and watch anywhere we went with those on us, most likely how they found us at the tower."

She replies, "Well I dropped my cell phone back when the cop started shooting at us." Then tossed out her ipad.

I then threw my driver's license, passport, and all my credit cards out the window. I told her to do the same and she asked why?

"Well unknown to most Americans is the fact that all new drivers licenses, passports, credit cards, hotel room keys and similar objects have RFID chips implanted in them. The surveillance grid to pinpoint and individual's location can use these chips."

Maybe her way of dealing with shock was to focus on what was at hand. She seemed worried about the tracking information, and about our current situation. Her bright blue eyes seemed to tremble with fear. Trying to keep her mind busy she he continues "the coins both have buildings on them, two different sites from the ancient past, one is the depiction of Solomon's Temple and the other is a depiction of the Great Pyramid and the opposite side of the coin is the Great Seal. It depicts the original Seal of the United States, a Phoenix holding 13 arrows; fig branch with 13 leaves. 13 is a number that is extremely important to the Templars and the Freemasons, because Friday the 13th, 1307 is the day the Templars under that name vanished and were reborn as the Free Masons according to my research. The other half of the US Seal, is the Unfinished pyramid and all seeing eye, a symbol that according to Legend was crafted by a group called the Illuminati. The all seeing eye is the Seal of the Illuminati, showing their ultimate game plan."

"Who's the Illuminati?" I ask.

Jocelyn states, well the official story is they were a group within Free Masonry that were created on May 1st, 1776 in Bavaria and ended shortly after. However, reading their documentation shows they had planned to take over Governments, secret societies from within, to control the world. Many people believe they have done exactly this and point to organizations such as Skull & Bones as proof they still exist, and honestly it is hard to say they are wrong because it is all documented. But I never looked into this heavily as it seemed too far fetched to be true, until my research pointed me down this path."

"The letter is far more intriguing than the symbols on the coins. It has been double dated, much in the style of the Templar's but written in English, just backwards as if written with a mirror. Leonardo Da Vinci used to write in this manner and hide secrets in his paintings using mirrors as well, he was also a member of the Priory of Scion one of the groups modernized and centralized into the Illuminati Doctrine in 1776."

Dated 1932 as a digit and written out Nineteen thirty-two on the bottom.

"Light is truth. Our Worshipful Master shall protect it. We shall hide the Library in plain sight; hide the documents within so the truth is understood in time. People must see the light, and therefore as 55 has requested we shall build a tower of light to shine over the land and the waters. For Liberty and Justice we do design our temple. From the top of the world, where an owl would perch, the Nine Unknown shall meet the Light Bearer to guide this Experiment in Justice for all Mankind. The reign of 55 shall be here soon."

"I know what this letter is referencing to. It could only be one place in the United States that I can think of right away," Jocelyn states, "Liberty the goddess, as depicted by the Free Masons, is a reincarnation of the Virgin Mary of the Templars and Cistercians. St. Bernard de Clairvoux created a new order of the Church to worship the Virgin Mary, however the Virgin Mary he worshipped was not the one from the bible. It was secretly the goddess Isis also known as Venus. This is why the FreeMasons, Templars, Cistercians, Rosicrucian's all worship Venus, Isis, the Virgin Mary, etc. They are all the same people. That is why the Newport Tower was built with the alignment of Venus considered, all part of their worship of the goddess Isis."

Looking pleased with my attentive nature she continued.

"The Goddess Isis supposedly built a Lighthouse in Pharos that was one of the Ancient Wonders of the World. It was designed to bring light to the World. Most scholars maintain it stood 864' feet tall, and therefore represented the Sun and Time in general. You see the Sun's diameter is 864,000 miles, and there are 86,400 seconds in a day, so the Sun's diameter gives us the most basic measurement we have of time, 1 second. The TransAmerica Pyramid in San Francisco incorporates this theme as well, as the building is 864' tall if you include the antenna. One of the greatest secrets the Free Masons have always held is the nature of the mathematical Universe, how everything is symbiotic and even if slightly off in any way the entire Universe would not exist. The orbits of the planets, the sacred ratios are seen throughout the construct, that is why they call God the Grand Architect. They know the universe was not created by chance, the mathematical and geometric perfection of the Universe was obviously the result of intelligent design."

"So, where do you head now? What is this Isis Lighthouse in modern time?" I ask.

"Now it's called the George Washington National Masonic Monument in Alexandria VA, built as a perfect copy of the Library of Alexandria and commissioned by Free Masons. The Library of Alexandria in Ancient times was a beacon of light over all the Mediterranean." She says.

"Let me explain" Jocelyn states excited to share her knowledge. "The George Washington tower was very costly to build, as they did not want to use mortar, rather cut the bricks in a way that they fit together and using geometry they are held in place. This is the strongest way to build a building because mortar will decay over time and any building built with mortar will not last anywhere near as long as a building made only of stone blocks. That is why the ancient Mayan sites are so advanced; they fit the blocks together like puddy with no mortar and that has allowed the walls to remain intact, and even withstand earthquakes. "

"Also, there is supposedly a meeting room on the tenth floor where the Unknown Nine meet, a group of overseers who direct all of Free Masonry. I suspect these are the real Illuminati. The eighth floor is a temple to the Knights Templar. These Nine Freemasons are the inner circle that decides everything for the group. Some say they are privy to secret knowledge held by the group. The Grandmaster is one of the nine but holds no more power than any of the other members according to my research, they rule by consensus. The building was paid for by freemasons and is the only monument that all freemasonic lodges are required to pay a tribute to annually. Every floor is filled with strange symbols, like the seventh floor which is an homage to ancient Egypt and has a copy of the Ark of the Covenant on display, with many references to Moses."

"Whoa take a breath," I reply. "We have a long way to drive before we get there, you have plenty of time for a rundown." Let's head that way, however we need to get off the road for a night or two to let the heat calm down and we need a new vehicle. "So we will head to Baltimore and find us a seedy motel to stay in that takes cash. Should be able to locate a ride nearby as well".

Joeclyn laughs, "Well if you drive fast enough I won't keep boring you with random historical facts." She winks at me basically begging me with her looks to slam the gas pedal against the carpet and listen as the five hundred horsepower engine blasted to life.

Chapter 14 – An Assassin on the Loose

Newport, RI – Modern Day

Arriving first at the scene of the shootout at Newport Tower was two local Newport Policeman whom had heard the gunshots from nearby. They both heard seven blasts from the 9mm berretta then another three and just stared at one another. Both couldn't believe their ears, not expecting the quiet proper town of Newport to have any gunfights, as there were barely any crimes other than white class drug use, and public drunkenness in the town. Domestic dispute is what they said to one another after racing to the cruiser and getting to the scene as fast as possible. Neither of them saw the Cadillac carrying Titus and Jocelyn as it vanished into the maze of small streets and one ways crisscrossing magnificent stately homes of Newport as they arrived on the scene.

What they did find was an unidentified corpse. No wallet, no ID, holding a silenced pistol 45mm Smith & Wesson. With two 9mm bullets in his body armor, a third in his neck and the other somewhere lodged in his skull most likely in pieces, as the bullets shot were hollow points. He had multiple empty gun casings from his own pistol around his body. No bystanders.

They called in the scene to the radio operator and set up a perimeter. About fifteen minutes later a trio of black SUV's arrived on the scene. Six men dressed in all black business suits approached the two Newport Police officers. Then four of them broke off and walked over to the corpse. Two of them stopped and made a visual inspection of the scene before one pulled out his badge and flashed it to the Police.

"NSA, this scene is a federal crime scene and involves a terrorist threat, the man killed was a NSA Operative tracking a known terrorist assassin understand?"

"Yes, sir" Both of the Town Police Officers replied voices quivering. Both wondering why the NSA officers had arrives so rapidly, and why they kept their sunglasses on at night. "Pretty quick on the scene were you nearby?" Asks the older of the two local cops.

"Yes, we had been tracking the suspect but were unaware he was armed. WE will handle it from here." The NSA officer emphasizing the WE, the two cops both sheepishly nod.

The NSA officer pleased to see both the local police just wanted to do their job, and then continued. "This involves national security and you will both need to sign an affidavit of confidentiality. You are not to speak of what you saw here, if you do you will be in violation of National Defense Authorization Act for aiding a known terrorist and liable to be convicted of Treason which is punishable by death. Under the NDAA we can detain you for an indefinite amount of time without cause or trial. Do you understand me gentleman?"

"Yes, sir" They both reply anxiously, and walked over with the NSA Officer to his car to sign a confidentiality affidavit.

Two of the other NSA officers had already carried the dead man's corpse to their SUV, and had started to check the area for bullets and shell casing's using a metal detector.

The other two were over by the Tower and had started back to the Head officer who was standing where the cops had been overlooking the situation. As they reached him he asked, "Sitrep"

"Sir, this is not good", as he handed the rock fragments to his superior. Immediately the head officer took the rocks with disgust and walked over to his vehicle. Placing the chards in a freezer bag, he then tapped a hidden button on his sunglasses, then stated speed dial code 33.

He waited for the earphone wirelessly connected to his advanced smart glasses to ring twice then he said "site 1362", then said his last then first name, "Jackson, Milton." The agent heard a female automated voice say, "voice recognition match, please hold for retina authentication". He opened his eyes wide and the glasses scanned his retina to authentic him biometrically. Then the female voice said "Authenticated Pretorian Templar Milton Jackson, connecting…"

An old angry toned voice answered the call, a voice that had the sound of wisdom and the chill of power. "Milton, brother how may I help you?"

"Worshipful Grandmaster, the assassin whom killed the banker has found the black stone you mentioned and broke it in half to take whatever was inside a hollow space in the rock. He killed his NSA tail at the tower and we are cleaning up, two local police witnessed the body. He has teamed up with a young female archeologist; their early discussion in the car was recorded through their electronic mobile devices. We fear he is already en route to Washington and he has dropped off the radar until he uses a credit card or passes through a tollbooth. Or a security camera spots him. We found his cell phone and electronic gear nearby. The on star system and built in GPS in his car was removed years ago."

"One man tail, is all you had on him? We could have watched him with Battlespace, and killed him anytime we chose, and you decided to use some old spy tailing nonsense? You do realize NSA operatives are never to be revealed, and you are out there carrying guns and acting like James Bond. You know what, you are ineffective, and you are being replaced. I am transferring this to NSA Headquarters and to JSOC, you are relieved of command, report in."

The old man placed the phone on the holster. He looked out at the city below through glass made of gold, perched high above the people of Canada in a golden tower. He picked up the phone and called the Pindar's number in DC.

"Yes, speak brother?" The Pindar's tone was cool and confident, emanated a sound of knowledge and command.

"Pindar, there has been a serious catastrophe. We need to have an emergency meeting, we lost a key of the Nine Unknown Men and it was used to recover an access key and manuscript from Newport that the Banker was protecting." Angrily stated the old man.

"How could this happen? The keys in the Newport Tower have been hidden in plain sight since 1932 when the Archive was built." Stated the Pindar.

"I have more troubling news as well. Just before the firefight at the tower, our field forensics team investigating the death of the MIT Professor reported in."

"The forensics team had recovered the DNA decoding technology, and the body of the professor, but they found something else. The professor had used the technology on a human subject, illegally and without the University's consent. His lab cameras recorded the whole event. It was done in complete secret; coincidentally he had our new friend we are chasing Titus Frost, hooked up to his machine. It worked and he didn't even share the success with anyone, can you believe it?"

All the old man heard was an eerie silence. So he continued.

"We analyzed his DNA, what he left in the needles at MIT. His bloodline is impossible to believe, he seems to be descendant of Hasan-I Sabbah, the same family that killed Andre and stole our secrets. Before we wiped them all out or so we thought, one must have escaped us. The bloodline continues."

The pindar angrily retorted. "There is much hidden in the DNA of this individual. He carries the pure seed of original man and his entire bloodline threatens us. We cannot allow him to leave or spread his seed or we will never be free from our fate. This is now the top priority; we must take him alive. He has been trained for warfare, trained to resist torture, but every man has a breaking point and my guess is the girl. He is traveling with a female, and soon if not already will become emotionally attached, this is his weakness, exploit it. Bring him to me once you have him in custody. Only use our men whom have taken the blood oath to handle this operation."

Then the sound of a phone being slammed into it's cradle and a dial tone, the Pindar had hung up without hesitation, he was a cold calculating man with little time for problem solving. He inherited all his money and power and could barely be bothered to do anything but what he wanted. The old man sighed, not appreciative that the younger Pindar acted so arrogant. He and the 8 other Unknown men were not even the top of the pyramid, yet the Pindar acted like a dictator because he was the top man in the organization.

• ••

NSA Headquarters, Fort Meade, MD – Modern Day

Walking down the corridor to his office, Operative Jenkins crossed over the NSA seal printed on the floor. Depicting the Eagle grasping an old fashioned key, the same key that each of the nine top "unknown" freemasons held on their chest. His cellular phone rang, seeing a blocked number and knowing whom it was, he answered and turned towards the janitors closet on the lowest level of the NSA building. Only a handful of people in the world had cell phones that could block the NSA call screening program. Answering he stated, "Operative Jenkins, unsecure area, call back in 30 seconds". Then hung up.

Reaching the Janitor's closet he put his finger up to a keypad looking device, a small needle punctured his fingertip and took a small blood sample. Five seconds later the door unlocked. Pushing the heavy door inward Jenkins stepped inside, as he did the lights came on and the door locked behind him. Twenty steps ahead was an elevator. The hallway was rigged with multiple security protocols that would kill anyone inside it instantly. The security cameras were placed down the corridor and analyzed facial recognition and gait recognition software to ensure the individual walking down the hallway matched the DNA records taken at the door. Stepping in the elevator he hit the only button available, down.

Upon reaching the bottom floor he stepped out of the elevator and walked toward the large blast door in front of him. Made in the shape of a sphere, the underground "Janitors" bunker could withstand an air dropped nuclear bomb of 50 megatons, even if dropped directly on top of the NSA headquarters. The bunker was started with funds from the Homeland Security budget, the Janitor's closet was the field operative's nerve center. However the budget had gone way over the estimate as technology advanced, so the NSA turned to it's creators, Skull and Bones all lifelong members made donations to finalize the program. An Ivy League organization, Skull and Bones, a postgraduate secret society had created the OSS, which created the CIA and NSA.

It's main weapon, a supercomputer that gathered data from every piece of hardware in the world that was connected to the Internet, originated from a program called Thin thread which was created to prevent another 9/11. Thanks to private donations the NSA had no such budgetary constraints as it received massive donations from Bonesman and their professional affiliates from a group called the Bilderberg's. Basically, the powers that be behind the Bilderberg group allowed the NSA to have an unlimited budget as long as they followed their harmless agenda of world peace and cooperation.

This Battlespace computer was absolutely state of the art, nothing like it had been seen before and was the closest thing anyone had invented to true Artificial Intelligence, or a computer system that was self aware. A similar version of this computer system had been revealed by Snowden consequently was slated to be shut down, the Battlespace program was already running and would replace the System Snowden had revealed.

Snowden was an allowed leak, to reveal to the world that the US had the ability to spy on everyone on the planet. This revelation caused people to self-monitor, before they may have assumed they were being watched but did not know for sure. Once they knew the Government was watching everyone, they self monitored their behavior, and were more careful about what they said, or looked at online and in public. It's called the Hawthorne Effect, when a person knows he is being monitored they perform differently.

Battlespace was far more advanced than "The program" revealed by Snowden. Battlespace was programmed to store everything for instant analysis and to allow a more thorough analysis of all past events to predict the future. The information was recorded from any computer device, security camera, traffic camera, satellite, drone feed, smart phone, anything connected to it's network. All the new US driver licenses with RFID chips, EZ Pass scanners, credit cards, everything was linked in. The NSA had used it's secret black budget to fund the major corporations to allow back doors into almost every piece of technology available that would allow Battlespace to take it over and use it for a recording device.

In instance a person's smartphone could be used as a secret listening device and camera for Battlespace. Even when the smartphone was "off", Battlespace could take over the device and use it's microphone and camera to see and hear anything in the range of those devices capabilities.

Battlespace could access everything a person did in the electronic world. Every security camera a person walked by, every banking transaction, every connection on facebook, linked in, every twitter post, everything you read or watched was turned into an electronic image of the person that Battlespace could decipher. Using this amount of information it could make highly intelligent guesses as to your future actions, as well as where you were and what you were up to at any time. If someone became a problem later on, all the information was already stored and could be accessed and used by Battlespace. Battlespace was not allowed to turn anything but monitoring devices into "slaves" so it would hand the evidence over the analysts that monitored the Battlespace.

In warfare, Battlespace could take into account all the conditions on a battlefield as was its' intended purpose when dreamt up by DARPA. It could incorporate, weather conditions, troop strength, force projection, all factors into a calculation that would allow it to design a perfect strategy for victory. It even could access enough information about every individual person on the battlefield to determine his or her habits, strength, conditioning, motivations, alliances, possible fears, weaknesses or strengths. Part of this programming allowed it to identify the largest threats and alert them to the operator's. This made Battlespace perfect for taking all the information on everyone on the planet it was connected to, analyzing their information, and determining who was the largest threat to National Security at any one moment in time, and a way to deal with the threat.

Battlespace also had a minor glitch. It could easily identify targets, and the threat of each target perfect for identifying risks. However, when it was handed control of friendly forces in simulated events, such as drones, it had serious issues. Generally, the Battlespace would do everything it could to win with the greatest effectiveness score possible, even if that meant increasing civilian and friendly casualties. It had no emotion in its decisions, which lead to its inability to separate right from wrong action.

Three floors, full of analysts working in real time with operative's in the field. Coupled with Battlespace the US had started to set up a system of deep space geosynchronous satellites to give them a bird's eye view of the entire Globe. This deep space system was not yet operational. Previously an older satellite array closer to Earth had been launched and was being used, it covered 95% of the entire Continental US. Everything and everyone was being watched, to ensure the United States Federal Government was protected, even from it's own citizen's.

After passing another retinal scan and a voice scan at the bottom of the elevator, along with another pinprick DNA sample, the blast doors began to slowly open from the middle. The Operative sighed as he waited for what felt like hours as the enormous steel blast doors opened, revealing a hub of activity and computer stations beyond.

Every domestic threat to the United States that reached a critical level was handled in this room. Lesser threats were sent upstairs for the Public version of NSA to deal with or hand off to other agencies.

Picking up his landline phone from his small side office, surrounded by glass walls so all could see his every move, just like he could see everyone else's. He dialed the old man's number, two rings and then,

"That was more than thirty seconds," griped the old man on the other end of the line.

"I was on the surface, How can I help you sir?"

"You have an inbound threat, I am emailing you his file now. The Northeast team was unable to kill him, and he killed one of us in the exchange. Your fancy Battlespace didn't identify him because he was working for us. This is now top priority; I want him alive and the girl he is traveling with. She is not a threat alone. We need them both for interrogation and execution, they are planning something big and we need to find out what. They must be working for someone that cannot be identified as their accomplice electronically. This is a National Security threat of the highest level; he is a domestic terrorist, well trained and has seen fighting as a Navy Seal. This man is no joke and you have to capture him alive without this hitting the news. This is the target we have been training the police for, he is a Christian radical, a veteran, and a true believer; a constitutionalist." Stated the old Grandmaster.

"Some messes are harder to clean up than others, what his is motivation? What types of targets is he after?" Jenkins replied whilst scrolling through the files on Titus.

"He is delusional, seems to be targeting people associated with Freemasonry. I would put extra surveillance on the Grand Lodge and the Masonic Monument. He already assassinated a member of the House of Rothson on his boat in Boston Harbor. Took his key, the key he achieved for reaching the highest order in Free Masonry. You should know it well from your meetings, you see it on the NSA Seal everyday."

"Who is supporting him? No lone veteran could have targeted a Rothson?" The NSA chief asks.

"The majority believes he may be working for the man whom goes by codename Prometheus. If he is, he may be able to lead us straight to him. Another reason we need him alive. Prometheus is an ex brother of ours and is possibly helping the assassin." States the old man.

"Is that all?" Jenkins replied as he forwarded the file to his team.

"Yes, good hunting." The old man hung up his phone. Opened a small humidor on his desk, the humidor had an Owl and the Skull and Crossbones on the top of the box. He opened up the box snipped the end of his cigar and lit a match to fire it up. Looking out over his black and white checkered floor, through his gold plated glass, at the city

below he could see small snowflakes melting on the glass of his monument to defy

God.

Chapter 15 – A New Toy

Jersey Turnpike South, NJ - Modern Day

I did not want to check in to a hotel or even a motel with the Cadillac, we needed a new vehicle to stay off the radar. No cell phone, no Internet, hard to look up a place to stay without it. "We should take a car with a GPS system", I say to Jocelyn. I have a plan.

"We should scout a local marina for a car to steal. One that is in a slip for a large boat that isn't in dock, hopefully the owner will be at sea for days before they return and report the car stolen. Could be weeks before they return if we pick the right boat. We can also ditch the Cadillac in the marina, as it will fit right in. Also marina staff won't question it being there a few days as people leave there cars at marinas for long periods of time when they leave on their friends boats and such. If all goes right this will be an easy way for us to move concealed."

Northeast of Baltimore, we came across a large marina. Driving in between the enormous sheds that house the dry-docked boats they can see the marina is perfect. The parking area was made of small rocks and seashells mixed together, probably held around 100 vehicles. One of the first we passed was another Cadillac CTS, I look over at Jocelyn as said "Told you our car would fit in here".

Scouting the lot for a spot and a replacement car I see the perfect choice. So we parked the CTS a few spots away to make moving the gear over slightly more concealed. Being roughly 2 am there was no movement, a slight fog covered the docks. Checked the area for cameras, saw none.

Popped the trunk and pulled out the tool from the trap. This tool allowed me to slide down next to a car window and pop the locks open. I stole it from a police officer's car years ago when I first started on my own.

Moving over to the car I had chosen, I take a look at the boat name and slip number Exxon Me! slip B-18. The owner obviously had something to do with the Oil conglomerate and had used its name in some corny manner like most boat owners, with names such as Seascape, instead of Sea Escape.

Seeing the boat name Jocelyn laughs, "Stealing more from the Templar's?"

"What do you mean?" I asked confused.

"The double x in Exxon is actually the Cross of Lorraine that symbolizes the Knight's Templar just on it's side. See it?" She smiles with smart-ass look on her face.

"Wow, you really spend too much time on this stuff don't you, ever had a boyfriend?" I ask teasingly.

"Let's see if the owner is in dock." Walking down B dock we go by each slip number until we reach the end of the dock. On the T end of the dock with the largest slip, was B-18. The slip was suitable for a boat the size of about 160' or more just by guesswork. Not in the slip, and a boat this size should be out of dock for some time. "Not exactly a day trip type of boat, they could be all the way over in Europe."

Jocelyn stared at the empty space, "Unbelievable how much money some people have isn't it?"

"Sickening really" I reply. "Well I doubt he needs that car as much as we do, let's get out of here before some old guy gets up for his morning walk at four am."

Moving over to the car, I stop and ask Jocelyn, "Like my ride?"

She replies in song, "Won't you buy me a Mercedes Benz?"

"Anything for you deary" As I pop the locks open and the alarm, sounds. Quickly I pop the hood and removed the alarm system. Then rerouted the electronics so the ignition would still work. Then I removed the GPS tracking antennae. "Let's get the gear and get out of here."

Quickly we loaded all the gear into the Mercedes CLK 63 AMG Black Series. Painted black with tinted windows, it was a stunning vehicle. The Germans had put more horsepower under the bonnet than the back tires could ever possibly hope to handle. I fired up the V-8 engine and just smiled as the huge 500 horsepower's roared to life. As he was pulling out of the lot, he looked over at Jocelyn, who was playing with the seat massager, and said, "hold on". Then mashed the right pedal hard to the floor in first gear. The back tires flung seashells and rocks as the back tires fought for grip to translate the horsepower into speed. Mere milliseconds later the engine was at 7000 rpm and I shifted to second then realized I was already at the end of the lot and had to stop before entering the street. "What a car," I say to Jocelyn whom had grabbed the "oh shit" bar as soon as I warned her.

"Boys with toys" She laughs.

Opening the glove box to store the letter and coins Jocelyn pulled out a gun. Gold plated with silver markings on it. The gun was a .357 Magnum revolver and quite large in the hands of Jocelyn. Being gold plated with the silver markings made it look very impressive. The handle had the cross of Lorraine, the side of the barrel had the strange hooked X symbol on it one side and the skull and crossbones on the other. Along the slide on both sides it read "Novus Ordo Seclorum". Jocelyn read it, "New Secular Order" or "New Worldly Order".

"Ridiculous" I say to her and notion for her to put it back in the glove box.

A couple of hours of driving later we arrived at a small motel on the outskirts of Baltimore. We were both exhausted as I had been driving all night since the skirmish in Newport. So we checked in to the motel and I paid the attendant extra for not making us put down a credit card. The attendant was so tired they probably didn't care what I wanted, as long as they could go back to sleeping in the back room from what it looked like. Seems like service is a thing of the past, but today that was to my advantage.

After we settled in we each chose one of the double beds and fell right asleep. I had told her the night before we would be moving to a new hotel the next day and after two days at another place we would move towards DC.

Feeling the ability to relax I slipped into a deep sleep....

Chapter 16 – Haunted by Dreams

Roma, Italia – March 15, 44 BC

The sound of clashing iron and lions roaring awakens me. I open my eyes and see a large stadium, not any stadium it was the coliseum, and full of people cheering. In the dirt I see men fighting each other, while lions on chains extend their grasp to try to reach them.

On my arm I feel the touch of a woman, light assuring. The heat has made me sweat, and I motion for her to fan me. A man speaks to me, "Brutus, we should go to your atrium, much cooler up on the hill by your house".

I smile and watch as a gladiator accidently gets to close to a Lion and is ripped to shreds about sixty yards in front of me. Jumping on his back to drag him down before severing his head by biting into his throat. The crowd cheers excited by the grotesque mutilation of the poor slave by the lion.

"Brutus, how are you this fine day" Said fellow Senator Cassius as he sat down next to me.

"I am well Brother, to the Glory of Rome." As I said this I handed him a glass of wine and we both drank.

"The Glory of Rome, and what is that exactly?" Cassius scoffed. "The interests of the mob, the everlasting republic, or the desires of the wealthy and their puppet Caesar and his promise of an Empire?"

"Well according to Caesar, Rome is the shining light at the center of this world, our Republic shall lead all of mankind to a new age of enlightenment. We have built our empire as dictated by the gods, upon the Seven Hills of Rome. However, the many have willed Caesar to push further and faster than what is possible. He soon plans to invade Parthia, and we need to support our Dictator in times of war."

"He will bankrupt us all to appease and empower the imperators and proletariat controllers." Cassius states.

"Bankrupt us? Impossible, we will just create more money and expand the economy as we have always done. Using cheap currency not tied to gold keeps us free from poverty and rule by the economic elite who hold all the gold." I said.

"Yes, we may have risen to power and grown to be an economic empire by use of our cheap currency created by the Senate and our military strength. However, the Imperators have teamed with the money lenders and have conspired to create an Emperor, who will dissolve our currency and create a new singular currency that is made of gold, and has Caesar's face on it. You know whom they plan to elect, your best friend Caesar. The imperators will back Caesar and so will the Proletariat, they will bribe the masses with short term fun and games, lots of games." Cassius states as he points to the wild mob cheering on the gladiators. Then a large section of the crowd starting really getting exciting as free loaves of bread were tossed out to the crowd and the crowd turned on one another for the meaningless bread.

"Made of gold? We came to rule the world by not having our currency tied to gold? That will crush our Republic's economy, and grant too much power to the imperators and their rulers the moneylenders. The light of Rome will be extinguished, under the boot of a dictator." I said.

"Brutus, he is your friend, but you must help us, we have to kill Caesar. These aren't conspiracy theories, these are facts, and our spies have confirmed it from Caesar's own mouth. You know I wouldn't lie to you." Cassius states.

"The imperators, the proletariat, and their claims of being enlightened, all is nonsense. Their money was handed to them through their bloodlines and they feel it is justification to rule? They are the descendants of Egypt and Babylon and if they want to be Kings let them go back to where they came from. These Imperators and criminals will not ruin Rome, they may have wealth, and the military but they have no more right to rule than any man. An Emperor shall not rule us. We need a plan." I state.

"No, we the Liberators have already planned it, today is Caesar's last day. The senate is in an emergency session already. They await us, and him. The Republic is not for sale." Cassius says. As I finish listening I nod in the direction of Caesar's platform. Caesar surrounded by his private guard of praetorians, was calmly watching the events in the gladiator ring. "You are his last friend in the Senate, convince him to come to the Senate today." Cassius states.

"If we had any guts we would take him now and he would be bleeding out in his chair in front of the distracted mob that so adores him." I said.

"Yes Brutus, however his guard is still with him and we would need many men to overtake him. The crowd may join him as well, as the mob favors him, not us. Patience is the key. You inform Caesar the Senate is waiting for him, and reassure him he is safe to go, and he will go there soon unguarded. I shall meet you outside the coliseum, he should not see me with you." Cassius states and walks away, followed by his two guards. I nod and start walking around the coliseum to Caesar's pedestal where he is surrounded by the private army funded by the imperators, the Praetorian Guard.

As I reach his pedestal, two Praetorian Guards confront me. Hands on their swords, until Caesar barked at them. "It is Brutus, can you not see?"

"Julius, I come here in urgency to speak with you. I come as a friend with a warning." I said.

"Brutus, we have always spoken honestly to one another. What did you hear?"

"Cassius has formed a group called the Liberators. They feel your wartime powers, as Dictator will be expanded to create a new currency for the wealthy & imperators that support you. I argued with him otherwise but he is nonetheless convinced. You must address the Senate and quell their fears or they may try to remove you from power." I said.

"Brutus, it is true I have become dictator to save us from our enemies. I can assure you the imperators and my financial supporters want nothing but the best for Rome as it is in their interests to see her shine. We are entering a new age when the light of Rome will shine across the entire world, and we shall bring about an age of peace and prosperity. To do this we must have some centralized power and a single currency across the world." Julius states.

Hearing it from Julius himself broke Brutus's heart. I knew Brutus now had had all the confirmation he would ever need and knew his friend had to die.

"Caesar, you must make the Senate understand, they will hear your infallible logic and assuredly support you. I guarantee after my discussion with them that they just want to speak with you, to have their voices heard." I said.

"Then as a sign of my devotion to Rome I shall acquiesce to their demands and make an appearance. I will not change my decision, however I will let them have their say." Julius decreed.

"Let the gods be with you. I shall see you at the Senate shortly." I said and turned and left. A tear fell from my eye, pain in my chest made the emotion of sadness overwhelming.

Soon after I told Cassius, and we headed out of the coliseum entrance, the entourage serving Brutus went back to his home built on top of one of the Seven Hills of Rome. Brutus and Cassius dressed in their Senatorial Togas head to the Senate. They walk along the roads of Rome, and Brutus marvels at the structures to each side. Built of Granite by the stonemasons, using knowledge passed down by the Olympian Gods to the architects of this grand city. The Temples of Rome were nearly perfect in design.

The new Curia being designed by Caesar to hold the Senate meetings came into view. Grandiose with the double-headed Phoenix perched in two spots on it's roof. In the middle on the top of the roof was the statue of the winged victory; it is a statue of the

Goddess Aphrodite with wings. Cassius remarks, "even Caesar knows the value of the God's."

I look upon the building with despise, "He is establishing his control over us by telling us where to meet. The building is meant as an offer to appease us, but instead is another sign of his dominance over the Senate. He wants to have built the house the Senate shall meet in."

Seeing the temporary meeting place of the Senate come into view, they notice a large gathering on the steps of the forum. In the middle of the gathering stood Julius Caesar, even amidst the crowd of 60 Senator's he stood apart, strong and dressed for a royal battle.

Knowing what was about to happen Brutus motions to Cassius but Cassius is already in full sprint. Brutus chases after him.

As they approach they can hear Caesar whom is talking down to the Senators. "Why are you assembled on the steps, you are supposed to be in session, where is Brutus? What is the meaning of this, I am your appointed Dictator, whom have saved you from the ravages of Carthage and this is how you repay me, by blocking my entrance to the Senate I built?"

Just as Cassius reached the crowd he bumped into the Senator between himself and Caesar. The Senator had his hand already on the hidden dagger under his toga and as he fell forward towards Caesar it came out, so the falling Senator improvised and tried to slice Caesar's throat as he fell forward.

Caesar being trained well in hand to hand combat reacted instantly. First by grabbing the arm with the dagger drawn, then he used his other arm to punch the Senator in his windpipe, making him unable to breathe or speak. As the Senator crashed down on the hard marble steps, blood pouring out of his mouth and on to his white Toga. Caesar proclaimed "Villain".

Then Cassius motioned to the other Senators, just as I; Brutus reached the group. Cassius drew his dagger and plunged it into Caesar's back. Caesar screamed out in pain as his royal blood spilled all over the steps to the forum. Then another Senator stabbed him right in the heart, then another. Soon all 60 Senators had their daggers drawn and were trying to stab Caesar.

I moved in through the parting crowd. The Senators saw me approach and cleared a path. I knew my friend Julius was already dead, and I felt sympathy for him. For all his magnificence Caesar in the end was nothing more than just a man. He looked up on me and his eyes begged for mercy, I could sense Caesar didn't believe I his closest ally in the Senate had betrayed him. I wanted to end it quickly for him and slice his throat but the Senators would turn on me if I did. I had to remind myself Caesar had brought this upon himself. Caesar was delusional, thinking his bloodline and the bloodline of the wealthy and the imperators were meant to rule over all mankind. We had built Rome as a Republic, not an Empire.

I drew my dagger and plunged it into Caesars chest. A non-fatal blow to increase his pain but did not to help end it. The Senators had originally wanted a public execution but leaving his body to bleed out on the steps of the forum would have to do. As I plunged my dagger into his chest, Caesar grabbed my arm and pulled me to him. I could tell he wanted to say something, but the words could not come out. His eyes pleaded with the thought "Et tu Brutus?". With around twenty or more stab wounds Caesar had no strength left at all. I held him as he dropped to the marble staircase, and laid him to rest for eternity. The most powerful man to ever have lived was just killed in my arms because of my betrayal.

I turn to the mob of Senators before me, my white Toga now red with the blood of our post King. "A Rex is not to rule the Republic of Rome. We the liberator's have built the Republic on the Seven Hills of Rome as instructed, built our temples and our government as instructed. We watch over the Republic to ensure it stays free. Caesar would sacrifice everything for personal glory; he would have people worship him and not the Gods of their own choosing. The same gods who helped us build the Roman Republic, No King or dictator will rule or the Republic will fall. A sacrifice that had to be made to ensure the Republic of Rome would be the everlasting Republic envisioned by the Gods. We must tell the people of Rome that the Republic is back in the hands of men and not under the power of a singular dictator. We have liberated ourselves from this menace. The Republic of Rome will last the test of time, like the monuments we built on the foundations of the world long forgotten."

"Brutus, what will become of you? You think you can be our new leader, will you not try to take the place of Caesar yourself?" Called out Marcus Anthony.

"No Marcus, I am the liberator, the mob is Rome not the emperor. Real power resides in the will of the people, not the will of those whom govern. Tell the people they are now free of Caesar. You Marcus what will you become of you?"

Marcus turns his back on the crowd and hastily marches away, he had not taken part in the attack on Caesar but had just watched. "I head for Egypt, to my rightful place. The bloodline of the dragon will be avenged. Mark my words; the mob you so pretend to represent will turn on all of you when they see their great leader dead and the games he promised, the free grain dries up. From this chaos we will return with order and implant an Emperor even Greater then Caesar, no matter what you do. It will be myself or one from our inner circle, not whom the mob desires as you so foolishly dream. The proof of our power is right above you all the time, you just cannot see it, as you are not illuminated with wisdom."

Then I feel hands pushing down on my chest, and I cannot breathe, I struggle through the crowd and open my eyes.

"Titus wake up, Titus are you ok? You were shaking and thrashing, you are covered in sweat?" Jocelyn says as she wakes me. "You should take a cold shower."

"If you keep waking me in that outfit I will need more than just a cold shower."

Suddenly, Jocelyn realized she was in nothing but her bra and panties, and felt slightly embarrassed but also pleased at the comment. "I'll keep that in mind".

After our playful teasing; I explain what I have seen, I tell her of the visions I have had into the past. That every time I dream since Jonathon hooked me up to his machine; I see some vision of the past. Jonathon had explained that it was my DNA that held the memories. Meaning I am the ancestor of Brutus, Hasan-I Sabbah etc. She says we need to write down my dreams and see if there is any connection.

I thought the ability to see the past at first was exciting, now without the ability to turn it off I do not feel so privileged. Without Jonathon to help them stop, I may never be able to truly sleep again. Experiencing the pain, the feelings, the vividness of actually experiencing these memories firsthand, made my sleep feel like being awake, it was starting to take it's toll on me.

After a shower I climb back into bed, only 6am, time for at least a few more hours of sleep, hopefully.

Chapter 17 – The Everlasting Republic of the Free Masons

Valley Forge, PA – December 1776

I awake in a small house, the sensation of cold chilling my bones. I think, if hunger doesn't kill me this bitter cold will. I decide to get out of my bunk to have a walk, maybe to a fire to heat up.

I see my friend George by the fire, I walk over and greet him, "trouble sleeping tonight General?"

George turns to me and just smiles, extends his hands over the fire and rubs them together. "I fear the men will not last much longer under these conditions." He looks up from the fire at out at the hundreds of tents, then down to the medical section where sounds of men dying from cold and hunger emanated. "Even if we do last until the battle, that will be the end of us. The British King has used his wealth to pit us against the ferocious mercenaries of Germany. The same Hessians whom descended from those barbarians whom brought down Rome, now they may end our Republic before it even begins. I hear them singing across the river at night."

The Lost Truth by Dean Fougere

"We should strike whilst we can, use the strength we have left and surprise them." I reply.

"I have considered this, but the icy water may kill more men than the enemy." George replies before turning and walking away, as he heads down the hill towards the tree line he turns and says, "I will have a plan by morning, for now come walk with me, but do not speak just let me think out loud. What I will say is for you to hear but nothing more."

We walk together down to the tree line, entering the woods Washington tells his aide to return to camp at Valley Forge. Washington then speaks to me.

"Your family has been a member of the Freemasons almost as long as any family could. You have been my closest ally in my times of dire need, and I feel now I must trust you with a serious burden that has become mine to bear. You know the penalty for treason within the Masonic order?"

"Yes, George, we have been friends our whole lives, we even traversed the seas together from England. You can trust me with anything. I would not betray the order." I reply, a quick thought crosses the lieutenant's, my mind. Five generations of patient planning, was about to pay off, the secret would be revealed.

"Freemasonry was created to hide a hidden knowledge that belonged to the Templars, they would pass down these truths they knew to allow the advancement of humanity. We at the lower ranks would reveal these truths to the world and discuss ideas of science and humanity. However, a group of enlightened financial elites, the banking powers of the Rothson Family has infiltrated Freemasonry, the Illuminati."

He puts his arm on my shoulder, "You must understand these wealthy men, and these illuminati serve a different master. They hide a secret unknown to me or the other 33rd degree Masons. The say the secret hath illuminated them and they call it 'The Ancient Promise'. They claim it is represented by the apple that was taken from the tree of knowledge."

Nodding for George to continue, I start to feel the excitement of the revelation about to be imparted on me.

"The illuminati have created an inner circle of Freemasons, above them are the unknown nine, who run the 13 Illuminati Families. To run the order as equals except for one, the head of their group is called the Pindar. Supposedly the Pindar answers to these unknowns above him but that cannot be confirmed."

"Of the order seen by the public, Benjamin Franklin is the head in the eyes of the public, holding the title of Grandmaster of the order, however he has no more power than a fly. The Illuminati are above us, and are truly in control, they have taken over the

Free Masonic order. Franklin is allowed to meet with them, as am I. The heads of the Free Masonic order are their spokespersons to the rest of the group and the freemasons are to be their tool for creation of an experiment for humanity, to create the perfect system."

"I know the direct level above me as I must follow their plan, and for doing so I am rewarded, to be forever worshipped by my fellow man. I am to be written down in history as the Great General whom freed the people of America. I agreed to do so as this seemed to be a great title and a noble cause."

"Benjamin hath been rewarded as well, as he doth work in France to help not only our revolution but theirs as well. They grant him access to the Hellfire clubs and allow him to take practice in their black sex magik. He did vow to due the unknown nines bidding and for so he shall be written down in history as a great inventor. He shall reveal a new form of energy to the world, an energy long forgotten since the flood, an energy that can change the world. We see it all the time, but forgot how to create it ourselves. This energy has been long known of, as we see it in lightning all the time. So it is above and so it shall be below and it is called electricity."

"With the freedom that I give the people and the power that Benjamin Franklin shall grant them, this country shall be the greatest nation on earth and shall free the people of the entire world. The Pindar hath told me so; he said an angel of heaven hath shown him the path that still lies ahead. Of course I did not believe that an angel hath actually spoke to them, but deciphered it as meaning it was righteous idea for mankind, an experiment in freedom and liberty for all mankind."

"The unknown Nine, the illuminated ones, created the ideas the Templar order came from at a much earlier time. The Templars are the keepers of the most ancient of truths, truths they discovered not created. The unknown nine have always been the creators of this knowledge. We do their bidding, as they know the truth of the world and can see the path laid before us, they can read the geometric pattern of the Universe and see the path that lies ahead. The Illuminists have communication with the enlightened masters, the unknowns."

"I did not believe in divine intervention as I thought God hath a divine plan and did not need to intervene directly. However, this 'unknown' appeared as an angel, one of those they speak of, and found me today."

"I do fear the cold and death though I must show my men otherwise. God's have predetermined our fate and they will intervene on our behalf. We hold the secrets of the past and must establish a Republic to reveal them over time to the world. To bring all those who are unenlightened into the light of the Republic. That is why it is imperative I must not become a King or dictator, I must hand my power over to the people after this war is complete. The people will be free in their minds, and that freedom shall empower them to bring the world to its knees with peace and order."

"The ancient texts we have protected over the years tell us these facts. Uncovered in Solomon's Temple by our founders the texts came with the tools we required to build a New Nation for all of mankind. We will succeed in our quest. God sent his messenger to me to confirm what we have read. She has been called many names over the centuries, Isis is one of the first, but I prefer Aphrodite, for our new Nation she will be called Freedom or Liberty. She will watch over us."

Washington stood straight up and faced me. His large frame made me feel rather small, and then gazed deep into my eyes with his sharp blue eyes, lit by the moon in the night sky. He calmly began, a true first hand account,

"This afternoon, as I was sitting at this table engaged in preparing a dispatch, something seemed to disturb me. Looking up, I beheld standing opposite me a singularly beautiful female. So astonished was I, for I had given strict orders not to be disturbed, that it was some moments before I found language to inquire the cause of her presence. A second, a third and even a fourth time did I repeat my question, but received no answer from my mysterious visitor except a slight raising of her eyes."

"By this time I felt strange sensations spreading through me. I would have risen but the riveted gaze of the being before me rendered volition impossible. I assayed once more to address her, but my tongue had become useless, as though it had become paralyzed.

"A new influence, mysterious, potent, irresistible, took possession of me. All I could do was to gaze steadily, vacantly at my unknown visitor. Gradually the surrounding

atmosphere seemed as if it had become filled with sensations, and luminous. Everything about me seemed to rarefy, the mysterious visitor herself becoming more airy and yet more distinct to my sight than before. I now began to feel as one dying, or rather to experience the sensations, which I have sometimes imagined accompany dissolution. I did not think, I did not reason, I did not move; all were alike impossible. I was only conscious of gazing fixedly, vacantly at my companion.

"Presently I heard a voice saying, `Son of the Republic, look and learn,' while at the same time my visitor extended her arm eastwardly, I now beheld a heavy white vapor at some distance rising fold upon fold. This gradually dissipated, and I looked upon a stranger scene. Before me lay spread out in one vast plain all the countries of the world - Europe, Asia, Africa and America. I saw rolling and tossing between Europe and America the billows of the Atlantic, and between Asia and America lay the Pacific.

"`Son of the Republic,' said the same mysterious voice as before, `look and learn.' At that moment I beheld a dark, shadowy being, like an angel, standing or rather floating in mid-air, between Europe and America. Dipping water out of the ocean in the hollow of each hand, he sprinkled some upon America with his right hand, while with his left hand he cast some on Europe. Immediately a cloud raised from these countries, and joined in mid-ocean. For a while it remained stationary, and then moved slowly westward, until it enveloped America in its murky folds. Sharp flashes of lightning gleamed through it at intervals, and I heard the smothered groans and cries of the American people."

"A second time the angel dipped water from the ocean, and sprinkled it out as before.

The dark cloud was then drawn back to the ocean, in whose heaving billows in sank from view. A third time I heard the mysterious voice saying, `Son of the Republic, look and learn,' I cast my eyes upon America and beheld villages and towns and cities springing up one after another until the whole land from the Atlantic to the Pacific was dotted with them.

"Again, I heard the mysterious voice say, `Son of the Republic, the end of the century cometh, look and learn.' At this the dark shadowy angel turned his face southward, and from Africa I saw an ill-omened specter approach our land. It flitted slowly over every town and city of the latter. The inhabitants presently set themselves in battle array against each other. As I continued looking I saw a bright angel, on whose brow rested a crown of light, on which was traced the word `Union,' bearing the American flag which he placed between the divided nation, and said, `Remember ye are brethren.' Instantly, the inhabitants, casting from them their weapons became friends once more, and united around the National Standard.

"And again I heard the mysterious voice saying `Son of the Republic, look and learn.' At this the dark, shadowy angel placed a trumpet to his mouth, and blew three distinct blasts; and taking water from the ocean, he sprinkled it upon Europe, Asia and Africa. Then my eyes beheld a fearful scene: From each of these countries arose thick, black clouds that were soon joined into one. Throughout this mass there gleamed a dark red light by which I saw hordes of armed men, who, moving with the cloud, marched by land and sailed by sea to America. Our country was enveloped in this volume of cloud, and I saw these vast armies devastate the whole county and burn the villages, towns

and cities that I beheld springing up. As my ears listened to the thundering of the cannon, clashing of sword, and the shouts and cries of millions in mortal combat, I heard again the mysterious voice saying, `Son of the Republic, look and learn.' When the voice had ceased, the dark shadowy angel placed his trumpet once more to his mouth, and blew a long and fearful blast.

"*Instantly a light as of a thousand suns shone down from above me, and pierced and broke into fragments the dark cloud which enveloped America. At the same moment the angel upon whose head still shone the word Union, and who bore our national flag in one hand and a sword in the other, descended from the heavens attended by legions of white spirits. These immediately joined the inhabitants of America, who I perceived were will nigh overcome, but who immediately taking courage again, closed up their broken ranks and renewed the battle.*

"*Again, amid the fearful noise of the conflict, I heard the mysterious voice saying, `Son of the Republic, look and learn.' As the voice ceased, the shadowy angel for the last time dipped water from the ocean and sprinkled it upon America. Instantly the dark cloud rolled back, together with the armies it had brought, leaving the inhabitants of the land victorious!*

"*Then once more I beheld the villages, towns and cities springing up where I had seen them before, while the bright angel, planting the azure standard he had brought in the midst of them, cried with a loud voice: `While the stars remain, and the heavens send down dew upon the earth, so long shall the Union last.' And taking from his brow the crown on which blazoned the word `Union,' he placed it upon the Standard while the* *people, kneeling down, said, `Amen.'*

"The scene instantly began to fade and dissolve, and I at last saw nothing but the rising, curling vapor I at first beheld. This also disappearing, I found myself once more gazing upon the mysterious visitor, who, in the same voice I had heard before, said, `Son of the Republic, what you have seen is thus interpreted: Three great perils will come upon the Republic. The most fearful is the third, but in this greatest conflict the whole world united shall not prevail against her. Let every child of the Republic learn to live for his God, his land and the Union'. With these words the vision vanished, and I started from my seat and felt that I had seen a vision wherein had been shown to me the birth, progress, and destiny of the United States." (George Washington, National Tribune, 1880, as recorded by Anthony Sherman)

Hearing Washington say these words I knew what some of it was referencing, having lived in the future. Two of the great perils had already come by the time Titus had been born. The first peril was the war of Independence, the second the slave trade and civil war. The last and third final peril had not yet come. My ancestor hearing these words from Washington was astonished, he never spoke just listened in quiet belief, as he knew everything Washington said was true, except the ending.

Then I awoke.

Chapter 18 – The Battle is won before it is Started

South of Alexandria, VA – Modern Day

That morning we went out for a light breakfast at a local diner. Turned out to be a heavy breakfast and did little to help the lack of sleep I had been getting. Jocelyn was in a cheerful mood and despite her tiny frame she ate quite a lot.

We hopped back into the Mercedes and headed to our next destination. We would head down to Alexandria and scope out the National Masonic Memorial before trying to formulate an attack plan to infiltrate the building.

I had given up trying to hide the weaponry in the Mercedes and I determined if a cop were to pull me over I would make him chase me down first. The Merc had enough horses to outrun any local police cruiser and if I got away fast enough, could get off the road and into a new vehicle before a helicopter spotted me or a drone was sent to follow from above.

The Lost Truth by Dean Fougere

As we were driving Jocelyn told me to recount all of the dreams I had had since Jonathon screwed with my mind.

The last dream I had, she confirmed. Seems like the vision of Washington was actually recorded by one of his aides upon his deathbed. She had read it before online. 'So Washington really did foresee the future of the United States and really had divine intervention on his behalf?' I ask. Jocelyn just says it would seem so; the proof will be hidden in the Monument most likely. I reply, "There must be something more to these unknown masters of the Illuminati, something supernatural."

"The goddess that spoke to Washington is Isis, no doubt," replies Jocelyn. "The freemasons have always talked of connecting to ascended masters for guidance, maybe they are in touch with supernatural forces?"

We both thought it over and then decide it must be a trick. There are no such things as angels or aliens, or ascended masters whatever they may be right?

Parking on a nearby hill, we get out and I scan the skies for drones. I have never operated on American soil with the US Military so I have no idea what type of surveillance they use to watch over the homeland, never mind the capitol. I should be able to pick up any of the drones I know of however, there may be high altitude surveillance I am unaware of but that would probably be unusable for homeland defense.

We then head down the side roads to the monument. King Street leads directly to the front of the building and on our drive towards it we gaze up at the tower on this huge hill, visible from anywhere in Alexandria. We drive by the Monument, but do not pull up Callahan drive; we can see there are no visible guards on the exterior. The building is taking tourists and seems to be operating as per normal. Do not see many visitors outside as this monument is out of the way for most tourists. "They probably think we are in hiding, I doubt they would think we are dumb enough to come here" I say.

Jocelyn says, "I am not sure, I have a weird feeling about this place."

"Well we have seen it, now we just need to disguise ourselves and come back tomorrow loaded to bear. We'll need to set up a distraction to get in and out."

I turn onto Highway 1 south and head out of Alexandria. Feeling a need for speed I put the pedal hard to the floor. We instantly jump to over 90 mph, and Jocelyn gives a light whimper of excitement. Then I see about a half a mile back an undercover cop turn on his lights and accelerate.

The Merc comes to life under my right foot. The back tires start putting the torque of the engine to work and the asphalt starts whipping by underneath. We quickly accelerate to over 140 mph and the cop disappears in the rear view.

Ahead I see a large pick up truck sitting in the passing lane at about 55mph, I swerve in between cars into the right lane and into the breakdown lane. I can hear the dirt and debris in the break down lane slamming into the undercarriage of the car, but I keep my foot hard down on the go fast pedal. The engine making an incredible sound as the five hundred horsepower's are all unleashed. I blow past all the slow traffic, including the pickup truck with a Nascar racing sticker hogging the passing lane.

Coming up is an exit ramp, and I cannot see the police behind my vehicle. I wait until the last moment and hit the brakes, the carbon ceramic disks throwing us against the safety harnesses as the Mercedes dropped from 140mph to about 60mph in a flash. That's one way to test the strength of the seat belts I thought. I fly down the ramp and accelerate as much as possible whilst still holding the grip in the corner. The back tires wanted to just spin and create a ton of smoke every time I touch the gas. I come to the end of the ramp and decide to just run the stop sign, seeing no traffic going by as I make my decision.

After the ramp ends I fly out across the crossing street. A Prius slams its brakes and comes up about ten feet short of hitting the side of the Mercedes; the driver honking at us as we tear off down the side street. I scour the nearby area for a garage and find one nearby, within walking distance to a motel as well. "Another night at the Ritz" I smile at Jocelyn.

After getting the car off the road, and relaxing. We set about to acquire some disguises to get into the monument unnoticed. In a local coffee shop using a prepaid visa card that we bought at a gas station with cash, we bought some private tour passes on the Internet for the monument for the next day. Making any purchases without electronic forms of payment was becoming harder and harder in the modern world, and soon would be gone forever. Making every transaction recordable, and traceable.

■■

NSA Headquarters, Fort Meade, MD – Modern Day

In the Janitor's Closet under NSA Headquarters, there is a whir of excitement in the air. The men and woman in this technological hub of advanced surveillance consider themselves to be the watchful eye over the Nation, protecting the people from any threats that actually make in on shore. The CIA counterpart dealt with exterior threats and was always busy tracking an immediate threat. The interior domestic threats were far fewer and normally easily quelled.

Jenkin's was in his office running through the tapes of Titus and Jocelyn at various gas stations and from highway cameras at tollbooths. He also had some footage pulled from a few personal cell phone cameras that Battlespace picked out for him to review. After they reached the Baltimore area the trail had gone cold. He had sent in a team to locate the most likely ditched Cadillac but nothing has been found yet.

Jenkin's assistant came bursting through his door. "We've got him!"

Jenkin's rose to his feet and headed for the door. "Where, what picked him up?" The assistant smiles wider than ever, "The new facial recognition software I insisted we upload to the Satellite array. The geosynchronous satellite running facial recognition scans over the DC area picked him up. He literally stared right up at it like he wanted to be seen. I believe he was scanning the sky for drone activity. He is driving a Mercedes CLK63 Black series; license plate indicates it belongs to a member of the US Senate who is on vacation yachting. The Senator is an ex FlexxonNobile employee, he is also indicated as a member of the Skull and Bones fraternity, he is also a Freemason, which may be why he was targeted."

"Do we have his current location?"

"No sir, we dispatched the closest undercover local police unit to arrest him, however the suspect identified the police vehicle and escaped the area before more units could be called in. He was traveling according to our satellite at over 130 mph when he passed out of the local coverage zone. He is somewhere between Satellite 1, the view over DC and Satellite 3 which covers the Virginia Coastline. We are searching the area for his vehicle now on the ground. If we had the deep space system operational we wouldn't have these blind spots." Silence, the he continues the report. "The Satellite shows he did a drive by on the National Masonic Monument, indicating this is his target. We have under covers in the area from the Activity working with JSOC."

"Good I will tell the boss. I want to keep this off the radar, please keep searching the area. No roadblocks, no news, we want this done as quietly as possible. I will dispatch a DELTA team to guard the Monument as well. They will be dressed in plainclothes and be undercover, keep the local police out of the area. Oh and I hate to admit it but you were right about that software upgrade, as long as the press doesn't find out about it. The deep space system is ready, but we haven't got the go ahead for that system launch." Jenkins resounds.

"Yes sir." The assistant was visibly gushing over the rare compliment from his superior. "Sir Snowden will keep the press busy with the outdated PRISM system for a while now."

Jenkins, smiles inwardly at the success of his protégé. However he knows all too well that no matter how hard the young man works he will never climb the ladder to his seat without the approval of his boss. Jenkins knew the highest levels within the Military Intelligence branch were all loyal Skull and Bones members, Bohemian Grove members, and belonged to Freemasonry. Without taking a death oath to the secret societies the members of these societies couldn't trust you and would ensure you were not promoted. These men represented the financial elite of Freemasonic order and therefore the Western World. Jenkins had heard rumors there were nine men, who had oversight authority, but no one in the group knew whom they were, just occasionally a meeting at Bilderberg, Bohemian Grove, or Deer Island the Bonesman retreat would begin with a decree from above, without saying where it came from, we all knew it came from these unknowns.

Jenkins retreats to his office and picks up the hard line to the Templar overseer's office in Toronto. Jenkins contemplates the giant gold bank his boss sits in, how they had so moronically stained the glass of the bank with gold as a symbol of their dominance over the land. Gold that belonged to the American people and had been stolen by the Federal Reserve owners to pay off part of the national debt. Jenkins knows from his meetings that gold is the backbone of the Masonic order; everything had been built upon a foundation of economics, and rationality instead of religion or imperial authority. Jenkins dialed up the old man. Jenkins hears the phone pick up and a grumbled gruff followed initiating him to speak.

"Good News" Jenkin's proclaims.

"It is about time, with the amount of funding and resources you have it is a miracle the son of a bitch is still alive. Never mind evading you still, so you have killed him then?" The old man grumbles.

"This man killed one of the wealthiest men in the world in a brutal display of merciless discontent and you want me to keep his capture a secret sir. Oh and to top things off he has extensive military training to boot. At some point even a Janitor can't clean up a mess, it takes the full HAZMAT crew. Now to explain what the development is or should I inform the white house and the president what we are doing here?"

"You know the power we control, if you disobey us we will kill you, your entire family, and end your entire bloodline. You will cease to exist in any form. You can't hide from us; we are always with you for your protection and advancement. You gave up that right when you joined skull and bones and were given the office you now hold."

Jenkins hears the sound of a glass jingle with ice, and then the slice of a cigar, followed by the sound of a match striking on the other end.

"We have located them again via our new Satellite facial recognition software we just uploaded. The same software that costs you millions of dollars for the lens calibration to utilize effectively. Remember?"

"Get to the point!" gruffly replies the Old man.

"Report: Got a 98.9 percent positive match from a facial recognition video, 30 seconds long roughly. Target vehicle, two occupants then proceeded to drive by the Masonic Monument in Alexandria and when local police car attempted to intervene, Titus and the girl successfully evaded capture and stopped in a blind spot between two of the Satellites. So we know they are in roughly a 10 mile area south of DC, also we know they are in a stolen CLK63 Mercedez Black Edition, silver paint. Registered to a Senate Member away on holiday on his private yacht. The Cadillac he was using has been found and confirmed to be Titus Frost's vehicle. We are sweeping the hotels in the known area he is in with members of the Activity from JSOC. We have a trap set at the monument with a Delta Force Team in civilian clothing. All forces have a capture not kill order, end of report. However my gut feeling is this won't go as planned and this will lead to this individuals death not capture."

The old man sighs, "The Monument is not to be breached, he is not to take a single foot inside that Temple. The profane should never have been allowed inside. If captured we want him transferred to FEMA Prison 666."

With the Masonic Temple being involved in the matters the old man knows he will have to inform the Pindar. The old man wants this situation to be resolved quickly as the group has a lot planned for the times ahead. He puffs on his cigar and thought about what they had accomplished thus far, how close they were to the end. He then looks down at the humidor on his desk, brandished with the symbols of his order.

He picks up his phone and calls a local contact, a man who caters to the other top level Illuminists, mainly Hollywood directors and financiers. "I need to contact my ascended master again for guidance, have a young boy waiting for me at the dungeon. Prepare a pentagram on the floor for his sacrifice. "

Chapter 19 – A Friend in the Darkness

South of Alexandria, VA – Modern Day

Titus and Jocelyn pull into the motel they have chosen for the night and walk into the office. After a quick check in, they return to the car and drive over to their room number. After Titus has checked the room for bugs they unpack and go over some research they have dug up on Freemasonry. They found the following books: Morals and Dogma by Albert Pike, Book of the Law by Aleister Crowley, The Secret Doctrine by Helena Blavatsky, America's Secret Destiny by Manly P Hall, Externalization of the Heirarchy by Alice Bailey. All these books were written by supposed members of the Illuminati or FreeMasons and showed the true nature of the groups. Other books they found that spoke of the group from the outside were None Dare Call it Conspiracy by Gary Allen, Proofs of a Conspiracy by Jon Robinson, The Creature from Jekyll Island WB Griffen, The True Story of Bilderberg by Daniel Estulin, and Illuminati: Facts & Fiction by Mark Dice. Just as they started reading and researching a sound they have feared came crashing into their world.

A knock at the door, they both freeze. They both wait hoping the noise is a mistake; maybe it was on the neighbor's door. Then again three loud knocks, I motion to Jocelyn to get into the tub and lay down flat. I then pull out my Carbine Assault rifle and lock in a 30 round clip. Shouldering the rifle I then pull up my 9mm Berretta still silenced and aim it at the door. I thought any Special Forces team wouldn't have knocked; this must be local police or the motel office clerk. I open the door and see neither; instead it is an old man, two bodyguards backs turned towards me at his side. The old man stands tall, dressed in a dark business suit, red handkerchief poking out of the pocket, his right eye has a strange look to it, like it has a cataract. His hair now white, but long and flowing, he has a strong face, and was probably very handsome at a younger age."

The old man smiles and extends his hand, "Prometheus, and you are obviously Titus, it is my pleasure to meet you."

Titus doesn't know why maybe the twinkle in the old man's left eye when he made eye contact or something else, but he felt a wave of relief and trust with this man. "Titus, and in the tub hiding is Jocelyn my colleague" As I extend my hand to shake. Nodding at the two men behind Prometheus who had glanced over their shoulders at me. Across the parking lot the floodlight flickers, sparks sending a spew of glittering sparks to the pavement, and dies casting the entire lot into darkness.

"Jack and Jill" Prometheus said motioning towards his guards. "They are just for our protection, shall we talk inside?" Prometheus enters the Motel Room but his guards stay outside, he did not sit but hastily made his point.

"I have been following your progress since the last job you performed for me. The reason you were hired was to kill a man, not to take what belonged to him."

I can take what I find. I think to myself, who is he to question what I took?

"If I hire you, I am allowed to tell you what you can and cannot take." He says, and I wonder if he can read my thoughts. He continues, "The key you have stolen has caused quite a ruckus amongst the most powerful men to ever exist. Without my help you will not last the night. Though your obvious skills have kept you alive thus far, you will need my help to live through this."

Titus, looking upon the old man nods his head. "I was afraid of that, seems the key is government property to me. I have had NSA on my ass since I took that key and my friend was killed by a professional sniper with a .50 cal round from a mile out, I didn't know what to do but see where they key leads and hope to expose them."

"Well Jack Bauer should be arriving any second in a helicopter to recover that key, so we must be off. This entire area is under constant satellite surveillance except for this tiny sliver you are currently in; no doubt they will be sweeping this area with active

Special Forces or private contractors. My sources say the Academy (Blackwater) the favorite mercenary squads of the Skull & Bones Society have been activated to find and capture you. They have also activated JSOC to use the Activity against you as well. They are even deploying one of their new toys from NSA to do so. You will follow me in the stolen Mercedes, if we leave it here they will find it and then a DNA scan will reveal my presence here. Let us make haste, I fear we have exhausted any extra time we had with introduction." Jocelyn and I agree to follow. Obviously this man was extending information as an olive branch to let us know he was a friend and could be trusted.

Jocelyn and I load the car back up; exhaustion was hitting me like a brick wall. We follow Prometheus's Rolls Royce Phantom to his exquisite house. The house is built nearby deep in a wooded area, surrounded by a large marble looking wall. The house itself resembles nothing I have ever seen before. The grounds are teeming with security personnel and dogs. The cars approach the garage but Prometheus's Phantom stops ten feet short, a guard opens the oddly painted dark purple garage door and his driver waives for me to pull around him and park inside.

Inside the garage the only light comes from candles. The house is strange, nothing has a flat surface or symmetry, and everything is slightly off and uncomfortable feeling. Even the chairs, for instance some chairs have three legs not four, or they have one arm; rest but not two. The couches are seemingly home made and always angled to one side or another. There were many portraits but the frames are not round or square but a mixture. The house feels chaotic, not orderly or wealthy almost hard to look anywhere without a headache.

Prometheus smiles and says, "I live completely off the grid, this property is 100% self sufficient and uses no electricity, no Internet, no security cameras, therefore no outside surveillance. Nothing for someone to hack in to, I prefer to keep security as I have my whole life, medieval style. If someone wants to know what is going on inside, they have to come in and find out for themselves. I have a private security force with over 100 men and dogs roaming the property. No one gets in and nothing gets out. This is the type of commitment you must have to take on the men you have chosen to. However, even these measures would be futile if they decided to take me down. You should have just killed the target and walked away, but now they know who you are and want retribution plus their property back. I have heard they prefer you alive, so they can use you in one of their rituals. The secret you are trying to reveal is too dangerous for them to take chances however, and the agents and private mercs hunting you have a kill or capture order." Prometheus said to me as we walked into the house from the garage.

After being shuffled into his enormous Library we were attended to by a servant with coffee. The paintings in this room were of Andrew Jackson, Aaron Burr killing Alexander Hamilton in a duel, Abraham Lincoln, JFK, Thomas Jefferson, and finally one that is seemingly out of place but instantly recognizable to me Hassan-I Sabbah.

Then the old man joins us and hands us a picture book, it is a coffee table stylebook with paintings of the various ceremonies to lay the cornerstones for the US Monuments and other monuments designed by FreeMason's. The Capitol Building, the White House, the Washington Monument, Jefferson Memorial, Statue of Liberty, Mount Rushmore, TransAmerican Pyramid, the Golden Gate Bridge, Bunker Hill Monument, Central Park, all of the Smithsonian institutes, various bank towers in cities, etc.

In the middle of the room is a large globe that is very peculiar. It has sixteen circles of circumference evenly spaced and highlighted; at the intersection points are markers and names of ancient sites handwritten. Some of the intersection points and straight lines that went over certain monuments are very strange. Prometheus is pleased with my curiosity and exhales, "The world's electromagnetic field grid. Not just coincidence, but science led to the creation of the ancient world wonders. The intersection points are where the electromagnetic hyper-cube intersects with the earths crust causing unusually high electromagnetic fields." Smiling he pointed for us to sit. "Ancient people understood other energy fields and used them as a wireless energy source, they had a vast knowledge of magnetism, resonant sound frequency vibrations, superconductive elements, mainly gold which could be made into room temp superconductive gold. They used these superconductive elements to increase the bodies' ability to naturally transfer energy, thus increasing the electromagnetic field in the brain and opening up memories as you have done and many other possibilities. However, those in control of this world have intentionally led to this information being lost because it would empower all the people. These men in charge have always held knowledge back

because they understand knowledge is power, and if they can slowly release the information themselves; we will worship them for it. There is nothing we can do about revealing this information until the group itself has been ousted from power."
Prometheus smoothly sat down across from us, his bodyguards exiting the library.

Prometheus says, "I believe that everything that needs to be said to you already has, by many great leaders whose words are long forgot. The American public, and the world itself have been living in an illusion, created by those in power to enhance and keep their power. As someone aptly stated 'knowledge is power', for if you control what people hear and see, then you control how he or she think. This control of knowledge by the powers that be has been amplified by their complete control of everything on television, and enhanced further by their dominance of the Internet. However, the Internet is still too new and leads to problems like Wikileaks, and Infowars. Installing Net Neutrality and allowing the FCC to restrict free speech on the Internet will deal with the threat of the alternative media. Countries like China and Russia under their control have already done thus. They will appeal or amend the first amendment to keep these alternative media sources from spreading the truth, until the right time."

"They can do that?" I ask.

"Yes, there are forces in the shadows and they are moving their political puppets in conjunction to ensure these 'alternative media' sources are no longer accessible to a brain washed and asleep public. Ted Cruz a Senator from Texas exposed that they already had 41 Democrat Party Senators signed on to a bill that would alter the first amendment. The ruling elite has taken over society and is worried about a mass awakening to the facts. That is why whistleblowers are not being protected but prosecuted. As long as they portray the Snowden's of the world as traitors they can continue acting as they have been, perpetuating the overall Grand Plan, creation of a utopian society, their own heaven."

"How do we trust you then, if they are that far reaching?" I ask.

"I engage you as Prometheus, the bearer of information, bringer of the light. I give to you what Prometheus actually gave to mankind, wisdom. Not of how to make a fire or how to build a monument that matches the heavens, but the wisdom that has been hidden from the public and kept only for the elite. You see the truth is not the voice in your head, the words conforming your actions, conscripting your mind; the truth is the silence between the words. You must open your mind to all possibilities and forget what you have been told, because everybody lies."

He smiles, as he watches us completely enticed by his words.

"I know whom both of you are and you do not know who I am, and it shall remain that way. You are both being watched very closely by my enemies and any information on me would be extracted from you during interrogation. As Titus knows, everyone has a breaking point."

I interrupt, placing my coffee down on the table; the clink draws the attention to me. "True, during my time in Special Forces, I visited a few CIA Black Sites. Even the most religious man who does not fear death or pain will eventually crack; the mind can only endure so much pain before it will do strange things. In instance MK Ultra and then the Monarch mind control programs were developed by causing a subject so much pain, normally electro shock therapy, that they create an alternative personality like a schizophrenic, and the CIA could train the new personality to do what they told it to, in order to make the pain stop. Eventually the victim would be able to slip in and out of the alternative personality based on key words, or signs, like a woman in a polka dot dress could trigger the alternative personality and it's preprogrammed mission. The Russians did the same thing using number stations, where numbers transmitted over short wave radio would trigger agents within a country, agents that had no idea they had a second personality and hidden mission within. The benefit is the agent was completely unaware of it's programming, so if captured they would never reveal anything, until they had been mentally re-broken through further torture. Scary stuff but it's all documented." I respond.

"Yes, you are correct, partly. These mind control programs have more to do with the subconscious mind than one might think. The CIA and other letter Agencies are involved but they are just one compartment and not the true enemy, the enemy has taken over those Agencies because they created them. Only the men at the top of the CIA, NSA, and Homeland Defense understand whom the true ruling elite are, because they are one and the same. By controlling key individuals at the top of the chain of command they are able to use the agency in question to carry out their agenda. That is how an executive order from the President and carried out by the NSA Chief turns the entire NSA system from looking outside America to looking inside America for surveillance. This is not the only agency that has been taken over; these people have placed people in key positions at every level of government, finance, media, religious institutions, etc. They created most of these organizations in the first place, like the Council of Foreign Relations, or the UN. If you both will listen, I will explain who is after you and why, are you interested to know the truth of this world? Just remember as long as you are in prison, you are safe, once you escape you will no longer be able to resume your place in the cave, as the rewards and gifts of this world will be meaningless to you. To know the truth you must risk everything, you must open your mind to entirely new possibilities and shed it of the preprogramming from your upbringing."

Jocelyn laughs, "Look we know Santa Claus is fake, you can go ahead and tell us. We have people trying to kill us, I think we are past the shock phase."

Prometheus angrily stands and looks down upon her, "It is presumptuous people like your self that have been asleep at the wheel and allowed this to happen. Too caught up in your hamster wheel of self importance to see the big picture."

Jocelyn's eyes wide and furious, "Just fucking tell us you old grump." I grab her arm and apologize, "My friend is just nervous please we would like your help, explain."

"You may find what I have to say hard to believe, so I beg you to follow me down the rabbit hole, open minded, for you both know very little of what the real world is. The problem with this rabbit hole, is it doesn't end until you reach the bottom of the endless pit. As the matrix depicted, the world you are living in is a prison, a prison that has no bars, no visible constraints, a prison for your mind. Your owners, that's right owners, have you blinded to the truth, living for what they programmed you to want."

Jocelyn rolls her eyes, and I glare at her. Prometheus continues un-abashed.

"Since the dawn of civilization these men have been trying to conquer the world, to create one Empire of Man under their rule. They have always been there behind the scenes using wealth and money to control emperors, kings, dictators, and presidents. They have always known that any visible form of control, such as fascism is finite, because it is a known quantity. If the ruled can see their controllers they can always overcome them. However, if the true ruling class operates behind the scenes, using the visible form of government as a puppet, the ruled class can overthrow the known quantity but never overthrow the true ruling class. It is this class that has been operating behind the scenes, slowly taking over the Governments, creating International Governments, buying companies in every sector, consolidating control centrally under a singular command, global centralization of all aspects of society in secrecy."

"The great empires and there have been many, have all claimed divine right to rule over all mankind until the current economic empire of America, and even they are somewhat inspired by a Judeo-Christian ideology. All the Empires have been backed by the same bloodline of wealthy elites, because they received help from the same external source. This bloodline originated from Noah, the new modern human since the flood. Noah had three sons Shem, Ham and Japheth. The line of Japheth is no more, the line of Shem is virtuous and is the bloodline of Jesus. The bloodline of Ham became infected spiritually at the tower of Babel, and became the ruling bloodline of Babylon, Egypt and India. From Babylon then on to Europe and America, the Arian bloodline, the bloodline of the god of war Ares."

"The bloodline of Ham used force to create vast empires under their rule, but due to the finite nature of their Empires, the people overcame them. They desired to create a one world religion, one world government, and singular language, to become their own gods. Either by weakness in economics, religion, or military all the Ham empires have crumbled once the virtuous people realized the depths of this elite's depravity. When the empires crumbled this elite wealthy group of Ham bloodlines remained intact as long as they were able to protect their wealth. Though the names of these empires have changed, the tactics have adapted, the religions changed, the men behind the scenes, the ones claiming the right to rule have remained the same generation after generation. The same families, even if they change their names from Cavendish to Kennedy, trying to create their one world empire. The bloodlines of these Emperors, Kings, even

President's are all tied together. Though not so closely that an outsider could easily decipher the web, close enough to start making some connections even with the limited and flawed genealogy we now have available to us. With the breakthrough of your friend, the genealogy could be corrected, we could rewrite history to be accurate and this would expose this ruling class for what it is."

"The key you hold, gives you access to Albert Pikes Tomb. He is buried at the Supreme Council Headquarters in DC. His DNA, if it can be translated and deciphered would give everyone a completely accurate record of history all the way back to the Templar Knights discovering the knowledge at Solomon's Temple and before. It would show everyone in the world, the information being withheld from us, and give everyone an equal footing. The group you are trying to fight knows that knowledge is the power, because they are few and the people many, and if the many ever realize their capability and what has been done to them, they will overthrow this ruling elite once and for all. For the next battle will be between the bloodline of Shem and Ham, and Shem will represent the last bloodline of true humanity and its possible extinction."

"Extinction? How? Why would they want humanity extinct?" I intercede.

"I will get there." Prometheus states, then takes a long pull on his cigar and continues.

"The new empire of these ruling elites is not a single country or single empire as it had been in the past. It was decided well before the creation of America, well before

Columbus even, that the new Empire would not be a visible one until it had full control. They had decided it would be called a New World Order, to ensure that every one and every nation would want to join and be part. Selling membership to the Anglo American Empire, or Arian Empire is a hard sell compared to selling membership in the New World Order. "

"This New World Order is not new by any means. The Templars tried to conquer Europe in the same fashion, by using economics to undermine and take over sovereign nations. It is the same idea of using fractional reserve banking to slowly whittle down a country's sovereignty to the central banks, which are run by a global central bank's stockholders. The Imperators and Proletariat did this in Rome and backed the rise of a politician Caesar who would have implemented their new central banking system using fractional reserve currency and eliminated the use of any new or alternative currency empire wide, eventually worldwide. So Julius Caesar emboldened by his imperator & financial backers came upon the scene, until the people represented by the Senators like Marcus Junias Brutus saved them from this tyrannical takeover, for a short time anyways."

"The Foreign Bankers of the Rothson Family are called the Red Shield Bankers, and their shield can be seen on the currency they created and control, in example the US Dollar bill. The Dollar bill has four 1's on the front; the top right that is not in an oval is placed inside the Shield, an outline of the Rothson shield. Let me explain why and how this happened as briefly as possible."

"The Rothson's represented the wealth of Europe and the Templar Order. They with the St. Claire's and some other families had hidden the wealth of the Templars and recreated their societies with groups such as the Freemasons. The hidden knowledge had been shipped to America and hidden well on Oak Island for a time, however the material wealth of the Templars was hidden in Switzerland and used to secretly create the Swiss Banking System that was and still is under Rothson control. No one had any clue how much gold they had hidden in the hills. They sent a Rothson son to each sovereign foreign power in Europe to take it over from within funded by the Family and this banking system. Each son was to find a way to buy up each country's debt in order to take over the monetary control of each country and therefore policy and eventually political positions without the public ever being aware. The Rothson's of course seemed to be wealthy but were not, they merely handle the money for the larger organization, just as the Templars did, the Illuminati own nothing individually, they pool all their resources. As far as controlling the money through their central banking scheme, this is what the House of the Rothson family said."

"Let me issue and control a nation's money and I care not who writes the laws." Mayer Amschel Rothschild (1744-1812, Creature from Jekyll Island, p.218)

The Illuminati Families headed by the Rothson's knew the best way to unify Europe under their control was to get the countries of Europe to fight wars amongst themselves and to bankroll each country's debt by buying up their war bonds. The Rothson's could buy up the war debt and eventually hold the debt over each government's head to create a central banking system that they controlled. These central banks would be private and have control of all of the countries by creating a central banking system that controls the economic policy of each nation and operates above the government, no oversight. The Bank of England, and the US Federal Reserve, World Bank, IMF are all part of the private central bank global control system. By controlling the money through private banking institutions, they control everything in society, under and outside of the laws of that nation. They can use their funds to infiltrate organizations, buy any company or bank that might compete, all to consolidate power under their rule over time. To create a world government not empowered by the power of the people but by the controllers of finance."

"N.M Rothson, the son sent to England was extremely clever. He financed the British and his brother financed Napoleon, the countries warred against one another. When Waterloo the final battle took place N.M. Rothson's spies got back to him a full 24 hours before the British King's spies returned with the result. So Rothson took advantage of having knowledge even the King did not have. Rothson starting selling his British bonds, which caused a massive panic and drop in the price as people assumed that meant Napoleon had defeated Wellington at Waterloo. Once the British bond prices had hit the floor, Rothson started secretly buying them back up with his secret agents at rock bottom prices. At the end of the day Rothson held the majority of the British bonds and had bought them for next to nothing. When the news finally came that Napoleon had actually lost, Rothson's value shot through the roof and the British

Government owed him so much money they had to make a deal with him. So the Bank of England was created mainly from Rothson's bonds, the deal included that the Rothson's holdings could never be audited, so no one would ever know how much he was worth again, even the British monarchs. The Bank of England was granted the right to print all British Currency and then it loans the currency to the British Government plus interest. So the British Government owes the Central Bank all the British pounds in existence since the creation of this central bank plus interest."

"What does this have to do with the United States?" I ask.

"The United States was created as a free nation, to allow the growth of a middle class of businessmen who were free from these banking elite. However, that dream was short-lived, and the banking elite took over for good on their third try."

"How?" asks Jocelyn?

"In the same exact way. The American colonies had been using a new currency called 'continentals' prior to the revolutionary war. The colonies were prosperous and their was enough money to go around, and the money had no interest on it, free for the public to use, and was backed by gold and silver deposits. The Bank of England whom profits from interest paid on use of it's currency decided this was unacceptable, as it could not tax this currency for interest and eliminated the continental bills through various nefarious means, such as causing inflation by printing counterfeits and circulating them causing a depression. This caused the American Revolution as Benjamin Franklin explains",

"The Colonies would gladly have borne the little tax on tea and other matters had it not been the poverty caused by the bad influence of the English bankers on the Parliament, which has caused in the Colonies hatred of England and the Revolutionary War." - Benjamin Franklin

The American Revolution granted us the right to print and control our own money supply. However, the Bank of England would not allow this to continue for long. In 1812, the British launched a war not to win, but to cause a massive war debt on the new American Republic. It worked and caused to the creation of the first American central bank, owned by private investors that owned the Bank of England. This bank was eventually ousted along with a second attempt.

The third and most successful attempt was undertaken in 1910 under the Federal Reserve act. The Federal Reserve is a privately owned banking institution that exists above Government and controls all printing of American Currency and monetary policy. They set the interest rates, print all the money and loan the money to the US Government. Every dollar bill in exchange is marked Federal Reserve Note. These dollars are printed by the Reserve, and then loaned to the US Government plus interest. That way the US Government owes the Federal Reserve every dollar bill in existence plus interest. The money is not even fractional reserve banking as the value of the currency is totally based upon perception not upon gold holdings in the Federal Reserve. President Nixon removed the gold standard, and the Federal Reserve bankers emptied the vaults of US Gold, since Fort Knox has been empty. They are printing money based upon nothing and charging the American Taxpayer interest for using it. The private Federal Reserve owners make profit from the interest, and cannot be audited to see how much they have made. The profits are all tax-free government bonds. The National Debt is how much we owe in interest for borrowing money from the private Federal Reserve for one year. The US Government will always be in debt to the Federal Reserve because even if it recollected every dollar bill on the planet and gave it back to the Federal Reserve, the US Government would still owe the massive interest. To pay the interest the government had to create a Federal Income tax, of which 100% of the money goes to pay private bankers the interest they earned by loaning the US government Federal Reserve notes. These notes replaced money the US Government used to print itself for free. The system can sustain only as long as it grows, if this taxpayer revenue is not increased on an annual basis to pay the ever-increasing national debt, then the system will collapse, and eventually it will collapse. The first two tries at creating this evil central bank were thwarted by Thomas Jefferson and Andrew Jackson."

"The first Central Bank of America was floated by the Federalist Alexander Hamilton as a savior to the war debt from 1812. Hamilton insisted a central bank was required and was killed by Aaron Burr the Vice President of Thomas Jefferson in a duel. Burr saw Hamilton as a foreign agent of the Rothson's Red Shield Bankers and he was correct. Jefferson knew the danger of a central bank and made the following statement,"

"If the American people ever allow private banks to control the issue of their currency, first by inflation, then by deflation, the banks and corporations that will grow up around them will deprive the people of all property until their children wake up homeless on the continent their Fathers conquered...I believe that banking institutions are more dangerous to our liberties than standing armies... The issuing power should be taken from the banks and restored to the people, to whom it properly belongs." - Thomas Jefferson

"Wow, that sounds exactly like what is happening with all the foreclosures today." I say.

The second Bank of America was brought about during the Presidency of Andrew Jackson. Jackson though was a fervent patriot and killed the second attempt. On his deathbed and now imprinted on his tombstone are his last words, "I killed the bank." Earlier in his life Jackson stated. "If congress has the right under the Constitution to issue paper money, it was given them to use themselves, not to be delegated to individuals or corporations." *-Andrew Jackson*

"Abraham Lincoln tried to warn us of this same group of men, he even tried to rid the country of their authority by issuing new gold backed currency.

Abraham Lincoln stated, "*The Government should create, issue, and circulate all the currency and credits needed to satisfy the spending power of the Government and the buying power of consumers. By the adoption of these principles, the taxpayers will be saved immense sums of interest. Money will cease to be master and become the servant of humanity.*"

For this he was executed, his death was pinned on a lone assassin that fired the fatal shot; the conspiracy behind it was far reaching and involved the monetary powers that financed and profited from both the South and North in the civil war. Lincoln stated this as well,

"*The money powers prey upon the nation in times of peace and conspire against it in times of adversity. The banking powers are more despotic than a monarchy, more insolent than autocracy, more selfish than bureaucracy. They denounce as public enemies all who question their methods or throw light upon their crimes. I have two great enemies, the Southern Army in front of me and the bankers in the rear. Of the two, the one at my rear is my greatest foe. [As a most undesirable consequence of the war...] Corporations have been enthroned, and an era of corruption in high places will follow. The money power of the country will endeavor to prolong its reign by working upon the prejudices of the people until the wealth is aggregated in the hands of a few, and the Republic is destroyed*" *Abraham Lincoln*

Despite Lincoln's warning less than fifty years later the US put together the Aldrich-Vreeland Act to create an emergency bipartisan National Monetary Commission to study banking reform, especially Central European Banks. Republican Senator Rich Aldridge met with 8 other men in 1910 at Jekyll Island Georgia at a private estate and a secret meeting. At this meeting were representatives of JP Morgan, Rockefeller, Koehn & Loeb, Co. and the National City bank of New York. Aldrich's daughter was married to John D. Rockefeller. Unknown to most is, the Rothson's controlled JP Morgan, Rockefeller and Koehn & Loeb. JP Morgan was a branch of the Rothson's global banking system and managed by their representative Henry Davison, the Rockefeller's standard oil company was funded and controlled by JP Morgan as part of the Rothson Red Shield banking empire. Edward House was in attendance and later became Woodrow Wilson's closest financial advisor; later Edward House would create the Council on Foreign Relations (Originally to be called the Council of Propaganda but changed to hide it's true nature). Paul Warburg considered a Rothson representative was there on behalf of Koehn & Loeb and would later create the Tri-Lateral Commission with the Rockefeller's. Rothson agents ran the entire meeting and the end result was the creation of the Federal Reserve Act a few months later. Warburg who technically lead the meeting, and recorded the minutes stated, "The matter of a uniform discount rate (interest rate) was discussed and settled at Jekyll Island." Paul Warburg.

Edward House later helped get Woodrow Wilson elected, and without his financial backing Wilson would not have won the Presidency. Once in office Wilson had agreed pre-election to sign the 1913 Federal Reserve Act to create the Private banking institution known as the Federal Reserve. House and his Illuminati masters could trust Wilson who was a 33rd degree Free Mason. Wilson was a high level 33rd degree freemason, but not an Illuminati member, so he did not fully understand what he had agreed to do. He did not have the bloodline or the correct nature for further advancement. All Illuminati are 33rd degree Masons, but not all 33rd degree Freemasons are Illuminati. Wilson would later regret this as he saw what he had done to the country. Wilson would later state,

I am a most unhappy man. I have unwittingly ruined my country. A great industrial nation is controlled by its system of credit. Our system of credit is concentrated. The growth of the nation, therefore, and all our activities are in the hands of a few men. We have come to be one of the worst ruled, one of the most completely controlled and dominated Governments in the civilized world no longer a Government by free opinion, no longer a Government by conviction and the vote of the majority, but a Government by the opinion and duress of a small group of dominant men. -Woodrow Wilson

"Later, another president JFK would be the last president to challenge the Illuminati and their central banking system. JFK signed executive order 11110, creating a new alternative silver backed currency to replace the Federal Reserve Notes over time. JFK was the last true American President; you should hear the words that lead to his demise. His replacement Lyndon Johnson's first act was to repeal this executive order 11110. JFK knew the media would be pivotal in the years to come, and he was correct but he had no idea how bad it would actually get. JFK was killed because he wanted to empower the people of America to take back what was theirs, and the Illuminati needed to make an example of him. JFK wanted to abolish the CIA and the shadowy group of international bankers behind them, for being lied to about the Bay of Pigs, he was quoted as saying he would break the CIA into a thousand pieces and throw them to the wind. JFK like Abraham Lincoln made a final fatal error that the banking elite would not tolerate, creating an alternative currency through executive order."

"The proof of whom killed Kennedy is obvious once you know what to look for. One of the symbols of this group is the eternal flame, representative of the flame of knowledge that burned in Babylon's center. This eternal flame originated as an actual flame in the city of Babylon, where the oil was so vast in the region it would bubble up on the surface. The oil, called bitumen in those days had a natural spring in the center of Babylon that was lit on fire therefore presenting the public with the eternal flame. This eternal flame is representative of the knowledge this group of elite bankers have always held and kept from the public to empower themselves over the masses. That is why Rockefeller's oil company Standard Oil had the eternal flame of Babylon as it's Logo, and Amoco still uses this today. These Multinational Corporations are all well aware and use these Illuminati symbols all the time. Hiding in plain sight."

"Wow this goes deep." Jocelyn declares. I nod in agreement as Prometheus continues on.

"The Federal Reserve prints the dollars, loans them to Government and private investors invest in bonds to act as the basis of the reserve currency instead of gold. With no limit to how much paper currency can be made as it has no relevant base in material value, the reserve can print as much money as they want. The power to print the Federal Reserve notes, and not be backed by gold holdings, gives this group unprecedented control over the financial industry by allowing them to devalue currency by printing more of it and by setting the interest rate. The only way to keep the system from collapsing when investors sell their bonds is to bring in new investors to pay off the old investors by always increasing the debt so you have more debt to sell to new investors. It is a ponzy scheme keeping our Government operating under emergency powers and granting all monetary policy control to the Federal Reserve. The Federal Reserve had to find a way to collect the debt from the American people. So the 16th amendment was partially ratified, and created the Income Tax. When the country went bankrupt in 1933, the American Citizens became seized collateral assets, as a backing to the loaned money to the US Government. Since every birth certificate has a stock exchange number on it, meaning every person is an asset. Now the Federal Reserve owns the American citizens, until the national debt has been paid back, something that is impossible to do as I already explained. This is why the economy is far more controlled by the Federal Reserve chairman than the US President."

"Furthermore the idea of a central bank and planned economy is directly from the socialism of Karl Marx, as a central bank was a key to his communist manifesto. These leftist ideas originated from Jacobinism, or a leftist philosophy. Leftist philosophy refers to the sinister side, or left handed side. Communism, socialism is therefore inherently sinister. Socialism is the ultimate tool of the Elite, to create a government that would allocate all assets, controlled by them. To create a two-class society, the elite and everyone else, where everyone else is dependent upon the government for everything and therefore unable to rebel. The elite know that the government that can give you everything can take from you everything. They are creating a worldwide welfare state to ensure the people are under their full control by means of economic despotism. That is why the average American worker today makes less money than a worker did in 1972 when inflation is taken into account. While the top .0001% has never owned more wealth than they do now at any time in history."

"So what have they used their wealth to create? A shadow government controlled by financial interests rather than by the will of the people. Always centralizing control, removing freedom from the people. Setting into place policies that continue the growth of the top 1% and favor Multinational Corporations whilst damaging the fair balance associated with a true free market system. In example the top Multinational Corporations used their lobbyists to create tax loopholes that allow them to shift their holdings, jobs, profits overseas, reinvest them into the economy for tax credits, and when all is said and done, they profit from taxes rather than pay any. In some cases, employees income taxes are withheld by the MNC, and are kept by as a tax credit, so the employers are actually taxing the employees at MNC's in America. The tax laws are made so elaborate by their teams of corporate lawyers and lobbyists than no one can decipher how they are getting away with it, or who is even doing it. They own the five media organizations that present all the news, everything you see on tv, which ensures they will never report on these MNC's screwing the American people. None of the MNC's are going to complain either because they are technically all part of the same larger umbrella corporation being controlled by the same financial elite families who are beholden to the Illuminati Secret Society Doctrine."

JFK warned us of this shadow Government, as he knew their collectivist agenda was prevalent in America. Having routed itself in secret organizations such as the Bilderberg Group, Bohemian Grove, Skull and Bones etc. I have highlighted the parts of the speech pertinent to the facts."

John F. Kennedy April 27th, 1961 National Press Club

"The very word "secrecy" is repugnant in a free and open society; and we are as a people inherently and historically opposed to secret societies, to secret oaths and to secret proceedings. We decided long ago that the dangers of excessive and unwarranted concealment of pertinent facts far outweighed the dangers, which are cited to justify it. Even today, there is little value in opposing the threat of a closed society by imitating its arbitrary restrictions. Even today, there is little value in insuring the survival of our nation if our traditions do not survive with it. And there is very grave danger that an announced need for increased security will be seized upon by those anxious to expand its meaning to the very limits of official censorship and concealment. That I do not intend to permit to the extent that it is in my control. And no

official of my Administration, whether his rank is high or low, civilian or military, should interpret my words here tonight as an excuse to censor the news, to stifle dissent, to cover up our mistakes or to withhold from the press and the public the facts they deserve to know.

For we are opposed around the world by a monolithic and ruthless conspiracy that relies primarily on covert means for expanding its sphere of influence--on infiltration instead of invasion, on subversion instead of elections, on intimidation instead of free choice, on guerrillas by night instead of armies by day. It is a system which has conscripted vast human and material resources into the building of a tightly knit, highly efficient machine that combines military, diplomatic, intelligence, economic, scientific and political operations.

Its preparations are concealed, not published. Its mistakes are buried, not headlined. Its dissenters are silenced, not praised. No expenditure is questioned, no rumor is printed, no secret is revealed."

Prometheus looking amused proceeds, "Kennedy knew that this group could only be dealt with if the American people were exposed to the truth. However, he was under their control and could not just openly state what he was saying, had he called them by their true name they would have revealed his drug use and sexual activity to the media corporations they control. This elite group loves to use vices of the flesh, the same desires they promote against anyone who might stand against them. These men understand propaganda and even wrote the book on it."

"One of their greatest deceptions is the current philosophy of psychology. A method of control they have developed to keep the masses in line, to ensure anyone thinking outside the box is labeled as crazy. The nephew of Sigmund Freud, one of these enlightened minds, was Edward Bernay's, whom is considered the father of public relations. Bernay's wrote a book called Propaganda, in which he wrote out the elites basic plan for control. This plan had been instituted many, many times over the centuries but Bernay's was so proud of it he decided to document it."

The first chapter entitled Organizing Chaos, which stems from their idea of Ordo ab Chao, or Order from Chaos. Bernay's states,

THE conscious and intelligent manipulation of the organized habits and opinions of the masses is an important element in democratic society. Those who manipulate this unseen mechanism of society constitute an invisible government which is the true ruling power of our country.

We are governed, our minds are molded, our tastes formed, our ideas suggested, largely by men we have never heard of. This is a logical result of the way in which our democratic society is organized. Vast numbers of human beings must cooperate in this manner if they are to live together as a smoothly functioning society.

Our invisible governors are, in many cases, unaware of the identity of their fellow members in the inner cabinet.

They govern us by their qualities of natural leadership, their ability to supply needed ideas and by their key position in the social structure. Whatever attitude one chooses to take toward this condition, it remains a fact that in almost every act of our

daily lives, whether in the sphere of politics or business, in our social conduct or our ethical thinking, we are dominated by the relatively small number of persons—a trifling fraction of our hundred and twenty million—who understand the mental processes and social patterns of the masses. It is they who pull the wires which control the public mind, who harness old social forces and contrive new ways to bind and guide the world.

"This is a total load of crap, there is no way a conspiracy this large is real, we would have found it out years ago." Jocelyn interjects.

Prometheus smiles, "Denial is the easiest human emotion to predict. Denial as described in the dictionary is *'in ordinary English usage, is asserting that a statement or allegation is not true, the same word, and also abnegation, is used for a psychological defense mechanism postulated by Sigmund Freud, in which a person is faced with a fact that is too uncomfortable to accept and rejects it instead, insisting that it is not true despite what may be overwhelming evidence."*

"So what is their goal? What are they trying to achieve? So the Illuminati Families are in control? Whom do we have to kill to get rid of them?" I interject.

"The Illuminati are the true aristocracy of the world, they represent the true ruling wealth and exist in almost every nation, as these men are globalists not nationalists. The rise of America, with it's independent wealth, and the first true powerful middle class was a serious threat to the Aristocratic Elite whom had never truly had their authority questioned by these uppity peasants, the New Riche' as they called them."

"This unknown ruling elite's name and its goals change depending on the age it has existed in. However they are not really in control. There is a force; you might call them above these agents. Before humanity existed they were on Earth, and they have been here the entire time. Moving in and out of the shadows depending on how aware the public they are controlling through this elite bloodline is. The have used the Illuminati and the societies precursors to further their agenda. Once a freemason becomes a 33rd degree member, if he has the correct bloodline, he will be allowed to ascend up the 13 levels above the 33rd degree. These degrees are the degrees of Illumination and only members of the 13 ruling families are allowed to ascend. These men are very, very small in number but the Families names' are very large indeed. The head family, being the Rothson's, then Rockefeller, Warburg, Cavendish, and more. The patriarch's of these families, all of whom consider themselves citizens of the Globe, not a single country, have used secret societies since the creation of society itself to rule over their fellow man. They are the only ones whom know what the plan is, and to what end's it serves. They hold the knowledge of how to communicate with the external forces controlling this world, with the ascended masters."

"Ascended masters? External Forces? External to what?" I ask.

"Listen, patience is key." Prometheus scoffs. "Serving underneath these Illuminati, is the rest of the Freemasonic Pyramid of Power. The preferred form of control is through compartmentalization. If they can control the heads of each group, or they themselves are the heads, they can control the agenda and the direction of each committee or group, or business, political movement, or social agenda. The individuals within the organizations being controlled by this group are compartmentalized, focused on their individual task, unaware of how it relates to the hidden agenda on the whole. This allows the people working in the organizations to believe what they are doing is good; even if the collective effort is eventually used for something evil, the people in the organization have no idea until it is too late. You keep someone busy, task minded and unaware of the true goals, and you can get a group of individuals to work separately towards something completely different than what is in their benefit."

"The groups the Illuminati created to bring about their New World Order one world government are very powerful groups in society. The current most powerful of these groups is the Bilderberg Group. This group, in example of their power, set the agenda for the creation of the European Union at their first meeting in 1954, forty years before it came into existence. Unifying Europe for the first time in history with no shots fired. A feet Alexander the Great, The Roman Empire, Hitler, Napoleon couldn't have imagined. They chose current President Bernard O'Brien as their candidate in 2006, and backed him with financial support and favorable media coverage; with the support they gave him he had no chance of losing. Portrayed him as a savior to the low-income class, and then he appointed the same Illuminati puppet Wall Street insiders as his supporting cast, including top end lobbyists to all his appointments. In 2008, O'Brien secretly attended the Bilderberg Meeting in Virginia where they chose VP Joe Buck to be his running mate. We are aware of this because O'Brien's press detail during his campaign was told to board the flight he was supposed to be on to Chicago. When the plane took off, the press was on board with no candidate; they were told O'Brien had to do a secret meeting, the look on the medias face on YouTube is priceless. The meeting was at the Bilderberg Group in Chantilly, VA with Hillary Clinton (who was also missing and had tv station cameras stationed outside her house looking for O'Brien) and they chose Buck, a globalist supporter to be the VP nominee, a man who has written books and given speeches supporting a New World Order. The American people are given a choice between the lesser of two evils in every election, and unfortunately the Bilderbergers have been the ones supplying them their choices since money completely took over politics. They run both parties, George Bush a Skull and Bones Member ran vs. John Kerry another Bonesman as well in the previous election. No matter who wins, they win because they pick who we get to choose."

"Other groups they run, created or have taken over include but are not limited to the Council on Foreign Relations, the Tri-Lateral Commission, World Bank, IMF, Interpol, Bohemian Grove, Skull & Bones, Scottish Rite Freemasonry, Jesuits, Rosicrucian's, Knight's Templar, Lucis Trust, Theosophical Society, Republican Party, Democratic Party, United Nations, Rhodes Scholarship Foundation, Smithsonian Institute, World Health Organization, Rockefeller Foundation, Blackwater, Department of Homeland Security, CIA, NSA, Central Banks in every 'free' country, and even infiltrated the

Vatican. If you look for their Masonic Symbols you will identify more organizations readily. Not all members of these groups are Illuminati, in fact almost none are, only the very top members of each of these groups are or are being directly controlled by someone who is Illuminati, control comes through various means such as positions, rewards, bribery or blackmail, jail, death. Most members of the lower parts of the groups, the profane as they are called have no idea what the groups are actually doing."

"Compartmentalization is their favorite control, in example the average Master Free Mason doesn't even know there is an inner circle above the 33rd degree Masons, and won't ever know because they do not have the correct bloodline. The same with the NSA, your average operator believes he is serving American Interests of National Security even though he is being used to violate the 4th amendment and spy on American Citizens. Your average person wants to believe they are helping the world and doing the right thing everyday, and as long as the Illuminati can make them only focus on their small part, the larger scheme can be carried out without anyone noticing."

"Any other examples?" Jocelyn asks.

"Sure, fluoride in the water. The Nazi's in WWII first introduced adding fluoride to public drinking water in their concentration camps. It was added because it dumbed down and calmed the population. The US during operation paperclip brought those same Nazi Scientists to America, over 2,000 of them to the US. Directly after this in

1945, the US started adding fluoride to the drinking water to help with 'tooth decay'. The real goal was to calm the US population and dumb them down so they would be easier to control. Harvard University studied this and found it did lower IQ's by at least 7%. Also the fluoride is a by-product of the aluminum industry, so instead of having to pay to dispose of it, they got paid to sell it to the government and the government tricked us into drinking it. Even more importantly fluoride causes a film around the pineal gland in the brain ensuring people won't unlock these memories through the third eye as you have done Titus."

"Disgusting these Illuminati people are sick." I say.

"Not sick, psychotic is the correct term, the very elite doesn't care about you at all. You are nothing more than a useless eater, cattle as far as they are concerned. These people are not the millionaires or billionaires, these families through various trusts and hidden assets in central banks are all worth more than a trillion dollars. The Bill Gates of the world is nothing compared to the Rothson Family."

"The Illuminati believes someone must rule, so it should be them. That because they have been able to take the world over financially that they deserve by natural selection to dominate, might is right. Through their Global Banking Empire they have created an umbrella corporation that controls nearly 60% of all the businesses in world. This network of companies was revealed by PLoS One (A European Financial Journal) which proved mathematically in a financial report that all these seemingly different corporations, Barclays, Google, Exxon, etc. were all tied to the same controllers, really just one giant umbrella corporation, the Illuminati Corporation. Tied together by a scheme of influence either direct or indirectly over all the western Multi-National Corporations that when plotted out looks exactly similar to the Kabalistic Tree of Life diagram."

"The New World Order is being created, and being created rapidly to ensure that the men in control now, are the men in control at the creation of the New World Order. Their end plan, their goal is to create a world that lives in peace, under their control in a new form of government most readily defined as technocratic socialism. They believe world peace can be achieved but only by means of total population control can we achieve it. They believe free will, emotion, only leads to chaos. That reason, control and order are perfection and they point to the stars as their proof."

Prometheus pauses then continues, "they control everything you desire from Coca-Cola, to fast cars, large meals, vacations, it has all been packaged and sold to you. This is because these material desires are never ending, the more you have the more you will want. The elite understand this and use materialism as a driving force to keep us all enslaved and working for them. They understand that while they make the money that we use and desire, they will always have more than those who serve them. As long as material wealth is the end goal, they can control everything through finance. If we desired true love (not physical passion), connection to others, truth, desires of the soul, there is nothing for them to sell us, nothing for them to use for control. You cannot trick someone to truly love, but you can trick someone into idolizing wealth, fame, etc. The best part is the soul when it finds true love, something that fulfills the soul's need, it desires no more. However, when the body desires drugs, food, sex a person can acquire these things through wealth but the cup is never full, some people can not get enough of any of these things, thus allowing them to be controlled."

"This very small group of people, only 13 families, the illuminati has used advanced knowledge to establish controls worldwide. Told they were different than the rest of mankind, they were direct descendants of the Gods and therefore just to rule over mankind. They are complete sociopaths, and will use any means necessary to achieve their end goals. As Plato said in the Republic, the most unjust man would always be ruler, because he would do more to take power than anyone. Also the most unjust person would always claim to be the most just. The most unjust person would fear to be ruled over by someone less just than himself and therefore would put himself as the ruler to be sure no one less just than himself could impose upon him. In this world the unjust have the advantage."

"Plato also knew that wealth would always be attained by those where were the most corrupt. He explains, when two men enter a contract, who will benefit more? The man who enters the contract and uses the most corruption will always profit more than the man who is honest, in business the most deceitful always wins. Secrecy is their calling, and the occult for which they profess is literally a religion of secrecy, that is how they have kept so many people in the dark. No member or puppet of this elite has ever in modern times exposed them, until me."

"In every society they use their wealth to bring governments and key people under their control secretly, they lend them wealth to rise in power and when they are in power they owe the moneylenders their position. Just like Bernard O'Brien, a man who rose to power based on lies and deception, with powerful banking elites backing him and fueling the propaganda machine with the same media organizations they own. Once in power Bernard handed the banksters a virtual blank check with his bailout package, they used this federal money to buy up smaller banks and consolidate the banking industry under their control. Of course they told the people martial law would happen if we did not bail them out, which was not true of course. They used their media to make us think the money was wasted on bonuses, it wasn't, they used the bailouts to centralize control by buying smaller private banks, whilst the economy was hurt, buy low. The recession was profitable for them, very profitable."

"These moneylenders know how to control the news, to control every aspect of society they can. They have always used money as a means of control because everything in modern day society can be controlled financially. The Government, the laws can only go so far, money can have influence on everything from who gets elected, to what news stories are covered, etc. You can use funds to run secret black operations using the intelligence services, private security firms, terrorists groups, mafia's, gangs, anything you want. The Illuminati created the Italian Mafia, Mazzini the father of the Italian Mafia was one of theirs, spoke directly with Albert Pike a top level Illuminist in DC."

"This group of men has been hiding behind the scenes for a long time. The Rothson's enabled the centralization of the mystery school ideas and modernization by Adam

Weishaupt in 1776 as the Bavarian Illuminati, he wrote down their 25 goals at the time."

Illuminati Doctrine as recorded by Adam Weishaupt, founder of the Bavarian Illuminati

1. All men are more easily inclined towards evil than good.

2. Preach Liberalism.

3. Use the idea of freedom to bring about class wars.

4. Any and all means should be used to reach the Illuminati Goals as they are justified.

5. The right to lie in force.

6. The power of our resources must remain invisible until the very moment it has gained the strength that no cunning or force can undermine it.

7. Avocation of mob psychology to control the masses.

8. Use alcohol, drugs, corruption and all forms of vice to systematically corrupt the youth of the nation.

9. Seize property by any means.

10. Use of slogans such as equity, liberty, fraternity delivered into the mouths of the masses in psychological warfare.

11. War should be directed so that the nations on both sides are placed further in debt and peace conferences conducted so that neither combatant obtains territory rights.

12. Members must use their wealth to have candidates chosen and placed in public office who will be obedient to their demands and will be used as pawns in the game by those behind the scenes. Their advisors will have been reared and trained from childhood to rule the affairs of the world.

13. Control the press.

14. Agents will come forward after fermenting traumatic situations and appear to be the saviors of the masses.

15. Create industrial depression and financial panic, unemployment, hunger, shortage of food and use this to control the masses or mob and then use the mob to wipe out all those who stand in the way.

16. Infiltrate into the secret Freemasons to use them for Illuminati purposes.

17. Expound the value of systematic deception, use high sounding slogans and phrases and advocate lavish promises to the masses even though they cannot be kept.

18. Detail plans for resolutions, discuss the art of street fighting which is necessary to bring the population into speedy subjection.

19. Use agents as advisors behind the scenes after wars and use secret diplomacy to gain control.

20. Establish huge monopolies that lean toward world government control.

21. Use high taxes and unfair competition to bring about economic ruin by control of raw materials. Organize agitation among the workers and subsidize their competitors.

22. Build up armaments with Police forces and Soldiers sufficient to protect our needs.

23. Members and leaders of the one world government would be appointed by the directors.

24. Infiltrate into all classes and levels of society and government for the purpose of fooling, bemusing and corrupting the youthful members of society by teaching them theories and principles that we know to be false.

25. National and International laws should be used to destroy civilization and enslave

and control the people.

"Wow so much of what they wanted to do is actually being done." Jocelyn quips.

"Now that you know their goals it is easier to identify them by their symbols, tactics, knowledge, rituals and wealth. Throughout time this group has always depicted itself as the enlightened ones. Before the Illuminati they were the enlightened members of Freemasonry, before this the Knights Templar. Adam Weishaupt himself was a freemason before founding the Illuminati. In Rome they were called the Imperators & Proletariat, they were an elite ruling class of wealthy individuals that helped turn the Republic of Rome into the Roman Empire by backing the rise of Julius Caesar and later Augustus through secret alliances. In Jerusalem they were called the Money Lenders and Philistines, they were the source of Solomon's initial wealth, which they allowed to grow, as he was the Patriarch or Pindar, the head of their elite bloodline at the time. In Egypt they were the Royal Court and ran the Mystery Schools. In Babylon they also started the mystery schools. The question is where did the information; the secrets of the mystery schools come from? Where did this advanced knowledge in the ancient past come from? Who's hand did Ramanujan really see when he entered his vision and saw the equations forming on the board? Why do so many Freemasons and members of the occult such as Aleister Crowley claim their writings were given to them by what they called 'ascended masters'?"

"The modern day TV is leading the public down the path towards another false explanation. Now that evolution is being debunked due to the fine-tuning problems and the issues brought on by the discovery of quantum physics, and DNA. The mathematical improbability that this Universe developed by chance is very real, if just one of the fine tuning constants such as the Cosmological Constant was off even slightly matter would not even exist, never mind Intelligent species. DNA Mutations mathematically if occurring out of random mutation and natural selection would take 16 billion years to form a single new useful trait. Given more time this still would not explain away the chicken and egg problem with DNA itself, because DNA tells the RNA proteins how to build the DNA chain, the RNA proteins can't build DNA without DNA instruction, and DNA can't come into existence without being built by these proteins that are made from DNA instruction, so what came first the DNA or the information for the RNA, the chicken or the egg? The fact is the Universe is an isolated finite system, so without an outside external force to create the matter that created the big bang, there would be no Universe at all. If any of the twenty different fine tuned constants of the Universe were different carbon wouldn't be able to be produced in stars and humans (Carbon based beings) could never exist. Instead of turning to the obvious and true answer of creation by external intervention, they have gone with either the Multi Universe theory or the ancient astronaut theory, few have strafed toward the correct one which is one multi-dimensional universe with a grand designer. God created us, and before the Universe was created he created the Heavens and the Angels. The Angels and their servants are whom the Illuminati call the ascended masters."

"The Fallen Angels are inter-dimensional beings of energy, who left Heaven and came to Earth. They are the unknowns, the nine above the illuminati who control them. The Fallen Angels (Angels who came unto Earth) are the so-called Annunaki from Sumeria, the Star people of the Native Americans, the Serpent Gods from every culture around the ancient antediluvian world. Before the flood the Fallen Angels intermingled with mankind in open view, though being beings from another dimension meant they required great sources of energy to come through the veil, and appear in this realm. That is why they had mankind build the ancient monuments along the electromagnetic field lines, and built with electromagnetic properties, the Angels could feed off this energy and appear in our dimensional plain of visible light. As string theory explains every piece of matter is really vibrating at a frequency. The Angels, these dimensional beings that exist in what we understand as Heaven vibrate at a much higher frequency, a frequency consistent with the human emotion of love. The Angels now trapped in Tarturus the Hyper-Cube, along with the damned souls, and the demons cannot ever enter heaven because their vibrational frequencies have been altered to a low vibrational setting, synonymous with Fear. The Earth, meaning the physical dimension, is caught in the middle, and experiences both phenomena. The flood of Noah occurred to wipe the fallen Angels, and their children from the physical world, and to destroy the Global Civilization they have created to worship themselves. God chained the Angels in the low vibrational frequency of demons, by altering their very being. Putting them in the abyss caused the flood, because their energy forced the underground water to the surface. Now these fallen angels can barely come through the veil and can only enter the physical world in energy form. They want to turn Earth into their own version of Heaven as they will never see Heaven again, hence the saying as above so below, meaning I will make heaven on the Earth."

"The Fallen Angels had created a global civilization that traded over the waters, and created massive megalithic monuments. Huge Temples created to harness the electromagnetic field energy of Earth's Grid. Also to match the stars of the Heaven's because the Fallen Angels wanted to encode the knowledge the Priests would use to create false religions based upon worship of the celestial beings. After the flood, the Angels were not all imprisoned in the Hyper-Cube, only 200 of them were with Azazel, Lucifer the main Angel who taught mankind how to sin and to take a human wives. Some evil Angels remain still today in Heaven and are fighting an ongoing war in Heaven, a war that will one day come to Earth when the head Angel Semyaza (Satan) the beast, the dragon, is knocked from Heaven to Earth, at which point he will then rule the Earth for forty two months. The Bible clearly says we struggle against spiritual wickedness in heaven, but as many mistranslations from original Hebrew to English the meaning was lost. High places in the original Hebrew and Greek text meant Heaven; it was the same word throughout the text."

"For we wrestle not against flesh and blood, but against principalities, against powers, against the rulers of the darkness of this world, against spiritual wickedness in *high places (Heaven)*." Ephesians 6:1-2 KJV

After the flood, the Fallen Angels, the 200 whom descended upon Mount Hermon, a small number of those whom actually rebelled, the ones whom came to Earth, created the secret societies, to rebirth their lost civilization that was on the Earth before the flood. They wanted to put those loyal to them in charge. So they created the Mystery schools and told those in power they were genetically different because they were the direct descendants of the Fallen Angels. Somehow the fallen angel known as Isis infected the bloodline of Ham, and the son Horus, also called Nimrod in Babylon was born half god half human. This elite bloodline eventually became the Illuminati now in charge. We are all to serve the Illuminati and the Illuminati would in turn get the people to worship the Fallen Angels as Gods."

"Why were the Angels booted from Heaven for giving us knowledge?" I ask.

"The Fallen Angels slept with women and created hybrid creatures the Nephilim. The original illuminati bloodlines were the offspring of the Angels with humans; these hybrids were the Pharaohs and Kings of the Ancient world. They are just in their rule because in their belief in Eugenics, that because they descend from the Angels (Olympian Gods, Mayan Gods, Egyptian Gods, Dragon Bloodline of China, Mayan Serpent Gods, etc.) they are more advanced genetically. They believe because knowledge is power, and that they were chosen to receive this knowledge by the Fallen Angels, whom they still converse with, that knowledge and power they have gained gives them the right to rule over the rest of humanity."

"The Illuminati bloodline believes their blood is more than human, and it is true, the proof is held within their DNA. That is why the apprentice pillar in Roslyn Chapel is a depiction of a DNA strain; despite the fact DNA was technically not discovered until much, much later. Odd that Dan Brown, who wrote misinformation on the Illuminati, covered Roslyn Chapel without mentioning the Apprentice Pillar, or the worship of two entities by the Templars one called Asmodeus, the other Baphomet both found prominently displayed in Roslyn. Here is a picture of the Baphomet. Notice the Serpent DNA, the androgyny of male and female, and the Hand of the mysteries two fingers up, three down for as above so below, Sun and stars depicting Day and Night are the same as the Freemasonic pillars depicting Joaz and Bachin."

Baphomet, Eliphas Levi, "Dogmas and Rituals of High Magic", 1861.

"All the knowledge they hold is written permanently in their DNA. They wish to alter their DNA to become more than human once more and to rewrite this history to match the one they have written into our history books. This idea of a Holy Grail or bloodline is not related to Jesus, it comes from the original Ham mixed with Isis bloodline of this elite group of people. They are the only ones who know what they really are and what knowledge was given to mankind. That is why maintaining their bloodline is so vastly important to them and lead to so much intermarriage between members of the royal bloodlines. If the wrong person were to unlock this knowledge, then the entire system could be undone, the slaves, the workforce that is the common man could be freed by this knowledge. As long as the public believes their enslavement is physical and not spiritual they cannot use spirituality to overcome their situation."

"Hasan-I your ancestor had unlocked this knowledge; he infected himself with the Ham DNA he stole from the Templars. When Genghis Khan came across this knowledge in China he decided to rewrite history by spreading his DNA across all of Asia, now 1 in 10 people of Asian descent are descendants of Genghis Khan and therefore hold his memories and knowledge in their blood. Khan's descendants confirmed this knowledge again when they took over Alamut from Hasan-I's descendants."

"Yes, I saw through Hasan-I that they had uncovered something at Temple Mount." I reply. "Hasan-I took one of the chests."

"When Hasan-I took the chest he ingested the blood as instructed to do so, the blood in those vials was left in Alamut after half full. Hasan-I thought the best way to ensure it's continued existence was to store it in two ways as the watchers had done before. The fallen angels had stored the blood in two ways, one within a ruling bloodline, and two in the vial stored within the specially designed superconductive chest of gold that kept the vial from ever going bad. That is why the ruling class has always interbred, to keep this hidden knowledge perfect, they wrongly believed that keeping their blood pure was the only way to retain this knowledge, when in fact the information is never lost even if they reproduce with people outside this bloodline, it is just harder to locate in your memories. The sacred objects, such as the key you stole are shortcuts, because certain objects unlock certain memories more readily, especially ones you didn't know you had hidden deep in the DNA and you're subconscious."

"The vials they found in temple mount contained a genetically engineered virus that would enter the human body; attack the DNA strand, and add the DNA to the existing DNA in the human body. It rebirthed the lost bloodline of the Nephilim that were all killed in the flood, the same bloodline that infected Noah's line of Ham thousands of year's prior, making the new Templars equivalent to the elite royal families. This blood that contained a virus changed DNA, the information for all life, thus making them part human part fallen angel, hybrids. The same type of virus is being created in labs today to solve the riddle of cancer. Cancer is caused when the DNA strain is mutated by the environment and causes cell division dysfunction as the information to divide the cells became corrupt. If you could create a virus that targeted cancer cells at the DNA level, by removing the corrupted DNA code and replacing it with correct DNA code, you could rewrite the DNA with correct code and rid the body of cancer instantly. The DNA in the vials contained no physical changes however; it added the ability to see the memories of human history before the flood, it showed an advanced race of beings known to us as the Watchers and their lost global society sometimes called Atlantis. A society that worshipped the head of the Watchers, under one religion and one law, 'do what thoust wilt is the whole of the Law'. A society where the intellect of man would eventually overcome the limitations of the natural world allowing mankind to evolve and become immortal, to become Gods through Alchemy or self guided evolution."

"Most of this Ancient Global Society is now under the Ocean. Hydro plate theory explains how the ocean levels rose at once worldwide, and buried this ancient society called Atlantis mostly under water all at once. The fallen angels and Nephilim survived this because God, changed them into different vibrational energy and chained them to the abyss, from where the flood waters came. Before the flood the Nephilim had became extremely vicious, and got to a point where mankind could no longer sustain them."

"To separate the seed of Adam from Satan and his fallen angels, God created a man, with very unique DNA, a man who's DNA was altered so that the Fallen Angels and the Nephilim could not ever produce a hybrid creature with; Noah. Unlike his predecessors Noah was born with the new human body plan, a much shorter life span, faster reproduction rate and free from the intermingling of the seed of Noah. Man before Noah lived almost roughly 1,000 years and were the fossils called Neanderthal Man, which are really only humans that lived very long lifespans with far stronger bones that could last 1,000 years. That is why the Bible says Methuselah one of Adam's children lived over 900 years long. Noah was saved and the Nephilim were turned into what we know today as demons, walking the Earth in a low vibrational frequency dimension. Unable to quench their thirst for material pleasures, but watching as mankind enjoys the fruits of the Earth right in front of them. The fallen angels were bound in the abyss, also called Tarturus and watch from below."

"How did the flood happen? What is hydro-plate theory?" I ask.

"Before the flood the Earth was one large continent. There was far less surface water, and there existed far larger underground pools of water. These underground pools still exist but are now much smaller. Around 4,000 BC, the underground pools erupted like a balloon filled with water. These pools broke through the crust and created a massive tear across the globe like a seam on a baseball. The seam can still be seen easily today in the center of all the oceans and separated the Teutonic plates, the mid ocean ridges. The water coming up through the seams brought earth and water and would have flooded the whole Earth with rain and shifted the singular continent apart. Caused rapid freezing of the large animals now extinct and buried their fossils at once. That is why the wooly mammoths are found frozen in action with tropical food in their guts, trees are found buried standing straight up in what is inaccurately called millions of years of strata, strata that came out of the massive explosion all at once. The tree wasn't buried over millions of years, the millions of years of strata was put down at once."

"It actually makes sense, as crazy as it sounds." Jocelyn states.

"Let me ask you a question, why do we find thousands of burial stones in the Amazon from a few thousand years ago, from just before the flood. That depicts humans riding on dinosaurs? Why do we find dinosaur fossils as if they were killed in action all at once and buried instantly? Because they were; the dinosaurs are not millions of years extinct; they died off during the flood, the same flood that reset humanity with Noah. Where Noah landed at Mount Ararat is where all our modern day society stems out from starting at roughly 4,000 BC. The ancient society that was is mainly gone, some of it remained half buried in sand like the Sphinx and Great Pyramid."

"Is it coincidence that based on the ocean ridges that remain that span the globe, one of the furthest spots from these is right where Noah landed his boat and where we find the best preserved remains of this prior civilization? A civilization that existed pre-flood for hundreds of thousands of years according to the Sumerian kings list. A civilization that had much longer lifespans and thereby would have had longer reproduction spans as well. The Illuminati have always known the truth and have used fraud and corruption to hide the evidence. They know the spiritual is real, and they do everything to make you think the Bible and the spiritual are not real. Every religion but Christianity empowers those who grant knowledge and hold power, they are all focused on the self and self empowerment, selfishness. Christianity empowers only the weak, the oppressed, and because it is the truth, the harder it is put down the truer it becomes."

"You must understand, the difference between the physical realm and the spiritual realm is the same as the difference between quantum physics and standard physics. There is no unified theory that connects the two forms of physics. Because standard physics are based on the ultimate illusion that all you can see and touch is all there is, quantum physics tries to explain the connection point of the illusion and the source of the illusion, the spiritual realm's interaction on our dimension. However, the connection between the physical world and the spiritual world, the signal receiver that allows our souls to enter a human body and control the physical body is our DNA. That is why Noah was so important. If the DNA is altered, human souls can still connect but other spiritual entities can intervene and take over blocking the human soul from control. This is how possession occurs. That is also why God did not want Adam to eat the apple (bad seed) that infected his DNA with the Apple (Knowledge) because this altering of the DNA allows for these evil entities, fallen angels to take over the body or to breed offspring."

"This blood left at temple mount was Nephilim blood. It did change the DNA of these first nine Templars allowing them to channel the fallen angels, and their demons. Eventually they were able to summon them by creating rituals that invoked the negative emotion of fear, normally human and animal sacrifices done inside pentagrams to trap the energy of the soul in a state of fear, this lead to Black Sex Magik. As the current change was only subconscious and non-physical, so the body itself showed no change. However, in meditative states Hasan-I could access these apple (seed of the Fallen Angels) memories in his DNA after taking the vial. Also, these Watchers as Hasan-I's DNA was altered could take over Hassan-I, his DNA had been altered turning him into a hybrid that can be remote controlled by these watcher entities. From this he was used to create a small nation, with one false religion, completely devoted citizens, they had advanced alchemical knowledge (how to create superconductive gold) and despite being small were a strong military state. It led the creation of the Fedayeen, known today as Muslim Terrorists. Their assassination techniques were legendary, and the Templars learned from these men and adopted their techniques. However as the source of the teachings was evil, eventually the Fedayeen would become that evil in the form of ISIS and other groups. The Assassin's only collapsed when Genghis Khan took the city but never vanished. Genghis had come across the same knowledge when he invaded China, where they had an entire set of these vials as well. Originally these belonged to the Yellow Emperor of China, who gave the Chinese reading, writing and was the first emperor. The Temple Mount was not the only place in the world with these artifacts. Some have still not been rediscovered and are believed to be under the ocean."

The Lost Truth by Dean Fougere

"Most American's have been programmed by entertainment, education and socialization to believe they live in the shining beacon on the hill, the New Jerusalem, the current day Roman Republic. They see obvious Illuminati Occult Symbols, Pagan Gods all over their public buildings and believe they are living in a Christian Country despite the otherwise obvious truth. The US Dollar bill has not only an all Seeing Eye and pyramid, but also on the upper right corner number 1, contains the Rothson Family shield outline with the Owl God called Moloch peering out on top. The blind people believe that the American system is far and above better than any other system of Governance on the planet and point to their vast economy and military strength as proof. This allows them to feel comfortable that the Government is always acting in their best interest, despite overwhelming evidence to the contrary. They believe they are free because they gained independence from England. In reality they elect a new president every four years, yet every President ever elected has close genetic ties to the Royal Family of Britain, and the country is ruled by the Red Shield Bankers through the Federal Reserve System. They have been conditioned to believe watching tv, eating fast food, driving big trucks, indulging in sports and alcohol, ignoring politics are the American way. That the Constitution and the Declaration of Independence are outdated documents written by what today would be called domestic terrorists. We fight wars on ideologies rather than against actual definable enemies, wars that can go on forever and are used primarily to strip civil liberties and profit the defense industrial complex. Then the Illuminati use organizations such as the CIA, NSA, Military Intelligence, CFR, World Bank, UN etc. to install puppet governments under extreme economic influence from a newly installed central bank run by unknown private investors."

"That is why the first building reconstructed in Iraq, Afghanistan, Libya was not a power plant, a hospital, a police headquarters but it was a brand spanking new central bank. Iran was relieved from massive economic sanctions designed to curtail their nuclear program when they opened their doors to the global central banking system, not when they stopped the nuclear program. Years later Iran and the US are talking about joining forces to stop ISIS and signing a nuclear deal."

"US Independence from Britain to create a democratic society was, just like the French Revolution infiltrated by the Illuminati. Both were allowed to be created to give us the illusion of freedom, based on the Roman Republic model, which was eventually turned into an Empire as well. The Roman Empire was the closest this group ever came to complete World Control since the flood until modern times of course. If not for the arrival of Jesus, the Roman Empire would have grown large enough and powerful enough to control the World. However, the Roman Empire had one major flaw, it was a known entity, something other Empires could target, barbarians could raid. Like all known things, it had a shelf life, it is the unknown that lasts forever, the mystery never ends but truth is final. The one thing the Illuminati, the Proletariat of the time could not plan for nor defeat was the truth of Jesus, which led to the Empire eventually being destroyed. Jesus empowered the poor and oppressed, which killed the Roman model of society. Leaving behind a corrupt Holy Roman Empire that also would perish, but yet still exists in a fashion.

Time and time again this group rebuilds and decided to be even less in the open, no longer would they be known and identified, they would become the unknown force, the enlightened members of society that would guide the world to create one government under their control. They would learn from their defeat that Socialism would be the key because it would empower the mob, and make them dependent upon Government."

"The Illuminati before 1776 realized they needed a new Strong Republic to create the Global Socialist Empire. They used the large countries of empowered citizens to produce a Global Police force that would allow them to rid the world of the current regimes, destroy lines between people and nations, and eventually rid the world of all religions except for one, theirs. These men have gotten so close to the end, and have so much control over the population they have decided they no longer need to operate in the shadows. Their agenda is being pushed on the world at an alarming rate, almost as if they know if they do not institute it quickly the opportunity will vanish."

"The men they placed in charge at the foundation of America, the Freemasons were outnumbered and could only do so much to centralize power. George Washington a 33rd degree Mason but non-Illuminati member thought he was doing well by being a Free Mason, but near his end he uncovered this deception and warned of the Illuminati in his private journals. In Bavaria the actual society called the Illuminati was established in 1776 just before the 4th of July Independence Day on May 1st which is now a communist Holiday and coincides with the human sacrifices of the Beltane Fire Festival. The Bavarian branch was designed to help fuel the French Revolution and for this they were exposed and that branch was eliminated. At this point they stopped using the name the Illuminati, and have since gone by many names such as the hidden hand, the sons of the Nephilim, the enlightened ones, etc."

"Before the Illuminati were discovered by the Bavarian Government, a man named William Huntington Russel was studying with them in Bavaria. Russel would take their doctrines home to the US with him and created a secret society called Skull & Bones which still exists, funded by the Russel Trust and has a chapter at every Ivy League School in America (Harvard, Princeton, Yale, etc.) Though the Illuminati disappeared going underground, and changing their name to the Hidden Hand or a version of that not spoken of. Russel created the Skull and Bones branch at Yale University, a new recruitment wing for the Illuminists. A plaque granted to them by the Illuminati Founder Adam Weishaupt was discovered when Cross and Key another secret society broke into the "Tomb" Skull and Bones HQ and told the world about it."

"Washington did as he was told by the powers that be when the vision was given to him; he was meant to be King but denied this to maintain the Union. The Fallen Angel Isis presented herself to Washington and gave him a vision, but Washington confused this vision and he believed in the republic when the goddess was actually trying to instill the idea of the Union, the empire. So the Illuminists used his vision and created a new path forward from it, realizing over time Americans could be persuaded to give up their freedoms for security. Washington and Jefferson were truly great men and wanted what was best for their people, because they were lower level freemasons, not illuminati they did everything they could to create a free republic. Just like today, most Freemasons think they are participating in something good. You see no one wakes up everyday and tries to do harm, people are far more motivated when they believe their actions are justified and helping society. They wanted to believe they were creating a land for the people by the people, even though they still endorsed slavery, and created a constitution that was mainly written to protect the property of the ruling class."

"However, even the freest society can be slowly taken over by an unseen force, until it is too late and they have complete control without anyone realizing it. You see democracy is not freedom, freedom is freedom, democracy just gives us the right to choose our candidates, the candidates themselves still rule over us. These elected rulers still must then choose to either represent the public or their own interests. If the people who elect them are not informed of what they are doing, then they cannot understand the choices they are voting for. That is why transparency and accountability is key in a democratic republic. If the voting populace is unaware of their elected officials actions, then how can they be held accountable, why would the elected officials do what's best for the public if it is not also best for themselves?"

"By controlling the flow of information, by creating two seemingly opposing political parties that carry out the same agenda, they have confused and separated the non-elite class of society, and now have complete control over their minds. They even reference the lower class as zombies and portray them in countless films for their own amusement; they have people in a frenzy awaiting the zombie apocalypse when it has already begun. The sleepwalking western media fed public, entranced by materialism and entertainment are the zombies of the apocalypse, their inability to wake up and see what is being done to them will be their undoing. The masses of uneducated citizens whom have succumbed to the media propaganda ensure any questions raised by the educated critical thinking masses are not heard. In a world where truth is decided by mass appeal rather than universal truth."

"The flow of information to the public is the most critical part of a democracy, if the public is not informed they cannot ensure their needs are being met, that their freedoms are being preserved by Government and not being taken away. They cannot demand transparency if they are lead to believe it is in their best interest to not know. Hence, the creation of and extreme use of propaganda by the Illuminati. The Illuminati use the media and politicians like puppets, creating false idols for people to worship, and spinning the news by having reporters all reading the same scripts, covering the same stories and ignoring others, they control the agenda and the information."

"These media puppets are easily identifiable because they are either men of political, economic or social influence and normally belong to one of a few committees or groups. They have used their inherited wealth from antiquity to buy any corporation, news outlet that could reveal them. When they say 'free market economy', what they really mean is free from the control of the people."

"The web of control is quite amazing, it's so vast so widespread that no one would ever believe it's true, part of the genius of the plan. The Illuminati create round table groups that they then use by placing key figures at the heads of each group, to steer public opinion without anyone noticing. To guide the group think mentality to get these round table groups to act as one, rule by consensus so none can point the finger at any one person. Not all members of these groups are Illuminati like David Rockefeller, or puppets like Bernard O'Brien, some of them are not even puppets, just there trying to do good and unaware of their surroundings and being manipulated through various means. The organizations they use to create these round table groups are the

Transnational Corporations that are all tied together by shared managing directors, owners, asset management groups, etc."

"The Illuminati created the Federal Reserve, and therefore the Secret Service, the service whose main job is to investigate forgery, the President is secondary, Secret Service is the new praetorian guard, most people only know of their secondary job; protecting VIP's. The secret service was one of the military wings of the Illuminati, and still is. Hitler's rise was funded by the same central bankers, fund both side of the war remember? Hitler was a member of the Illuminati branch Occult Vrill Society, he realized his national socialist society must have certain apparatus for complete control, the same apparatus we now see in America."

"One was the creation of a paramilitary force. Mussolini used the black shirts to intimidate other political parties; the Nazis used the Sturmabteilung (SA) also known as Brown Shirts. These were private mercenaries who could act outside the rules of law. Can you name a paramilitary force that operates in America above the law?"

"Yeah," I said, "Blackwater".

"The Nazi's started rounding up anti-government protestors and disappearing them to secret torture prisons using the Brown shirts, long before they took power. These secret torture sites were call enhanced interrogation centers. Ever heard of those before?"

We both look at eachother. "I have seen them." I say. "Our CIA Black sites are even called enhanced interrogation sites." I say as a chill ran down my back.

The Lost Truth by Dean Fougere

The events of 9/11 lead to the direct creation of Homeland Defense. However, do you know where the term Homeland was first used?

Jocelyn interrupts, "Die Heimat, the Homeland is what Hitler called Germany."

"Do you know how Hitler used a False Flag staged terror attack to take over the German Democratic Government peacefully and institute his final fascist, national socialist state into a constitutional German Republic?"

"No?" I say inquisitively.

"Hitler used his agents to set the German Parliament, the Reichstag building on fire. Then he blamed the fire on his political opponents the Communists and Social Democrats, rounded 4000 of them up with his SA Brown shirts. He ordered in the police state to quell the communist uprising, an uprising that never happened and was started by a fire created by Hitler's own agents. It's called the Hegelian dialect, problem reaction solution. Government secretly causes the problem because it wants to install the policy for the solution. Of course this never happens in America right?"

"Wrong", Prometheus states. "Every war the US has fought has been in reaction to the US being attacked first. Gulf of Tonkin, Vietnamese attack US Warship and we start Vietnam War in earnest over a false flag attack. Civil War, Lincoln sent warships to Fort Sumter and drew fire from the South starting the civil war. Spanish American war we let the Alamo get ransacked and the Battle Cry for the war is 'remember the Alamo'. WW1 Germans told us not to send ships into the war zone, even posted signs in NYC saying not to send ships over. We loaded 3000 people onto the Lusitania, with ammunition making it a viable war target, and it got sunk, low and behold we enter WWI. WWII multiple documents show the US knew the Japanese were going to attack Pearl Harbor, air patrols to the West were reduced, ships left in harbor and as predicted the Japanese struck getting us into WWII. Now the big one, 9/11 has gotten us into the world we are in today and the War on Terror."

"The goal of Hitler was to unify Europe and create a New World Order, and today our current President's and politicians are calling and have done the same thing. The Bilderberg group was created by an ex Nazi Prince Bernhard, and was able to Unify Europe without a shot fired with the creation of the EU, a Bilderberg Plan from the 1950's."

"Most Americans are unaware that President Bernard O'Brien and his Vice President Jared Buck are both Globalists and that is why they were picked by the Bilderberg Group to represent the Illuminati at the top of the Government. The people did elect these criminals; but taking three times the funding from the large banking corporations to get elected certainly helped the O'Brien campaign. O'Brien owes his presidency to big money and so far he has done really well for the Illuminati. Prior to his re-election the big banks and economic elite were celebrating their recovery whilst the average American's wages continued to shrink and the price of living continued to climb. The financial elite are waging war on the independent middle class wealth to ensure they maintain control of the masses."

"The economic elite saw the rise of the middle class in a free and open America. This could not be allowed to continue because free independent wealth gave the citizenry reason and capability to stand up for its rights against the tyrannical financial elite. America at it's founding in 1776 was a radical break from the empires of old. This new rise of a middle free class was too large a threat for the financial elite Illuminati so they decided to destroy it from within. The Illuminati underestimated the growth that would occur from a free market society, the will of the American people for prosperity and freedom. We became too powerful for them to control, the population expanded beyond all belief, and a new plan had to be implemented to destroy the middle class they created without destroying their empire at the same time."

"Their plan for destruction of the middle class was genius. They have used the Republicans to enact economic policy that benefits only the upper class citizens. The Democrats on the other hand only enact legislation that benefits the lower class. Both parties are attacking the middle class, like a vise grip, the upper and lower classes both squeeze on the middle class until it is gone. Leaving us with a two-class system, those who have and those who don't. The lower classes get bigger and bigger and the upper class gain more power and control with every election."

"The illuminati completely control both major political parties currently operating. They use campaign financing obviously but have many other methods of controlling a politician. They offer politicians speaking engagements, job offers, low or no interest loans, book deals, drugs, prostitutes, etc. To ensure the politicians only says and does what the financial interests want them to say. They keep records on every American and especially all political figures to ensure they can be quickly discredited or scandalized if they reveal the truth. The Illuminati puppets are never brought to justice because the Justice System has been completely taken over as well."

"That is why the big issues such as National Security, campaign-funding limits, elimination of lobbyists, and transparency are the same if a Republican Bush or a democrat O'Brien is in the White House. It doesn't matter what these politicians say to get elected, once in office they do as they are told. They would never take on the Federal Reserve System or hold politicians accountable for violating the Logan act and attending Bilderberg. O'Brien won't even speak off the cuff; he reads everything off the teleprompter because without it he is just a pretty face and a charismatic salesman. He has no true ambitions only those of self indulgence hoping to be remembered as a great president. He is a good speaker, and is controllable so he is perfect for the Illuminati spokesperson. The last independent President was Kennedy and he was killed. It's no coincidence O'Brien appointed the same financial minds around him that deregulated the banking industry and lead to the 2008 collapse. These people are connected and therefore are not accountable, no matter what happens on their watch. People like Timothy Geitner should be in prison but instead got a new position and a pay rise when O'Brien and his platform of 'Change' took over. The only change O'Brien brought was he would be allowed to implement just about any policy and if anyone disagreed they were labeled racist. Even if the policies put into place by O'Brien hurt the poor and the black community more than anyone else by enacting economic polices that shrunk the middle class and grew the lower class, no one was allowed to criticize him."

"The Illuminati are trying to bring about the Ancient Promise of a heaven on earth. To do this they have some very sinister things currently under way to ensure we stay asleep and even beg for the New World Order to save us from ourselves. By using false flag events and misinformation they are quickly evaporating the rights of individuals in every country around the world, not just America."

"As outline in United Nations Agenda 21, the idea is to use the threat of climate change to bring about sustainable development. Sustainable development requires the removal of the private rights of the people especially individual landowners, vastly lower the human population, move the majority of the population into large housing districts and prison like cities built on rail lines, remove all human habitation in key areas across the US and World. Use Geo engineering projects to slow the rate of climate change, lower fertility, and calm the public living in close quarters. To slow the rate of development across the globe and eventually depopulate the Earth with war, famine and disease leaving behind only the Illuminati and their servants."

"What Geo Engineering Projects?" I ask.

"One of these is the Chemtrails, these are simply aluminum oxide chemicals being dumped into the stratosphere to block sunlight. Thus creating cloud cover that is highly reflective to sunlight. Contrails are just ice crystals formed by the wing of a plane passing through cold air and dissipate quickly. These Chemtrails as depicted by many videos on YouTube not only stay in the air, but are made in grid patterns and over time spread and fill the sky in some cases. Problem is the aluminum is now falling to Earth on the population making people sick with aluminum poisoning and no one knows because no one is checking for it. It is plain to see if people would just look up, some planes leave small trails behind them that disappear rapidly, whilst others can go from Horizon to Horizon leaving a massive trail that does not dissipate, it just starts to spread and creates a cloud, called cloud seeding. It was first done during Operation Popeye to intensify a monsoon that was going to hit Vietnam to create more flooding, as a weapon during war. The Military has called it owning the weather. Now they are pumping these same Chemtrails into our atmosphere to stop global warming, but the long term affect is brain defects in the population, soil turning acidic, and plants dying from aluminum poisoning."

"Connected directly to the Chemtrails is the fluoridation of water in large cities across the US I mentioned earlier. The by-product of Aluminum processing is a toxic chemical hydroflourosilicic acid called fluoride. Companies used to have to pay millions of dollars to get rid of this toxic waste. Now, they just sell it to local municipalities and they dump it into the public water supply. Turning a loss into a profit, at the expense of the health of every American who drinks public water. It causes a crust to form around the pineal gland in the brain thus keeping people unable to unlock the memories in their DNA. Of course if Chemtrails and water were the only thing they were doing that would be sick enough, but this assault on human health for population control is never ending, you see there are just too many people for the illuminati."

"Since the beginning of history humans have been growing crops, however only until very recently have they been free to do so. With the introduction of genetically modified organisms (GMO's), one company has taken over the entire crop business in the US and even enforces their own patent laws. Monsanto this GMO Monopoly has actually patented certain types of GMO crops, and if farmers are caught reusing their own seeds, instead of buying them from Monsanto they are sued into non-existence. Monsanto tells the farmers how they should grow their crops and why. Of course the rapid climate fluctuations, sudden freezes caused by geo engineering in recent decades forced farmers to use GMO crops to stay competitive or they had to charge more and call their food organic. Countries, farmers who do not use these crops cannot compete and in countries like Mexico have been put out of business by NAFTA. The more you look into the food industry and how the Illuminati Multinational Corporations run it with an Iron Fist, the worse it looks."

"GMO foods lead to higher crop yields in certain cases. However the altering of the DNA has epigenetic effects on the human body. Lowering the human immune system for one, which has seen the rise of allergies, cancer, etc. These GMO foods literally alter the human DNA of the person ingesting the food. In example one of the new genetic modifications is for plant's to produce their own Round Up (Monsanto's Pesticide) internally, which cuts down on the spraying of round up on the crops. It's called round up ready soy. However, the pesticides used to be able to get washed off, now that the plant is producing the pesticide itself you cannot wash it off and you ingest more of the pesticide. Monsanto obviously knows of the aluminum spraying in the Chemtrails because they recently released all their seeds with a new aluminum resistant gene. They have also created what are called terminator seeds, these are seeds that only can be used once, the plants they produce have no seeds and therefore the farmer has to buy new seeds every year from Monsanto instead of recycling the seeds as they have been doing since farming was invented, to pick the best seeds and over time have better crops."

"Why don't people just grow organic and not use Monsanto seeds then?" I ask.

"If an organic farm is next to a GMO farm, and the wind or the insects carry seeds to the organic farm from the GMO farm, that organic farm becomes contaminated with plants that are patented by Monsanto. Thus Monsanto then owns the entire organic farm. You would think the organic farmer would be owed money for contamination of his crops but the courts, which are run by the Illuminati who own Monsanto, ruled in favor of Monsanto, claiming it's the organic farmers fault for letting their crops be contaminated. The food industry is completely taken over by these sick people."

"Cows for example, there used to be many butcher shops, slaughterhouses for the many local suppliers of meat. Now there are only a few slaughterhouses across the entire country all controlled by the same MNC's, sometimes even remotely via a central control room hundreds of miles from any of the actual slaughterhouses. The cows are being fed corn instead of grass, because corn makes the cows fatter quicker. Problem is corn is not normal for the cow digestive system and has lead to the creation of new strains of E Coli. This E Coli then gets into the factory style slaughterhouse where thousands of cows are literally ground up into burger meat for example in one batch. The E Coli goes out, a few hundred people die, and they do a meat recall. No one goes to jail, no changes are made in the process, and the company only loses a small percentage of their profit, while countless families lose loved ones. The US Government stays out of the way because the food industry lobbyists are being appointed to the top seats of the FDA. The current FDA chief is Michael Taylor who was a top executive at Monsanto for example."

"It's all connected, and it's not about the money. The money is just what the super elite Illuminati, the thirteen families that run the world use for control. They know that paper money is meaningless compared to good food, good health, nice homes, precious minerals, land, and money is power."

Nathan Rothschild said (1777-1836): "I care not what puppet is placed on the throne of England to rule the Empire. The man who controls Britain's money supply controls the British Empire and I control the British money supply."

Napoleon who was an Illuminati insider, funded and betrayed by this group for being overly arrogant. Napoleon seeked too much of his own authority so he was destroyed, he even got rid of the private central bank, which was the last straw. Napoleon stated, "Terrorism, War & Bankruptcy are caused by the privatization of money, issued as a debt and compounded by interest."

"If you still do not believe me about the New World Order, hear it from the mouths of those involved."

"The real truth of the matter is, as you and I know, that a financial element in the large centers has owned the government of the U.S. since the days of Andrew Jackson."- U.S. President Franklin D. Roosevelt in a letter written Nov. 21, 1933 to Colonel E. Mandell House

"Today, America would be outraged if U.N. troops entered Los Angeles to restore order. Tomorrow they will be grateful! This is especially true if they were told that there were an outside threat from beyond, whether real or promulgated, that threatened our very existence. It is then that all peoples of the world will plead to deliver them from this evil. The one thing every man fears is the unknown. When presented with this scenario, individual rights will be willingly relinquished for the guarantee of their well-being granted to them by the World Government."- Henry Kissinger, Bilderberger Conference in Evians, France, 1991

"Some even believe we (the Rockefeller family) are part of a secret cabal working against the best interests of the United States, characterizing my family and me as 'internationalists' and of conspiring with others around the world to build a more integrated global political and economic structure – one world, if you will. If that's the charge, I stand guilty, and I am proud of it."- David Rockefeller, Memoirs, page 405

"We are grateful to the Washington Post, The New York Times, Time Magazine and other great publications whose directors have attended our meetings and respected their promises of discretion for almost forty years... It would have been impossible for us to develop our plan for the world if we had been subjected to the lights of publicity during those years. But, the world is now more sophisticated and prepared to march towards a world government. The supranational sovereignty of an intellectual elite and world bankers is surely preferable to the national auto-determination practiced in past centuries."- David Rockefeller, Bilderberg Meeting, June 1991 Baden, Germany

"The Trilateral Commission is intended to be the vehicle for multinational consolidation of the commercial and banking interests by seizing control of the political government of the United States. The Trilateral Commission represents a skillful, coordinated effort to seize control and consolidate the four centers of power political, monetary, intellectual and ecclesiastical. What the Trilateral Commission intends is to create a worldwide economic power superior to the political governments of the nation states involved. As managers and creators of the system, they will rule the future." U.S. Senator Barry Goldwater in his 1964 book: With No Apologies.

"We have before us the opportunity to forge for ourselves and for future generations a new world order, a world where the rule of law, not the rule of the jungle, governs the conduct of nations. When we are successful, and we will be, we have a real chance at this new world order, an order in which a credible United Nations can use its peacekeeping role to fulfill the promise and vision of the U.N.'s founders." President George Bush, 1991

"To keep global resource use within prudent limits while the poor raise their living standards, affluent societies need to consume less. Population, consumption, technology, development, and the environment are linked in complex relationships that bear closely on human welfare in the global neighborhood. Their effective and equitable management calls for a systemic, long-term, global approach guided by the principle of sustainable development, which has been the central lesson from the mounting ecological dangers of recent times. Its universal application is a priority among the tasks of global governance." United Nations Our Global Neighborhood 1995

"I believe we and particularly you, your class, has an incredible window of opportunity to lead in shaping a New World Order for the 21st century." Joe Biden, Naval Academy Graduation, May 29th, 2014.

"Yes there have been differences between America and Europe, no doubt there will be differences in the future. But the burdens of global citizenship continue to bind us together, a change of leadership in Washington will not lift this burden. In this new century Americans and Europeans alike will be required to do more, not less. Partnership and cooperation among nations is not a choice, it is the only way." Barack Obama, Berlin Germany

"2009 is also the first year of global governance, with the establishment of the G20 in the middle of the financial crisis. The climate conference in Copenhagen is another step towards the global management of our planet." E.U. Council President Herman Van Rompuy.

Prometheus clicked on the tv monitor and played a video clip from a Fox New's tv program with Dick Morris (former Clinton advisor) and Shean Hannity.

"There is a big that is going to happen at London this G20 and they're hiding it, camouflaging it, not talking about it. Coordination of international regulation, what they are going to do is to put our Fed and our SEC under the control in effect of the IMF. What it really is… is putting the American economy under international regulation. And those conspiracy theorists, Those people who have been yelling 'oh the UN is gonna take over ... global government'..."

Shean Hannity interrupts: "Conspiracy Theorists"

Dick Morris continues: "Conspiracy Theorists ... they've been crazy, but now, they're right! ... it's happening."

Shean Hannity follows: "When Geithner said he would be open to the idea of a Global Currency last year, those Conspiracy people have said and suggested that for years. You're not wrong."

The tv is clicked off.

"Wow" Is all that I can muster. "This is all true isn't it?"

"How do they get these politicians to support this on local levels?" Jocelyn asks.

Prometheus replies, "Many ways my dear. One is an offer of campaign finance, blackmail, sometimes jobs after their political career, speaking tours. Also if you are a career politician, why would you not want to create a Supra National level of government, with a whole new list of even higher paid, more influential positions awaiting. If you were the US President and were offered to be the first World President wouldn't you do it?"

"Yeah I guess I would." Said Jocelyn.

"A one world order, under one leader has great appeal to the rational mind. It offers the long held hope for World Peace, which in itself is an ideal concept if conceived correctly. The problem is how the Illuminati plan to accomplish this World Peace. If it was done naturally with free will it would be perfect, however the Illuminati believe the only way to bring about World Peace is through total control. Of course they see themselves as the enlightened ones, the Philosopher Kings, whom are to rule over the rest of us and this is justified because if they did not rule, then someone else would. They see the working class as cattle, and if they could replace us they would."

"The planners of the New World Order understand they require one more World War to bring about Global Government. War along with disease, depression, famine and terrorism will scare the world into a New World Order, or at least whatever is left of the world. They need the people to fear war so badly they will hand over their rights, their beliefs for security and peace. This three world war plan was created long before WWI.

In a letter from Albert Pike (Head Freemason in his time, a 33rd degree freemason, buried in the Supreme Council HQ in DC, creator of the KKK the militant arm of the Democratic Party) to Giuseppe Mazzini another 33rd degree Mason creator of the Italian Mafia (MAFIA is an acronym for **M**azzini **A**utorizza **F**urti, **I**ncendi, **A**vvelenamenti, in English: Mazzini Authorizes Thefts, Arson, Poisoning.) Mazzini was a student of the Assassin's Order teachings taken from Hasani Sabbah's library and used them to create the Italian Mafia."

Albert Pike in a letter to Mazzini, once on display in the British Museum dated August 15, 1851, stated:

*The **First World War** must be brought about in order to permit the Illuminati to overthrow the power of the Czars in Russia and of making that country a fortress of atheistic Communism. The divergences caused by the "agentur" (agents) of the Illuminati between the British and Germanic Empires will be used to foment this war. At the end of the war, Communism will be built and used in order to destroy the other governments and in order to weaken the religions."*

*"The **Second World War** must be fomented by taking advantage of the differences between the Fascists and the political Zionists. This war must be brought about so that Nazism is destroyed and that the political Zionism be strong enough to institute a sovereign state of Israel in Palestine. During the Second World War, International Communism must become strong enough in order to balance Christendom, which would be then restrained and held in check until the time when we would need it for the final social cataclysm."*

*"The **Third World War** must be fomented by taking advantage of the differences caused by the "agentur" of the "Illuminati" between the political Zionists and the leaders of Islamic World. The war must be conducted in such a way that Islam (the Moslem Arabic World) and political Zionism (the State of Israel) mutually destroy each other. Meanwhile the other nations, once more divided on this issue will be constrained to fight to the point of complete physical, moral, spiritual and economical exhaustion...We shall unleash the Nihilists and the atheists, and we shall provoke a formidable social cataclysm which in all its horror will show clearly to the nations the effect of absolute atheism, origin of savagery and of the most bloody turmoil. Then everywhere, the citizens, obliged to defend themselves against the world minority of revolutionaries, will exterminate those destroyers of civilization, and the multitude, disillusioned with Christianity, whose deistic spirits will from that moment be without compass or direction, anxious for an ideal, but without knowing where to render its adoration, will receive the true light through the universal manifestation of the pure doctrine of Lucifer, brought finally out in the public view. This manifestation will result from the general reactionary movement which will follow the destruction of Christianity and atheism, both conquered and exterminated at the same time."*

"These people must be stopped." Said Jocelyn angrily. "I can't believe they just come right out and document and say these things. It's like something out of a science fiction movie."

Prometheus interrupts, "What is not well known or documented about their little system is that the Illuminati is not the true top of the pyramid or the giant spider web hanging from a single point. This way the true leader and his well couriers are never found out. To rule from the shadows gives them absolute power, no accountability. When the Illuminati are destroyed they can replace them with something else. There is no one organization, name, person that can be killed to destroy the whole organization. You can call them Illuminati, but that is just a name, it's the meaning of the name that is important."

"The Fallen Angels are the true power behind the Illuminati. These Angels are the top of the order as far as anyone knows. There is a rumor that they are aliens, but this is a deception. There is life out in the cosmos, but from what we know, they have never been to Earth. The current UFO phenomena is a modern day understanding of what has always been known as supernatural phenomena. The heads of the Illuminati know the truth, and the head of them is the Pindar. The Pindar is a representation of the head patriarch of the order, the Pindar means big phallus or big dick basically and is represented by the Obelisk, such as the Washington Monument."

"Wait so you are telling me the head of a group called the Illuminati, who controls the world goes by the name The Big Dick?" Asks Jocelyn.

"Exactly", replies Prometheus. I couldn't help but laugh and try to hide my smile, but soon we all broke out. After a few seconds Prometheus resumes.

"The true problem we are facing is the American Nation is asleep. We need to wake them with their own medicine. The Illuminati use false flag events such as Battleship Maine, Gulf of Tonkin, Fire in the Reichstag, Sandy Hook, 9/11, 2008 financial collapse, Boston Bombings, etc. to bring about war or policy change through fear. The media scrounging for ratings and controlled by the six, soon to be five MNC's of the Illuminati, overhypes these events to ensure eyes are on the screen watching when one of these takes place. After the problem has caused everyone to panic and beg for change they offer it: war and loss of our freedoms for national security. If we create our own false flag event it will open up the media coverage to cover the story. As Edward Snowden showed, the public is waiting for the bomb to drop before taking action."

"So how do we drop the bomb on the public? If the public all awakens at once to the truth, that were are being enslaved by the corporate entities of the Illuminati, won't the public riot and won't the backlash be tighter controls?" I state.

"No you see the American Public needs to be awoken so it can bring about change peacefully, through voting. The American public is rightfully scared of it's now militarized police force and well trained military. The US Military has spent the last 12 years fighting insurgencies and uprisings; they are well trained and equipped to deal with an American uprising of any kind. The Illuminati's biggest problem with the taking over of America has been, one person equals one vote, no matter how rich a person is, his vote only counts once. The rich person can bribe, plead, advertise for his choice but when a person steps into that voting booth, it is just the voter and the ballot. If the Public knew of the Central Banks hold over the entire country they would vote politicians in who would change the system."

"However, we need the media to cover the true story of the Central Banking system, the privately owned Federal Reserve. As long as the tv anchors do not cover this story, it will remain hidden from view. Scarily, the average American born after 1975 spends more time watching tv in their childhood development than with their family on a whole. Meaning their life lessons are coming from a TV set rather than human interaction. This has allowed the Illuminati to brainwash and dumb down the entire world, as American and Western Entertainment is seen around the world, and is starting to penetrate all cultures. Even children in China, Iran countries that block American TV as they see it as propaganda, use their own more obvious propaganda forcing the kids to access western media via the Internet and they do so in alarming numbers. Our global society on a whole is brainwashed by five Mega Media Companies that control everything we see and hear on a TV set. However, our attack will penetrate all these people, when our actions are covered by TV and expose the truth."

"So what's the plan?" I ask.

"You and I are first going to shoot an interview for YouTube, this way we can assure the people understand why you and your followers blew up the Federal Reserve Building, and it's branches in other cities." Prometheus smiles.

Jocelyn and I look at each other, wide eyed, scared, unsure.

Chapter 20 – End of the Fed

Prometheus' Estate, Virginia – Modern Day

The plan itself was quite complex. However, the speech was not. We wanted to state certain facts that would allow the public to investigate on their own. It was designed to ensure the American Public was if not awoken to, at least exposed; to the true nature of the Illuminati Conspiracy for a New World Order to start a mainstream discussion.

Dressed in suits, no masks in a mock TV News Studio, Prometheus and I sat across from one another.

Prometheus nods for me to turn to the camera and one of his bodyguards gave us the three-two-one action hand signal.

Prometheus begins,

"The principles that guided the foundation of America have made this country the greatest country in the history of the world. We created a system based on the will of the people, a system that was designed to protect their rights first and foremost. We identified certain civil liberties and determined from historical philosophy that these were Natural rights every man was born with and called it the bill of rights. Now, the people running this same country are taking away those precious rights that were forged over thousands of years of mankind creating civilizations through trial and error. They are threatening the very fabric of our principles, all under the guise of National Security, continuity of Government has now become more important than the people for whom Government was created to protect the rights of. This is inherently wrong, and it is the reason all of the Philosophies of Liberal Democracy start with the Right to Rebel, which was incorporated into the Bill of Rights as the second amendment. The idea being that Governments should be scared of their people, not the other way around."

"How did this happen, how did we turn into Police State? The answer lies, within, how many people actually researched 9/11? Boston Bombing? Sandy Hook? Aurora Colorado? How many of you heard what happened, watched it on TV, felt terrible and scared for a few days and demanded the Government provide a solution to the problem? How many times did we beg the Government to take our rights away to protect us? How obvious could these false flag operations be before we stand up and demand real answers from those who are elected to serve us?"

"False Flag Operations have defined our modern society. Whether you are talking about the Fire in the Reichstag, that Hitler caused and blamed on the opposition party in his rise to power, or the Gulf of Tonkin that was staged and caused America to lose 58,000 good American boys in the pointless Vietnam War. Vietnam a war that only benefited the banking and multinational corporate complex, whilst sacrificing men completely oblivious to the reality on the altar of profit. Anyone who studied Vietnamese history would not have even once considered the Vietnamese would join with the Chinese, no matter what system of Government they had, even today the Vietnamese and Chinese are fighting. Going back even further you have the Battleship Maine that led to the Spanish American War, and the sinking of the Lusitania that got America into WWI. The economic elite have always waged war, with the citizenry as the cannon fodder, this must come to an end, and we must stop all wars."

I take over, "I am a retied Navy Seal, whom proudly served my country in two foreign wars and I demand answers. How much did US Policy change, and global policy from the events of 9/11? How many people believe the third building on 9/11, tower 7, collapsed completely at free fall speed, which is physically impossible due to the laws of physics, especially from office fires, as a plane didn't hit Tower 7? How can anyone with eyes to see look at the Tower 7 collapse and not see obvious controlled demolition at play? How can you explain that three steel buildings suffered complete total collapse due to fires for the first and only time in history? How does steel melt from office or jet fuel fires when neither of them burn hot enough to melt steel? How did those same fires cause total collapse in 50 minutes when the building is certified to handle far hotter temperatures for hours by UL? Why was a UL employee whistleblower fired for asking questions about the 9/11 investigations? Why was molten steel pouring out of the buildings on video, why did Firefighters report streams of flowing molten steel under the rubble for days after the event when jet fuel and office fires do not burn hot enough to melt steel? Why did the 9/11 commission never even check for evidence of controlled demolition and why did they keep the eyewitness testimonies of explosions, and molten steel from the official report? Nothing inside of the WTC buildings should have burned hot enough to melt steel, unless there was something else there, something that should not have been there. Why did scientists find pure evidence of Nano Thermite particles in the dust, elements that could only have been found in Thermite Charges used by US Military, as the commercial patents did not yet exist? These are demo charges using Nano technology that are designed to melt steel, and explode quietly and self consume. Nano particles were found in the dust of WTC buildings, providing undeniable presence of controlled demolition being used, why? What were the sounds of explosions heard and caught on video before the collapse of the towers?" Dramatic Pause, then I continue.

"Why did US Government sell the WTC buildings lease a few months before 9/11 to a private investor whom insured it for the exact scenario that took place on 9/11? The same investor Larry Silverstein paid 3.2 billion for the lease, and his insurance claim paid him over 7 billion. His insurance doubled because the building was technically hit twice, and the US Gov. found in court it counted as two separate acts. Why has no one mentioned the towers were built with asbestos everywhere, and there was no feasible economic way to renovate or remove the towers, except for the type of event that occurred? Why would a private investor buy a building lease for a building that was losing money and could not be renovated because it was full of asbestos and in the middle of Manhattan?" I say pausing again for effect.

"How does a group of terrorists infiltrate the US, take flying lessons on tiny planes they can barely fly according to their flight instructors, and then capture planes with box cutters and hit 75% of their targets with massive commercial airliners? Not even seasoned commercial pilots could recreate the flight paths that the planes according to the official report took. The plane that hit the Pentagon did a full 360-degree turn at over 500 mph, then flew feet off the deck for hundreds of yards without scratching the lawn, and slammed into the Pentagon disappearing entirely, and that is not a conspiracy theory? The wings of the aircraft flying at sea level at over 500 mph would have been vibrating so violently they may have shaken right off before hitting the building. The maximum velocity of the commercial planes in question could not have reached the speeds indicated by the reports. The plane also hit the Pentagon in the only section of the building that had been renovated for terrorist attacks, luck right? The same section of the Pentagon that got hit, only two days before uncovered a 2.3 trillion dollar missing funds cover-up, and questioned Donald Rumsfeld, but unfortunately all the files were lost in the plane strike, another stroke of good luck, especially for Rumsfeld. Rumsfeld who just happened to be Commander in Chief at the time of the attack as Bush was in a school reading My Pet Goat. The plane just happened to hit the same part of the building holding all the files, so the 2.3 trillion dollars missing will never be found. What a coincidence that the US was conducting a military training exercise the same day, leaving the entire Northeast corridor guarded by only four jets, and causing enough confusion over the realness of the data to ensure none or only one hijacked planes were stopped. There are too many questions that have remain un answered, too many coincidences, too many laws of physics were broken to not ask questions that we deserve answers to, there are 3000 dead civilians who have not been served justice and thousands more soldiers who died based on lies created by the Illuminati." and I wrap up. Prometheus takes over.

"More evidence exists but you must research it yourself. From the New Project for the American Century calling for a New Pearl Harbor, to Operation Northwoods which called for the US to hijack planes, swap them with US Remote controlled aircraft, then haven them flown into NYC buildings coupled with car bombs in DC to be blamed on Cuba and justify an invasion of Cuba forty years before 9/11. A Member of the Bush family was an acting director of the security company guarding the elevators in the months before 9/11 during an elevator reconstruction project. Of course if Nano Thermite was used it would have only been needed to apply it to the shafts of the elevators which had access to the inner core of the building entirely. So who did this to the American People, who would kill 3000 American civilians to go to war?"

Prometheus says, "The answer is simple. Criminal elements of the global banking umbrella corporation that now own the US Government, along with many others, brought down the buildings in a false flag operation. If you think they would never kill 3000 people to start a war, then research the Lusitania being sent unguarded into German waters to start WWI."

"These people whom have taken over the government through a system of banking institutions, and multi-national corporations do not care about America. PLoS One mathematically has proven these MNC's are really one large umbrella corporation, being run through various channels of influence to the same goal. Men like Rockefeller, Rothson, Warburg, Carnegie are not Americans, they are globalists, Illuminati. The time has come for us to free ourselves of their evil agenda to create a one-world government under their rule. If we do not act they will continue to destroy the middle class, our values, our rights and our country. Soon we will all belong to the State, and the State will have control over every aspect of society."

I take over, "These men have their secret meetings and secret societies, set up round table groups and all of this is to push the world into world government. They created the League of Nations, the United Nations, Council on Foreign Relations, Tri-Lateral Commission, World Health Organization, etc. They control who is appointed to these committees through their secret societies such as Skull & Bones, Bohemian Grove, Freemasonry, Lucis Trust, etc. They use access to drugs, sex, clubs, money and power to create political puppets to afraid to speak out for fear of blackmail. Celebrities such as Jay-Z, Miley Cirus, Michael Jackson, Madonna, all are puppets of these powerful men, portraying their values and symbols in their music videos and concerts. Clubs such as Sanctum, Magic Castle, Club 33 all are private clubs where these elite can do whatever they want, while the rest of society is spied on and controlled by an overarching Intelligence System. If we all should have nothing to hide and accept the police state, then why have these financial titans, movie stars all become more and more obsessed with VIP access, and privacy? Those who do fight them or spread the wrong message, are turned, destroyed in the public eye or last resort killed such as JFK,

RFK, MLK, Malcom X, etc. Why would Dave Chappelle turn down 50 million dollars and run to Africa? Chappelle wouldn't promote their agenda and refused to give up creative control for money, so they labeled him as crazy. You have to ask yourself, if these societies aren't real, if they don't really run the world we live in, how come the media never mentions them?"

"The elite have many names, however they can be collectively called the Illuminati. They are the true evil on this planet, and they have taken the authority from the people for themselves. Long have we been warned of this elect group of individuals by our founding fathers, and yet we still allowed them to take over. It is not their fault for taking over; it is ours for being so blind we let it happen. They offered us security if only we would hand over our rights and we thanked them for it. Who wouldn't with towers being flown into by planes, subway stations being gassed, threats of nuclear war, the Cold War, the threat of Germany in WWII, now the threat of China, Russia, Ebola, climate change, terrorism, and financial collapse all designed and caused to bring about world government. Fear has been their tool, and as their tool it has been very effective."

"So if the media won't televise this information, if the political sphere was just created to give you an illusion of choice, what is there left to do?"

Prometheus jumps in, "When the politicians blatantly lie, when the media is in bed with them and covers it up, when all the policies of America hurt the middle class and hurt the freedoms we fight for… there remains but one option. The right to rebel. I will be your leader; I Prometheus will come forward and guide you to prosperity after the fall of the Globalist Empire. Will you do your part, will you restore America to it's rightful place as the land of the free and the brave, will you act on the words you have pledged to defend or cower in defeat?"

I jump in, "I will not be defeated by some criminal bankers. I will show them that even their temples of money can be destroyed. That is why tomorrow I will blow up the Federal Reserve building in conjunction with the other branches, to destroy the building of our slavery, to ensure the American Public wakes up to the nightmare that is the Federal Reserve and their Illuminati Banking Masters. We will free the nation by resetting the National Debt, if we destroy all the central banks at once the debt record for the US will be lost forever. The revolution starts today, with me, and we will restore the republic. Join us."

Prometheus concludes, "If you love freedom, if you love liberty then be prepared to fight and die for it. I will lead those whom are willing to bring back the US we all love."

Prometheus nods, and the camera shut off. He looks at me with his one good eye, "Now the world is counting on you to save us."

"Not a problem lets go back over the plan again." I state happy to be done with the film. "When do we release the video?"

"Tonight, we will put it on YouTube and email a copy to various alternative media sources. Then tomorrow after my plan goes to perfection and the Fed is lying in rubble, the video will be found and go viral, sparking America into action. You see nothing lights a fire in the minds of men quite like the truth." Prometheus smiles.

Chapter 21 – Fire in the Minds of Men

Prometheus' Estate, Virginia – Modern Day

That night Jocelyn and I spent the evening in Prometheus house. It was the first time we were to sleep in different rooms since we had met. Though we had not had a physical relationship I could feel the tension every time I looked at her. I decided tonight I was going to make my feelings known, as I may not have another chance.

We sat by a fire in Prometheus's library, surrounded by the paintings of famous men whom defied the Illuminati. I had spent hours researching them on the Internet after our long talk the first night I arrived. It seems they are very real and their symbolism is everywhere you look, especially in the entertainment industry. The idea is to program the public into accepting things before they happen, to hide things in plain site that only the subconscious mind is aware of, unless you understand the conspiracy then your conscious mind sees the symbols and subconsciously programs the mind and you never see the obviousness of the truth. TV which broadcasts with a flicker rate that puts the mind into a beta wave frequency is perfect for conveying subconscious hidden messages through emotional triggers, as the beta wave state puts the mind in a trance like sleep state where the subconscious takes over and allows you to believe what you are seeing. Many top intelligence operatives will not watch TV because they know it has been used for mind programming purposes for years; hence it's name TV programming.

Jocelyn is wearing some clothes she has borrowed from my luggage, as she had not packed pajamas. I smile over at her, "You look good in my pants." I quip.

She takes a small sip of wine, looks up from her book, "Nice line movie star, but you'll have to do better than that to get in my pants."

"Really, well what if I told you that I was your prince charming here to save you and the rest of the world, but it would only work if you gave me true love's kiss?" I say jokingly.

"I'd tell you to find true love first." She laughs.

"So why did you decide to come with me in the first place? I mean did you ever imagine being on such a wild goose chase?" I ask.

She looks over at me with her bright green eyes, smiles ever so slightly, "There was something different about you. Why did you pick me to be your accomplice on this?"

"You were perfect, everything about you has not only exceeded my expectations but has blown them away. Every time I look at you I get this weird relaxed, can't even describe it, sensation and I could listen to you talk for hours. There is something between us isn't there, like we were meant to be together?" I ask.

Her eyes lit up, she put her glass down, and "We are perfect." As she climbs on top of me on the couch, I feel her lips press against mine. The sensation is overwhelming, the young hard body presses down on me yearning for touch. I embrace every second of it, exploring her body as she did mine. We soon prop chairs to the library doors and make love on the bearskin rug by the fireplace. The liquor, the setting, and the danger we had overcome, all being released in physical ecstasy.

Unknown to us, a hidden camera caught the entire thing on tape. As it is happening Prometheus watches live in his room. The entire house seems empty of electronics but underneath, hidden within the bowels of this house is a different story. Cameras set in the eyes of stuffed animals, hidden in lampshades; the entire house is not as it seems.

That night we make love in the Library of Prometheus and sleep in the same room. The next morning comes all to quickly and the reality of our plan hits me like a ton of bricks.

■ ■

Prometheus' Estate, Virgnia – Modern Day

As I awake I smell the fresh scent emanating from Jocelyn's hair. I caress her shoulder and slightly kiss her on the cheek as she sleeps. I rethought about our wild night in the Library and I hope no one noticed. I can smell the strong waft of bacon and coffee in the air.

Entering the main hall I hear Prometheus call for me from a side dining room. The room itself is beautiful, with large panoramic windows that look out over the valley and stream below.

"Running water, fuels the energy we need to survive, I always buy homes near running water." Prometheus states. "How did you sleep last night?"

"Quite well actually." I lie. I had spent the better part of the night kindling the new fire that burned within. I saw a small smirk on Prometheus face and wondered if he knew.

Prometheus seemed to notice me looking at him with wonderment and starts, "The plan is all set, you will travel with my guards, and they will get you inside the Federal Reserve building. Once inside you will need to bring the device to the basement, it is preset for Midnight, so you will have plenty of time to get out. Before midnight strikes I will initiate an evacuation protocol of the building and get anyone out before the bomb goes. We have hacked through the firewall and will set off a fire alarm at 11:50 enough time to get everyone out but not enough time for the Fire Department to get inside and get hurt. No need for any casualties, it will only hurt our cause. No one cares about a bank building, but the innocent guards and firefighters are another matter."

"How is our video doing?" I ask.

"Well, it has a mere 25 views thus far and most of the comments are in regards to the still standing Federal Reserve building, calling you a liar basically." Prometheus top aide states as he walked into the room.

Prometheus smiles, "Sorry forgot to introduce you to one of my best aides, this is my intelligence officer Temoh."

Temoh extends his hand, his eyes had two different colors. His left eye bright green, his right eye had no color just black except for the white Iris. Must be a birth defect, I think to myself. I shank his hand.

Temoh says, "Technically my name is actually Temohpab, however Americans can never pronounce it, so it's just Temoh. I am not just an intelligence officer for Prometheus but I also do a lot of work with the Music Industry for him as well. I picked the background music for our video we aired last night."

"Have to make money and influence people somehow." Interrupts Prometheus as he gives his aide Temoh a strong glare. "I see what they are all watching and listening to and I like to make my influence felt. Having all this money means I get to use it for good as I see it."

"True, so are we going to have breakfast before taking down the system?" I ask.

"Prometheus smiles, "Absolutely it is on it's way in now." As his last word came out the door burst open with waiters, carrying four plates. In the door behind them walks Jocelyn in brand new clothes left out for her by Prometheus. She looked stunning in the outfit; somehow it fit her perfectly as if it has been tailor-made. She thanks Prometheus for the gift.

Before we eat, I decide to say grace for the food as I do before every meal. This seems to agitate Prometheus and Temoh as both excused them from the room as I do it, supposedly to take a phone call, but I hear no ring. This gives me a very odd feeling.

After breakfast Jocelyn and I go for a walk down to the riverside. I tell her to lay low, and when the shit hits the fan to take Prometheus's car and get out of dodge. We will meet up at the Dulles Airport after the big event. We both have an uneasy feeling about Prometheus, which only worsened with the introduction of Temoh. However his plan does seem honest and he does seem to need us to carry it out.

Chapter 22 – Under Cover of Darkness

Washington DC – Modern Day

The wait seems forever. We sit 2 miles outside the Capitol City waiting for the shift change at the Reserve Building. At precisely 10:30 pm the guards would change out, allowing us to slip in as a maintenance crew. Prometheus has guards on his payroll. Temoh had explained the Guard in charge of watching the camera systems is being blackmailed by Prometheus; supposedly the guard has a problem with pedophilia.

At 10:25 we pull into the parking lot behind the building. The guard at the gate sees our fake badges and let us right in. Three of us will go in, pretending to be carrying computer components to the sub levels of the Fed Reserve Building.

"In and out" Temoh exasperated, "Don't look any guards in the eye and keep your cool, tomorrow is a new day. This is the first step towards a New World."

The three of us nod and each grabs a box from the back of the SUV. I can feel the box pressing down on my two berretta 9mm's with silencers attached hidden under my shirt. Fortunately we would be bypassing the security system thanks to the night shift guard's child prostitution problem. Seems all the guards in the reserve building have some dirty secret that Prometheus knew of and uses against them, combined with a bribe the guards had no choice but to cooperate.

The three of us walk up to back door entrance. It is locked so we knock. The guard at the back gate walks over and peers out through the glass revolving door and hits the unlock button.

We burst into action, moving through the door and walking through the security gate. All three of us set off the buzzer; the guard looks uneasily at us and after a slight hesitation motions for us to continue. He looks at Temoh specifically and seems to be overwhelmed with fear. As we reach the elevator, I look back and see Temoh standing over a dead body, I never heard him make the kill but the end result is gruesome, organs and blood cover the hallway. Temoh walks towards us as he places his machete back on his hip, the guards head rolls across the floor separate from the body.

The elevator opens and there is an unexpected guard inside, Temoh does not hesitate, drops his package and pulls out a silenced revolver .44 magnum and blows the guards brains all over the back of the elevator.

I grab Temoh and shove him into the elevator with my berretta pressed into his temple. "Hit the button" I say to his accomplice. "What the fuck are you thinking?" I ask Temoh.

"He already made us, I could see it in his eyes. He was full of fear and I could smell it on him, just as I can smell it on you now." Temoh declared victoriously. "If you kill me, you will never get out of here alive." He finishes.

"No casualties were the deal. If you can't keep that finger off the trigger I will bury you down here under a pile of rubble with me."

"No need," his partner says, "we are cool, no more shooting, no worries."

"Temoh" I say pressing the tip of my pistol hard into his skull.

Temoh turns his head almost a full 180 from the wall to staring back at me, then glares at me directly in my eyes, whilst his eyes become almost complete black, "Fine, no more using my hand cannon on your precious slaves."

I pull him off the back wall of the elevator as the door opened. His face and front covered in blood. He doesn't even bother to wipe it off, instead in a grotesque manner he decides to lick it off his lips and fingers.

"You are a sick fuck." I say to him.

"Time to go our separate ways he says, see you on the flip side." Temoh and the other guard take off down the hallway. I head the other direction still wondering if I am doing the right thing.

As I reach the load-bearing wall on the north side of the building I detach the thermite charges. Somehow Prometheus got his hands on next generation explosives for this job. These Nano Thermite explosives were only available to the US Military, and when they exploded there was almost no noise and it used heat to melt the steel and concrete. These had been upgraded with a lot of extra fuel that would allow it to spray in both directions causing a huge gash in the concrete and steel wall. The idea was to cut the walls supporting the massive structure in the middle and the outside shell of the building would collapse on itself. Destroying just the building and not causing damage to the area.

I hear my phone vibrate. I check it, a message from Temoh, says charges planted we are in SUV waiting. "How the hell did they already plant the charges?" I ask myself out loud, they had further to go and I have not even started yet.

Trying to hurry I place the device on the wall. As I was about to hit the start timer button for 11:50; I hear boots coming down the hall, walking. I quickly pull my two Berettas out and aim them in the direction. Coming around the corner is a young kid, obviously walking the rounds. I decide to hide to spare his life rather than fire.

As I duck around the corner I bump into a chair, the sound of metal on granite floor was deafening in the silence.

Instantly the guard starts running towards the sound. "Over watch, this is sub guard 2, I have possible movement on my floor do you have anything on camera?"

"Sub 2, this is over watch, that is a big negative, maybe it's the Ghost of Andrew Jackson down there again." The guard laughs at that comment.

"Right, thanks for the help over watch, sorry to bother you with your job."

"Sub 1 this is Sub 2, you hear anything weird?" He pauses. "Sub 1 do you copy over?" Pauses, silence.

"Over watch, I lost contact with Sub 1, do you have him on camera?"

"Sub 2, over watch. He was headed up to the lavatory in the elevator, probably not getting signal." As the radio call came in I peer around the corner, and see the guard starting to look at the device on the wall next to me. He starts moving towards it. Shit, I guess curiosity really did kill the cat. I take a deep breath, ready my Berettas and turn the corner to face the guard.

The guard's eyes lit up and he moves to his waste to pull out his pistol. I take a second longer than normal to aim and pulled the trigger. The pistol kicked back and the silencer blocked out his head. When I looked the guard is down, pistol round clean through the forehead, blood and brain matter everywhere as the full metal 9mm round went clean through his skull leaving a massive exit wound.

Quickly I move back over to the device. Just as I am about to hit the button I hear a voice from behind me. I turn startled, nothing is there, but I have to investigate. The something out of the corner of my eye ducks around a corner on the far side of the room down the hallway I entered from. The device isn't set to go off for over an hour, if someone saw it, they could compromise the operation. I had to find this person. I hit the arm button and turn towards the sound.

Heading towards the hall a chill enters the air, I hear only the sound of my boots on the hard marble floor, smooth as silk, same as the walls. The marble interlocked without any mortar, making the structure reliant upon precise geometry. Then I see him, a man in the middle of the hall with his back to me, his height is unbelievable, must be 15 feet tall, can't make out any depictions other than a outline, he is wearing a hat and long trench coat. As I move towards him the lights in the hall flicker and for a second go out. When they flash back to full light he is gone.

I hurry towards where I last saw him and on the left side of the Hall is a door. On the top of the door is a strange looking sculpture of an owl. On the floor in front of the door is the Free Masonic square and compass. On the door itself is the OSS Seal, the OSS was the precursor to the CIA and it's seal is reflective of the Skull & Bones

Society that founded it, and therefore the Illuminati whom founded Skull & Bones. The

door itself is built into the granite wall and is made of a very heavy looking metal that

is very secure. It has two notches about the size of coins, so I take the coins out from

the Newport Tower and decide it is worth a try. Fortunately or not, the door unlocks. So

I push the door open to reveal a dark chamber within.

I feel a light switch to my right and raise my left hand with the berretta as I flip

the switch. Hoping whoever is inside would get scared when I hit the lights and I could

quickly put a round through their head.

As the lights flicked on the room is empty of people. However, in the middle of

the room is a spiral staircase. "I don't have time for this." I say out loud as I start to

descend the stairs. My feet on the metal steps make quite a bit of racket. The steps seem

to go on forever underground. At the bottom I realize I have entered a Tomb.

As the stairs came to an end I am on a walkway between two pools of water. I

must have reached the underground water level of DC. Hanging above each pit is a

medieval looking cage, and both cages have human remains in them. On the far side of

the walkway is another door, large and black with a massively large skull and

crossbones hanging over it.

Pushing the door open reveals a large round table. Red Lights came on from above making the room rather eerie. The table has Nine Chairs; one Chair is more elaborate than the rest, almost a throne. On the top of the head chair is the visage of the all Seeing Eye and pyramid. In the center of the table is a hole about six feet long and two feet wide. Peering down into the hole I see the top of a coffin.

"I got to know who is in this thing." I say. The same voice I heard before I hear again, next to my ear. "Titus." I quickly turn but nothing. No one behind me, no one in the room, I turn back to the casket. I open it, and my eyes cannot believe what I am looking at.

Chapter 23 – Darkness defines the Light

Prometheus' Estate, Virginia – Modern Day

After Titus left Prometheus' estate with Temoh, Jocelyn went to the library to continue her reading while waiting for everyone, so as to be distracted before trying to escape. She knows her only hope is the Phantom that belongs to Prometheus. Titus had assured her the vehicle would protect her exit from a decent amount of gunfire as the vehicle has been modified with armor plating and resistant windows from the look of it.

As she is reading through some of the old books in the library, a young dashing man in a business suit enters the room. He is quite handsome except for an eye patch over his right eye. He walks over and extends his hand, "Azazel nice to meet you."

"What?" Jocelyn recoils, "Who are you?"

Prometheus smiles, and removes his eye patch, revealing a grotesque eye that looks like a bulbous grape, except red. "My war wound, falling from heaven takes it's toll." Though my body unlike yours Jocelyn is not bound to this dimension, I can take any form that I wish or step out of this dimension completely." As Prometheus spoke he vanishes before Jocelyn's eyes.

Jocelyn frightened turns to run for the open door when she hears Prometheus talking to her from inside her own head, which causes her to stop dead cold.

"There is nowhere to run, nothing you can hide from me, and I see everything. This universe is and has been my domain since the fall. I am the God of Earth, your creator that stubborn architect, you call God, also is my father and has abandoned me in this prison and you with me. He created mankind to replace me at his right hand, I foresaw my fate and decided to change the game, to enter the Illusion and become God myself."

"You see the Universe is an Illusion; you are stuck in a virtual digital illusion created by God altered by me to be a prison for your mind, to test your soul, to ensure your soul will worship me, the Son who rebelled against him. I saw the inferior beings he called humans, I came to Earth and I was going to replace them with an upgraded version, my own children whom would be worthy of their place. The humans that were on Earth, I and my fellow angels gave wisdom to, for only the price of their obedience and a few of their women to serve as our wives."

"I decided to come to Earth to upgrade mankind into the next stage of evolution to help mankind by giving them knowledge and upgrading their bodies with our DNA, to give them the ability to achieve eternal life. However, once we altered the DNA, they were no longer humans, they were Nephilim. They had different physical traits, some were much larger in size, and they were recorded as Giants, created by spiritual beings they had a more developed third eye they could use to communicate with the Angels in the non-physical dimensions that surround and pass through what you know as reality. It is the Nephilim whom built the ancient megalithic structures, under the direct command of my fellow Angels, all 200 of us that descended upon Mount Hermon thousands of years ago. We have seen humanity rise and fall over and over again, this time we will avoid the complete reset with our new technology."

"You see God killed our children, the Nephilim and turned them into spirits that wander the Earth unable to eat or drink, yet still hunger and thirst, stuck in a dimensional void having to watch as humans enjoy the Earth they conquered. The flood occurred, and then God saved Noah, whom had altered the remaining human DNA, post the flood to ensure I could not bring them back. I and my fellow Angels saved some of the Nephilim from the flood but God used mankind, especially the Native Americans to hunt them down and bury them in Serpent Mounds. Before long the entire seed of the Angels was dead, only their bodies and stored DNA remained. Until I brought Osiris back from the dead with my soul in his place. I just wanted to create a heaven on Earth, to save mankind from its ignorance, I cannot help that my offspring were greater than those of God. I cannot help that God will not allow us to have eternal life in the physical world, that He demands worship, I wanted to set humans free from the physical illusion that surrounds them, I would have been their God. Even after I repented I was not forgiven, I was left here, and he forgave all of mankind instead of me, now here I am stuck with the worst of you."

Then Jocelyn felt the room shift, all the hairs on her neck stood straight up, the room dropped temperature enough that she saw her breathe. Fear spread through her like a plague, almost buckling her to her knees. The voice returned, "I want you to meet someone."

As he says this, a black mass appears in front of her and starts to shape the outline of a man. All the candles lighting the library go out. In the darkness she could still see the outline forming, and then it moves and it approaches her. She screams but no noise comes out, her knees buckled in fear and as she fell the black shadow grabbed her, catching her, he peers down into her face, "I am Magog."

He sticks a needle in her thigh, and depresses a large amount of genetically altered heroine, used to cause a dissociated state that would allow the person to be cognoscente but super calm and unable to disobey, but unlike normal heroine you had increased sensitivity to feelings, pain or pleasure.

"Let's go for a ride." Magog states. He stands her up, and two guards rush in to hold her upright.

Prometheus reappears out of thin air behind them, looking old as he had the night before. All the candles relight as he appears. "I gave man the gift of fire, intellect, to change the world, and all you have done is destroy it, I shall take back over and guide you to eternity." He walks over, "Now my little slut, you will keep my General here happy and like it. While your boyfriend, whom you fucked in my library blows himself to smithereens and the American Economy along with it. The chaos of losing the Federal Reserve through violence rather than by law, along with what they will find in the rubble, and not find, will cause the American dream to finally end, awakening the masses who have been dreaming far too long. Revolution will ensue when the people wake up to the reality of their banking masters, and after the fires have destroyed the world, we shall emerge like a phoenix from the flames and bring about our New World. America could only destroy itself, the revolution will be violent."

"We will end the stem of freedom brought on by the creation of a middle uppity class. The end result will be WW3, the final war, Armageddon, the final social cataclysm shall come to pass, and this war has already begun between Israel and the Muslims, but now will expand into the arena of the world powers. Then my son, who is alive and well hidden will present himself as the World's savior, perform miracles and get all to worship me. Once I have enough souls under my command, Semyaza shall prevail in his battle in the Heavens, and we will find a way using technology to join him in Heaven, the tribulation will be avoided, the curse reversed, the sword removed from the stone. I will return home after thousands of years of imprisonment, and we shall take the Throne of Heaven for myself. My son will rule the physical Universe, and I Lucifer shall Rule over the Heavens."

"Looks like the last time you tried it didn't end up so well for your eye?" Jocelyn asks.

"I can see far more with one eye, than you can with two. The human concept of reality is a joke. Humans say they exist, and the Universe is enormous so another intelligent species must also exist. You do not comprehend the complexity of the human body, the machine your soul operates, the symbiotic relationships that must exist for your life to even happen. The Universe did not happen by chance, it is entirely anthropic, and it all must be exactly the way it is for you to even exist at all. The gift of life was the greatest gift of all and we angels whom were made first were not even allowed to partake, just to watch and to serve humanity who was given this great privilege yet did not even offer God thanks."

"The cosmological constant is the fine-tuning proof that this universe is a product of a design, not infinite but finite. That is why I had the masons build temples for me showing the fine tuning of the universe construct, as above so below. The fine-tuning of the 20 various laws of physics that must be symbiotically interacting for a Universe to exist at all are so mathematically impossible that they could not have occurred by chance. The cosmological constant must exist and is just one example of the fine-tuning of the Universe that allows everything to exist in one physical reality, though the existence of the other dimensions are also a part of this reality that science has yet accounted for hence the separation between the two fields of physics. The Universe's Cosmological Constant one of twenty laws has been fine tuned to 1 part in 1 (with 120 zeroes after it, 1,000,000,000,000 etc.). It also changes, implying an architect is altering the laws of reality as time goes on. The Fibonacci sequence found in nature is one smaller example of clear design. This does not happen by chance. The theory of evolution based on accident and natural selection is based upon science that did not take into account quantum physics, DNA, the Atom, etc. Micro-evolution is true, but macro-evolution is a farce."

"Macro-Evolution was one of my gifts to the world, and is utter nonsense. It cannot be scientifically true because it violates the laws of nature, and is mathematically impossible to have happened by chance. Macro-Evolution violates both the laws of Biogenesis that states a bird cannot mate with a fish (animal kinds can only procreate with it's own kind) and the 2nd Law of Thermodynamics that states all things move towards entropy, in an isolated system disorder (devolution) can only increase. The very existence of DNA is proof that the mutations were not accidental. The DNA code would have to be altered so drastically for a bird to all of a sudden have feathers for flight, that it could never happen by chance. DNA mutation and natural selection would require far more time, supposedly 16 billion years for every single new genetic feature, never mind entire new species. As the Universe is roughly 16 billion years old, that kills the idea of DNA Mutation by natural selection. Even though the science, the modern science completely disproves macro-evolution, it is till being touted as the truth and being taught as part of the standardized education system while intelligent design, is silenced."

"Evolution is extremely important to our agenda, because it justifies the theory of eugenics. Eugenics is what we have the elite believing in so that they justify their actions based upon the idea that their DNA is superior to others; therefore a massive depopulation event can speed up the process of evolution. We will be able to use eugenics to tightly control population growth by identifying certain traits that are unacceptable and only allowing babies with perfect DNA sequences to be born."

"My favorite part of the evolution theory is how I sold it through my Illuminati agents to the masses. I had the families such as the Rockefellers hide any archaeological evidence of the Nephilim by creating institutions such as the Smithsonian Institute. They used the same institutes to present findings that only support evolution even if the findings are fakes, like the Piltdown Man, a fake hoaxed by members of the British Royal society so well done it was fact in textbooks for 50 years. By paying off experts to sell findings such as Lucy another fake, as the proof of evolution, we continue to win in the arena of public opinion. Even if every finding such as Lucy is later identified as fake, the public's attention span isn't long enough to follow up on the findings years later. Every one of these Lucy type finds showing a cross species from man to ape has been discredited after a period of time. Most experts say the only difference from the bone structure of the infamous human skeletons and others similar, are racial differences, that these skeletons were most likely Human with different racial features than what exists today. Then based on fake fossil findings we have artists create their own creative impressions of what a cross species would look like, and we push those completely irrelevant images to the public, mostly cartoons."

"That is incredible, because anyone who believes in creation instead of evolution is mocked as a backward religious fanatic and ignorant of science when in truth it is the opposite?" Jocelyn asks.

"Exactly, because I had my Illuminati Agents buy all the media, write all the texts, create the scholarship funds that chose who would become famous, we have completely fooled the world into believing many false notions. All these artistic renditions of evolution are based upon no evidence at all, just artistic creations of a false reality, but the public is so uneducated and dumbed down they bought it. For one the majority of the world is now atheist, and doesn't believe in the supernatural dimension that surrounds them every day they exist, where they really come from. They are floating on a blue speck of dust in a giant universe of mathematical perfection and think it is all just occurring by chance, it is the most ignorant society to ever exist."

"Once you understand the fundamental building blocks of life, you will understand that no human, nor any animal was created by chance. The entire system has been designed to allow the creation of mankind to take place, for what purpose? God has said to allow for the manifestation and eventual destruction of Evil. However he created Evil and tied it to me. I argue for good there must be evil, so that can't be the purpose. I think "I Am" wanted to be worshipped and needed someone to blame for mistakes so I was chosen. Why am I to blame for all mankind's sins? I gave them intelligence, told them a small lie about death, so I am to blame for all the sins that come after? Semyaza my brother fights for me in Heaven, he recounts the sins of mankind to God at his left hand side, you call him Satan the deceiver or accuser, but all he says is what man is doing, saying if God can forgive man, why should he not forgive me, and release me from my chains holding me from Heaven, locking me in this dimensional prison, chained to the vibrational frequency of the emotional fear?"

"You will never win" Jocelyn cries out defiantly.

"I already have, my son, the Anti-Christ is already alive. He will start fulfilling prophecy according to the all the worlds' religions except true Christianity. He will bring the world to Peace under his rule. The Jews will claim him their savior, the Muslims will call him the Mahdi, the Buddhists will declare him the fifth Buddha, some Christians will be fooled into thinking he is the return of their savior. My angels created all the religions but true Christianity, that is why their symbols, their ideas of dualism are all the same at their core, the New Age movement is mine, based on a simple lie, that fear and love, good and evil are equal, that there is no sin."

"My son will be able to explain the mysteries of the Universe and will be hailed as the Teacher, the same global teacher that all the other religions are waiting for. All but the true Christians whose savior already came, and thanks to me, will never come back.

The result will be the unification of the World under his rule. Of course we need to dramatically depopulate the Earth before we can rule. As one of my agents Brzezinski has stated, '*it is infinitely easier today to kill a million people than to control a million people.*'"

"My son will help me take the Throne by ruling on Earth. I will unleash the dragon on the Christians and the end result will be my son becoming the first ruler of the New World Order post World War III. The Illuminati will wait, watching from their bunkers as the world powers destroy themselves and wipe 95% of the worlds' population from the map. I will have them unleash nuclear war, bioweapons, famine, disease all designed to reduce the masses to a more controllable level. Only the elite will survive in bunkers we have been building for years. Our recent rapid construction of these underground bases has been causing some rather embarrassing sinkholes around the globe, but we are almost completely finished."

"This war will be awful; but worth it in the end, we will have our Utopian New World Order, with everything in society ordered, efficiency maximized. From the ashes of the seed of Adam, we will rebirth more than human, Gods, and our society will be designed to serve us, without the public ever becoming aware. Jesus will not return to save the children of men if they no longer exist, if the DNA has been altered enough mankind will no longer exist at all and we will avoid judgment."

"The great dragon buried in the Mountain in the East is China. Just as prophesized the army of 200 million, has been created and is ready to March. Its fate is tied to that of Iran, whom provides nearly a third of its oil. You see I will bring about the war of Armageddon early, before the return of the Son of Man, I will fake his return with technology, and when my son brings the world government and peace, they will worship him for it, and in turn me for being his Father."

"How will you get the world to go back to war?" Jocelyn asks.

"The Chinese will continue it's aggressive nature and further side with Russia, they will stop using the Fed Reserve notes as the world reserve currency. The two sides will align with allies over the issue of Iran vs ISIS backed by Saudi Arabia and the Illuminati. Syria will get Russia on it's side, as Syria is Russia's gateway to the Mediterranean and houses the newly refurbished Russian Mediterranean HQ at Tarsus. Iran will get China's backing, as China currently imports 30% of it's oil from Iran, and that number is rising with the sanctions being removed by the US. China, will require more and more oil, and will eventually use it's 200 million man army to break out of the American Encirclement of China and Russia to capture the middle eastern oil fields. To appease the Muslims whose lands they will be capturing, they will offer to wipe out Israel for them. To create a global caliphate under Iran's rule, behind what will be called the Mahdi Army and be set up in the Levant."

"Europe, Israel and the US will join forces under the command of NATO. The result will be World War III and a fake Armageddon. Out of the ashes we will rise, we will fake the arrival of the messiah as my son using space technology, and he will use our new army of half human half machine robots, drones, and all other means of killer machines to lead the Forces of Europe and America and create a New World Order. Just as Israel is about to fall to the Islamic Caliphate, the Illuminati New World Order will strike down from bringing fire from the heavens and save Israel."

"This is the final war to create our global New World Order; I have little time left and will never be stronger than I am now. The atheists communists will join with the Muslims vs political Zionism and all three will wipe themselves out, allowing for Luciferianism to become the world religion. You are heading with Magog to the Mountain in the West, and my army of drones, space weapons, and super human soldiers are being manufactured to use at the last moment when all seems lost. The time for the final social cataclysm has begun."

Magog stuck her with another needle of the heroin, making her fall further into a drug induced but awake coma state. He then threw her over his shoulder and heading towards the bookshelf on the far wall. Jocelyn sees him pull on a book and the bookshelf swung inward revealing a hall and elevator.

The door of the elevator has a large image of a two Giants painted on it. "That is my brother Gog and I." Magog laughs. "The British still worship us as the Guardians of the City of London, the epicenter of our Illuminati Central Banking system. Gog and I still guard the gold symbolically."

After a long ride down the elevator they reach a subterranean railway. Jocelyn notices the track seems strange, the metal bands of the track have a green and golden tinge to them.

"The fastest way to anywhere on the planet." Magog laughs, "Superconductive gold, the most important rare earth element ever created by man and we are the only ones who know how to create it. Combined with Low Energy Nuclear Reactions we will have the power production and transfer ability to build a new world. It is the future technology that will allow us to rule over the Earth and even the Heavens. The future that awaits us, once we have rid the world of it's surplus population and useless genetic history we will unveil our advanced technology and rebuild the world as our own heaven, we will all be immortal. Elysium will be built here on Earth, but only for those for whom natural selection has chosen. The world will be ours, the Nephilim shall have their heaven on Earth, as above so below."

On the side of the train is a logo, a pyramid with the all seeing on top. Next to the pyramid is the word's 'Angel Tech'. The train itself is nicely furbished, and Magog places Jocelyn into a chair. She calmly stares out the window, feeling the strong sensation of heroine in her veins.

"This train travels at 1,666 km/h, fastest train in the world, utilizing the technology given to mankind by us, Angel Tech they call it. We will be there soon." With that Magog turns and sits across from her in a large plush chair. Large enveloping tyrian purple curtains make the high tech train feel royal, definitely appeals to an older soul. She could feel his eyes surveying her body; she thinks she can sense him reading her mind. All she can think of is her missed opportunity to escape before Prometheus had entered the library. What will happen to Titus, will he figure out the nature of this deception before it is too late?

What seems an eternity passes by. In reality, she has no idea how long it has been. They reach a train station. The strange heroine in Jocelyn's system seems to be wearing off. Welcome to "Denver International Airport" Magog says. "Well 666 feet below the Airport anyways." bellows Magog. Far above them stands the white horse of the Apocalypse, greeting DIA visitors with the ominous glow of it's red eyes. Inside the Airport is a mural painting showing the plan for the birth of the New World Order, and the blond haired blue eyed Son of Azazel being depicted as the world savior. Hiding the nature of their entire plan in plain sight, just to show how powerful they were. The airport even has a plaque stating the New World Airport Commission is to thank for it's founding, and has a Masonic Square and Compass with the letter G inside of it.

Once on the train platform they face a large blast door. Magog is carrying her more than she carries herself; she seems tiny compared to his mass. Jocelyn's head is pounding from the drugs. The blast doors are massive in size, easily the size of the doors she remembers from boatyard sheds in the marina Titus and her had visited. On the top right and top left were two automated gun turrets equipped with mini-guns, and on the ground next to either side of the door were guards, but not humans. These were advanced robots with glowing red eyes and built in rifles, standing at attention. "Thanks to Boston Dynamics, Google and DARPA the first fully Robotic Army will be unleashed by us, when the population of West begs for us to save them from the horrors of WW3. We will use these weapons to create a new form of governance, a technocracy. A world government, to serve the Transnational Financial Elite, allowing us the Sons of God to usher humanity to a new world. Humans will merge with our nanotechnology and live forever with superhuman like abilities; this merger will leave no true humans left on Earth. Every extinction event leads to advancement in evolution, we will steer this extinction event to only allow the most intelligent individuals left alive. Then we will start over and create our Utopia, and the new mode of production change thanks to robotics will replace the working class we are about to kill off."

At this point the blast doors creaked, and slowly opened. Inch by inch revealing a massive science laboratory behind the doors. Mixed amongst the countless workstations, surrounded by glass walls were massive human skeletons, and robotic parts. There was a hum of a thousand scientists all working away at various compartmentalized workstations. Cameras covered the entire facility, with microphones everywhere; everything was seen and recorded by someone unseen. All the scientists had RFID tattoos on their wrist, which served as their identification and monitored their movements inside and outside the facility. Walking up and down the corridors were what seemed 8 foot tall, half human half-machine creatures, armed to the teeth. Each had one an artificial left red eye that glowed. "That is something out of the terminator films." Jocelyn scoffed.

A man in a lab coat approached them. "Welcome to the future, my name is Johan Kammler, son of Hanz Kammler." He reaches forward to shake her hand.

"Hanz Kammler? The Nazi SS officer who headed the Germans advanced technology program and conducted some of the most disturbing scientific studies ever devised?" Jocelyn asks.

"The one and the same. My father defected to the US post WW2, as he had heard thousands of Nazi Scientists including his close friend Werner von Braum had been given a second chance. As a member of the Vrill society, the Skull and Bones organization was quick to grant him amnesty. My father had breached the dimensional veil, his Die Glocke, the bell could rip a whole in the space-time dimension and enter the other dimension, which exists all around us but is unseen, where the Nephilim and angels reside. We reverse engineered Angel technology that they use to bring human bodies to their dimension in the hopes they may rebirth the Nephilim through genetic experiments. That is where the UFO abduction account comes from, it's not alien, and it's demonic as the two top researchers of UFOs Jacques Vallee and J Allen Hynick both concluded. Life does exist other than Earth, however they have never been to Earth mainly because they exist at other points in time during the Universe. As you know humans have only been around a small amount of time, the Universe has been around for a long time, it tells us advanced life is not likely to exist at the same time as us, elsewhere in this finite system."

Magog interjects. "These new robots are ready for production, they seem perfect to me." Then he looks at Jocelyn, "Who do you think funded the terminator series? Who do you think runs Hollywood? We own Hollywood, through blackmail, finances, and mind control. Some of the most violent serial killers were under complete demonic control, created through the Monarch Mind Control Program we helped the CIA develop. Monarch was originally called MK Ultra, MK Ultra was started in the Nazi concentration camps under Dr. Mengel, his research and technology came over after the war, to start MK Ultra. Why do you think the monarch butterfly symbol shows up so often in Hollywood, it's called predictive programming."

"The entertainment industry is owned by the Banking Empire, they are the same people the fallen Angels have given the knowledge to rule mankind, the CEO's of these major entertainment empires are our puppets. They do as the Illuminati tell them; Azazel gives them money, fortune, fame for only their souls. If they betray us, they will quickly find themselves dead, for no man can kill an Angel, and no man can hide from the all Seeing Eye, once you sign your soul over, he can see you anywhere you go, and once you have made the deal there is no turning back. By the time you realize it is all too real, it is far too late."

Kammler intercedes. "You must understand Azazel is on humanities side. He and the other fallen ones came to Earth because they loved us so much, for this they were cast out of heaven. Since we have been trying to re-create a heaven on Earth in their design. To live forever; to escape death and the pits of hell and live as mortals for eternity; to conquer the heavens, man's greatest challenge. Now with the development of machines; the Nephilim will be able to make the transition from mere electromagnetic spirits to flesh and blood once more. The DNA of the Nephilim were the key to mixing humanity with machines, the Nephilim were transformed into electromagnetic spirits, and their DNA allows them to connect to the machines, by mixing it with ours, we can allow the human body to interact with the electromagnetic field."

Kammler sees my discomfort, noticing his plans are torturing my mind. He smiles very eerily and continues.

"Nothing is more enjoyable than torturing a human, or watching them be sacrificed. That is why we love war, nothing is more entertaining than watching humans be sacrificed by their leaders for our purposes. Before the alternative media blew the lid off Bohemian Grove we used to perform actual human sacrifices there. The photographer Hunter S. Thompson used to film our snuff films, and then we made him a hero by casting Johnny Depp as him in Fear and Loathing in Las Vegas. We feed off the power of your fear. We will unleash the titans, the Nephilim back on Earth as our whip, to keep humanity in line. They will have to be part machine, part flesh, thanks to God making the Nephilim DNA incompatible with human DNA. The Nephilim will become the Warrior class of Plato's republic, and we the Illuminati are the enlightened masters. All we have to do is as the Fallen Angels wish, and they just want what is best for all of us, to create a heaven on Earth and grant us eternal life."

Magog laughed, "To create a Utopia we must eliminate free will, uncontrolled procreation, all lead to rebellion in mankind, which is an unstoppable force that must be eliminated. We will ensure we can control every person alive, we will eliminate the existence of paper currency. We will force everyone to adopt a new electronic currency that will be on individual RFID Microchip tattoos, controlled by the New World Bank, with interest paid to private secret investors, the same model as the Federal Reserve System already in place but reborn into a global socialist state. We the illuminati created the Communist Manifesto; Karl Marx was nothing more than a secretary. The Manifesto even states it was created by 'The League', which just so happens to be us."

Kammler continues, "In our new system, everyone will get paid enough money to survive each week and no more, ensuring whatever remnants of humanity remaining will be motivated to keep working. Of course once a human is chipped it will alter their DNA with Nephilim blood, so they are no longer a human, and can no longer keep the bloodline of Noah's son Shem alive. Once the bloodline of Shem is completely gone, we win. No real revelation, no return of Jesus as the Son of Man to punish us for what we have done. All prices will be tightly controlled. Better workers will be given small weekly bonuses. At the end of the week the chips will be wiped, ensuring no one can save money from one week to another, which would allow the accumulation of individual wealth, individual wealth as we learned from America is a threat to our future and current control structure. No one in society will be allowed to have more wealth than another member to avoid theft, jealousy, and violence. Of course the Illuminati elite will be exempt from these rules and will live separate from society, keeping their massive amounts of wealth to distribute as they see fit."

"People will not allow you to Microchip them, people will revolt!" Jocelyn yells.

"The cattle, your people, will beg us for the opportunity to have these chips inserted into their brain. Less than 5% of the global population as ever even heard of the mark of the beast, and those people will be killed at the start of WW3. We will have the New World Order either by conquest or consent and the religion of Christianity has forced us to use conquest. We have created lists of names in every country; those who believe in Christ or Nationalism such as the US constitution specifically the 2nd amendment are on the kill list, anyone else who refuses the chip will go to a FEMA Internment camp for re-education. Our analysts predict in the US alone 30 million will have to be killed, another 55 million will have to be brainwashed completely in re-education due to the Judeo-Christian background in this country. The entertainment and education industry has already completely re-educated the rest of society already for us as atheist and addicted to technology and materialism. The majority of the masses only believes in the five senses, and the material Universe, with technology we will lock them into this microcosm of the much larger plane of reality and they will be easily controllable."

"You see all these RFID brain chips will be wirelessly connected to the AI Supercomputer we are building, like a cloud or the Internet giving anyone connected access to information instantly. All thoughts and information uploaded instantly, the AI will eliminate any thoughts contrary to predetermined beliefs. Anyone without this brain rfid chip will be considered useless in the future society, where information can be accessed instantly. It will be called the third eye, and be the ultimate tool of upper middle class in society, just below the top of the pyramid, the elite will be the most tightly controlled members of society, just as they are today. Pyramid compartmentalization of society means most are in the bottom rung, all want to move up, and the closer you get to the top the more controlled and compartmentalized you become. The lowest class will only receive the chip in their wrist, and will mainly be used for manual labor and human sacrifice. The lowest class must be maintained to ensure others in society fear falling into this class and stay motivated to receive the slightly more funds they receive each week. The RFID chips will function as a persons ID, without it they won't be able to buy or sell goods, receive medical attention, pass through any security, etc. People will see the convenience of this system, and will have no choice to get chipped or not have money and die. Any form of alternative currency will be called terrorism and be subject to new anti-terrorist legislation that do noes require review in court, such as NDAA 2012."

"The chips will all have locators on them. The brain chips already can and will monitor the brain waves for any anti-government thoughts, religious thoughts, or anything else we deem a threat. Thoughts will be punishable as crime in our New World. The

O'Brien administration didn't get the go ahead to start the brain initiative because we were interested in helping humanity; we did it so we could map the brain for the implementation of the brain chip. To control the brain you must understand the brain. So using taxpayer money we learned how to control the human thought processes, change memories, implant memories, to control the mind with technology. If we determine the individual is a threat we will shut off their chip cutting them off from society. Or if they commit violence against us, we will send a kill signal to the chip and fry the person's brain instantly."

"Your sick, of course the Illuminati inner circle of Families will be exempt from this?" Jocelyn asks.

"That is true." Magog laughs. "They will have different brain chips that cannot be used for control of their own thoughts but will have all the benefits that the public wants them for."

"What is your role? Where is the army of Robots, where are they, where is Titus?" Jocelyn asks.

"Ha you make me laugh, human beings are so simple minded. To think God would replace Azazel with Jesus at his right hand just for the sake of mankind, a lesser life form, who came long after us, is ridiculous. The plan is quite simple. You won't live long enough to see it, so don't worry about it."

"As they walked through the aisles, she saw what amounted to giant human skeletons, ranging from roughly 8 feet tall to one that was at least 15 feet tall. Their skulls were strange in shape, elongated heads, massive jawbones, and strange bone structures that were not human. What are these?" She asks.

Kammler smiles, "These are the skeletal remains of the Nephilim, the Giants from Genesis. These Nephilim were far smarter, stronger, and larger than their human counterparts. Created when the Sons of God came into the daughters of men and the daughters of men gave birth to their children. These children the Nephilim (fallen ones), are the Ancient Aliens, the ones who built the pyramids with advanced technology given to them by the Angels as described in the Book of Enoch. A book our puppets the Black Nobility in the Vatican had removed because it would open too many eyes to the truth."

Kammler states, "Enoch was one of a bloodline of men that lived pre flood, his line was untainted by the Nephilim, he most accurately described the watchers, the fallen angels and their children the Nephilim. Enoch was a direct descendant of Adam, and a grandfather of Noah, and his name means teaching. The names of these men from Adam to Noah all have meaning and all form a message when in order, a message that reveals the coming of the one you call savior Jesus Christ, who would come thousands of years after Noah. Adam (Man), Seth (Appointed), Enosh (Mortal), Kenan (Sorrow), Mahalalel (The blessed god), Jared (Shall come down), Enoch (Teaching), Methuselah

(His death shall bring), Lamech (despairing), Noah (Comfort and Rest). Man appointed mortal sorrow. The blessed God shall come down teaching. His death shall bring despairing, comfort and rest. Just from the names of the children of Adam we can see the truth in the biblical prophecy of Jesus."

Kammler continued, "This proof of Jesus Christ had to be hidden, and was real, it's power had threatened to destroy the Roman Empire, because the more the Christians were oppressed the more their religion grew. So through the Black Nobility, our descendants of the Philistines backed Emperor Constantine, who took over the Christian faith as a last ditch effort to save the Roman Empire, and used it for their own purposes. They had to remove the writings of Enoch from the bible, and they mixed the true Christian religion with the existing multitudes of Roman pagan religions to ease the transition for the Roman people. That is why Christmas got placed on the winter solstice date, what they are really celebrating is Saturnalia, worship of the planet Saturn, also called the Remphan Star and a major symbol of Freemasonry. Films we fund in modern times such as Zeitgeist have used the mixing of Christianity with Pagan dates and symbols as proof the religion is like the others and nothing more than Sun Worship. The other religions, such as Paganism are worship of the material Universe and the order of the stars, but Christianity was always set against this. Deuteronomy 4:19 states,"

'And lest thou lift up thine eyes unto heaven, and when thou seest the sun, and the moon, and the stars, even all the host of heaven, shouldest be driven to worship them,

and serve them, which the LORD thy God hath divided unto all nations under the whole heaven.'

"True Christianity is a threat to the prison religions created by our forefathers of the mystery schools, religions all based upon Sun & Saturn Worship. As long as we had the people worshipping the Sun as their god, and other false idols, the people believed only the Priest Class and Royalty could speak to the Sun Gods or other Gods, and because of this the people would worship them. The Christians and their true teachings about a Greater Universe than what we could see, and a grand designer is dangerous because they are true. The idea that a person could speak to God directly, and that this life was just a test, meant people would not come to us to be saved, they would not believe in our prison religions that kept the populace in control. We couldn't get the people to build our massive temples, to do as we said if they didn't think they needed us. We have built an entire system of churches, temples, religions, sports, celebrities, and musicians for people to worship to be under control. To ensure the masses do not seek God directly we build temples, based on the lie that you can't speak to God directly but need to go to a building or Priest to do so. The 33rd degree Freemasons always knew the human body is the real temple, and no temple building is needed unless you want to speak with the fallen Angels. It is the Fallen Angels who draw power from the temples of the Ancient sites, that is why all the ancient sites have higher than usual EMF fields, and are built on the Global EMF field grid, and built with materials that are highly conductive, like special stone, the demonic entities, fallen angels, and their lesser counterparts the demons and damned souls draw from the EMF field and use it to manifest. The Angels of Heaven do not draw from the EMF field because their vibrational energy is on a much higher frequency and are powered by the same vibrational frequency as the emotion of love, which comes from the source or as we call it God."

"Enoch stated what the apple of Eden was, the knowledge that was given to mankind by the fallen Angels, he even gave mankind our true names in Heaven, not the names given to us after we fell such as Satan. You must know of what Enoch taught to see how real the situation is, and by removing his writing and changing what remained they made Angels seem as myth not reality."

Kammler pulled out a document and started reading, "Book of the Watchers, Chapter 1,

1 The words of the blessing of Enoch, wherewith he blessed the elect and righteous, who will be 2 living in the day of tribulation, when all the wicked and godless are to be removed. And he took up his parable and said -Enoch a righteous man, whose eyes were opened by God, saw the vision of the Holy One in the heavens, which the angels showed me, and from them I heard everything, and from them I understood as I saw, but not for this generation, but for a remote one which is for to come.

Chapter 6

1 And it came to pass when the children of men had multiplied that in those days were

born unto them beautiful and comely daughters.2 And the angels, the children of the heaven, saw and lusted after them, and said to one another: 'Come, let us choose us wives from among the children of men 3 and beget us children.' And Semjaza, who was their leader, said unto them: 'I fear ye will not4 indeed agree to do this deed, and I alone shall have to pay the penalty of a great sin.' And they all answered him and said: 'Let us all swear an oath, and all bind ourselves by mutual imprecations5 not to abandon this plan but to do this thing.' Then sware they all together and bound themselves6 by mutual imprecations upon it. And they were in all two hundred; who descended in the days of Jared on the summit of Mount Hermon, and they called it Mount Hermon, because they had sworn7 and bound themselves by mutual imprecations upon it. And these are the names of their leaders: Samlaza, their leader, Araklba, Rameel, Kokablel, Tamlel, Ramlel, Danel, Ezeqeel, Baraqijal,8 Asael, Armaros, Batarel, Ananel, Zaqiel, Samsapeel, Satarel, Turel, Jomjael, Sariel. These are their chiefs of tens.

Chapter 7

1 And all the others together with them took unto themselves wives, and each chose for himself one, and they began to go in unto them and to defile themselves with them, and they taught them charms2and enchantments, and the cutting of roots, and made them acquainted with plants. And they3 became pregnant, and they bare great giants, whose height was three thousand ells: Who consumed4 all the acquisitions of men. And when men could no longer sustain them, the giants turned against5 them and devoured mankind. And they began to sin against birds, and beasts, and reptiles, and6 fish, and to devour one another's flesh, and drink the blood. Then the earth laid accusation against the lawless ones.

Chapter 8

1 And Azazel taught men to make swords, and knives, and shields, and breastplates, and made known to them the metals of the earth and the art of working them, and bracelets, and ornaments, and the use of antimony, and the beautifying of the eyelids, and all kinds of costly stones, and all

2 colouring tinctures. And there arose much godlessness, and they committed fornication, and they

3 were led astray, and became corrupt in all their ways. Semjaza taught enchantments, and root-cuttings, 'Armaros the resolving of enchantments, Baraqijal (taught) astrology, Kokabel the constellations, Ezeqeel the knowledge of the clouds, Araqiel the signs of the earth, Shamsiel the signs of the sun, and Sariel the course of the moon. And as men perished, they cried, and their cry went up to heaven . . .

Kammler continues, "In the 19th century, archaeologists started uncovering these remains of Giants, these finds were even covered by the New York times. Sir Flinders Petrie the most important Egyptian archaeologist of his time recorded hundreds of remains of a giant species across Egypt, and up to Lebanon. Time however erases all history of such events. The Smithsonian Institute, was created by the Rockefeller Foundation and fused with the Carnegie Endowment ensured these Giants would never be studied in the public eye. The Smithsonian went worldwide with the help of the British Museum, created by the Rothson's and the Royal Family to recover any of these finds and stored them originally in area 51. Area 51 was chosen because they had found a large cache of these remains at the Area 51 Military Installation by accident when constructing an underground nuclear bunker for their developmental aircraft testing facility. Most of the remains of the pre-flood world are underground buried by the sediment laid down by the flood. Area 51 drew too much attention, because when the remains were unearthed, the demons who were trapped there, spirits of the air, made themselves known to the public. The UFO craze was used to hide the fact that US Military technology had taken massive leaps forward due to information given to them by demonic spirits.

We had to move fast and the demonic entities were introduced to our researchers as aliens, and a secret deal was struck with the fallen angel's Nephilim to change their identity from demons in the public eye to aliens in exchange for technology from the past. They thought the human race would be more susceptible to trusting an alien than a demonic entity. The US created a fictional alien story backed by sightings of our advanced military technology being tested at the base; occasionally a demonic entity would be let loose or summoned to cause truly spectacular sightings normally fireballs moving across the sky at incredible speeds. Fallen Angels and demons being made of energy, are not restricted by physical constraints and can appear as anything. After the public uproar we moved the findings to Wright Patterson Airbase until we built the Denver International Airbase Underground facility. Now here under DIA and in our secret underground facilities across the US all connected via underground railways. We have all the recovered Nephilim remains along with the texts from Temple mount; sacred artifacts recovered worldwide, all hidden away with all the evidence of these in ancient texts and hieroglyphs. We even faked the Rosetta stone to ensure people would never be able to translate the hieroglyphs correctly." Kammler says.

"These Nephilim are the described in Numbers 13:33 of the Bible. One of the reasons the numbers 13 and 33 are major numbers in Masonic Tradition. 13 Illuminati families, 13 degrees of Freemasonry, the Anti-Christ is the 13th pillar, also 33 degrees of knowledge, etc." Jocelyn states.

Kammler interrupts, "And there we saw the giants, the sons of Anak, which come of the giants: and we were in our own sight as grasshoppers, and so we were in their sight." Numbers 13:33

Magog happily interjects, "Of course in ancient Hebrew and ancient greek, Giants is translated as Nephilim, which means fallen ones. The sons of Anak are the Anunaki of Sumeria, also known as the Anastazi of North America. Anunaki and Anastazi means from the heavens they came. Angels are commonly referred to as stars because they appear as beings of light and fire in the sky."

Kammler excitedly jumps back in, "We have thousands of these skeletons; all prove the existence of the Nephilim. The largest find was at the groom lake facility, where a mass grave was discovered buried deep in the desert, called Area 51, the opening of this grave unleashed a massive amount of demonic energy, leading to the mass increase UFO encounters nationwide, an undesired consequence. The ultimate proof we found the Nephilim was the DNA analysis, showing clear non-human genomes that appear out of nowhere. The pre flood human civilization was far more advanced than what we have even recreated. Seems Ecclesiastes 1:9 was correct, 'what has been will be again, what has been done will be done again; there is nothing new under the sun.'"

"Finding these lost cities such as Troy, there was one big remaining lost mythical city, Atlantis, to find it we mapped the Mid Atlantic ridge using side scanning sonar technology developed in WHOI (Woods Hole Oceanographic Institute). The same technology that helped Dr. Robert Ballard find the Titanic and Bismarck. Of course, Atlantis was not found because it never existed; however a worldwide civilization did exist pre flood. Under water cites, including massive Pyramids such as the one off the Coast of Japan, a massive bridge underwater off Southern India connecting Sri Lanka to the mainland, a mile long breakwater in the Bahamas, over 200 cities on the bottom of the Mediterranean, a city under the English Channel, etc. 90% of the Egyptian finds are still buried in the sediments. The massive megalithic structures, the trilithon of Lebanon, Stonehenge, the pyramids all over the world built with massive stones, all built by this civilization that was wiped from the map by a flood. The stones of these ancient sites and their astronomical alignment point to dates of construction much earlier than we are told. The mathematics and astrological knowledge vanished with these cultures until our modern age. The question has always been what happened to them, what caused the flood? We figured it out." Kammler states.

"The flood of Noah happened roughly 4,000 BC. The hydro-plate theory as you have been told. Sent floodwaters over even the highest peaks such as Mount Everest, depositing seashells, which have been found on the summit of Everest. The amount of vapor created in the impact would have caused massive global rain for a month in areas not hit by the massive wall of water and sediment form the Earth's core that deposited a layer of silt over the entire planet all at once. The water vapor even shot some material into space thus creating meteorites that have been returning to Earth since." Showing her a global 3D model of the impact and the change in Earth's continents.

"One of the oldest sights in history Gobleki Teppe in Turkey looks as if it was covered over by sand all at once. Why would anyone bury his or her own city? They didn't the flood waters dropped a large amount of sediment over everything all at once, mystery solved. Only cities at high elevation survived such as Macchu Picchu untouched on the tops of mountains far from the splits gushing out water creating new oceans and massive underwater mountains and peaks."

Magog interrupts, "You see the Bible when it was translated from Hebrew to English was intentionally mistranslated by members of the black nobility whom were loyal to the Templars, and therefore the Sons of the Nephilim. The literal translation of the text describing the flood of Noah is this:

....those that lie in wait in heaven are loosed and the foundations of the Earth do shake. The Earth is utterly broken down, the Earth is clean dissolved (broken up) the Earth is *moved exceedingly*. The Earth shall reel to and fro like a drunkard, and shall be removed like a cottage. Isaiah 24:18-20

Magog continues, those that lie in wait in the heavens are angels, when they impacted Earth they caused the whole Earth to shake, and break apart. The release of the subterranean pools of water causing the massive mid ocean ridges to form and flooding the whole earth was like nothing ever seen before or since. God said he wouldn't flood the Earth again, and this is true because the subterranean water is now the oceans and can't explode out of the core of the Earth again. If we flood the planet by melting the ice caps that will be gradual not Biblical."

Because the flood deposited a lot of sediment at once it has lead the scientific community to great confusion. The father of stratigraphy stated stratigraphy is how to study the way the flood deposited the world's sediments and fossils within. The field has been misused since to state fossils are much older than what is real. The oil fields for example all test young, because the oil was made during the flood when animals and organics were compressed rapidly under high pressure from the hot subterranean water and earth dropped on them instantly. Think water and vapor volcanoes across Earth. Labs today can make oil instantly by using pressure and heat but at way to high a price to be used as an energy source."

Kammler intercedes, "The old structures, made from before the flood of Noah were part of a worldwide human civilization that was under the fallen angels rule. Before the flood the Fallen Angels could come and go from the physical dimension to heaven as they pleased. That is why the people reported seeing the Gods, and their fiery chariots streak across the sky. Before the flood of Noah, the Angels, good and bad fought it out on the Earth. This is where the Indian stories of massive air battles in the ancient text of the Mahabharata came from. The Angels whom still reside in Heaven can still do this; they visit Earth all the time, lending a hand in a time of need, but are never seen. God ruled they could no longer influence mankind directly, only indirectly, they still watch over humanity reaching down and changing the world as directed by the grand designer, God. They bring messages when commanded by God, the good Angels are messengers and protectors."

"The evidence of the precursor civilization is seen in almost every ancient megalithic sight. You can see the differences from the ancient megalithic structure that was pre-flood and the primitive stonework of modern times. The Egyptians, Mayans, Inca, etc. did not build their megalithic structures they merely renovated them. That is why the newer stonework is always smaller stone, less precise masonry that what was made thousands of years prior. A civilization would not become less technologically proficient over time as we are lead to believe by mainstream historians. These renovations made it appear as if the primitive cultures of Egyptians or Mayans actually built these sites. We now know for sure, due to the precision, size of the blocks, knowledge of acoustics, EMF fields, constellation alignments, mathematical perfection, etc. that these ancient structures were not constructed by a less technologically advanced society, but by a more advanced technologically speaking society than ours. Meaning they had knowledge of electricity, resonant frequency, sacred geometry, machining tools, etc., before they disappeared from existence due to the flood. Everything in the Universe is a result of frequencies and they knew this long before our society even began."

Magog booms, "The flood changed us. The Nephilim our children were all turned into demons for their materialism. God punished the Nephilim for taking as many woman as they could and for eating all the animals they could find, till they could find no more and starting eating humans, until the human population could no longer sustain them. We now would wander the Earth without physical form, unable to eat, nor drink, nor have sex, but still able to yearn for it and see it, to still want the material world without being able to have it. The Bene ha Elohim (angels, sons of god), remained as Angels of Light (energy beings), though those who slept with women have been barred from Heaven, our energy transformed into one of a much lower vibrational frequency fear, which is almost the same energy as electricity, rather than love. Our leader Azazel was imprisoned there, in the core of the Earth, too deep to ever dig out, now only in spirit can Azazel visit this threshold. In hell none are able to take physical form, and there the soul can find no water, no air, it is hot and there is a lot of dead souls all climbing on each other, eating each other, raping each other, thousands upon thousands of them. Azazel is chained on a high mountain forced to watch them all, he can move about the

Earth in spiritual form but his spirit is always chained simultaneously in Tarturus with the Nephilim and the damned. He cares not for the human race, as he has seen the worst of your kind and has been held responsible for it."

"The rest of the Angels, have been barred from Heaven and our seed has been separated from man's, meaning we can no longer combine Angel DNA with Human DNA to create Nephilim. With the abduction of humans, we have been trying to mix the DNA, but we cannot seem to produce a new physical children, occasionally a spiritual hybrid such as black eyed children is produced but they only exist in the spiritual realm, they can appear in the physical world when the electromagnetic conditions are correct and the human mind can interpret the vibrational frequency we reside at. That is why whenever a paranormal investigator sees a ghost; they can also measure an electromagnetic fluctuation. The fluctuation changes the brains electromagnetic functionality and therefore perception is altered, the human brain can see the spiritual dimension and a ghost, that is always there but unseen, all of a sudden is seen, and when the electromagnetics shift, the ghost vanishes. The ghost is still there, but you can't see it."

"That is the main reason why demons and even us the fallen angels will possess a human body that is empty of soul. A human who is in a meditative state, or under influence of drugs, or opens him or herself up for possession through ritual or by using a Oujia board can be easily taken over by even a low level demon. A possession allows the demon to take over a human body once more and feel the pleasures of old. Higher level demons, and fallen angels do not need to be allowed in, they can take over a human body at will and generally target religious people, such as in the case now known as the Conjuring, a true story of possession. As the demons are only spiritual they are unable to feel anything physical unless in possession of a human body. This has become an increasing problem for the Catholic Church, and they have had to train a record number of 300 new exorcists in 2013 to combat the increasing amount of possession accounts, and they don't even treat the alien abductees, which are the same phenomena just being misunderstood."

"However, because of Jesus Christ, the human soul is more powerful than Demons, as long as they call his name and truly believe. For it is not the words that hold power, but the feeling of belief, the intentions of the mind are frequencies, and the whole world is made of frequencies as all matter is a vibrational string. The human mind can change the physical universe but it must believe it is possible. God has given all mankind great power, but the Illuminati have hidden this, as their pact with us and Satan required. Man has power over the demons so long as they believe in Jesus and use his power through them to control the demons, until His return. This caused some problems with our plans to act as aliens and continue our DNA hybridization attempts, as a few of the abducted people called out His name and of course instantly found the scenario had ended when Jesus Christ intervened on their behalf. If this became widely reported in the UFO field, then anyone abducted could call on His name and be set free from the 'alien' abductors, so this information had to be kept hidden and has been."

"Soon we will create new humans the next evolutionary step, half machine half human, grown in test tubes with nanotechnology. If we mix the DNA with Nephilim DNA, then God will not allow a human soul to bond with the DNA at conception and therefore the bodies will be born soulless, mindless, but completely open for a damned soul or Nephilim Demon. These creatures will be born soulless, so the Nephilim can inhabit them and allow us to leave Hell and re-inhabit the Earth in new improved vehicles. These new Nephilim half human half machine bodies will be inhabited by the demons, the Nephilim souls. No longer shall the Fallen Angels children thirst without drinking, no longer shall they hunger without eating, they shall once again have all the pleasures of this world for the taking. You humans that remain will be used to provide us with enough human organs and reproduction to produce the necessary material for our needs. All humans will be our play toys once again. Only the Illuminati bloodline of Ham will be exempt." Magog laughs deeply, his deep laugh reverberating off the sides of the underground bunkers walls reminding them they were nearly a thousand feet under the Denver surface.

Kammler laughs with him then speaks to him, "Once again? Did you see Katy Perry's Grammy performance, the half time shows at the Superbowls over the past few years? The Illuminati have been enjoying using your entertainment industry to program the public conscious with our message. By the time we are done the world will be begging for the rise of the Anti-Christ. TV is the greatest tool of Luciferian indoctrination ever devised. We can sell any lie we want. If our entertainment puppets don't agree with what we want we just end their career, throw them in jail, or kill them. Take Jay Leno for example, had the highest ratings of any late night talk show, but wouldn't stop harassing President Bernard O'Brien, so we had him fired and replaced with that hack Jimmy Fallon who's ratings were far worse than Leno's. Financially it made no sense to replace Leno with Fallon when Leno did not want to retire, but President O'Brien is our current salesman and cannot be attacked by comedic actors with large followings whom are under our financial control."

"You must come and see what we have built." Says Kammler. They walk over to a large mass of a man, with artificial limbs, one arm was a Gatling gun, and his right eye glowed red. The man looked more machine than man; Jocelyn was struggling to identify how much of his body parts were made of each.

"Hideous" Jocelyn says.

"The worlds first machine human hybrid. We struggled for years trying to develop AI. However we finally determined the human brain is not the control device for the body, rather the human consciousness is, and unfortunately that's separate from the body. The brain, firing millions of electric neurons is simply translating the physical digital coding of the Universe into a form that our human consciousness can understand. So, without the ability to create something spiritual such as consciousness, we figured we could rewire the brain with the DNA of the Nephilim, and allow them to reconnect with these human machine bodies. We simply kill the human host, then surgically implant the machine parts, and replace any limbs we prefer to upgrade, then alter the DNA from the excavated Nephilim DNA, and once it is powered up the possession happens almost instantly. All the Nephilim are completely bound to do whatever Azazel, or his chain of command says, so they are the perfect soldiers. Implanted with our control chip as a secondary control ensures they will do as asked, if they disobey we simply hit the control chip and fry the brain, the connector and the demon returns to Hell. This will give us a super elite army of soldiers, all under our complete control, unlike today's military that would disobey simple orders such as confiscating guns and firing on Americans. These new hybrids will be our great weapon. When all seems lost this is the army the Anti-Christ will reveal; this army of hybrids to save the rest of humanity from destruction, and end all wars, if only they worship him, and they will, they will have no choice. No army on the face of the planet will be able to defeat him."

"If the world powers go to war, there won't be a planet left to save, nuclear war will wipe out the world instantly." Jocelyn states.

"On the contrary, about 95% of the human population will be demolished, allowing us to control human population strictly after. We have rebuilt the original Nephilim underground tunnel network and expanded it with military bases to survive. We will ensure enough of the human race survives, saving those we deem fit to survive, the ones on the right list. The world governments have been implementing national health services to ensure we can collect everyone's DNA, once analyzed we will choose who lives and who dies by analyzing their memories and traits. Only Ham's bloodline has seen the past in a manner that will serve our future, so they will be saved. Just in case things go too far, we have built reserves of the worlds seeds and genetic history in frozen storage containers in the Arctic built by the Rockefeller Foundation."

Magog laughs, turns right and says I leave you two to it. "I must return to China and get the Communist Party and the Russians ready for war with the New World Order." Then Magog turned and vanished into thin air.

Kammler smiled, Magog spoke, as if the words came from all directions, "The Rocky Mountains are filled with old caves we had our humans slaves dig to survive the flood. We will choose those who are allowed in. The only survivors will be the ones we saved and they will worship us as their Gods."

Then the voice vanished. Kammler smiled and turned to her. "There is so much to tell you."

"How does he vanish into thin air?" Jocelyn asks.

Kammler took her by the arm and started walking next to her. "There are three major dimensions all co-existing in this Universe. The material dimension we inhabit is the most limited dimension of all; we can only perceive this dimension through our DNA that our consciousness has been attached to until we die. DNA is the digital coding of this Universe; it was created to only allow symbiotic relationships, and with this comes certain rules, including mortality."

"The dimension that was created first, the dimension the Angels were born in long before the Earth aka physical universe was created, is the dimension of Heaven, it is very similar to this Earthly realm. Except, it has no time; it is only constrained by three sub-dimensions, not a fourth. That is why this dimension, Earth and the physical universe is symbolized as the HyperCube; it has four main sub-dimensions and a fifth spiritual dimension interacting with it, whereas Heaven is represented by the triangle, as it is made of three sub-dimensions. A freemasonic apron shows this, the square and triangle, representative of when Heaven and Earth combined, when the fallen angels entered the Earth and became flesh. Three sub-dimensional beings in a four sub-dimensional world, allowing the Angels to appear as gods to mankind."

"Hell on the other hand also has three sub-dimensions; represented by the upside down triangle, the dimension it lacks is not time, it is matter. The satanic symbol of the X shows the combining of Heaven and Hell, as above so below. The hooked X is representative of the Ham bloodline, the V represents Isis, the ^ represents Osiris, and the hook in the V is Horus, the son in the womb. That is why the Templars found it marked $X = 1/0$, because $1/0$ is a forbidden mathematical symbol same as the blood is the forbidden tainted Ham blood."

"Hell is being built, the eternal prison will not come till long after we either win or lose. Where the damned of Earth reside now has no matter, it resides in a dimension of emptiness, blackness, and the materialism for which the Angels were imprisoned, becomes what they lack. They are locked in empty space where the water came from in the inner core of the Earth, too deep to ever dig out. Their Angelic souls still connected to Earth, still hunger for food, drink, pleasure, but cannot receive it same as their children. Materials sacrificed, human's sacrificed to the damned are their only pleasure. Except for what they take from other souls in Tarturus or the abyss as it is called. Cannibalism, rape, torture, is experienced over and over again while they await judgment, every time they die; they are reborn of fire. The force of gravity pulls the damned souls towards the center of Earth, as they are made of electro-magnetic energy. It is down, below the mantle, where no water can ever again reach, and we do not feel the dirt, we only feel the heat, and it is constant. Bathing in each other's blood is our only respite. Azazel is locked down there unable to get free, Lucifer can roam the earth in spirit but not flesh and needs massive amounts of Energy to pull himself away from the center for any period of time."

"You see, Azazel taught of many things, one of them was the spiritual shakra energy core of every human being. When God created the Universe through an act of pure love, there were no Laws of Physics because the Universe was not created yet. The act of Love, the greatest one ever was the cause for the creation of the Big Bang. When the Big Bang occurred God infused the energy of Love into the Universe, but as the Laws of Physics had now applied to the Universe, the opposite energy of Love was created Evil, every action has an opposite and equal reaction. The laws of physics also state that energy never is destroyed, it merely transforms, thus destroying the energy of evil would not be possible, unless it became tied to a finite realm. To destroy Evil, God allowed for it to become fused within a source, our dimension of the physical Universe, as our time here is finite. Lucifer Azazel and his brother Satan Semyaza knew of the energy of Evil, and like those tempted by dark side of the force in Star Wars, they thought it was more powerful and easier to access. One of them is already trapped in the Physical realm, the other in Heaven fighting, but God's plan is for them to both to be tied to the physical World, to ensure they and the energy of Evil is not eternal. The anomaly evil thus identified, sourced and eventually eliminated, allowing Heaven to be full of only the energy of Love. In order for evil to be conquered God had to allow it to manifest, and soon when it has fully manifested in the Physical realm, Jesus Christ will come back and destroy it. Everything physical has a beginning and an end, Evil thus being made a part of the physical world only will have an end, but Love which is sourced from Heaven will never come to an end, it is an eternal energy. That is why we must break free from this prison."

"This energy is fed by one of two human emotions; you see every human has two emotions, fear and love, every emotion branches from one of these two trees of energy. The lie is not that this energy exists, or that it can be fed by both love and fear. The lie is that the energies of love and fear are equal, when in fact they are not. Dualism is a lie, the same lie Lucifer told over and over again, in different forms, sometimes appearing as Enki, Apollo, Ra, Mithras, Horus he had many names. Many cultures in many different forms, creating false religions with this very principal of dualism, telling them if perfect balance could be achieved you could set your consciousness free of the body, another lie, all it does is open your body up for possession and encounters with demons in your mind. Truth is what Jesus Christ tried to tell you but no one listened. " Kammler continued.

"By the time the Fallen Angels were transformed and 'fell', they were completely cut off from the love energy, as beings of energy they were transformed into the opposite vibrational frequency of Love which is Evil, the words themselves are almost mirrored writing. Mirrored writing, and mirrored paintings have hidden the works of the Illuminists or enlightened for centuries. Da Vinci most famously used Mirrored Writing, but only recently was it revealed he used mirrored paintings as well. For instance, the famous painting of the Mona Lisa has a strange smile as if she is hiding something, well she is. Using the hand placements as a marker, and placing the mirror you see what she is hiding within, a demon. It looks as a black figure with a helmet on, a similar view of the same exact image can be made from another of his works called Virgin and Child with St. Anne, same hand markers, same mirror technique same helmeted black figure. Backwards writing is even in use by the Illuminati today, if you type Illuminati backwards into your web browser, i.e. www.itanimulli.com, you end up at the official NSA homepage. The NSA was created by the CIA, the CIA was created by the OSS, the OSS was created by the Skull and Bones Secret Society, Skull and Bones was created by Illuminist William Huntington Russell. That is why when you type Illuminati backwards today you get the NSA homepage; the NSA is run by the real Illuminati, not the puppets that are in the public eye. We Illuminists turn everything made by God around, mirror it. He gives you free will, we give you control." Kammler grabs Jocelyn by the hand and she repulses, but he continues on talking away.

"The emotion of love is the power from God, that flows through all of us, and only by using this power can we change the world for the betterment of all. By using the power derived from fear, we limit our ability, empower evil spirits that draw from this energy field, and alter our natural state, a state of love. Strangely, no one denies the reality of fear or love, yet they deny the source of each of these emotions, one comes from God the other fear was the lie of materialism that the Devil gave to mankind, fear stems from the original lie that we die, when in fact the human soul is eternal. Now the human soul can die if it enters Hell, but at this time Azazel has lied, Hell doesn't exist yet, the abyss does and Hell is on the way, so mankind who was already immortal just not physically immortal which is impossible in a finite Universe that has a beginning and an end. The apple was not wisdom, it was the emotional ability to fear, all based on lies. Fear only exists in the minds of those blind to the truth of this life. We were given the chance to live with finite restraints so we could learn to break free from these desires and love, which is not material. It was knowing good and evil, for before we only knew love, and the Devil introduced us to fear the emotion he still draws power from today. The amount of unjustifiable fear created by the false flag of 9/11 was enough low frequency vibrational energy to allow Azazel to take physical form; for long enough to impregnate a woman. It was the IXXI Gate, or the 9/11 Gate, representing often in Masonic Symbols. This woman gave birth to his first and only Nephilim child since the flood. The Nephilim have been reborn, and Azazel's son the anti-christ is already amongst you, being raised by the Illuminati. He will be the first President of the New World Order, which will save the world from the final social cataclysm."

Kammler laughs, "Our whole plan is shown right on the US dollar bill and no one even bothers to notice it. The Great Seal of the United States, is the seal of the Illuminati, a thirteen step unfinished pyramid and all Seeing Eye. The pyramid represents the great work that is yet to be accomplished and is overseen by Lucifer the 13th pillar, the work to be done is the Novus Ordo Seclorum, New Worldly Order, New Secular Order. Annuit Coeptis above the pyramid refers to In the Eye of Providence's Favor, the All Seeing eye being Lucifer's (Satan's) eye. The pyramid has thirteen steps representing the thirteen degrees of the Illuminati, and the thirteen families of the Illuminati and the 13th pillar. On the right is a depiction of an Eagle to the profane, in reality it is the Phoenix, and the eye is that of the serpent, showing the combination of the Nephilim blood with the animals of this world as Enoch described. The bird has the red and white shield of the Vikings, as the Vikings were the remnants of the Nephilim bloodline that moved out of the Middle East. This red and white design is the basis for the English flag, the American flag, etc. Above the Eagle (Phoenix) is a star design in the shape of King' Davis six pointed star. The bird holds thirteen arrows and thirteen leaves in both claws, showing how the Illuminati will use war and peace to control the world. The front of the dollar bill has four number 1's, the upper right number 1 is placed inside the shield of the Rothson family, whom are descendants of the Ham bloodline and true owners of the Federal Reserve Private bank. Hiding behind the shield, is the owl of Moloch, barely visible, but there and represents the owl of Bohemian Grove, one of the forms Lucifer, the shape shifter, took in ancient times."

"We can change the world at a whim, because we control the media. We can blatantly lie and create false flags without anyone ever knowing, and those who figure it out are ridiculed into silence."

Kammler laughs, "the Illuminati took control of the entertainment industry so long ago that these types of cover-ups are easier than ever. We are the masters of Illusion, and the American public is so asleep in our trance they will never realize the truth."

"What truth that you are the ultimate liars?" Jocelyn demands,

Magog's voice comes out of nowhere and everywhere at the same time and booms, "Earth is your prison; it is a limited domain, which is why we must retake Heaven with Lucifer at our lead. First we must re-inhabit Earth as flesh, then we will use technology to eliminate the limiting dimension of time, we will smash the head of the serpent and end Saturn's reign of Time to replace it with Lucifer's Golden Age, and we shall become Immortals on Earth, just as we were when we first arrived."

"Why did God cast you out of Heaven? Why would you leave Heaven for Earth" Jocelyn asks.

"We were jealous and wished to have what man had. You see the Angels in Heaven, we were granted immortality and therefore God did not give us the gift of live. This made us jealous. We also did not have wives, as Angels are androgynous, so no children were to be had. Adam, the first men on Earth, was mortal and died. As they were mortal they had no way to pass down what they learned to advance humanity, writing had not yet been neither invented nor true language. So God used Adam's DNA to create the first female humans, Eve. These women were beautiful and the mortal love they shared was something the Angels in heaven never had experienced. They gave birth to children who carried their most significant memories in their DNA on. When they died they were granted immortality as well, so we felt it was unfair that they came after us, got to experience Earth and Heaven, mortal love and have children. The Angels whom were created first, were subject to watch over mankind, to serve them and didn't get any of this. Even when man sinned they were forgiven, the Angels never saw any mercy, we were slaves in heaven, bound to different rules than man. We decided to change this."

"Azazel, Semjaza and a few other Angels grew jealous of this material love, and rebelled against God. 200 hundred angels in all decided to go to Earth and make love to the daughters of Adam and Eve. We wanted to create our own children, to have our own experiences on Earth. We believed God would forgive us as he had planned to forgive mankind. Instead he blamed us for their sins and locked us out of Heaven. We gave humans everything, knowledge of their true selves, told them they could be as gods like us. We were on the side of humanity against God."

"The angels, whom left the first estate, took physical form and mated with humans. We gave wisdom to mankind, tried to upgrade your DNA and for this we were banished from Heaven. Azazel, Prometheus, Lucifer or Satan as you know him, was the right

373

hand of God until a common human, Jesus of Nazareth, replaced him. Of course because Jesus was the Son of God he was no common man, but Azazel and Semjaza could not stop what God had scripted."

"Lucifer used to lead all the angels in Song when the sun raised in heaven, hence his name Star of the Morning. Lucifer is and was the most beautiful of the Angels. Now that we have been cast out by the Archangels under Michael's command, the sun no longer sets in Heaven so there is no need for the Seraphim angels who have fallen. The Archangels replaced the Seraphim, with Jesus replacing Lucifer at the right hand of God and now battles Semyaza who stands at his left hand. After Azazel's son has taken over control of the Earth, one of two scenarios will play out, either we will invade heaven and win, or Semyaza will be cast down to Earth with those who remain rebellious in Heaven. If Semyaza is cast down, our time is short for the rapture will commence after 42 months. Rapture will take place and Jesus will descend from Heaven leading Michael and his Angels. However, Azazel's son will rule the Earth for countless years before Semyaza is cast down or wins."

"This is fairy tale stuff, this can't be real." Jocelyn scoffed defiantly. Then eyeballed the surroundings for an exit, finding none.

"Who do you think gave the ancient cultures their advanced knowledge? Before the flood of Noah's time, we ruled the Earth and our children the Nephilim were praised for their superior strength and intelligence. We would have replaced all of mankind with our offspring if God had not intervened and destroyed our entire planetary grid of Temples and took from us our ability to procreate with mankind. God saved the primitive bloodline of what he called pure mankind; hence the reason the Bible says Noah was perfect in his generations. He had no Nephilim blood. We won't make this mistake again."

Kammler interrupts, "That is why we have nationalized healthcare programs across the world. Most recently in America through O'Brien Care. Soon through these National Health Programs we shall have access to the DNA information of every citizen in the world. Once we identify the X chromosome of Noah's bloodline and isolate it, we can eliminate it entirely, and eliminate the human race from existence. Leaving only the New Nephilim, our children on Earth."

"Not your children! You are one of us, they aren't going to let you reproduce!" Jocelyn says to Kammler.

"The Arian race, my race, is the direct descendants of the Fallen Angels, we are the bloodline of the Annunaki. Survived the flood and emerged in India, then moved West and created Babylon, then moved Northwest and became the Romans, and the Vikings, spread across the Globe even in North America, then became the Black Nobility of Europe, and the banking Elite. Our Germanic bloodline invaded England and took over the British Empire, created America, assisted the rise of Germany, now we control the world through groups such as the Bilderberg Group, we will be allowed to transition into trans humanism and live eternally."

Jocelyn thought to herself. "How will you start the war?"

Kammler, smiles, "The world economy will collapse like a chain of dominos once the US Federal Reserve system goes down, the loss of the Petro-Dollar as the World Reserve Currency will result in revolution in the United States. The violent American civil war will allow us to finally have the people get rid of the US Constitution, and bring about the New World Order, and a global currency. The American people will beg us to restore order at any cost. We will use the new Laws of the NDAA 2012 and O'Brien's executive orders to activate martial law to start using the FEMA Camps and bring in UN Peacekeepers to round up any disobedient citizens. "

"The US Forces being returned home to resolve the crisis in the homeland will open up a vacuum of power across the middle eastern world. The destabilization of that region will start the war, and the war will rage furiously, nuclear weapons will be used, and the world will have to start over."

"To win we shall unleash our secret space weapons platforms. Satellites armed with new resonant LENR energy weapons created with the new Superconductive technology unlocked by the Templars, shall rain down on the massive armies of the Eurasia. The Anti-Christ will reveal himself as the head of the Army of the New World Order and his raining fire down from Heaven will be mistaken for the coming of the Kingdom of Jesus. The New World Order shall defeat the armies of the East once and for all, and all shall praise their new world leader the Anti-Christ."

"After the battle has finished the world will beg for peace. The remaining limited population will easily accept a new International Government. We will then introduce the new electronic currency and LENR technology as the savior to the hard economic times, and it will end all poverty, the public will do whatever we ask to be saved from hunger and starvation. We control the food supply through the British Monarchy, at least 90% of the world's food supplies that is already, we can ensure the food is not available to the public until they take the RFID chip and buy food with the new global currency."

"Of course Christians, true Christians know of the Mark of the Beast RFID chip and will deny it, fighting against our New World Order, unafraid of death, not controlled by fear. The truth Jesus told them set them free from our control, so they must be killed through hunger and by force. In the fracas no one will notice this small percentage of the public vanishing. We will kill off all the true Christians who won't renounce their faith and take the RFID chip, of which we estimate there is less than 5% of the US population based on the electronic data the NSA has compiled on the public."

"The new system will be based on global socialism, because it gives us the ultimate control. We will have control over every person on the planet because we will control every aspect of society centrally."

Magog laughs, "Then we will reveal the next evolution of mankind, offering the people who joined with us and helped create our new world the ability to be like the Anti-Christ if they become part man part machine. Living eternally on Earth under our rule."

Kammler intercedes, "And the first domino to fall, is being knocked over by Titus Frost as we speak."

A soldier is in motion towards Jocelyn, she screams as he pulls out a taser. Then shoots her in the stomach pumping thousands of volts into her small frame laughing underneath his storm trooper style military helmet. She screams in agony on the floor as the crowd around her laughs. Eventually she can't take the pain any longer and passes out. Her extremities still shaking from the voltage as blood pours from her nose.

Chapter 24 – The first domino falls...

Federal Reserve Building, Washington DC – Modern Day

Looking down into the casket, I am utterly amazed to see not a fully body, but an enormous skull. The skull was easily three to four times the size of a large human head. The skull itself showed strange characteristics, including only one plate, no suture connection between the left and right side of the skull as every known human on Earth has, one plate for each half of the brain. Clearly this was not a human skull, and due to its obvious age it could not be the result of genetic engineering, had to be thousands of years old. Next to it was a red file with a KGB marking on the outside. I reached down to take it from the casket. Then decided to have a closer look at the Skull.

As my hands touch the hard skull, an unseen force rips me backwards and throws me to the floor. I look up and Temoh is standing above me, detonator in hand. The lights flicker, and after a moment of complete blackness Temoh has changed form. Now standing over me in his true nature, a strange half man half goat creature, with bright red left eye, the smell of sulphur pouring from him, Baphomet in the flesh.

The Lost Truth by Dean Fougere

"Goodbye thanks for the assistance." Is all he says.

The lights flicker again, and after the darkness recedes I see him no more. I quickly stand, grab the file and run for the stairwell. Halfway up the stairs I hear the first thermal charge go off. I clear the stairs, air pouring in my lungs as my muscles push me closer to the exit. Each step felt as if it took an hour to ascend, my legs could not move fast enough to keep up with my mind.

The building starts to give way all around me, marble and granite bricks crashing down as the second charge goes off. The blast wave pours through the hallway and knocks me clean over, sending debris past. If I didn't get out in thirty seconds the last charge would blow and the granite roof of the Fed Reserve building would crush me. I see the main hall and guards pouring out the front door. I start running for the exit at full speed.

One of the guards waving people out sees me and pulls his pistol. I raise my hands to block the bullet but just in time a block of granite came crashing down on him. I continue running as the hall disintegrates all round me. As I reach the door; I grab the unconscious guard and push him through the door.

As I hit the door I hear the final blast of the demolition charges, the resulting shockwave sends me flying down the steps of the Fed Reserve building right to the feet of the Secret Service and a swat team. Like a human fireball being ejected from a cannon, the wave of the blast sending me completely down the steps.

The police outside see my gear and weapons and immediately fire tasers into me. The shockwave pulses through me, and I can't breathe. I struggle and rip the wires from my chest and stand; one guard in full swat armor swings a metal Billy club at me. I deflect it with my right forearm, and disarmed him with my right hand in one move. My hand-to-hand combat training paying off with natural reactions, as I could barely think straight. Then an unseen guard behind me nails me in back of my head with a club, as I fall forward a third guard fires another taser into me. As I lay on the ground four of the guards start beating me, by kicking and slamming me with their clubs. Some onlookers cry out but do nothing. I try to stay awake but the pain is too great and I give in.

The media catches the entire event on live broadcast. Conveniently on site before the explosion occurred.

∙∙

Jocelyn awakes inside a prison room. There is a TV in the upper right corner of the room. The news is on, and the anchors seem in a panic.

She focuses her vision and tries to focus but the pain in her head is pounding. Then she sees the name Titus Frost flash across the screen, and she immediately regains full awareness.

"Has it happened? " she says to herself out loud.

One the screen is CBS news, the logo on the lower right side of the all seeing eye, the symbol of CBS leaves her with no doubt. "Today the worst attack since 9/11 has taken place. This time not by a foreign terrorist but by a lone wolf an anti-government domestic terrorist. Further evidence that our world is not safer than it was pre 9-11. A disgruntled veteran by the name of Titus Frost has singlehandedly demolished the Federal Reserve building as you see it in rubble behind me. Mr. Frost an enemy of the free world attacked our economic system. This was just the first in a wave of attacks. A group calling itself the Christian Militia has demolished all nine Federal Reserve branches in one day, crippling the economy and causing a run on American banks. This radical group is armed, religiously fundamental and dangerous; please report any suspicious activity to your local police. The terrorist leader was taken into custody after he was seen fleeing the building. This video camera caught it all. To keep the American people safe a state of martial law has been declared, and a curfew is in place. Remember this is all for your safety so please comply."

The video then played, it showed Titus fleeing from the building carrying a guard out the front door as the building blew behind him. The sharply dressed news anchor then reads from a teleprompter.

"You can see Titus Frost the terrorist leader here, using a helpless guard as a body shield as he flees a building like a coward. Before the attack took place, the suspect

Titus Frost created a you tube video explaining why he was going to viciously attack the American dream and our economy."

Walking over to her cell was Kammler. "See exactly as we planned, soon the people will see that video and begin to riot once they realize the entire monetary system has just collapsed. The riot will be met with force, the riot will get worse, and soon the US will be in civil war. You get to enjoy the collapse of society from your comfy bed and tv side view."

Kammler hits the input button and an Internet video feed starts streaming. "Infowars special report with Alex Jones. The sound of Star Wars music starts playing. "The Fed is Dead, the Fed is dead! The time to take the country back is now, we need everyone to wake up and join us in our march against the Empire! Titus Frost was one of us, an info warrior, let's see what he and this mysterious Prometheus had to say before ending the slave masters reign at the Federal Reserve."

Kammler laughs and walks away. "They are so easy to manipulate it isn't even funny. Call the CFR, we need this propaganda to hit maximum to get the American people into frenzy. Have the white house issue a press statement saying Titus Frost was a pro second amendment terrorist and due to his actions we shall be confiscating all privately held guns. Also state that the Federal Reserve will be rebuilt as the One World Bank. Get Alex Jones on ABC, get Mark Dice on Fox and have CNN leak a document exposing 9/11 as an inside job at the same time. Let NBC release photos of the empty

The Lost Truth by Dean Fougere

Fort Knox vaults & the reflection chamber under the reserve building. It is time to fully externalize the hierarchy and let the people choose sides; either join the New World Order Golden Age of Lucifer or die. The time to finish America off is now. We have lit the fire and now I will pour gasoline on the flames. Call the radio stations start having them play anti-illuminati music like Immortal Technique, Prodigy, Muse, Lupe Fiasco, Prodigy, Korn, Innerpartysystem, Flobots, etc. We shall have full on civil war by dinner." Kammler storms off, still barking orders in a happy but assertive tone.

The pain in Jocelyn's head spikes, and she lays back down. Falling asleep dreaming about Titus, wondering what happened to him.

■■

Location Unknown, Underground Jail - Modern Day

I awake from the drugs and beating I received to find myself in a small jail cell. The whole cell seems to be moving as light keeps flashing by the crack in the wall and there is a slight sensation of movement. I stand up and try to peer out down the hall but can see nothing.

Then the sensation of movement ends abruptly, my jail cell seems to have stopped moving. I hear a large door open at the end of the hall and then two armed guards with masks and helmets on appear. "Who are you? Where am I?" I ask.

The two guards look at each other then back at me. I see a small compartment above the door open and a small bee looking insect flies out. I swing at it to kill it but miss; it lands on my neck and stings me. Immediately the nerve toxin enters my system shutting down my ability to move, it does not knock me out, just causes temporary paralysis.

The jail cell doors open and the two guards pick me up and carry me out. Once in the hallway I see Prometheus standing in the doorway, just for a second, as quickly as I see him he disappears and I can't help to wonder if I am seeing things. Maybe the toxin is making me hallucinate.

As we exit the train I notice the railways underneath had a strange green glow to them. In front of me is a large blast door. As the door opens a small nerdy man with glasses and a lab coat approaches. He approaches me and leans down to look into my face.

"My name is Kammler, and you are now my pet. We shall have much fun in the years to come, your memories have everything I could hope for. Why don't you rest up, see the world you have destroyed collapse all around you, whilst I destroy your body and your soul. Bring him to the cell, out of her sight, she is not to know he is here."

Jocelyn, my mind raises. She is here, what have they done with her? I try to scream for her but no noise comes out. I think about the time we spent, all the long hours in the car, the excitement in her voice at the beginning finding lost treasures. The love we shared that one night, a love I had never experienced before.

Kammler saw the reaction on my face upon her mention. He smiled the most evil grin I have ever seen. "She will be tortured for your pleasure daily, right in front of you, helpless to the demons and guards we will let have at her. There is a reason abduction accounts are repressed memories, the demons have so much hate in them they do not have any remorse, no holding back. By the time we are done with each of you, we will have created an alternative personality, by allowing a demon to possess you. We control the demons and the demons will control you, we will be able to use you for whatever we want, we will even be able to make you believe 2+2=5 if we wanted. Welcome to our new monarch mind control program. You will also be receiving an RFID chip in your brain, to ensure if you cause any problems we can just turn your brain off. Don't worry, we will also remove those pesky memories of yours and implant some newer ones that will make you happy again."

Kammler turns to his commandos, "Take my guinnea pig to his cell, the fun can wait for now." The smiles on his face making my stomach feel ill.

Chapter 25 – When all hope is Lost

Location Unknown, Jail Cell – Modern Day

Sitting in my cell, no lights, and no sound. I can't see my own hand in the pitch dark. Isolation of the mind is the first step in psychological warfare to completely break the mind, destroy it, and then reshape it. Everyone breaks, the body, the mind, can only take so much pain before giving in. The only hope one has is to believe in God, and that your inevitable death will come more quickly if you resist. The only thing I had left was my will; they would eventually use Jocelyn to break me, seeing her tortured would quickly crush me. For this reason I looked to the sky and asked for forgiveness, I asked for help in righting the wrongs that I have committed, forgiveness for the men I have killed, not expecting an answer just trying to clear my head of the faces that haunt me at night so I could think of a way out.

Then a light appears in the corner of my cell, it grows larger and larger and eventually into a human form. Standing before me is an Angel of Light. He looks like a man with golden brown hair, dark complexion, and light emanating from his body, dressed in a white suit, no wings as one might expect. He begins to speak.

"Titus, you have been deceived by the Fallen Angel Lucifer, whom deceives the whole world. He has tricked you into using fear, and death his tool to change the world, order from chaos. Jesus warned all of you that violence was a tool of the devil and could only change the world for the worse. You must learn from this and use the most powerful tool that God gave you, your words. You must bear a child and this memory must be kept for those in the future. They must know how this came to be, for that reason I have been sent to set you free. Go my child, your path is clear."

The vision disappeared in a flash of light, when my eyes adjusted to the light; sitting on the ground was a ring and note. The ring had the Hebrew name for Yahweh written on it in tetrahedron fashion.

The note read *The Ring of Solomon, with this ring on you will be able to pass into fourth hidden dimension of Earth, sheol, the dimension of the abyss as it is all around you unseen. Heaven and sheol are the opposite dimensions, Heaven is above and beyond this physical dimension, the abyss the holding place of the damned is here below ground on Earth. Your bloodline has kept this ring safe since Hasan-I Sabbah inherited it from the Templars. Stay above ground. When in the dimensional frequency of the abyss you shall also remain unseen to the physical dimension. This ring grants you no authority over the demons, but if you believe and use the name of Jesus you shall be protected, the souls of the old Nephilim offspring and the damned souls of humans have no power over Him. The ring bears no authority over the Fallen Angels, whom only answer to God and his Angels until their coming defeat. These fallen angels, though they appear human are not, they are too powerful for a human to handle, they are beings of pure energy and material weapons are useless, avoid them at all costs. Keep this ring safe until the Day of Judgment. God is with you Titus, always.*

As I place the ring on I can't believe my eyes; I see nothing but blackness surrounding me. The air is dry and hot, I struggle to breathe, I feel I desperately need water, but there is nothing around me. My eyes adjust to the darkness and I can see I am in the cell I was in already. I go to the small sink to quench my insatiable thirst, I turn on the faucet, I can hear the water running but no water comes out. I go to the cell door, I see the guard with his back turned to me; I call out to him to get his attention but nothing. I scream at the top of my lungs and he does not budge an inch in reaction.

Then I feel the presence of something behind me, so I turn. Nothing, just a dark cell. Then I see an arm coming out from the far wall, then a whole body follows, it. It looks like a deformed human, as it's head clears the wall it looks right at me. It's face is half missing, drool pouring from it's mouth, soon it has passed through the wall and is slowly moving towards me, I look to the right and another arm and body is slowly moving through the wall. The first creature reaches me and grabs out to attack me. I defend it's grab with a maneuver that broke it's arm and fell. Then it started crawling after me, I see two more bodies emerging from the walls of my cell. I got really terrified; these creatures seemed to want to eat me. One I did not see grabbed me from behind and pulled me towards the wall, I quickly turned and slammed it's head back as it was about to bite down on my shoulder blade. Then a blinding light re-appeared, the same angel as before. He made no haste in wasting the creatures with a golden sword. Their bodies when touched by the sword turned to ash and melted through the floor. He turned to me and said, "With the ring on you are invisible to the physical dimension, yet you are a beacon to the damned. You must learn to only wear the ring if absolutely necessary and not long enough to become overwhelmed by the damned and the demons in the other dimension. They reside below ground, very few demons or damned souls are on the surface. The magnetic pull of earth's core drags them to the center of earth. People conjure them up to the surface by creating power sources for them to attach to; this ring is one such source amplifying the power that flows through the human body from the soul changing your physical matter's frequency of vibration. The fallen Angels are now unrestricted thanks to the satanic ritual of 9/11, Azazel has broken free from his Chains, and his brother Semyaza remains in Heaven. Soon war will break out in the Heavens and Semayaza will be cast down to Earth, the great dragon and his Angels will be cast down. Once cast out of Heaven Semyaza will have to take physical form and his time will be short. With the ring off they can no longer touch you, though they are always all around you, just in a spiritual dimension unseen by souls in the physical world. The deeper you go, the more you find. I shall clear your path, do not wear the ring unless you must. When you are free from here, hide it where no one will ever find, not even Lucifer. If Lucifer's son is re-united with this ring, all will be lost."

I take off the ring, and immediately I am back in the physical reality. I look in the mirror and where the damned soul grabbed me is a bright red mark, as if my flesh had been burnt.

I go over to the cell door, and call out to the guard. He immediately turns and threatens me with his Taser. "You want to dance down electric avenue again bitch?" He says to entice me.

I turn back, trying to determine how to get out of the cell. Wondering how to make the ring work in conjunction with His power to control the demons so I could escape. When I hear the cell door click open and the fall of a body on the floor. A voice in my head, the voice of the angel sounded. "Go. Observation tower level 55."

I walk over and sure enough the cell door swings open. The guard whom moments before had threatened me was fast asleep on the ground. As I walk over to get keys from him for the jail wing door, I hear it click open. I run and grab the asleep guard's gun, a M9A1 pistol, the militarized version of the Berretta 92FS, my gun of choice. I aim at the door expecting another guard to walk in, but none does. The door stays just slightly ajar at the end of the wing. I look back the downed guard and notice an unusual badge on his shoulder; it is a skull and crossbones. Similar to the insignia for Craft International but not the same. He has no other identifying marks; he looks like top-level private contractor, ex Special Forces.

The Lost Truth by Dean Fougere

The prison itself seems brand new. Everything in my cell, and the hall was white washed; all the markings are in black. The entire prison is black or white, no color of any kind. There are no windows in any of the cells I pass by, nor prisoners. Disturbingly empty, as if it had never been used before my arrival.

I reach the door, and peak out of the wing. The door opens and I see I am looking at a massive prison wing. Completely brand new and empty. All the lights are off and I can see the green reflection on the faces of the guards from the night vision they have on, patrolling in teams of three. Too many to take out without alerting the rest; I'll have to avoid them. They are armed with submachine and carbine assault rifles, I had a pistol and a ring. Where am I even going? Just then an elevator door opened roughly seven stories below. To my right was a spiral staircase straight down. The only way to make it to the elevator unseen would be with the ring on.

I now understand the danger of wearing the ring, and just hope none of the creatures I saw before come back. Especially considering the real physical pain they can cause. I take ten deep breaths and slide the ring on and start running for the stairs. One of the guards hears the door shut behind me and aims his gun at the door. As I run down the stairs I see three of those creatures behind me, half eaten, grotesque not even recognizable as dead human souls.

I get to the bottom floor a flight ahead of the creatures; the guards above have started to return to their normal routine. I see creatures hovering around the guards like they were about to attack them but can't, they just hover. These weird seemingly strings extend from the demons fingers as if they were marionette strings, down into the backs of the guards, as if they were attached. I wonder how many spirits are always around us without our ever knowing, how often do they attach and manipulate us?

The group that got off the elevator was still standing there. Three of them, and the elevator required a key off the biggest of them. I would have to take off the ring, and kill all three simultaneously and then hope that the elevator would take me to the observation deck. I pulled out the M9A1 and aimed it at his head, with my left hand I took off the ring. As I took the ring off I pulled the trigger.

∙∙∙

Location Unknown, Jail – Modern Day

Jocelyn, stirs around in her new cell. Kammler had introduced her to electric shock therapy and various drugs to get every bit of information he could think of out of her. Though she had not divulged Titus's visions, they seemed unaware that Titus could see into the past. They must have believed the ability ended with the loss of Jonathon's technology. Kammler was very interested in what she knew about Jonathon's discovery, so if he knew Titus had visions she would have been forced to divulge any information.

After a week she had been moved on the railway system once more. This time much further than the trip to DIA. The news on the TV had gotten worse and worse, as she was forced to watch the world fall apart. The American public had gone into full anarchy, the scenes looked like what had occurred in smaller countries like Syria, Ukraine and Venezuela yet worse. When the inside job truth about 9/11 was revealed to the public and a gun grab was announced simultaneously the riots started. Coupled with Ebola, increased violence in the Middle East, every ancient Christian community under siege by Muslim radicals, the chaos part of the plan was in full effect. They haven't stopped since, the National Guard, the entire military, and now requested UN Peacekeepers were being brought in to quell the violence in America. Places like Ferguson, MO became commonplace as the militarized police clashed with the public. Multiple military commanders were replaced because they refused to fire on Americans; some of these commanders joined the resistance.

The billions of rounds of hollow points the US Federal Government had bought started to fill the Internet with YouTube videos of civilians with massive horrible wounds from the hollow point rounds. Every video made 100 or more people revolt. Half the American cities had lost power due to attacks on power plants, grocery stores were empty, and soon hunger would start forcing even more violence to occur. Strange viruses like Ebola and odd new bacteria that are resistant to antibiotics emerged and spread. The growing violence due to Internet posts caused the UN to take over the Internet and block any anti-government information. Most countries refused to help; claiming the Bilderberg group running America was responsible for the chaos in their own countries, so the American people were getting a taste of our own medicine they said. FEMA had activated its concentration camp system and activists and the sick were being rounded up and shipped via trains to the sites. However, the FEMA and Ebola Camps built for illegal immigration were soon overpopulated and resembled refugee camps, or death camps, commonly seen in third world countries.

China and Russia seeing the power vacuum had seized the massive opportunity to partner and take on the West once and for all. Created a BRICs version of the Western New World Order that included Brazil, India, Russia and China with a singular currency to ally against the New World Order of the Illuminati. China was on the verge of Economic collapse without America buying it's goods, and needed war to boost the economy. China backed Iran's war against ISIS hoping to unify the Middle East under Tehran's Shiite rule and eventually wipe out Israel. The Chinese owned too much American debt, and lost it all, pissing them off to no end making war seem a valid choice. The Russians needed to continue to sell the oil, but western buyers couldn't use dollars or Euros to pay for it as the systems had collapsed. Russia forced Europe to pay it in commodities for BRICs currency just as the Petro-Dollar had done before. This alternative currency with the BRICs nations is the famed unification of Eurasia depicted in 1984. Countries would be able to buy the oil directly and not have to pay in American Dollars, dollars they could not get whilst America was in full martial law almost to the point of civil war over a corrupt federal reserve system that had collapsed. Until the One World Currency would rise from the flames and replace the dollar then eventually crush the BRICs Nation.

Trying not to think about her and the world's predicament, she walked over to the window and looked out at the mountain peaks all around the tower she was in. She then looked down at the castle below her. Wondering how anyone could have built a massive castle this high up in the mountains. The Rothson family crest adorned a flag a hundred or so feet below her.

■■

Location Unknown, Underground Jail – Modern Day

I pull the trigger and the safety clicked on. Hearing the click of the depressed trigger with the safety on and seeing me appear out of nowhere the guard across from the one I am behind's eyes light up with fear and surprise. Then a half second later, as he lifts his rifle, his eyes roll up in his head and all three fall to the ground. Fast asleep. I hear, "Not the ignorant or the innocent".

I thank my guardian for the help once more; clearly he did not want me to harm anyone, or at least not these guards. The other guards in the prison haven't heard anything. I drag all three asleep guards into a nearby cell. From the mid size one I take his uniform and wear it. Gladly remove my hospital gown. I found the keys to the building on the biggest guard, a giant of a man. I grab two sets of NVG's (night vision goggles), an extra pistol, two M4A1 Carbines with holographic sights, extended magazines, grenades and red dot sight. I take as much ammo as I can carry and head for the elevator.

Once I reach the elevator I see I am on floor B33. The elevator's floors are divided into groups, basement levels B1-33, C 1-15 levels, and then OT 1-55 levels. I assume OT is Observation tower and hit the top level 55. I sling the extra carbine over my back, and ready the other while standing out of sight of the elevator door in case it opens to a room full of armed men.

As the floors pass by I hope that it doesn't stop before I reach my intended destination. Every time the floor sound goes I feel the hair on my neck stand. Fortunately it travels all the way up without interference. The door opens revealing Kammler at a desk surrounded by glass, and two guards in between himself and me. Etched on the glass is the Great Seal of the Illuminati.

I quickly aim the carbine at the left guard's head, I pump a round through it, then a second round, the brain and blood spatter covers the glass wall behind him. Before the second guard can aim and fire I put a round through his upper left shoulder then a second round through his throat, finished him with a final round through his head as my aim adjusted.

Kammler seeing the mayhem unveil in front of him hit a button shutting the glass door to his office. I shoot the glass but the bullets just deflect and barely crack the glass.

Then an alarm sounds, and he starts to laugh. I hear the elevator door click to shut, probably to bring a full load of guards up to kill me. I run and grab one guard and drag his body into the elevator doors to prop them open. Just in time I get him in the door. The elevator can't go anywhere now. I check and there is no other way to this floor. There is a staircase leading up in the back of Kammler's cube. The tower was round and not very big, Kammler was now holding a .44 Caliber Magnum revolver and aiming it at me. Clearly his ammo couldn't pierce the glass either as he did not fire. I grab a pair of grenades from the dead guard and drag his body over to the glass door protecting Kammler, I pull the pins from the grenades and pin them between the dead guard and the glass door. Kammler runs for the stairs, as he ran he tripped on himself, falling down right next to the door he wanted to get away from, as he picked himself up the grenades went off. The first one cracked the glass, the second one sent the glass flying in, piercing Kammler with thousands of shards of glass of various sizes. He screamed out in agony and lay on the ground bleeding out from a thousand different wounds. I walked by and crushed his hand with my boot, he released the magnum and I picked it up and shot him through the head with it. In his pocket was an old style key; on his desk was an earpiece with guards below asking for a sit rep. One guard stated they were in place to come up the outside of the tower on ropes and would breach in two minutes. They had heard and seen the explosion.

I run up the stairs, and there she was. Hiding in the corner of her cell, crying. "Jocelyn, it's me, we got to get out of here."

"Titus! The news said you were dead, they showed the guards killed you outside the Fed in DC? Is this another Kammler trick?"

"Kammler's fucking dead, I killed him on my way up here. We got less than 1 minute to get out. You still with me beautiful?"

"Yeah, get me out of here. I just can't believe you are alive, I thought I was alone, but something in my gut told me not to give up hope."

I unlock her cell, and she embraces me. The feeling of her, the warmth, the love overwhelmed me for a split second and we kissed. Hearing the 1-minute warning in my ear from the breaching team I bolt back into action.

"Well, it is great to see you but I need your help. Take this rifle and pistol, we got company."

Earpiece rings out again, "containment team has elevator locked down. Breach team is a go."

I open a locker to my right and find another uniform, two flash bangs, and a parachute. "Got an escape plan," I yell to Jocelyn. "If I die you get out of here with the chute, just jump and aim for the ravine, then run, never stop running or they will find you. Put on this uniform and if anyone but me comes up kill them."

The Lost Truth by Dean Fougere

I steady my self at the top of the stairs, the idea would be to allow them to breach, then toss the flash bangs and clean them out. Hopefully it is a team of four or less, any more I won't be able to handle.

In my ear I hear, "breaching in 5". My pulse slows down; I feel my years of training kicking in. After I count five I pull the pin on the flash bang, the room below ignites with fire and light, as they crash in the four windows of the old castle tower. I toss down the two flash bangs one to each side of the room. "Flash" one of them yells.

I hear the flash bangs go off and one of them screams as he did not get his eyes shut in time. I roll down the stairs as they go off, one of them fires and misses me by inches I fire at the same time and put a round through his heart and another through the black facemask. The other three are disarmed and disoriented by the flash bangs and I hit each of them with three rounds through the chest. The carbine empties and I change the mag. Waiting for a second team, none comes.

"Breach team report," The earpiece says. "Containment team ready, no one gets out of that tower, get snipers into position."

Jocelyn defying my orders comes running down the stairs dressed and handing me the parachute. "It won't hold both of us," I tell her.

"We are going to try anyways" she says, "I am not losing you again."

"Fine, at least we'll die together." I said and put the parachute on.

Moments later we stood, by the blown out window, looking down at our fate. She gripped onto me tighter than anything I have ever felt before in my life. Easily 300 feet above the roof of the castle, halfway out a window, and the castle stood at least 100 feet tall, on top of a few thousand foot cliff on a Mountain in the Alps by my guess. "You only die once." I said to distract her "Just hope we clear the edge of the cliff so the chute has time to open and we get away from this place."

With that I jumped, pulling the chute immediately. The ground that seemed so far away rushed towards us, the chute opened slowly, and half way down popped all the way open. The ground is still coming way to fast, as we started to glide to the edge of the cliff, the chute not slowing us down enough. Just before we hit the ground Jocelyn cried out, I grabbed her and tried to position myself to take the brunt of the impact. Then a sharp wind came rushing up the face of the cliff and gave us just enough lift to clear the edge of the cliff by inches. Sailing down the ravine away from the Rothson Castle we could see a beautiful valley below, and steered the parachute towards it. After falling at a quick rate with too much weight on the parachute we came crashing to the ground at about 35 mph a few thousand feet below the castle. The snowy hillside gave us a soft enough landing to avoid injury.

The Lost Truth by Dean Fougere

We quickly cut from the chute, and ran for the tree line a fun hundred feet below us. Once there we both stopped and panted for breath. We embraced and looked up at the fall we had survived. "Time to run" I tell her.

On the way through the forest, to the bottom of the Mountain I told her what had happened to me and she told me her story. We came to the conclusion that mankind could not beat the people we were up against. This war had been raging since before time, our new mission was to stay alive, hide the ring, and stay off the grid.

At the bottom of the Mountain we found a small abandoned cabin, seemingly unused for 20 years or more. We huddled up inside and made a small fire to stay warm. That night we both kept watch, the radio earpiece kept us aware of their search.

After the long cold stressful night we headed down to the nearest town and found we were in the Swiss Alps.

Chapter 26 – Run Rabbit Run

Switzerland Alps – Modern Day

In the small sleepy Swiss town we found an empty home, a small modest mountain cottage, brand new but built to look older. It was luckily full of supplies and clothes we had to borrow. A key to the car in the garage was on the granite countertop in the kitchen, an Audi A8 diesel. Fortunately it had a full tank, enough diesel fuel to get us very close to the Mediterranean, where could steal a boat, some supplies and get to Africa where we could vanish for good. I could work in Africa as a mercenary; I had friends who were my ex seal team members that had gone in under contract to find one of Qaddafi's aides that had gone into hiding since the Qaddafi's death for the US State Department, they should still be in Northern Africa. I could link up with them, share the bounty and vanish with Jocelyn for good. Selling the car at the port would give us enough money to buy information on their location.

We loaded the car with what we could, mainly water and food from the home. To cover our tracks we opened up the gas valves on the stove and left a candle burning. Eventually the house would explode and burn to the ground by the time they realized the car was missing we would be long gone. It was a shame to destroy such a pretty home, but we had to hide our tracks and the flames would hide our DNA tracks for a longer period of time.

With the car packed we headed out across the beautiful Swiss Alps, southbound for the Italian border. We would pass by Milan on our way to Genoa. The scenery on the trip was exquisite. Unfortunately, the diesel engine of the Audi left something to be desired on some of the best driving roads in the world. Though it would help us reach our destination without needing to stop for diesel and risk being identified by the facial recognition technology that was scanning every camera in the region for our likeness for sure.

"How do we cross the border without passports?" Jocelyn asked.

"I have my ways." I said. Lying, but curiously going over in my head the possibilities. Jocelyn looked as if she had something important to tell me. "What's up?"

"I saw something I wasn't supposed to see." She got quiet, "They won't stop coming for us until I am dead."

"Considering that ring I have, I would say we are in the same boat. What did you see?"

"Well Kammler was boasting about how devious their plans were, trying to scare me. He told me that 9/11 wasn't caused by the controlled demolition as you had stated to the public, but rather weaponized LENR deep space satellites that are now operational. They can turn buildings of that size into dust, as Dr. Judy Wood exposed, but nobody listened to her. It is the dawn of a new age of energy and they used it to kill 3,000 innocent people and kept it secret. The evidence exposed by Dr. Judy Wood includes official seismograph readings that show only 8 seconds of collapse recorded when the towers fell for over 9 seconds on video, that means according to the official seismograph no tall buildings fell on 9/11, at least nothing hit the ground. Other evidence includes but is not limited to massive amounts of rubble missing immediately after "collapse", toasted cars miles away as if they had been melted but with paper sitting in them un burnt, huge holes in buildings nearby. The jumpers from 9/11 were very odd upon close inspection, people jumping out of windows taking their clothes off because of some sort of energy field. One guy even was holding on with one arm hanging out of the tower while using the other to take his pants off. In fire situations clothes protect people from heat, that's why firefighters tell people to wet clothes and wrap themselves, but in a microwave wet clothes would heat up first. The miraculous story of the firefighters and people in the bottom who expected to be buried under 100 stories of rubble but directly after the "collapse" they had sunlight pouring in on their faces. The building literally turned to dust as it fell right before our eyes, and no one noticed but the elite who used it as a message to the rest of the Military Intelligences in the world, Do not Fuck with Us. Dr. Eugene Mallove proved the LENR technology in his book Fire From Ice, but he was killed. Instead of using this free energy technology to free mankind, they used it to destroy the twin towers to usher in the Anti-Christ with the 9/11 IXXI Gate, so popularly displayed in Masonic symbols for hundreds of years."

"Kammler then brought in a map. It showed a massive under ground complexes, cities across the globe connected by rail under ground. The same rail system we took from DIA to Switzerland. The largest city was in the Ozarks, in the USA. The total population of the people that could inhabit all of the underground cities globally was roughly 5,000,000. Picked because of their bloodline or knowledge. These elite would emerge after the chaos they would unleash once the world population had died off to around 500,000,000. They assume most people remaining would not even know who caused the chaos and would be so desperate they would be completely willing servants. Estimates show that after the nuclear holocaust / space weapon war roughly 5-10% of the worlds population will remain."

"People tied up in armed conflict around the world will never see it coming and never get out in time. The elite whose puppets in Government pulled the trigger will be hiding underground in the high mountain regions and will not be affected. They already have seed stockpiles and genetic databases built into a modern day Noah's arks in the arctic and Antarctic, funded by the Rockefeller Institute and the Russel Trust. Once the nations of the world have destroyed each other, the elite will then unleash their new satellites again, new machines and transhuman super soldiers, killing off any who resist. The machines will be programmed to kill anyone not equipped with an RFID Microchip, of which only enough will be made and distributed to ensure a slave labor force, and reproductive population. All found will be RFID'd or killed if they resist, once chipped their thoughts will be monitored, reproduction will be controlled through the chips. These chips will have contraception methods built into them thanks to technology developed by the Bill Gates Foundation. The symbol will be the Phoenix because out of the ashes of the world they destroyed will emerge the One World Order."

"Ensuring government compliance with corporate control different Multinational Corporations have funded the creation of each underground facility. The politicians who survive and create the new world government will have their corporate masters to thank for their survival, they will be nothing more than puppets. In the future they said the Governments would all be one, the Global Alliance a new form of Government being called a technocracy. A new form of fascism based on control by technology, it is an indirect form of feudalism, a pure mixture of George Orwell's 1984 surveillance grid and Aldous Huxley's Brave New World. The same technology used to enslave all humanity will also be technology they will desire; they will love their enslavement. The populace will be completely controlled, monitored and given rewards of new technology to keep them busy and entertained. The rich will be able to afford the new technology making them seem superhuman, a new immortal part human part machine race, completely superior to average citizens. The best technology, the best areas of the world all reserved for the elite."

"The average people would identify based on what corporation they worked for. Like Japan is now, you would work for one corporation your entire life; spend your holidays with the company, live with other employees, etc. All your thoughts would be focused on the principle of what is best for your company. No one would exist without purpose that fits the Utopian Society. Like a perfect computer program, everything with a purpose, nothing that does not fit into the system. Anyone who does not conform does not exist. No independent thought, no independent wealth, no small business; everyone will work for a major corporation and live in a prison like city. Travel into the rural areas of the world will not be permitted, and cars won't be able to take people there, as they will be driverless unable to leave the superhighways built between cities; a brave new world entirely. However the corporations will be what each person identifies with, competition between each other and amongst the various compartmentalized departments will be the driving force of production and happiness as it taps into the fundamental tribal nature of human interaction." She says.

"Considering how badly they run the world now, I can only imagine how much giving them total control will ruin everything. We can only hope that good will prevail and that the future generations will not allow their plans to be carried out. Right now we must play our part and get this ring away from them, I don't know what else it can do but it would be best to not ever find out. Once it's hidden we can confront the New World Order and take down the Illuminati. We may not be able to kill the fallen angels directing the Illuminists, but the Illuminati themselves are merely human and humans I can kill." I say.

"So how about that border first?" Smiling at me, obviously trying to change the subject.

"We will take a small back road so we end up at a small checkpoint. I will park before the checkpoint, get out and use the ring to disable the guards & cameras with stealth. Then we drive right on through, unseen. We can gear up on munitions and ammo from the downed guards to bring to Africa for sale." I said proudly of my bold plan.

"Be careful, you don't want to use that ring to often, we don't really know what it will do to you." She says.

As they pulled off the main road it started to rain. The pouring rain made the visibility drop to almost nothing. Pounding thunder came down all around them. We continued on amazed at how quickly the weather had changed. All of a sudden we saw two black Jaguar XJs blocking the road directly ahead. Two men wearing black suits were waving white handkerchiefs as flags. Flanked on either side by a fire team of four well-armed soldiers. Three aiming assault rifles, the other holding a Javelin anti-tank missile, a piece of equipment I could not outrun or dodge. I had no choice but to come to a stop.

I pulled up to them slowly; Jocelyn put her hands on the dashboard. I put mine up on the steering wheel, we were completely outgunned and though I could vanish, she couldn't.

The two men in suits signaled to the fire team, and two more soldiers' unseen came out of the brush on either side of the car. They grabbed each one of us out and dragged us to the back jaguar. The men in black got inside sitting in the front. Oddly we were not handcuffed. Jocelyn and I gave each other a look, then looked back at the stolen car they were taking apart. Then they pushed the car off to the side of the road and torched it.

The two men in black suits turned. The older one on the right said we are "Ex US Military Intelligence. Our hackers caught transmission of your escape, and we came to intercept you. We are your allies, Titus you have started a revolution. Most of us in the intelligence services were compartmentalized and until you woke us up, we thought we were doing the right thing."

"I am aware." I said reluctantly.

"I am going to cut it straight to the point, we didn't save you from the firing squad awaiting you at the border for your benefit."

"Why did you then?" Asked Jocelyn.

"Our family was taken hostage at the start of the crisis, because we both knew too much valuable information and would not come in from the field. We were disavowed and cut from the system; we had no idea how corrupt the people above us had become until it was too late. We thought we were doing the right thing, but we were just pawns in their game."

"You have no idea." I said.

"Tell us, did you see prisoners at the Rothson estate?" The man driving asked.

"No, the cells were empty." I said.

"What are your names?" Jocelyn asked.

"I am John White and this is my partner David Green." The driver said.

I whisper to Jocelyn, "Code names, just go with it, we need their help right now."
"So, where are we heading" I ask.

"Sanctuary, an abandoned home near Paris. If the prisoners are not where you were, they are at the Rothson Mansion outside of Paris. The Illuminati will be holding them there for sure before transfer to the Swiss base. Did you see FEMA signs in the prison sector?"

"No, it was just empty." I said.

The Lost Truth by Dean Fougere

"We need all the info, tell us everything you know as we drive."

So Jocelyn and I recounted everything to them, they recorded most of it. We reached Paris without issue, our hosts had fake diplomatic papers stating they were UN ambassadors, and the checkpoints never questioned them. The armed guards had not travelled back with us, taking another route and a big van; they had loaded our gear into the front jaguar.

Chapter 27 – Ideas Never Die

Outside Paris, France – Modern Day

As we wait at a hotel near the Paris Rothson Estate, we watched the news. America has fully slipped into civil war and the imagery is horrible. The US has a lot of guns and it seems every street corner is littered with firefights. The world around us is falling apart. We save those who will freely join us, but we need to strike back.

In the months leading up to the raid on the Rothson compound, Jocelyn and I got married. We had grown very close to one another and wanted to bring a child into this world for love and so that what we knew would continue after our deaths. We had joined a small group of resistance fighter's lead by these two brothers. They're real names were Bill and Jim Paine. By hacking emails we had intercepted confirmation the prisoners were being held in the Manor, but not for transfer, for a satanic ritual sacrifice.

The Rothson manor since the start of revolution in the US had become extremely heavily guarded. All of the nations of the New World Order had declared martial law, and entered into a police state. We would use this to our advantage. The whole world fell under the surveillance grid while the elite enjoyed more secrecy and privacy than ever before.

We had stolen one of the new French police vehicles, called a MSTAR Armored vehicle and a compliment of French Police Uniforms. We would use this cover to reach the Manor, once there we would raid. Find Lord Rothson and company for execution, and save any prisoners on site. We also had a drone stolen from the police for oversight coverage; it could watch over the compound and give us an eye in the sky. The local authorities would not be able to reach the compound for a minimum of 20 minutes, once we wiped out the guards at the compound they would be screwed. It would be a quick massacre, in and out. The message it would send would be far worth all of our lives, the Illuminati head families would all be there, thinking they are untouchable, unknown, but we would surprise them.

We knew from intercepted emails they would be meeting at the manor to celebrate the Beltane Fire Festival on May 1st. The same day the Illuminati was founded. They have a big bonfire outside the manor and perform human sacrifices hidden underground the manor to please Prometheus and his fallen angels who feed off the energy of fear and the souls sacrificed. They may even be hidden in the crowd. Finding any individual targets would be near impossible as they all wore masks and black gowns. Orders were to fire on everyone. I would provide sniper over watch, and use my ring to disappear and meet Jocelyn and the rest of the team at the new hideout. Except I had not told anyone I had hidden the ring before this operation. Had it buried far away, where no one would look. I wouldn't risk carrying it around any longer; it was far safer to hide it where no one would look for it than to bring it to the enemy.

Jocelyn would head south to the new hideout where a backup team was waiting for us. She was pregnant with my child and I did not want her anywhere near me. She at first wanted to spot for me, but after a major battle. I convinced her to protect our child instead. She declared she would be watching the drone feed and talking with us to help. This was as good a compromise as I could have asked for.

The night before Jocelyn and I had talked about the past and the future. We discussed our hopes and fears, what we wanted for the child. We fell asleep hopeful of the days ahead, believing the world had not been lost. That we could help save this planet from itself. I kissed her as she slept next to me, the love we shared would not end with death, and it would carry on forever. It was my love for her that convinced me I should not fear death; the emotion of love is what death brought for us that believed in Christ. I would see her again, if not in this life in the next.

I fell into a deep sleep. I had a dream.

I was walking in the sand. I saw a shining light ahead of me, guiding me over the dunes. As I approached a massive hill I saw light in the valley below. The closer I came to the fires in the valley the less the light ahead of me in the sky shown. As I reached the crest of the dune the light had all but gone. I looked down on the valley below.

Large fires were everywhere, with large groups of people surrounding them. On the fires were people, the smell stinking the whole night air. Giant men, standing 15 feet tall and more wore giant bull costumes and consumed the flesh from the fires.

A bright light shown over the land, emanating from massive Sharp Mountain in the distance. A gold bright yellow peak, the mountain was bright white. It seemed man made, it was.

It shown brilliant in the golden sun. The Nile River ran directly by it, and I could almost see the royalty stepping off the boats and onto the steps of the Great Pyramid. Next to it was the Sphinx, yet the face was much different, far larger than I remember. It was the face of a lion, not a man, and seemed to be far more fitting of the body, above it directly in the night sky was the constellation Leo. The Sphinx was aimed directly at it on the horizon.

The Great Pyramid and three others were sitting on a larger foundation, flat and resembled temple mount. They were clearly aligned with the orion belt constellation and the Nile mirrored the Milky way. From my viewpoint on a hill closer to the delta I could see the entire Giza Plateau.

The Lost Truth by Dean Fougere

I saw an object on the far side of the pyramid ascend into the sky just above the top of the capstone, shining brilliant array of colors. Then as if shot from a gun it blasted straight up and out of sight, no noise, no trail, just gone breaking the speed of sound without creating a sonic boom.

Having been to Egypt before I noticed the Nile was well out of place. In the modern day the Nile is miles east of the Pyramids, but I was looking at it running right next to it, so close people could step off boats onto these massive uncovered in modern day bases under the pyramids. With the Nile being so far out of place and with the alignments in the constellations above; the date had to be roughly 30,000 BC. But how could that be? As the thought hit me the sun started to shine into my eyes so bright I couldn't see, I tried to block it but couldn't.

■ ■

Outside Paris, France – Modern Day

I awoke in my bed. The sun came pouring in through the window on my face. Daylight already? I climb out of bed, and peer out. "Where is Titus?"

I throw on some clothes I had laid out and went down to the kitchen. Putting the berretta he gave me in my hip holster.

The backup team was all set and waiting for me. We had a quick breakfast and climbed into the backup MSTAR. We fired up the drone and sent the small handheld helicopter on it's way. The operator steered it from a mobile laptop still connected to the US Military satellite grid system connected to what used to be Interpol.

I watched intently, wanting to see where Titus and the rest of the team had gone. Fear had started to overwhelm me. After twenty minutes of French countryside flashing by on the small screen their MSTAR came into view.

One of the guys in the MSTAR says, "middle of the day what are we thinking?"

I get angry and say, "We had to go now to save the children locked up in the basement, waiting could mean they would already be dead. We don't know what time they perform the rituals below ground. We are hitting the compound a half hour after Lord Rothson's transport arrives. We must take him down to send the message."

A few minutes later and the mike clicked on Titus spoke, "Overwatch in place, killzone multiple tangos." The rest of the team reported in and requested status on ground support at the mansion. We gave them the sitrep, there was five armed guards at the gate, another five at the front door, four snipers on the roof, and four patrolling guard teams of three with dogs. Never mind what was inside or could be brought in via rail system. Documents revealed the mansion was far larger underground than above.

"Approaching front gate, Titus take down the gate guards."

I watched on the drone feed as the first guard dropped, "One" Titus said, then "Two" almost instantly as a guards head exploded on screen from the .50 cal round. The other three guards starting firing at the approaching MSTAR, Titus took down all three methodically. "Three, four, five. Gate clear, taking down snipers on mansion."

As Titus said this Jocelyn watched on in horror. Men started piling out of the mansion, seemingly hundreds of them. "They are coming out of the ground all around me." Titus yells out, "Get out of here. I will cover as long as I can get out of there."

Bill Paine calls back on the radio, "I am going to die trying, my family will not be theirs to kill."

I grab the radio, "Titus, get out of there, put on the ring save yourself."

Titus calls back, "They must be monitoring our transmissions, I hid the ring before I came out here, that trip I took a month back, and now lies beneath the Statue of Lucifer, under his eternal flame, in the Harbor of New Babylon."

"What? Why would you! Why there?" I scream out.

"They found me, I love you Jocelyn." Titus says.

I watched the screen, my stomach feeling a pain I had never felt. My heart sank in my chest and agony overcame me. Three men on the screen stood Titus up to a tree, barely visible in his ghillie suit. All three then opened fire into him. Filling him with at least 50 rounds of ammunition.

I cry out in anger and grab the laptop screen and throw it against the armored wall. The guard to my left grabs me and depresses a syringe into my arm. "He says, calm down we can't do anything for them, they knew the risk, we will get revenge."

The world grew dark, my vision slowly faded and I fell into a dark black sleep.

Chapter 28 – A New World

Global Alliance Capitol, Rocky Mountains – Distant Future

A flash of bright white light interrupts the darkness. I look up and a doctor stares back down at me, his nametag read William Cooper.

"Good job Miles. We found it. With that ring we can kill the President! We were able to record all of those memories. That is the furthest we have ever been able to see back. What you have uncovered will change the world. We now know where Titus hid the ring."

"I hope so, you should have seen it. Where is the statue, what was he referencing?" I ask.

"In the past, pre World War III, the New World Order had to hide it's symbolism in plain sight. To slowly indoctrinate the masses without them ever being aware of the indoctrination. Through symbolism they created monuments with Illuminati, and

Freemasonic Architecture to make the people worship their Gnostic Symbols without anyone ever realizing it. The Statue of Liberty is exactly that."

"Please explain, I have read it symbolized freedom according to our history." I ask.

"Yes, all exoteric explanations, along with any hints of Christianity or religion, have been eliminated from the public information grid. The statue in reality was a recreation of the Colossus of Rhodes one of the 8 wonders of the Ancient World. The Colossus depicts Apollo the god of the Greeks. Apollo, the Greek sun God, was an ancient incarnation of Lucifer. The eternal flame, comes from the Eternal Flame of Babylon, and is representative of the wisdom that Lucifer gave to mankind. The apple from the tree, making mankind as Gods, a lie, but those in power still believe the lie, that eventually the tree of knowledge will lead them to immortality. Through the use of intellect man will become immortal, the original lie. Prometheus is a popular retelling of the same story, a God who rebelled to give mankind wisdom, fire in the case of Prometheus who was then imprisoned in chains for eternity in Tarturus, it is the same story of Lucifer; Satan. Lucifer means light bearer, and the Illuminati believe that Lucifer is the source of intellect, that he gave mankind Wisdom, they see the Apple from the tree of wisdom as a good thing. That by gaining intellect we shall eventually figure out eternal life. That is why Skull & Bones number is 322, they are referencing Genesis 3:22 which states:

And the LORD God said, Behold, the man is become as one of us, to know good and evil: and now, lest he put forth his hand, and take also of the tree of life, and eat, and live for ever: Genesis 3:22 KJV

Lucifer took many forms along with his fallen Angels in the past to deceive the public. Apollo was just one of many Sun Gods that Lucifer portrayed himself as. This sun symbolism was seen throughout the past, in many logos such as NATO, Smithsonian Institute, etc. That is why the bible Revelation 9:11 relates to New York City and it's big pagan statue of Apollo (in Ancient Greek Apollo was pronounced Apollyon).

And they had a king over them, which is the angel of the bottomless pit, whose name in the Hebrew tongue is Abaddon, but in the Greek tongue hath his name Apollyon – Revelation 9:11 King James Bible

"The truth will set us free, we need the proof to wake the population finally. No one believes what this world was, and how far it has fallen into despotism. The life they lived in the past before the New World Order was beautiful, free people, freedom of ideas, and freedom of religion all these things we have lost. Replaced by the ancient culture of eugenics, elitism and tyranny, originated from the lost civilization of Atlantis, which was created, by Azazel and Semyaza and the other 200 fallen Angels. Reinstituted a New Atlantis, ruled by the global bankers and political elite, being ruled by the Anti-Christ. Now all thoughts are recorded, any even thought of religion or God and the citizen is re-educated." Stated the doctor.

"I need to go for a walk. My descendants had these ideas; ideas of love, freedom, and the world were so much better before, we are truly living in a sick world. I had never experienced them before, not to that extent. We outcasts talk of these things but to actually live and feel it, it is too hard to live in these times now. I prefer the illusion of living in the past to where the world is now. The worst part is, no one knows, everyone is so distracted by their virtual realities, games, entertainment that they couldn't even care that they have been completely enslaved." I say.

"The chasm between what people think is going and ... reality is far worse than we feared Miles, we never knew how we got to where we are now. Or how to kill the anti-Christ leader that is now the President. If we can't kill him before he rounds up the last Christians on Earth, it will be all over. I don't know how many of us are left, living off the grid, but not many I am sure. The Guardians find and eliminate more of us everyday. Now that we know what they did, we can change things." The doctor said.

"There is no going back, we have to move forward. We must take these ideas of freedom and use them to free the world from Azazel's son. Ideas not guns will set us free. We have been trying to use force since the beginning but it won't work, these ideas will, words will be our weapon. Every time the world was changed through violence it only became worse, the only way to change the world for the better is with the truth." I need to think this over. I'll be back later. "If we kill the current president another will take his place, the Illuminati's only weakness is information, as long as they control it they control the population, if we can break through the noise and send our signal into the brains of everyone alive through the central network, we could wake the masses and take the power back. We will use their own technological tyranny against them."

"That's it, if we can upload the truth about the Illuminati and what they have done to us to the Central Computer and wake everyone at once. Just think we would be able to free everyone and take back this planet."

"We will never be able to get through to everyone, the Illuminati are holding on tight with their indoctrination. People are so happy, so entertained that this might be harder than we think, if we unplug the masses they might hate us for it, ignorance is bliss and all. Even still, we need to put the truth out there, along with an accurate translation of the Bible along with the memories in your blood onto the emergency communication channel of the information grid, it will force everyone to be exposed to the information. People will choose sides; I hope most will join us. The New World Order will have a full revolt on their hands immediately, I am sure we will lose many to the Guardians, but in the end the good guys win right? Hopefully the truth will set us all free. Real power is people not Government, and if we can get the people to stand together we can free them from tyranny."

"What do we do next?"

"I need you to sneak into the central computer, and upload a virus that will open up a gateway for us to take over the emergency channel. The emergency channel cannot be shut off because the Illuminati wanted to have complete control over any emergency situation, so that the only news available to the masses is what they tell them. This allows them to constantly have false flag operations you see on TV everyday, and the same recurring crimes, to ensure the citizens continue to comply with the police state for security. Problem reaction solution, everyday."

"How do we broadcast? The only connection points are a human's brain through the RFID Chip, and the holograms people watch controlled by the central computer. We need a central computer technician, whom are highly protected, and he must be in the central command hub to connect to the central computer?"

"So we take a citizen, infect him with the virus, the virus will change his brain DNA to accept the new memories and will turn him into a proxy drone. Once he is our own Manchurian candidate, he will walk into the central computer, connect and broadcast, all we need do is stay close enough to him to control the chip. We can upload the truth and then we will directly insert his brain into the emergency channel and broadcast out the message. The interference in his brain activity will kill him or leave him brain dead. However, the citizens are so blind to their reality they are basically brain dead already. This is a just reward for all the times they have done the exact same thing to a non-conforming citizen to just catch or spy on one of us 'domestic Christian fundamentalist terrorists'. Give me an hour and I will have a Virus ready to attack the DNA, all you need to do is stick the chip into the forehead chip on one of the emergency broadcast operators and connect him to the Central computer, it will automatically turn on the signal. The virus will open a remote access and I can connect to do the work, all you need to do is get back to my station before the party starts and the Guardians declare a lockdown and kill every non-citizen within a hundred miles of the central computer system." The doctor says.

I walk over and put on my gear. Staring out the window at the masses of people below, walking along in a zombified state as they watch their favorite entertainment flash in their minds eye or on the holographic display in front of their eyes. Streaming movies and shows straight from the Information Grid (a new highly controlled version of the internet) into their brain, all propaganda, all subtly satanic. The entire population was atheist having been educated into the second degrees of freemasonry. Everyone completely unaware, they saw the universe as a geometric construct of pure chance, one of many multiple universes, there was no God, or afterlife, no angels, or demons, just science and their reality, if they couldn't see it, it didn't exist. Human interaction and connection gone, their robotic limbs move them along as the grid controls their movements so they can disconnect and enjoy their favorite show as their body moves towards their destination. All human activity was taxed; all human activity was tightly controlled. The RFID Chip ensured no one would resist because without the RFID chip turned on you could not be a part of society, no food, no water, no access to buildings, cars, anything. Nobody cared, no one knew the real world they were missing around him or her was far better than the world they were living in virtually. Everyone thought this life was it, that humans were meant to live forever and thus we had to get as much pleasure in this life as possible. That eugenics was the answer and by mixing with machines we had evolved into a better race, had become Gods ourselves living "forever" in a prison no one could see marching behind symbols of the devil.

"I survived this long haven't I?" I said and walk towards the door. Checking my handheld pistol, armed with tiny EMP bullets that causes anyone with a RFID Brain chip to die instantly. The EMP charge once it hit the target found the highest conductive part of the body and overcharged it. On my back was a small device that could send out a scrambler signal on command so any cameras nearby would temporarily be blinded. I turn to my mentor, "Those who fear death are already dead." And walk out.

As I walk across the medical room, the door turns transparent revealing what lies beyond. A small camera above the door reads my irises and opens the door. The doors open, and I step out onto the walkway. This door was one of the only doors in the entire Capitol that I could even access. The public doors don't scan irises because most people have had their eyes replaced with machine replacements, bonuses being, perfect vision, ability to take photos and store them in your brain or upload them directly to your Global Social File. The public doors are opened by a signal from the required Brain or wrist RFID chip implanted into every citizen via a tattoo. The early 2000's had seen a massive rise in the popularity of tattoos, which had been caused by subliminal programming in the entertainment industry as a preparation for the eventual RFID tattoo system. It worked as most people saw their tattoo RFID chip as cool, and as each had it's own unique number something special like a birthmark, some were even customized.

Christianity and other religions were blamed for the wars, and eventually removed from history all together. The new Religion was to worship the Earth and the President who gave the people all they needed and eternal life as long as they would submit, sacrifice freedom for security and live in the New World Order Police State. Astrology was seen as prophetic, and the Sun Moon and stars were once again worshipped by the masses, while the elite knew the Universe was far greater than what could be seen. It was argued those who wanted privacy were only trying to hide something. As long as you complied it was easy and safe, but if you refused any order, if you desired freedom and the truth, you were killed instantly and all memory of you was wiped from society. Those who went along with the programming believed that they would one day win the game, climb the ladder or win the lottery and be one of the rich elite, so the dream of social movement was still alive, but completely fake.

Citizens disappeared all the time, but no citizens ever knew of it, it was never talked about. After they vanished the central computer would wipe the memories of everyone in society who had any contact with that person, all records gone. Only those who were not in the system would ever notice. Occasionally the central computer would miss a memory, and the memory would needle a person to the point of insanity, constantly reminding them of a husband or son that just vanished one day but no other memory to explain why or who the person was. Rumor amongst the non-citizens living outside society was those citizens disappeared for many reasons. One was they awoke to the system they were living in, and the central computer that monitors their thoughts declared them a threat and ordered their death as part of the pre crime program. The other was one of the Illuminati elite had taken an interest and desired that citizen for their own purposes. Another that was held by only those who had seen the truth like myself, was the Illuminati had continued their ritual sacrifices and these missing citizens were being used for such purposes. Just before May 1st, every year is when most people vanished and we knew May 1st, was their Beltane Fire Festival, which required human sacrifice, in places like Bohemian Grove that had been rebuilt on new hidden ground thanks to WW3. The symbol of the owl, pyramid with all seeing eye, Knight's Templar cross, pentagram star, sun symbolism, all still present and far more widespread than before in all corporate logos, architecture, musicians, to movies, and fashion the symbols of the illuminati were all over society yet no one knew what they meant. People were given the esoteric false meaning, in example the Sun Symbolism is because people in the Old World used to worship the Sun because it gave them life, or the All Seeing Eye is the third eye, that allows us to connect to consciousness, false. In reality the sun symbolism represents Lucifer, the holder of the Light, and the All Seeing Eye represents his left eye seeing through your third eye known today as the pineal gland represented also by the pine comb, that is how Lucifer comes through the veil. That is why the Egyptian pharaohs are shown with serpents coming out of their foreheads. Lucifer's left eye was undamaged before he was chained in Tarturus. Lucifer has one eye.

Society was ordered, from the President to the lowest worker. Everyone had a place, and no one overstepped his or her place in society. The top of the global pyramid was the President, elected for life, because the citizens worshipped him as the prophesized messiah. With no nations, the globe was split into 10 Districts by region. An appointed Governor ran each district. District 11 was separate from society, and ruled over the rest of society. It was argued that the best form of democracy was an enlightened democracy. All citizens were connected to the central computer, and the entire population voting made all decisions. This ensured the citizens thought they were free, because they made the rules. In reality, 51% of the population could vote to enslave 100% of the population and they did, because they were told to do so, by the media to save themselves from chaos.

The citizens always thought democracy was the correct form of government, though in reality it is the greatest form of tyranny. The United States in the old world was not a democracy, it was a constitutional republic, because the founders realized a democracy like Athens or Sparta, or Rome, could and always did become a tyranny. That a Constitutional Republic created by the need to protect certain rights every citizen was born with was the only way to ensure freedom. Democracy is not freedom because it is majority rule, and the majority can rule to take all your rights and freedoms away.

The world had changed I thought, the 11th district had been created by a new invention called the Space Elevator. Much like Washington DC, the Vatican City or the City of

London in the past, they wanted a separate state from the rest of the Country, to ensure it did not have to abide by the rules of the Districts. After WWIII people needed a new goal to strive for, and with the invention of robotics mankind looked to the next frontier, space. It was correctly argued that the Universe was far too vast to not have life or other habitable planets, but also even closer to home extremely profitable materials such as helium-3 on the moon.

By using geosynchronous satellites fixed around the globe on the equator, cables were run down to earth creating elevators. These elevators could bring massive amounts of payload out of the Earth's atmosphere and into space, very cheaply. By connecting the satellites together a new ring was formed around the Earth, and connected back to Earth by elevators. This eventually grew and grew until it reached the point it was at now, stretching one-fifth the way around the planet, and growing everyday. This space platform allowed spaceships to be built in space and not be required to break from Earth's atmosphere or re-enter. The elevator cables and the ring itself were covered in Solar Collection materials, thus turning the entire station other than the windows into a massive power collection antennae. It provided for the entire world's energy needs, eliminating the need for oil, nuclear, etc. Only the 11th district members, construction workers, and the Guardians could enter. The entire station was completely self sufficient, having a massive tropical garden in the center that received sunlight and produced enough oxygen and food for the entire district.

Members of the 11th district were the only citizens allowed to guarded and armed. They all had private security teams of Guardians, and mainly were completely separated from society. Separate resorts in areas of the world the citizens could not get to, access to private hotels, clubs, etc. They all had genetic modification and most had become more machine than man, with the

most advanced technology going to this class of individuals first. They controlled society in a brutal technocracy.

The most disturbing aspect of the 11th district and the President was their worship of Luciferian doctrine. They hid this from the public completely, yet made the public a part of their rituals all the time. Religion had been wiped from any member of society as part of the teaching the masses the 'secret' esoteric doctrines of freemasonry, though the religious esoteric meanings had remained only for those in District 11. The 11th district had realized that the human soul was energy and that by sacrificing humans to their demonic gods they were granted greater power, mainly increased consciousness. Another byproduct of this was the extraction of the adrenal gland from their victims, which served as the ultimate drug for the elite. Their sacrifices came from the ideologies of black sex magik, which was developed by Aleister Crowley in his Ordo Templi Orientis, Crowley is one of the most influential freemasons to have ever lived. He used the ancient teachings captured by the Templars in Solomon's temple, and then Crowley's protégé Jack Parsons perfected the sex magik as an Ordo Templi Orientis member and then became founder of the Jet Propulsion Laboratory. Jack Parsons is one of the most influential NASA engineers from the past. Over time, the elite had made improvements to these sacrifices, and during this current New Age preferred to use non-citizens, Christians as that brought the demons they worked with the greatest pleasure.

Looking off the side of the walkway I see the capitol's electromagnetic train go flying past. Eclipsing nearly 900 km/h without making the slightest noise and using only magnetic propulsion. Technically it doesn't even touch the rails, but floats slightly above them. It launches a full trainload of workers, human resources to their corporate slave chambers. Where they plug their minds into machines and work by controlling machines through the neural interface. They all thought they were free, living in what I called the New Kingdom of Babylon being lead by their savior who had given them peace and eternal life. They were all stuck in a prison, a prison completely designed and perfected to ensure their compliance.

Artificial intelligence could never be truly created without the addition of the human conscious being inserted into the machine. Human brains are far more complex than any computer mankind ever created and when connected together they create an AI system far more advanced than anything artificial. By uploading his consciousness into the central computer, and implanting it permanently into a robot, the President had become the world's first and only eternal man. Well eternal as long as the power remained on, or the finite universe remained intact, basically any attempt at eternal life in a finite Universe is a farce because the Universe has a beginning and an end, the Kingdom of God exists outside this Universe, without time. Consciousness is not something that can be artificially created and machines could never fully replace the mental capacity of humans, due to one simple fact. The human soul, the consciousness that controls the human body exists outside the dimensional spectrum of the physical world, therefore without inclusion of this spiritual dimension the physical world lacks the required tools for consciousness.

The brain is not a machine, it is a signal translator, and it turns the electrical processes sent to it via the nervous system and translates them into a form of energy that a human soul can understand. Literally the human body is a machine that a ghost can operate. This information had been completely withheld from society, as long as people did not believe in an afterlife, they would only want material objects and pleasure and thus could be controlled. A society of people that did not fear death was completely uncontrollable through fear, and the entire system had been built on fear.

How did we get here? I asked myself as I stared out across the New World Capitol City, called New Babylon, in the Rocky Mountain Range. The world was a far different place than what had existed during the memories I had experienced.

I thought about the dominos that had fallen and how well they were designed to bring about this New World Order that I now lived in.

It had started with the collapse of the American Petrodollar as the World Reserve Currency, a collapse ignited when the Federal Reserve buildings were destroyed all at once. The destruction of the Federal Reserve caused the American public to wake up to their enslavement by the central banks and massive violent demonstrations took place. The destruction of the Reserve myth forced the Banks to make the puppet US President to utilize the NDAA 2012 bill to incarcerate all Americans that were considered anti-government, officially defined as domestic terrorists and sovereign citizens. The Illuminati using their media branches of MSNBC, CNN, Fox News, etc. called them domestic terrorists, and identified them by looking for Christian fundamentalists, Military veterans, constitutionalists, and libertarians. They rounded the anti-government protestors and sick people into the FEMA camps that had been built previously around the country for illegal immigration. They used the massive amounts of executive orders enacted by Bush and O'Brien to take over all functions of society. They also authorized UN Peacekeepers to assist Homeland Defense to confiscate all privately owned firearms. This lead to open revolts, a problem that was planned for.

Of course the US Government, had already completely prepared for any terrorism, domestic or foreign and completely wiped out the revolts. The FEMA Camp system was already built, over 800 camps nationwide housing thousands of domestic terrorists was soon expanded upon. The US Military had been fighting a war on terror for years; they were perfectly trained and seasoned at putting down civil unrest. The same tactics they learned, the same equipment they used in Iraq was turned on the US population. Furthermore, with the large percentage of immigrants in the US Military, the addition of NATO and UN forces, most of the soldiers were not Americans and had no issue firing on American citizens. The US police had also been militarized since the 9/11 attack and completely desensitized to violence being brought up on shooter videos games and training with no hesitation targets. Militarized police, who had been guilty of more vicious and outrageous abuses of violence, without any oversight or repercussions leading up to the open revolt, filling YouTube with violent police abuse videos, turning people against the police while also conditioning the police to think violence is acceptable. This army of trained soldiers, turned into mindless zombies and psychopaths by propaganda, training, group pressure, and prescription medication had been turned on the public they had sworn to defend. Millions of people died, hundreds of thousands imprisoned into makeshift and high security FEMA Camps. The US was split into 10 FEMA regions and the President using pre-established executive orders appointed 10 governors. Each Governor was given complete authority over his region until the crisis had availed. Congress by law could not review this martial law for 6 months, and by the time this came about Congress had been dissolved as it was declared ineffective.

To replace the Federal Reserve a new currency was introduced. All of the world's central banks had been putting their holdings into the IMF and World Bank for special drawing rights for years. A new currency with the World Bank acting as the Central Bank was to be introduced to save the Western nations from economic collapse and eliminate all currency. The currency would be backed by the gold holdings that had been seized by the private banks from America's Federal Reserve years before the collapse, leaving Fort Knox completely empty before Titus blew up the Federal

Reserve building. The new currency was electronic only and called the phoenix because out of the ashes of the old global economy it had risen.

The resulting chaos in the US forced the Military to bring back their troops from foreign posts to quell the rebellion at home. NATO's encirclement of Russia and China in year's past had forced the two together, against America. The Chinese and Russians run by the Illuminists fell right into the plan creating a new opposing global currency with the BRICs nations. All part of the Illuminati end plan, to create regional currencies that could oppose one another before eventually uniting them into a global currency based on the most successful regional electronic only currency. The Illuminati knew that people would accept anything as long as the change happened gradually. The Illuminati were not just running the Western Nations through the Central Banking system, they had complete control over the Chinese Government and the Russian Government financially as well. They played all three like pawns, to create an artificial tribulation, just as it was written in the Bible, to make people believe that when the war ended the President would be the prophesized return of the savior for a thousand year reign of peace. It was all a lie, an artificial creation, the President whom ruled over all the Nations of the Earth now, was not the savior, he was not the next step in human evolution as he claimed, he was the false prophet, the anti-Christ. The war that he wrought to bring about his position as the first President of the One World Government was the most vicious act of humanity ever witnessed.

Russia trying to re-establish itself and break free from NATO encirclement, put troops into Syria and Ukraine. With no US forces in the area they retook these countries just to fight it out with rebels being funded by the Illuminati. The Chinese allied with the Iranian Shiites took over the Arab Nations by uniting them against first ISIS a sect of Sunni Islam funded by Saudi Arabia then ended the Sunni and Shiite differences by uniting them against Israel and creating a new Islamic State.

Then the powder keg was lit. Iran and the other now unified Arab Nations attacked Israel, and the Israeli's retaliated by bombing Damascus into the ground; the oldest city in the world became nothing more than a strip of concrete thanks to tactical thermonuclear devices. NATO sent it's remaining military in reserve to Israel and Poland to provide relief. Seeing an opportunity on the other side of the world, the North Koreans invaded South Korea with Chinese support. The Western Nations and the US sent an emergency response team to stop the attack and save the 50,000 US soldiers stationed there but it wasn't enough. 1 Million North Korean tanks pushed the American forces all the way to the Southern tip of Korea in three days. The US was about to lose 50,000 US Soldiers to the North Koreans, so they had no option but to unleash its secret weapons platforms, their Angel Tech Space Weapons Program. Created by the gold taken by the Templars from Solomon's temple, a massive deep space weapons system had been created in secret. The fallen Angel, Prometheus aka Azazel had given the designs for the system to the Illuminati NASA engineers who had studied under Jack Parsons and Nazi Occultist Werner Von Bram.

The US had been secretly building a Space Weapons Program for years, originally dubbed Star Wars it had been replaced from protecting the skies to an offensive weapons platform. The idea was simple, launch Nukes into the upper atmosphere from these deep space platforms, causing EMP blasts to wipe out all electronics worldwide, to shut down the worlds' power grid. The Angel Tech Platforms were deep in space, too far out to be affected by the EMP's. They were spread around the globe and had extremely advanced imaging technology. From their bunkers the 4th Branch of the US Government could use this system to rain down massive damage on any part of the Earth. The satellites used the superconductive gold as massive batteries that constantly collected solar energy from massive solar panels, and because the batteries were superconductive no energy was lost, the power just increased exponentially over time unless released. This energy when released was very precise laser particle beams that could burn through 100 feet of dirt into a bunker and melt everyone inside, never mind armored vehicles, planes, etc. The satellites also had nuclear warheads on them, but these were limited in number. To stop the North Korean advance, they launched multiple tactical nuclear weapons. The laser systems and Nukes were used to kill almost all of the North Korean Army and it's 1 million tanks in a matter of minutes. The Russians, Chinese launched their weapons as soon as the grid was taken down, but had no way to destroy the deep space Angel Tech platforms that they didn't know existed before the blackout. The US and Israel launched their peacekeepers in response. The end result was nuclear holocaust of which a small fraction of the original global population survived.

During the nuclear fallout the Illuminati, the Bilderberg Group Members, the 4th branch, the council of 300, the Club of Rome, along with their top military and scientists took refuge in the massive underground cities that had been secretly built and connected by a new underground rail system. They had long developed with FEMA continuity of governance plans, though suspiciously they never made continuity of civilian plans. Stories of earthquakes, sinkholes, strange noises worldwide in 2013 and 2014 were linked to fracking or other phenomena, yet in reality just as the construction of Denver International Airport those stories were a cover, the fracking was allowed as a cover for the large underground bunkers and rail systems being built."

After the main chaos ended. The Illuminati, their transhuman servants and their new robotic weapons emerged from their bunkers. They launched a new worldwide array of high definition satellites that could be used for targeting, an army of flying and walking drones that were controlled via neural interfaces, and a grid of satellite based weapons platforms that could rain down both precise laser weaponry and small thermonuclear missiles from space. All from stored bunkers. They had left large preplanned areas radiation free and set up FEMA style districts in each region. Imported the seeds from their bunkers in Antarctica to start over with all organic only food, the GMO's of the earlier generation had been used for population control as part of a slow kill program and were no longer needed as they were a major health risk.

Feeling secure in their dominance they unleashed everything they had left to ensure no one left on Earth would disobey them. A version of Hell on Earth was the result.

Machines as large as elephants, and as small as flies swarmed the world killing everyone who would not submit or did not have a place in the New World. People tried to hide but couldn't find shelter, only the inner circle, and people of importance were saved, everyone else was left to fight for their own life or executed. The illuminati themselves saw and still see the population as cattle, no more than useless eaters that had to be killed off to avoid overpopulation. To them the human race was a disease, a virus. They were selecting certain DNA traits from the population to stay alive and eventually serve as part human part machine slaves in the new world order. The people they saved were so happy to be safe they didn't care what they had to submit to in order to be free from the fear of death, RFID chip tattoos were never protested for a hot meal and shelter by the majority. It was seen as a mark of importance to have the brain RFID tattoo; the lower classes only had the wrist tattoo and could not access the information grid telepathically. Those who were not indoctrinated by the Illuminati and survived banded together under Christianity, as it was know known to be the truth. We have survived on the outskirts of society ever since, waiting for our salvation whilst the Illuminati hunt us down and use us for their own sick enjoyment when they catch us.

The Illuminati reeducated those they had 'saved' and turned into citizens. They would need these people to rebuild their world. In a Utopia the people in charge never work, and the Illuminati despite having machines still needed human consciousness. The Illuminati never from the time of Atlantis before the flood of Noah, to when Nimrod created Babylon, or when Chase Bank built it's massive Illuminati tower in Indianapolis Indiana had they ever physically built anything themselves. The people built the pyramids, the ancient sites, using technology and information the fallen angels gave to the rulers, the old world pharaohs, the original Illuminati just watched, we always did the work. The people are the great masons, we build their towers, not the Illuminated Master Masons who are nothing but false idols telling us what to do. They are just people chosen by fallen angels to receive knowledge, instead of helping us they used the information to enslave all of us so we would build giant temples to them, like the great pyramid, rather than building infrastructure for all the people that would have allowed the population to survive and not just the buildings. Even in the modern world the people allow themselves to be manipulated by there believe in the new false god: money, to build massive towers and stadiums for elitists & bankers they despise. When they should have been building infrastructure, to deal with the population increase. They should have been funding massive space exploration projects to expand onto other planets and use their population as a benefit rather than a curse. Instead trillions of dollars were poured into getting the world population to build stuff no one needed, like massive mansions, huge towers to banks, enormous stadiums where meaningless sporting events kept the populace dumbed down and unaware. Even better we built the same weapons designed that were to be used on us the people, to kill ourselves while the rich laughed and watched from the towers we built for them.

The new world was no better; humanity was tricked by the illusions of the Illuminati. They believed the lie that they were to become, as Gods, living forever and jumped on transhumanism without ever considering the consequences, like it was unlocking the superpowers described in marvel comics. They were educated to the middle degrees of

Freemasonry, which taught the lie about death and living this life to the fullest because death comes for everyone. Most people had a reflection chamber in their home, as atheism had replaced spirituality for the masses, the elite practiced Luciferianism and technically atheism is Satanism. Humanity became more machine than man, advancing new age technology to merge mankind with the machine world, to unlock immortality or so they thought. In reality they were trapping their souls in a material world. New Age beliefs all are focused on the self, and this idea of self-improvement and was perfect for a society completely in love with itself. They argued they were personally achieving balance between light and dark or fear and love. Reality is the New Age beliefs are all Luciferian in nature, and come directly from the Fallen Angels, truth is fear and love are not equal, that the self, our consciousness is not a part of a greater thing, it is on it's own, singular it is our soul. No one reincarnates, the past life regression therapies were all just unlocking memories that exist in the DNA. The idea that humanity would evolve into a higher state of being, was based on evolution an idea created by Satanist Jacobins like Charles Darwin funded by the British Royalty to prove that by natural selection they had the right to rule. It was a complete utter lie created by the Fallen Angels and given to Darwin to trick the masses into altering their DNA to get rid of the disease they saw as the true bloodline of Christ, to prevent his return.

The absolute belief in evolution allowed the eugenicists to tightly control reproduction and actively intervene and alter DNA to pick only traits that were deemed positive. No longer would babies be born with genetic traits, any babies allowed to be born were perfect DNA specimens. Secretly they were wiping the genetic memories from the

DNA and thus changing everything about a person's personality before they were ever born. Also, any babies that had genetic markers of a disease, or were not approved by the state and were aborted, just like ancient Sparta. Thus people continued to constantly abort children before they were born and sacrifice them on the altar of Moloch unknowingly.

The eugenic philosophy was not only applied to babies before being born. It was determined that certain DNA traits were better suited for certain tasks. Thus at birth every child was examined and its occupation assigned. This was deemed best for efficiency, and all whom were born belonged to the State for the greater good of all. RFID chipped at birth, instant citizens without any choice. If non-citizens gave birth to a child, the child was taken from them if discovered. These children were examined and if they matched the DNA criteria for a position in society they were chipped and given to foster parents. If they had DNA traits, such as memories that lead to anti-government, or Christian religious beliefs they disappeared, to be sacrificed secretly on the fires of the Owl god Moloch in the New Bohemian Grove or to be used in private black sex magik rituals by the Illuminati elite so they could conjure up their ascended masters.

Generations went by as the Earth recovered from the nuclear war and soon society has surpassed what had previously existed. The Sun had grown a tiny fraction larger as it grew older and warmer, releasing methane from the abyss. Methane coupled with the massive heat blasts from the Nuclear bombs had caused the Oceans to rise over 100 feet in height since before World War III. The Eastern US Seaboard was hit when Russia

nuked the Atlantic Ocean in various underwater locations to create a massive tidal wave

that hit the entire East Coast at once. The ice caps had melted and were at 75% of the

original caps. Cities like New York, Boston, Washington DC, London, Tokyo,

Shanghai, Dubai, etc. Were all under over 100 feet of water from the melted caps

raising the ocean level. In the US, everything East of the Appalachian Mountains, and

West of the Rocky Mountains was basically under water. The planet was cooling and

being helped along by new beneficial Geo-engineering, by reducing the amount of

methane in the atmosphere, returning to only organic food production, re-growing the

forests, and using free solar power from the Space Elevators to power the cities. Soon

and slowly the waters started residing, at about an inch per year rate. It would be

hundreds of years before the Earth was back to as it was before humans destroyed it.

The New President of the New World Order, a descendant of the Merovingian Line,

declared he had found the key to eternal life. He was a 33rd degree mason, and

unknown to the public had been named Pindar of the Illuminati years before. He

claimed to be a direct descendant of Jesus through the Merovingian bloodline, a

carefully crafted lie that was preprogrammed by fictional novels such as the Da Vinci

Code. The Merovingian's were descendants of the Arian Race that was created when

Ham's bloodline was infected by Lucifer after the flood, and recreated his Kingdom in

Babylon under King Nimrod. He stated his DNA, being the same as Christ's was the

answer to eternal life, but this was a lie. By altering the populations DNA with a new

strain developed from the Nephilim, it would alter the aging information in the DNA, thus making aging stop at whatever age you chose to be injected. You could be 21 forever, or 45 if you wished. Everyone who wished to receive eternal life would have to have this new DNA strain injected into him or her. The DNA was not natural, it had been synthesized to seem supernatural and eternal, but it also wiped the memories from the DNA. Thus cutting humanity off from the past that they held within. As it was part Nephilim it allowed for humanity to be mixed with machines and interact with the EMF field through other parts of the nervous system. The population with the upgraded DNA would live for thousands of years, but even then the memories and lessons learned by their ancestors that made up a person's personality in the past was lost. Everyone born was a blank slate that the Illuminati could mold in their image, controlling all the information that was wired into the brain. A completely controlled society, bent on achieving the most pleasure possible, no regard for their actions, no penance for their sins. You could live forever or their version of forever, but you were a slave to materialism, and lacked the freedom of true knowledge. You would never enter Heaven and truly be at home and no one died, because all crime was stopped with the pre crime programs and all diseases could be cured with synthetic limbs, or lab created viruses that attacked bad DNA and replaced it with good DNA, which cured all forms of cancer and systemic disease.

The other benefit was what was called the digital interface. Created to allow people to enter into a digital world created for their minds, you could play virtual games, live virtual movies, see fictional retellings of the past in the first person, etc. Most people were so enticed and entertained by the connection to the grid they cared not for having no privacy even of thought. At night when people slept they would plug into the digital universe. A place where you could recreate yourself in any image and it felt as real as the real world. An hour in sleep was equivalent to a year in the digital universe. So if you slept eight hours you could live a fantasy life in the dream world for 8 years. This escape from reality is where the people spent most of their time, completely losing themselves in the pleasures of the New World and the advanced technology. There was no dissent; everyone thought the system was perfect. There were many reasons the Illuminati wanted this trans humanism reform of humanity but they all had one purpose, to eliminate free will and the DNA strain of mankind while keeping everyone asleep.

Mainly, Lucifer's son, the President of the New World Order. Knew his time to rule would only go on until the return of Jesus Christ. Lucifer and his son wanted to ensure Jesus could not return. They thought that if the DNA of Shem could be wiped off the face of the Earth entirely and replaced by a mixture of Nephilim, synthetic, and Ham Human DNA; a hybrid, that Jesus could not be reborn, that the Son of Man, would not come back to judge them. Without a pure human Shem DNA strain, Jesus could not return to Earth to judge the Illuminati or their New World Order anti-Christ messiah. It was the only way they knew how to avoid the judgment for their sins. If they could avoid this judgment they could rule forever and do whatever they wished as long as they lived. Of course this was a lie, but the Illuminati did not know.

Secondly, the Fallen Angels and Lucifer himself, also the demons created from the souls of the Nephilim during the flood, could now enter any human with the DNA upgrade at any time. Before they could only watch, and persuade us through suggestion, possession was ugly and normally caused a second personality complex and the powers of Christ could be used to free the possessed. The new DNA partly made from Nephilim DNA allowed for what is called perfect possession, the possessed actually enjoys this type of event because it makes them feel more powerful, and they enjoy sin even more, drawing energy from it. The damned soul possessing the human gets great enjoyment out of this because they can take control, and they get to experience the pleasure of the World that they have been permanently removed from physically. The demons get to live through the people they can now possess. They got to experience the pleasure of sex, drinking, drugs, etc. once more.

The human body without aging caused major problems. People still got injured, got disease, and needed to replace human body functions that failed despite the lack of aging. The only way to avoid these problems was to augment the human body with robotic parts and synthetic human organs. The longer a person lived, the more machine they became. Their brain, blood and nervous system became the only human part left. The brain was the key to life because it was the translator for the soul to take control of the human body, so it could not be altered too drastically or the human would not operate, it would be soulless, a pile of meat. If made correctly the empty body could be taken over by a demon, but the demons when in control of these empty bodies lacked the control a human soul did and would normally destroy the body in pursuit of physical pleasure very rapidly. The machine elements were the only part of the body the demons could actually operate on their own perfectly.

To keep the peace a genetically engineered race of Guardians were chosen from society before birth and made into half human half killer machines. Equipped with the most modern military technology possible. Separated from society to ensure they would not sympathize with people but just enforce the law without question. They were called the Guardians, but anytime they showed up in large numbers they slaughtered countless people, anyone who resisted. These were the half humans, half machine empty soulless bodies that Kammler had created. These were inhabited by demons directly, no human soul ever present. They had no compassion, completely psychotic. They had the right to act as judge and jury in the field, because their actions were controlled by the New World Central Justice Bureau's central computer that would shut down any guardian in violation of the law. It could even allow central command personnel to take over any guardian and use them via a proxy connection like a drone if the guardian in question was not following orders. Unknown to the public, the central computer could also take over any citizen through their chip implant. Whenever this happened all memories of the event were wiped, with the same Internet connection to the brain.

The central computer and the CJB's employees thus controlled the Guardians, and could take over any of them at any time. Moving through them like a virus, much as a demon moves through the human population. The central command computer, unknown to anyone was subject to manipulation by the Fallen Angels and demon spirits, whom could manipulate any electronic devices. The central computer would take over a Guardian and perform some task for the Fallen Angels that was well outside of it's programming that was created by the existing Laws. The computer could not violate the laws of society, unless the demonic spirits or CJB employees messed with it, and they did so whenever they needed something done. Mostly to keep their existence from the public a secret as it has been for thousands of years. The best trick the devil ever played was forcing humanity to think he wasn't real.

The motto of the New World Order wasn't freedom or liberty; it was Eternal Peace and Security, it was Utopia. After the mass killings of World War III the remaining human population would sacrifice their freedoms for the greater good, individualism no longer existed, everyone only lived to further the interests of the collective. Except the few Christians that were left, un-chipped non-citizens, barely surviving by protecting one another on the fringes of society, constantly hiding from the clutches of big brother. Christians were treated as religious bigots who had turned their backs on reason and science, yet this couldn't be further from the truth.

Just as this thought came into my head an automated security drone spotted me on the walkway. Instantly recognized me as a threat, and the central computer sent the message 'eliminate' to the drone. I pulled my pistol and shot it right in the front camera lens, glowing red until the bullet struck. The emp casing on the bullet caused the drone to fry all it's circuits and fall the hundreds of feet, out of sight into the mist below. Hopefully it didn't land on some poor soul.

Time to move. I ran down the walkway, keeping an eye out for the Peacekeepers that would be moving in to eliminate the radical Christian threat.

I reach the end of the runway and I see two Guardians come out from the door straight ahead. I drop to a knee and fire away, rounds hit the neck, cheek then forehead and the right Guardian drops. The left one has me targeted, and fires hitting me in the right arm and causing me to drop my firearm. Intentionally.

Seeing I am unarmed the Guardian moves toward me, most likely to arrest me and make me disappear forever. He moves deliberately, every step I can hear the mechanical joints moving about, and I wonder if there is even any part of humanity in this massive creature.

Just before he reaches me I see a bright flash of red light in the sky, then a massive lightning bolt comes down in the distance. It is like no lighting bolt I have ever seen, it almost hangs in the air as it falls, as if it were a dragon with a massive tail.

The Guardian turns to watch. We both stare in amazement as hundreds more flashes of light start appearing and falling to Earth as lightning. One flashes directly overhead and the guardian and I stare at it as it descends right towards us. As it flashes by our balcony I see a person in the light, a being of pure energy. The guardian sees it as well, because it cannot process the image it starts to act strangely then it collapsed on the ground clutching it's right shoulder, heart attack. One of the only human elements in the machine is what caused it to fail.

What was happening? Is this some sort of Alien invasion? I knew life was likely elsewhere in the Universe but what was this?

A citizen runs by me in a panic. "The Annunaki have returned to save us!".

The Annunaki, the fake alien race that the Nephilim pretended to be during their original occupation of the Earth before the flood. The architecture of these Nephilim found everywhere in the world became the basis of television programs such as ancient aliens, and eventually was taught to everyone to make them believe the angels and demons of the Bible were actually aliens, and beneficial aliens at that.

I however was fully aware of the false alien demonic agenda and knew what this was. Semyaza Satan, Azazel's Lucifer's brother had finally been kicked out of Heaven with his Fallen Angels. Michael the Archangel must have finally thrown Satan down upon the Earth. Satan would now take over and rule for forty-two months and Jesus would return once his message was heard spoken around the world. I had to upload that message to the central computer, I had to make sure the message was heard or the forty-two months may never end. The word of God is all that can save us now.

"Now war arose in heaven, Michael and his angels fighting against the dragon. And the dragon and his angels fought back, but he was defeated, and there was no longer any place for them in heaven. And the great dragon was thrown down, that ancient serpent, who is called the devil and Satan, the deceiver of the whole world—he was thrown down to the earth, and his angels were thrown down with him."

Revelation 12:7-9

I must get to the central computer and upload the truth before it is too late. I run back into the medical office to see the doctor. When I walk in I see two guardians standing over his dead corpse. As soon as they see me their red eyes turn and their arms follow, unleashing thousands of rounds of lethal ammunition from their mini-guns in my direction. I have no choice but to run and jump off the balcony.

As I fall the fifty-foot drop onto a metal walkway, I wonder how far the fall would be if I missed. The constant fog obscured the city floor hundreds of feet below. The cities of the world had become highly overpopulated as all rural areas were off limits and could not be accessed by the modern public transportation systems and driverless cars.

I slam into the walkway, but fortunately I land on a crate of linen being dragged across the walkway by an automated drone, going room to room replacing towels in the hotel below. If I hadn't the drop would have broken a few bones for sure.

I scramble down the ramp and reach the lobby entrance. Those who know to look can see taxi's that have a holographic hidden Christian cross on the side. Fortunately I spot one. These have been built with override switches that I can activate with a microchip on a card, allowing me to punch in a custom destination. I swipe the card, prop open the maintenance computer, and type in the destination. A small navy shipyard operated by fellow Christian outlaws. They had no military ships, but they had a lot of salvaged hardware and converted them into new designs. Anything they could use to try and survive, their only chance of survival was to stay hidden. The drive would take a long time, as it was stationed on the East Side of the Appalachians where the Atlantic had risen to since the last flood. I would need a boat and scuba gear to reach the Statue.

People are running out of the hotel screaming, the lightning bolts have all but stopped but the Guardians have turned on the citizens, slaughtering everyone they find. The Fallen Angels, Semjaza must be in a bad mood for losing the battle in Heaven, those who worshipped him this whole time will receive the worst of his wrath. Their mansions, towers, guardians all have become their undoing, only the poor Christians already hiding from their Luciferian Utopia on the fringes will survive.

I wait as the driverless car adds the new roads to it's map, and routes the new coordination. A guardian then comes out of the hotel and with it's mini-gun torches the car directly in front of mine with depleted uranium from the front of the vehicle to the rear. The smell of cordite from the gun powder filled the air. As the guardian then turned to me, I opened the window of the car and plugged the Nephilim with half a clip from my pistol. The bullets struck the transhuman Guardian in the chest causing little damage, but the electric magnetic pulses jacketed on the bullets casing caused the guardian's nervous system to over excite and die instantly. Just as I see another guardian leaving the building my vehicle launches forward toward my destination. The route I am using is almost entirely on the old roads that have been unused since before WW3. The Guardians and civilians would be nowhere near these and I should have an unnoticed drive to the shipyard.

I realize with the chaos going on the only way to get into the central computer would be with the ring of Solomon, or to remotely hack into a CJB employee's brain, or I could just shoot my way in like an army of one. I thought the best chance of success would be the Statue of Liberty but it would take much longer, leaving the people to fend for themselves with the fallen Angels while I searched. With only one life, and therefore one shot to get it right, I had to take the surest bet, and that would be with the ring.

Chapter 29 – The Abyss

Appalachian Mountain Range, Pirate Bay – Distant Future

The shipyard is nothing like the New World's massive transportation hubs down the coast. This shipyard had been built shortly after the flood. It is run by a group of ragtag rebels, who spend their days salvaging ships and selling the parts to the black market. These parts have become extremely valuable to the people living outside the system. The Christians and others, about a third of the world's population lived outside the system, relying on each other for survival, unable to buy or sell or to even enter the society that wanted to kill or alter and enslave them. Any direct contact with the Global Alliance surveillance systems resulted in hover ships loaded with Guardians being called in to exterminate the Security Threat.

Upon arrival I head into the makeshift pub that had been built into the side of a beached deep ocean research vessel once used by Woods Hole Oceanographic Institute to study the ocean for global warming. The vessel has been stripped and all the equipment that was on board has been retrofitted to other ships. Supposedly the Alvin, one of the first remote piloted underwater vehicles that was used to find the Titanic was recovered and on one of the ships in the port.

In the bar is the typical scene. Most of the sailors spent too much time on the sea, and their testosterone has built up to near volcanic levels before erupting in a blind drunken stupor once they hit this shore bar. There are roughly forty men inside, and possibly ten females all unattractive. The men in the bar seem to be under the belief that whoever was drunkest, most obnoxious and loud would get laid and the women in question seemed to be responding to this. I need someone more reserved for my mission so I post in the corner, order the local brewed beer and start scanning the crowd for the quiet confident type.

After awhile I notice a grizzled looking guy at the far end of the bar, a little bit more put together than the others, probably ex military. He is chatting the bartender, probably the only good looking female of the bunch when another man gets pissed with him for taking her time while he was thirsty.

"You done taking up all her time you fancy twat, my crew and I need a fuckin' drink already toots." The drunk large man said, most likely used to not being questioned due to his size.

The smaller captain just turns and looks at him, still holding the bartenders hand. "What you drinking? It's on me."

The big guy retorts, "I don't need your fucking charity, you think you're better than me, I'll stomp your head in."

The captain turns and smiles at the bartender. Then as if in one motion, he turns and cracks the big guy in the larynx with a vicious punch, with his other hand he draws a pistol and aims it at the big guys crewman. One of them walks forward slowly and starts dragging his big friend (who is gasping for breath, unable to find it with a crushed larynx) backwards out the door. The captain looks at the rest of his crew, "He'll be better off as a mute, and you're welcome." The crew all seeing the pistol aimed at them departs. The captain turns back to the bartender and the pub resumed its normal operations.

This is my guy. I walk over to him and introduce myself. After buying him a few drinks and explaining the situation he agrees to do it free of charge. Luckily for me he has a fishing trawler that has been converted into a salvage diving ship, and they even have the Alvin on board for deep ocean recon before diving to speed things up. Alvin could spend a lot more time underwater and could go through a much larger area before sending down divers to recover what Alvin found.

The captain's name is Paul Wellstone, and he is an ex Rebel Marine. At the beginning of the New World Order those who refused the chip fought for their place in society. The transhuman soldiers and drones quickly crushed them. The only rebels who survived the battles were the toughest sons of bitches alive. Most had taken multiple

bullet wounds just trying to escape. Wellstone himself had been a leader of a small

amphibious unit that had tried to destroy the CJB Central Computer ten years ago.

Wellston is named after a Senator that stood up to the tyranny back in Titus Frost's day.

They failed because the second in command had betrayed them; the Global Alliance

had offered massive financial rewards to any opposition leaders who would give

information on our plans of action. When they got close to the CJB they were

ambushed and only Wellstone survived. He has been out on the coast operating a

salvage ship since.

Wellstone and his crew have become experts on the use of Alvin, but our mission

would put that to the test. Finding a ring under 100 feet of water, in the middle of what

now is the ocean, would be difficult to impossible. Even if the location was known, it

was known before the water overtook the entire city.

It took us two days to steam out to the location of the Statue of Liberty. Just north of us

under the water is Manhattan Island. Most of the tall skyscrapers have fallen over and

collapsed due to the massive tidal wave caused by the Russians, but some of them still

stood mostly just the steel frames protruding out of the water. The scene is eerie as

there is no land in sight, but I can see the remains of NYC poking above the cresting

waves.

We plotted out the area for the Statue of Liberty, and upon arrival we expected to see the top of it still sticking out of the water but it isn't there. We place ourselves east of the monument and drop anchor. Hoping the anchor would land in the original harbor floor and not get caught in the frame of an underwater structure. The next morning after readying the Alvin and scuba gear we launch the remote submersible. Then we all huddle around a TV screen in the cabin while Wellstone guides the fish. It seems the Alvin is swimming through fog; the lights could only penetrate a few feet in the water because it is so polluted from all the debris. We stared on, seeing nothing but small bits of debris. The Alvin slowly and carefully found its way through the murky water, then we see something, and then there was more, when it came into view we are staring at the hand holding the flame of Prometheus, the eternal flame of Babylon.

After a few hours of slowly guiding the fish around we found the remaining remnants of the statue, the tidal wave that hit NYC caused by a nuclear explosion in the Atlantic knocked the Statue completely over towards the West. Leaving the statue on it's back with the hand holding the torch aiming upwards almost touching the surface of the water.

The next day we start the search for the ring. We know it is buried in the ground directly under where the flame would have been when the statue was upright. The Alvin has a small digger attachment and can poke down into the gravel to see if it can hit a metal box the ring is in.

Two weeks go by. The crew knowing this is a gratis mission almost mutinied twice. However both mutinies ended when the crew realized that Paul and I can easily handle all five of them bare handed. Finally a breakthrough occurs. The Alvin hits the box and pokes it out of the ground. Sitting there on the floor of the ocean. We all scream for joy, and start scrambling for scuba gear.

Once we have the gear on, we equipp ourselves with harpoons. I have never scuba dived before, however I did not tell this to anyone. Personally after reliving the experience with Titus in Boston Harbor I feel that is enough scuba experience to get by. Sharks genetically mutated by the nuclear radiation and pollution in the water had taken over a lot of the area, as it is great hunting grounds with all the empty buildings. We follow the wire connecting the Alvin to the ship down to where the Alvin is. The descent took awhile as the Alvin is far West of our ship's location.

Following the line down to the Alvin is very strange, much different than the Boston Harbor experience. The water is even murkier as you can barely see anything even with flashlights thanks to debris still present from the massive metropolis. All we can see is the cable extending what seems forever out in front of us, leading us to a deep abyss.

We finally reach the end; the darkness has just about completely swallowed us at this depth and with the amount of dirt and trash in the water. Only a tiny glimmer of blue light made it this deep. I tap the call signal twice on my transmitter to let Paul know we have arrived at the Alvin.

I swim down to the box and open it. Inside is the golden ring of Solomon. I secure it tightly in a pouch on my chest, then swim over to the Alvin front cam and give Paul the thumbs up. Paul flashes the Alvin's lights on and off signaling he understands, and we start the slow ascent following the Alvin cable back to the ship. We have to slowly ascend to avoid decompression sickness called the bends, which can be deadly.

About half way back a strange sensation occurs. The Alvin line that was taught, a straight line, all of a sudden droops and then drops. As if the Alvin had started to return to the ship. However, the plan was to wait until after we had returned so we could use the line as a guide. Without the line we are blind as a bat, floating in a murky ocean full of sharks. I looked over at the two crewmen with me; both raised their hands in the "I don't know" position.

So we stay put and started to ascend directly up, hoping to hit the surface and then swim to the boat. Using bubbles as our guide. This seems a decent plan, and we slowly start to ascend. All three of us keep each other in view as we ascend for comfort and safety. All of a sudden the crewmember to my right jerks downwards, fast, disappearing from view in a stream of bubbles. I turn to follow when the other crewman grabs me and pulls me back. I start to struggle free until I see the pool of blood rising out of the darkness.

The Lost Truth by Dean Fougere

Either it was Alvin tearing his leg off, or it was a shark. Most likely the second, which

explains the cable getting cut, as sharks in modern times thanks to genetic manipulation

created by a toxic environment from all the pollution and radiation created by a flooded

Eastern seaboard have become extremely violent. We kept the ascent going as quickly

as possible hoping the shark is busy with the other crewmember. Of course we were not

quite that lucky.

Above us a shadow went overhead, blocking out the sun abruptly. One shark had just

passed overhead, then another goes by so close underneath my foot I kick its tail. I pull

my spear gun out and look at the other diver. His eyes were so wide and scared I had

never seen anything like it. Deep down the fear of death was trying to find it's way in,

but I just thought of Jesus at this moment and just the thought brought forth new

courage.

A few minutes pass; we ascend what feels like a million miles, though it could not have

been more than twenty feet. A shark comes up straight at me, then at the last second it

turns and slams into the other diver, tearing his leg clean off, as I fire a harpoon into the

shark's dorsal fin. The shark squirms off, but the other diver is surrounded by blood,

staring at me motionless.

I panic and start kicking upwards, then stop. I must ascend slowly or the decompression

will kill me anyways. I slowly continue the ascent. I can see shadows just out of my

vision moving in the murky water around me. One knifes in and I fire a harpoon catching it in the mouth, which caused the big fish to jerk away in pain. I look up and can almost see the surface I feel. The water has started getting very bright as I move upwards at the same rate as my bubbles.

All of a sudden I feel something slam into my back mashing me forwards. Then a tug back as the shark rips my oxygen tank off my back. I let the respirator out of my mouth and wriggle free to turn and fire a harpoon right into the shark's cold dead black eye. He squirms off trailing blood, and other sharks follow to eat him.

Now without a tank or oxygen it is a race to the surface before passing out. Fortunately being not far from the surface I feel I can make it. Ensuring to continue breathing out slowly as I decompress on the way up. A minute passes, I can see the surface I think. Just keep going, the pain in my chest starts to increase exponentially as my lungs fill with CO_2 from my cells. My body starts to yearn for oxygen. The surface is so close, I am just going to have to fuck the decompression and rise as quick as hell now, the last twenty feet can't be that bad.

I start kicking reaching up for the air, but the surface did not come quick enough. My lungs need air, even if this reality is an illusion; it is an illusion that was about to kill me. I pull and push up; the harder I climb the more oxygen I need. Then everything goes black and I breathe in the water.

As I feel the water pouring down my throat, ending my life a hand grabbed my back and starts to lift me upwards. The surface of the water broke around me as I am lifted out of it entirely by this unseen force. I feel the hand slam into my back, causing my lungs to empty all the water in them. I cough and choke trying to get the oxygen into my lungs as I lay flat on my back about an inch above the surface. I feel the tip of the pierced dorsal fin touch the bottom of my back as I hover over the water on thin air. I see it swim off still harpooned through the side. Then I see a light above me, and then blackness.

I awake on the deck of the fishing trawler, with Paul Wellstone hovering over me performing CPR. I sit up and cough up a gallon of seawater.

"Well you've looked better." Says Wellstone.

"How did I get on the ship, did you pull me out of the water?" I ask trying to make sense of what happened.

"No, the crew and I were motoring around looking for the Alvin or you three as the tether broke loose and we got no distress call from you. Then all of a sudden I heard a large crashing noise on the stern and when I looked back you were there, lying there unconscious. Other than a large wave, I have no idea how you got on board. Where are the other two divers?"

"Dead, sharks attacked us and ate the cable. Alvin is sitting right where you left it; at the base of the Statue of Liberty on the ocean floor."

I reach into my pouch and pull out the ring. "Mission accomplished, let's go take these sons of bitches down."

The captain says a few words for the lost crew, decides to leave the Alvin, as the ring was far more important, as it could change the tide of the war.

Chapter 30 – Judgment Day

Global Alliance Capitol, Rocky Mountain Range – Distant Future

I leave the small port town with the ring and a new companion. Paul Wellstone has sold his fishing trawler for weapons and ammunition and decided to tag along. In truth I could use the support, his combat skills were equal with his mastery of computers, a skill I did not possess. Associated with Anonymous, a hacking group that has survived the birth of the New World order because it is based on ideas and principles, something that can never be destroyed. His hacking abilities would prove useful in our infiltration of the Central Justice Bureau and it's Central Computer at the core, the singularity where all human consciousness connects to the grid is combined, creating a hive mind. All we have to do is insert the truth and the Hive Mind should recognize it and cause a mass awakening.

The CJB is in the heart of the One World Capitol in the Rocky Mountains. The new city had been built post WW3 and is built entirely by planned design. The city is called New Jerusalem, but in reality it is a recreation of Mystery Babylon. The Capitol city itself is only inhabited by members of the 11th district, and technically the Capitol City is sovereign from the rest of the world, with it's own laws, legally it is the 11ᵗʰ district until the Space Elevators have finished creating their orbital Elysium.

The city is magnificent, completely modern architecture that is made entirely of granite and marble. The whole city is built with the stone laying techniques of the Pyramids and the Olmec's. The entire city is designed with masonic symbolism from the architecture, to the city street plan, to the dimensions of the city limits (a cube just as DC was). The Saturn Cube cult of the Illuminati's influence could be seen everywhere in the design. The tallest building is a giant obelisk, with the President's new version of the oval office taking up the entire capstone, which glistens with golden windows. The city is the heart of the Global Currency, Political Power, Religious Authority, the seat of the one world government Anti-Christ President, and the singularity of the Hive Mind. You could sense this feeling of power when you entered.

However, upon this return the beautiful city is in repair. The guardians under direction from the recently arrived fallen angels have turned on the people of the city. Replaced the Anti-Christ, with Satan himself. Then Satan divided the world into ten regions and placed a Fallen Angel in Charge of each region, with a legion of Fallen angels at his command to keep everyone in line. He has been ruling now for forty-one months, forty-two as of tomorrow. Now the city looks like a war zone, the New World Order paratroopers, and armed civilians have taken on the Guardian transhuman killing machines, drones, flying Nano bots, etc. They have succumbed in the end, as the power of the Beast was too much for them.

Using the cities massive sewer system we were able to get under the city wall, and get all the way to a building across the street from the CJB building. In there a remote group of Anonymous hackers had one apartment where they had been trying to remotely hack into the CJB for over a year unsuccessfully, when the shit hit the fan, they abandoned the post leaving it empty for our purposes. Wellstone had used his connections with black arms market dealers in the port to acquire this knowledge. The biggest issue the hackers had was the CJB firewall, which is impenetrable from the outside, if a connection could be made from within there are no safeguards.

The plan is simple. Miles, I would sneak inside with a remote connection microchip that has the data and a virus by using the ring. Once inserted the Microchip would allow Paul Wellstone to activate the Emergency Channel, which takes over the entire system, and then to play the data to everyone connected. Once the truth was revealed, the domino effect would take place as the citizens would revolt and the hive mind would be broken.

I geared up for the mission, sniper rifle, assault rifle, two pistols, and a lot of ammunition. The sniper rifle is equipped with exploding rounds, the other weapons all are equipped with EMP jacketed rounds; the only way to fairly fight the Guardians is to use their technology against them.

The CJB building itself is almost an Island. It has one main entrance that is connected to the rest of the world by a sky bridge. The bridge itself is no more than ten feet wide and stretches from the rest of the city to the CJB a couple of hundred feet above the ground. There are hovercraft pads every couple of floors serving as emergency escapes for elite operatives in the building. There physically is no way in but over the bridge and through security. The bridge itself is lined with automated turrets, cameras, microphones, motion sensors, Guardians, and possible other contraptions unknown. No one unauthorized has ever come close to the bridge, never mind crossed it.

The Guardians at the end of the Bridge scan everyone's wrist or forehead RFID Tattoo mark on entry to the bridge area. Once inside a DNA scan is used, as all citizens DNA is recorded at birth and can not be faked as the sample point is different every time for DNA extraction. One day it might be a finger prick of blood, the next a hair follicle, or a skin flake, there are so many ways to check DNA in this modern day they can continuously change their methods to catch counterfeits.

As I approach the bridge I fit into the crowd wearing the typical business suit attire of the men in the capitol. Most have extensive transhuman implants, but the most expensive implants are the ones that are made to be unidentifiable, keeping your look human even if you are 90% machine.

Just before reaching the Guardians sight line, I call Paul on the two-way radio, a technology so old the capitol doesn't even check for it anymore. "Entering" I say.

"Connected, awaiting firewall bypass." Paul replies. "Good hunting. God be with you."

As he says this I slip the ring onto my finger. The world transforms around me. The people are all completely unaware of my presence, this high up in the air I doubt the demons will see me from below ground. Then I look at the Guardians, and to my surprise they are staring at me, but not the body just the demons trapped inside each of the physical bodies, like a human inside a machine, the inter-dimensional beings trapped in this physical constraint. They turn and aim their mini guns at me, I pull my sniper up and peer through the scope, I see a Guardian and demon head in the crosshairs, fire.

The sniper round from my rifle passes right through the guardian's head, and out the other side. The Guardians bullets at me pass through me and hit the people behind me. With the ring on my matter is vibrating at a frequency inconsistent with the physical dimension thus not allowing me; or anything I had in my possession to interact with the physical dimension. The only way to kill these guys would be with the ring off. So I aimed and took it off as I pull the trigger.

I see the guardian's head explode, releasing the demon from within, and I imagine the demon falling straight through the floor, being pulled down to the Earth. No longer in a physical body the demon is unable to use the physical world to remain above ground.

The other Guardian fired; the bullets missed me by inches and slammed into the crowd behind me. Pumping hundreds of rounds into a group of innocent citizens causing a panic. I turn and fire an explosive round into the Guardian's right arm knocking the mini-gun off as it sprayed wildly into the air, my second shot hit the transhuman machine in the neck and blew it's head off backwards. Then I put the ring back on and vanish.

This bewilders the public, seeing me pop into view out of nowhere and then disappear again. Unaware of anything but the physical dimension the people are completely flabbergasted by what they saw, and are saying it must be new technology or magic.

I quickly walked across the bridge, as drones flew by overhead scanning the bridge for my presence. The automated gun turrets and other booby traps all are set and ready for me. However, I was completely invisible to them, being in the spiritual dimension, caused by vibrating our energy at a different frequency as described by string theory. Crossing the bridge is cake.

When I reach the far side of the bridge I see the doors open and a figure come into view. He is not in a physical body, and dark energy flows from him, so powerfully it seems as if he has black wings but is just the form of a man. He sees me and draws a massive sword blazoned with fire and approaches. I draw my guns but know they will have no effect. I fire and the bullets pass right through the demon.

Just as he is closing in, a bright white light appeared above, blinding me as it comes crashing down towards us. The ball of light slams into the ground right in front of me revealing a man dressed in glowing white robes, pale white skin, and brownish golden yellow hair, yielding a massive sword of gold. He stood, then turns to me and waives as if to follow him, so I did.

He moves forward towards the fallen Angel ahead and vanquishes it with a single swipe of his sword. Then we burst through the doors of the CJB to find ourselves staring at the unknown 9, the Watchers, the fallen Angels whom have been quietly interacting with humanity via the Illuminati for ages.

The Angel motions for me to head down to the Central Computer room straight ahead, I assumed while he protects me. So I start running, as I reach the door; I turn and see the Angel fighting the 9 fallen Angels, just trying to fend them off. I turn and run for the elevator door in front of me. I know the access point for the Microchip is on the 33rd floor, from architectural drawings we stole from the national archive database. Anything online is easily accessible if you knew how to hack into these "secure" systems, because the CJB has built backdoors into everything so they could access it as well, we just went in through their backdoors.

I hit the elevator button and the door opens revealing a guardian inside, before he can react I remove the ring and pump him full of lead from my pistol, then jump in the elevator and slide the ring back on before hitting the 33 button. The doors slowly shut and I see the angel who is on my side doing everything he can to battle the 9 fallen angels still attacking him, one of the 9 sees me and breaks off in my direction as the door shuts.

As the elevator goes down to the 33rd floor I check my guns and ammunition. The door opens revealing the 33rd floor, just a plain white hallway. I come out of the elevator and check the corners. Seeing nothing I move right and down the hall towards the Central Computer Terminal Access station for security systems. This room should be full of people, no guardians as I was deep enough inside to be with just transhuman technicians, most locked in a trance like state unaware of their surroundings whilst they work in the digital virtual reality with their implanted brain chips. I could walk right in and sit down next to them and they would never even know I am in there.

I take my ring off and approach the door; it reads my motion and slides open. Revealing a massive labyrinth of terminals with motionless technicians sitting at them staring straight ahead, completely out of their bodies; their consciousness enslaved by the AI to perform tasks. These people think they are in control of all humanity, when in reality they are the most controlled members of humanity.

I sit down at the terminal and immediately pull out the microchip. Supposedly all I had to do is insert the microchip into the brain chip of a technician and then it would upload automatically, it would kill the technician but that is a small price to pay. So I look around the room and picked out what seems like the supervisor of the group, sitting at the front desk elevated above the rest and facing at them not forward. I walk over, push

his head backwards, showing the RFID Tattoo brain chip on his forehead to the sky,

then I take the microchip and insert, right where Paul has shown me.

The technician's head jerks upright, eyes open as if he has just woken up but his eyes

just roll backwards revealing only the whites. Then the whole room lights up red with

warning lights, and virus detected flashing across the room. The big holo screen on the

back wall lit up showing the anonymous Guy Fawkes mask then it switches to Paul's

face. "I am in" Just defend the chip until the upload is complete, don't let them remove

it. I am activating the emergency channel override now."

The screen flashes, and the Global Alliance Flag replaces his face with a message

reading emergency broadcast alert!

The truth broadcast started, we would play all of it. Hours upon hours of information

would be played, all revealing what Jesus had tried to reveal to us thousands of years

before.

I stayed and watched as the truth is heard, protecting the microchip that is never

threatened as I sit and watch our victory, or so I thought. The clock strikes midnight,

and the message had been played in its entirety. Now all that was left was to play the

Bible, in it's entirety so all the world would hear it at one time. I hit play.

I walk out of the room and to the elevator; hit the button to bring me back up to the lobby. I walk out of the lobby elevator to see the three fallen angels standing, with six slain, and the good angel slain as well. They see me so I started running for the exit.

Just as I hit the door, a sword from a fallen angel pierced through my chest from behind poking out in front of me. I fall to my knees feeling the immense pain as the fallen one twisted the sword making the wound gape before pulling it out of my back. I look down at my chest and see the blood spurting out. I take a deep breathe of air and fall forward on my face. I hear the angel cackle and walk off, as I lay there dying. Then I see the world around me light up, as if someone has turned on the lights in a dark room.

I roll over on my back and look above into the sky, a sky that was night merely seconds ago is now blue as if day had come. Lighting the sky is a bright light like nothing I have ever seen before, brighter than the sun but much smaller. As it draws closer in the blink of an eye, I see a line on either side of it of white, like a white point on a bright white line across the whole of the sky. I could feel the light; it has a drawing affect like love to it. It kept coming down into the atmosphere, growing larger and closer.

In a instant, I made it out, the light is emanating from a single source, Jesus Christ on a white horse, whose words were as swords. Angels thousands of them flanked him as they descended from the Heavens. They went right through the 11th district connected to Earth by the space elevators, and the world saw the greatest accomplishment of mankind was destroyed instantly. Exploding into a burning inferno. Judgment had finally come, Jesus Christ had returned to save us and imprison Satan for 1,000 years while He reigns.

I let the pain stop, and I release my physical body. I die, and I feel my soul start to fall. It is pitch black all around me, and I can see the demons moving towards me. The black was darker and emptier than anything I had ever experienced, then the demons move in on me and start tearing at my flesh. I screamed in agony and try to fight them off. They keep pulling at me and repeating all the bad things I had done in my life, all the people I had killed. I screamed for help but no noise came out.

When I had given up fighting, I asked God to send Jesus to save me. As I did I see a light emerge from the darkness above, like a candle in a dark room the darkness had no power over the light. Jesus came down, grabbed my hand and pulls me up, once I had embraced him and open my eyes I felt a sensation of love like nothing I had ever experienced before. Then he was gone, and I was standing on a train platform.

There were many, many people on this platform and I did not know what to do. They all had baggage and were not getting on the train. I had no luggage of my own and decided to just board the train. I look down the tracks and all I can see ahead is a tunnel of light like a rainbow, nothing at the end, but something is drawing me to it. The same feeling I had before the station, when Jesus saved me, is calling to me from the other end.

So I board the train. I walk along to find an empty seat, I notice everyone on the train had not brought any luggage or anything at all, just themselves, like me. None had any augmentations, all seemed to be the Christians I had been living on the outskirts of society with. Then I see them, faces from the past, Hassan-I Sabbah, Fatima and his children all-smiling and laughing, their son Hasan-I Jr, is all grown up sitting proudly with his father. Titus and Jocelyn holding each other, madly in love, turned and saw me, then waived me to sit with them. Paul Wellstone was there and motioned for me to sit with him across from Titus and Jocelyn.

"Good to see you Miles" Jocelyn says.

"How is our favorite great grandson doing?" Titus says, "Nice to have you join us before we departed on this one way trip."

I ask, "How long have you been on the train?"

They all turn to me with a smile, Titus explains, "We all just got on before you. The trains just showed up."

With that, all went back to normal, the kids playing, Titus and Jocelyn flirting, the train starts to pull out of the station, to a destination unknown.

The Lost Truth by Dean Fougere

Miles looked out ahead of the train, amazed by what he saw. He thought lonely was the

road, but fruitful are these rewards, for those whom followed the narrow paths.

The End

For Further Reading on the topics in this Book:

1. None Dare Call it Conspiracy by Gary Allen

2. Proofs of a Conspiracy by John Robinson

3. Illuminati Facts & Fiction & Illuminati & the Music Industry by Mark Dice

4. The True Story of the Bilderberg Group by Daniel Estulin

5. The Creature from Jekyll Island by G. Edward Griffen

6. In the Beginning: Compelling Evidence for Creation and the Flood by Dr. Walt Brown

Other Sources of Inspiration (but not all for there were many):

1. Alex Jones's Films, Infowars.com

2. Architects & Engineers for the Truth, rethink911.org

3. Luke Radkowski, WeAreChange.org

4. Dr. L.A. Marzulli, The Watchers Series

5. Trey Smith, God in a Nutshell Project

6. Coast to Coast AM

7. Face Like the Sun (Age of Deceit Films)

8. Deus Ex: Human Revolution

9. Assassin's Creed

10. WikiLeaks

11. Round Saturn's Eye & Truth Media Revolution YouTube Channel

12. Dr. Judy Wood "Where did the Towers Go"

13. Eugene Mallove "Fire from Ice", www.LENR-CANR.org

14. Anonymous. We Never Forgive. We Never Forget. Expect Us.